IN HOLLYWOOD ONLY ONE TH[...]
STYLE!

When exclusive London boutique employee Amber Green is
mistakenly offered a job as assistant to infamous 'stylist to the stars'
Mona Armstrong, she hits the ground running, helping to dress
some of Hollywood's hottest (and craziest) starlets. Awards season
turns Amber's life upside down as dazzling designer gowns are
paraded on red carpets in Los Angeles, London and back.

Suddenly Amber's catching the attention of two very different
suitors, TV producer Rob and Hollywood bad boy rising star
Liam.

How will Amber keep her head? Which man will she chose?
And what the hell will everyone wear?

The Stylist is a fast-paced, fun-packed rummage through the
ultimate dressing up box.

Rosie Nixon lives in London and is joint Editor of *HELLO!* magazine. She previously held senior positions at glossy women's magazines including *Grazia*, *Glamour* and *Red*. Ever discreet and protective of the big stars she has worked with, Rosie's experience has undoubtedly enabled her to write her debut novel, *The Stylist*.

THE STYLIST

ROSIE NIXON

HARLEQUIN®MIRA®

Harlequin MIRA is a registered trademark of Harlequin Enterprises Limited, used under licence.

First Published in Great Britain 2016
By Harlequin Mira, an imprint of HarperCollins*Publishers*
1 London Bridge Street, London, SE1 9GF

© 2016 Rosie Nixon

ISBN: 978-1-848-45459-0

58-0216

Our policy is to use papers that are natural, renewable and recyclable products and made from wood grown in sustainable forests.The logging and manufacturing processes conform to the legal environmental regulations of the country of origin.

Printed and bound by
CPI Group (UK) Ltd, Croydon, CR0 4YY

For Callum and Heath

Prologue

The car door swings open and bright white lights flash before my eyes, blinding me for a few long seconds. *Flash! Flash! Flash!* Like a firework has been let off at close range. I wait inside the car while she makes her big entrance. Getting out of a blacked-out limousine in an exquisite, glittering gown complete with vertiginous heels is no easy task, even for a seasoned pro. *Knees together, swivel hips, feet on the ground, smoothly push up, rise gracefully, and straighten gown and SMILE!* A thunderous cheer erupts around us as she emerges—*Ta da!*—a Hollywood goddess in the flesh. Then come the voices.

'Jennifer! Jennifer!'

She is under siege. Paparazzi shoot off hundreds of high-resolution frames, their faces hidden behind the long, prying lenses of their black state-of-the-art DSLR cameras. When they get too close to this tall, willowy, shimmering beauty, the minders rush in to hold them at bay.

'Hey, Jennifer!'

'This way!'

'Give us a smile!'

When the flashes subside, I tumble out of the car, dart hastily round it and slip through the entrance, flashing my invitation pass. I crouch down at the side of the red carpet, beside the cold metal crowd-control railings, and sink into the shadows, desperate to keep out of sight. But I've been rumbled. An autograph hunter taps me on the head and shoves a glossy photo in my face.

'Hey! Can you get this signed by Jennifer?'

Another pleads in my ear: 'Ma'am, ma'am, do you know her? Can you get her to come over?'

'Yeah, you got out of her car, get her to come here!' Others join in, like a chorus of extras in a low-budget film. I pretend not to hear, taking my eyes off her for only a few seconds; time enough to readjust the zip and pull down the hood of my grey towelling sleep suit. I'm breaking into a sweat. I look down at myself, in my deeply inappropriate, stale outfit, and then back at Jennifer in her stunning gown, all clean and super gorgeous. I'm so tired and embarrassed I almost want to laugh. It's rarely cold in Los Angeles, even on a February evening, and the Oscars—the biggest night in the entertainment calendar—is no place for a pasty British girl in a baggy onesie, flashing her saggy bottom at unsuspecting fans, never mind the world's paparazzi, who might snap an unexpected exclusive. Inside, I'm seething. *Bloody Mona!*

* * *

Jennifer makes her way along the carpet, spreading pneumatic glamour wherever she goes, thrilling the crowds of fans with high fives and making a point of waving to those at the back standing on their tiptoes, camera phones lifted skywards, straining to catch a glimpse of their idol. She stops to pose for a few photos with admirers, all of them less aesthetically blessed than she is, and an explosion of air kisses ensues. They have to be air kisses, they can't make actual contact with her skin—she can't risk a germ and she certainly can't mess up the immaculate, dewy make-up that took two hours for the steady hand of a leading make-up artist to apply. She signs a handful of autographs, using the black permanent marker pen I have learned to keep in my kit for such occasions.

Soon we are being ushered along the red gauntlet by her bossy publicist, brandishing a clipboard and a firm permasmile, to reach the main bank of paparazzi. Time to make my move. Pouncing out of the shadows like a leopard stalking its prey, I'm suddenly visible under the bright lights. I dash to the corners of her skirt, pulling down layer upon delicate layer of pure silk scarlet organza, embellished with shimmering beads and tiny sequins that catch the lights, sending sparkles in every direction. It is breathtakingly elegant.

'Jennifer! This way!'

'Over here, Jennifer!'

The cries are more urgent now. This is the main photo opportunity.

The paps are penned at least five deep, some standing on stepladders to get the view from above. She takes her time, moving elegantly this way and that, adjusting and tweaking her pose ever so slightly with almost every click. It's second nature now: right hip lifted, left foot crossed over right, enhancing the natural curve of her body; right shoulder pushed back, chest out, but not too far; left arm on her left hip bone, right arm hanging behind to create a slender profile. Head held high to elongate the neck, face turned slightly to the right to present her best side, chin raised just so for a youthful jawline, belying her forty-something years (she stopped counting at thirty-nine). She is textbook perfect.

'That's it, love, nice big smile for the camera!'

'This way, once more!'

'Beautiful!'

I look up. Both hands are on her hips now, slender silhouette perfectly shaped by the structured internal corset. Not so tight that she can't breathe properly, but plenty tight enough. A hint of crystal embellishment on satin sandals peeping out from beneath the gown at the front. Elaborate diamond-drop earrings, worth ten times the gown itself. It's such a timeless, romantic, pure Hollywood look. *Just perfect.* I glance back to check the security guard is still with us. He winks back in acknowledgement, earpiece and discreet microphone on the lapel of his slick black suit, ready for action should we run into any trouble. The fine jewellery houses don't take any risks with a loan this expensive. She moves on, floating down the carpet now, enjoying the attention, gliding gracefully, a beautiful swan. With her honey skin, wide smile and dewy eyes, she bewitches everyone in her path. She's so mesmerising, it's actually a little overpowering. *How incredible to put a spell on so many people, purely by turning up.* On to the bank of waiting press and TV crews. I shuffle back against the railings into the shadows cast by the hazy early-evening sun.

'Mind out, you're standing on my cables!' a small angry American man shouts to my right.

'Sorry, sorry.' I inch out of the way. Then I lose my footing, stumbling backwards, and a Japanese woman elbows me in the ribs.

'Hey! Watch it, miss. You almost lost my sound!'

Aargh, jet lag. I should be asleep by now. More bright

lights. This time microphones are being thrust in her face, a barrage of questions thrown from all sides. The faces of the entertainment reporters are so familiar to me now.

'Jennifer, you look stunning tonight! Who are you wearing?'

'Is it couture?'

'Did Mona Armstrong style you?'

'Can you twirl so we can see the back?'

'How much are the earrings worth?'

'Can we get a close-up of your shoes?'

'Were you influenced by the style of your character in the film?'

'Do you feel confident about tonight?'

And repeat. Over and over again, for entertainment shows from Boston to Beijing and everywhere in between. Finally we reach the entrance to the Dolby Theatre—and my phone vibrates in my pocket. But it's not the person I'm aching for it to be, and I'm disappointed. One text from him and this would all be exciting again—another crazy night in la-la land to chew over and laugh about later on. The onesie would give him plenty of ammunition. And though I'd protest, really, I'd love every minute. Instead, it's from Mona: Are you with Jennifer? *Seriously? Bit late now.* But I've learned it's best not to reply when I feel like I do right now.

* * *

As Jennifer is swept into the auditorium to deafening applause, thousands more flashbulbs and some ear-splitting whoops, I discreetly make my exit wondering how I ended up in this circus, in a slightly smelly onesie. Oh, if only this was just a bad dream…

Part One:
London,
Pre-Awards Season

Chapter One

We gathered on white stools around the cash desk as Jas, our boss, delivered the news.

'It's about Mona Armstrong.'

Kiki's eyes lit up. This sounded infinitely more interesting than a discussion about who was responsible for the smelly lettuce in the fridge. And her short attention span, after years of social media abuse, meant she *really* needed to concentrate.

'I've had a call from an assistant director at *20Twenty*, the production company,' Jas explained.

Her motley crew—the staff of Smith's boutique, consisting of Alan the security guard and the store assistants, Kiki and I—listened intently.

'They're making a pilot episode for a reality show about Mona,' she continued. Kiki flashed me a told-you-so look, but I pretended not to notice, willing her to topple off the stool.

'The working title is *Mona Armstrong: Stylist to the Stars*, but for now they're calling it *The Stylist*.'

Big Alan was the only one of us who blatantly wasn't bothered about this news. But it didn't come as a complete surprise to Kiki or me—style bloggers had been buzzing about the pilot for several weeks, and Kiki had been monitoring the situation closely. Her latest bulletin, gleaned from various fashion blogs and breathlessly delivered over her daily litre of Super Greens, had informed me the show was 'rumoured to be airing on an American network in the coming months'.

Mona was one of the few things Kiki and I bonded over. You see, Mona Armstrong was not just any old stylist, like the ones you saw on daytime TV turning Sharon from Wolverhampton into a sort of Sharon Stone. She was Britain's most famous—make that *infamous*—celebrity stylist; a personality in her own right, thanks to her minuscule frame, achingly hip, self-coined 'boho riche' dress sense, and close friendships with most of the names in *Tatler*'s Little Black Book.

Now, just a few hours later, it had suddenly become a reality. *My reality.* Little did I know today's news was about to change my life, forever.

* * *

'The TV guy—Rob, I think—asked if we can keep it to ourselves for now,' Jas went on, the American twang to her English accent a reminder of her two decades working as a top New York model. 'That means no Instagram, Twitter, Facebook, *nothing*—they need to keep it under wraps until the network has confirmed.'

But that wasn't the half of it. 'Oh, and the *20Twenty* crew want to come to the store tomorrow to do some filming, *with Mona*, as she prepares for awards season,' Jas said, 'so it's highly likely we'll appear in the pilot, too.'

Kiki and I looked at each other. I stifled a giggle—laughing was my default when I didn't know how to react. Kiki's jaw had dropped so low it looked like it needed a stool of its own. Jas carried on, ignoring the mounting hysteria emanating from her staff.

'We'll each have to sign a release form, in case we're in a shot the TV people want to use, and a non-disclosure agreement—an NDA.'

Kiki surreptitiously pulled her iPhone from the back pocket of her tight grey Acne jeans and held it in her lap, her finger hovering over the blue bird icon.

'Release forms and NDAs are legally binding,' Jas added, pointedly.

Sucking in her cheeks, Kiki turned the iPhone over. Updating her followers would just have to wait. But this was big news for both of us. In fashion circles, Mona Armstrong was a legend. AKA a #Ledge.

'*The Stylist* crew will be here to set up at eleven tomorrow, and Mona will arrive soon after,' Jas continued, already off her stool and itching to get to work. 'So we need to get this place looking camera-ready. Amber, can you refresh the windows—let's go monochrome. And Kiki, work with me in store.'

We nodded as the enormity of the situation began to sink in. This visit to the boutique, on a Tuesday morning in late January, was to be Mona's first this season, just before awards season kicked off in Los Angeles with the Golden Globes. Mona's visits were always an 'event', even without TV cameras rolling, so this was set to be off the scale.

Kiki, visibly about to burst at the seams of her skinny jeans, couldn't hold it together any longer.

'Oh. My. God. A camera crew! What the hell are we going to *wear*?'

We both cracked up. Kiki and I were both obsessed with Mona, though for different reasons—Kiki from a bona fide fashion perspective (she would regularly study the minutiae of Mona's outfits, to an extent bordering on OCD). For me, it was more of a morbid fascination. I wondered how she could function on a seemingly liquid diet of Starbucks, water and champagne. (There were no paparazzi photos in existence that showed her eating. Fact.) But what could not be denied was that Mona's celebrity power was off the scale. Practically a celeb in her own right, the careers of the stars she counted as friends were built on column inches secured through the clothes *she'd* put on their skinny backs. For up-and-coming fashion designers, she was a 'dress trafficker', able to kick-start a label simply by placing their creations on the model of the moment. Yes, in our world, Mona was massive news, so it wasn't surprising that today we were bordering on hysterical. *What* will *we be like tomorrow?*

* * *

On the morning of Mona's visit, Smith's was a flurry of activity as we vacuumed, steamed, straightened, dusted and generally tarted the place up. In the centre of the shop was a loosely set noughts-and-crosses board of square leather pouffes and two small glass-topped tables holding Diptyque candles and mineral water—though a glass of champagne was offered to those who looked like they had money to burn. This was one world where you mostly *could* judge a book by its cover. You could spot our customers a mile off: latest It bag hanging off her arm, rarely wearing a warm coat (who needed one when you cab-hopped around town?), sunglasses whatever the weather, breezing around in a delicious cloud of expensive perfume. Some of our best clients, many of whom were old friends of Jas's from her catwalk days, frequently stayed in the shop for hours at a time, chatting, gossiping and, of course, buying clothes, especially once the champagne flowed. One regular recently bought the entire Chloé collection on a whim following four glasses of Perrier-Jouët rosé.

'Her head will be aching tomorrow,' Jas commented, as the woman left the store with eight immaculate shiny white Smith's bags tied with bows. 'But she won't bring anything back. She'd rather die.'

Smith's did that to women who were usually highly self-controlled. The thought of spending nearly two thousand pounds on a few items of clothing, in one shopping trip? It made my eyes water. I still couldn't comprehend what it must be like to inhabit a world where a cheap bag cost three hundred pounds. That was almost half my rent for a month! But working at Smith's, it had begun to feel like we were ringing Monopoly money through the tills.

Of course, most of the store's reputation was down to its owner, Jasmine Smith—an elegant, fifty-something ex-model with cheekbones that make Kate Moss's look fleshy. Jas's talent for spotting a bestseller on the crowded runways of New York, London, Milan and Paris was second to none. But it was her skill in mixing up cutting-edge items from the designer collections with carefully chosen pieces from the debut lines of the fashion stars of tomorrow—often fresh from their Central Saint Martins graduation show—that had made Smith's the most successful, long-running, independent luxury fashion outlet in central London and a destination for stylists and shoppers alike. 'God is in the detail,' is Jas's mantra, and neither Kiki nor I would dare argue.

I was often mesmerised by my chic manager and her stylish customers. It was only now, after working here for the past twelve months, that I felt just about cool enough for this store. The truth was, I got the position by default. It was originally offered to my fashionista best friend and flatmate, Vicky, who then got her dream job as assistant to the fashion editor at *Glamour* magazine. I was temping at the time, which everyone knew was a fast track to nowhere, so she passed this job to me, and Jas said yes.

* * *

Until this position, I was more your average Debenhams devotee and Gok Wan fan. Topshop was my fashion front-line and Armani simply the fragrance my parents gave each other for Christmas. Yep, beneath this shiny new surface, I am one hundred per cent fashion fraud. I often see the real me, in the form of typical Westfield shoppers, peering into the window of Smith's and looking confused.

'Recession's hit hard, this place is halfway to closing down,' they remark, passing on by. At first glance, the shop's white walls and oh-so-sparse rails might look as though we're missing half our stock or have fallen victim to a Bond Street raid. But, as I have swiftly come to learn, true fashionistas know differently. The hardcore style set have Smith's in their Smythson address books because this boutique is a fashion landmark.

Once you step through the glass doors and enter the inner sanctum, you are in an Aladdin's cave, featuring a small, fully alarmed section of haute couture, rails of hot-off-the-catwalk pieces and Jas's 'ones to watch'. Either side of the cash desk stand two tall, highly polished, glass jewellery cabinets, filled with rings set with rare gems, shoulder-grazing earrings, waspish friendship bracelets and sparkling necklaces in pretty, contemporary designs, boasting price tags to make even the most fearsome fashion director pause. Then there are It bags, killer heels, painted pumps and chain-mail belts dotted around on white plinths and shelves, each presented as a unique work of art. Everything is to be admired, stroked, Instagrammed, Pinned, oohed and aahed over by every passing customer in turn. Smith's has it all. But only in small doses.

'Nothing makes an item more covetable than if you have to sit on a waiting list for six months before you get it,' Jas informed me early on. The minimalist interior is down to our strict instruction to put only one of every design onto the rails. Of course, mostly, it's just an illusion—we have all the sizes, colours and crops in the stockroom, downstairs in the basement, which is the size of the shop floor again but packed with polythene-wrapped clothing. It's a clever ploy; thinking your size isn't available only makes you desire something more. And then when we pop out of the stockroom, excitedly exclaiming, 'You won't believe it, Mrs Jones! We do have a 14 after all!'—well, they're already punching in their PIN.

Of course, the hefty price tags at Smith's *are* very real. That's why, like most of the high-end store managers, Jas employs a full-time security guard to watch over the stock—in our case, a burly silver fox affectionately known as 'Big Al'. He works here full-time, patrolling the boutique and keeping a trained ex-army eye on the very expensive items, which have actual alarms fitted. Though his six-foot-four frame doesn't suggest it at first, he's a teddy bear at heart and, like me, is now able to offer an informed second opinion on an outfit if a customer requires it. In fact, despite the fact he's happily married with two grown-up children, Big Al *loves* the opportunity for a gentle flirt with a 'lady who lunches', especially when she's in a quandary over whether to plump for the DVF wrap or the Hervé Léger body-con dress. He must be nearing retirement age, but when he removes his stiff guard's cap to reveal a full head of salt-and-pepper hair, and you notice his bright blue eyes, it's easy to imagine Big Al was a heartbreaker in his day. You'd be surprised how many phone numbers he's had surreptitiously thrust into his big, capable palms. *Uniforms really do work.*

As for me, I know that, in Jas's mind, what I initially lacked in fashion credentials, I gained with my 'artistic eye'. My art foundation course wasn't going to turn me into the next Tracey Emin, but it had given me the confidence to believe I knew what looked good when it came to dressing the shop, and the windows had become my specialist area. Our visual merchandising isn't on the scale of the world-class windows at London department stores—Selfridges, Liberty or Harrods. But, for a bijoux boutique just off Bond Street, right in the heart of London's designer shopping enclave, our little shop and its two bay windows gets a *lot* of attention.

* * *

On the morning of Mona's visit, we had all come in early to ensure the store looked more dazzling than ever. I'd even brushed the shag-pile rug—a first, even in our bonkers little world. The candles sent an intoxicating aroma of gardenia into the air, and the room-temperature Evian and best cut-crystal tumblers were set out. Mona didn't do Buxton or ice cubes, I discovered to my cost the first time I was dispatched for water without having received this important memo. And Kiki had spent the past ten minutes painstakingly assembling a pyramid of dark chocolate truffles on a white porcelain saucer next to the till (not that anyone was likely to eat one). Big Al was watching her with a mixture of awe and amusement.

'Dare you to take one from the bottom, Amber,' he whispered as I passed.

* * *

When I started at Smith's, Kiki had given me a crash course in preparation for a visit like this. Kiki was two years older than me, and boy did she let me know it. She'd been working at the boutique for nearly three years, and she was Jas's senior assistant. For me, the job was a full-time stopgap while I searched for a 'proper' career, ideally in visual merchandising, but Kiki adored everything about it. Waif-like, effortlessly hip and permanently looking as though she'd stepped off the pages of *i-D* magazine after a huge night at The Box, she had bags of attitude and I was intimidated by her from day one—a situation she seemed to relish. At first sight of me, Kiki had taken it upon herself to educate me in the intricacies of the fashion scene, because I so evidently needed it.

'There's a major hierarchy in the industry,' she explained, as I sat on a box of Diane von Furstenbergs once during stocktaking. Though she claimed to hail from the East End, Kiki still had a clipped, public school voice.

'At the top are the designers—the holy grail of Valentino, Giorgio Armani, Donatella Versace, Stella McCartney, Dolce & Gabbana and so on. Beneath these are the A-list stars who wear the designers' creations on red carpets everywhere from Hollywood to Cannes, at the Golden Globes, BAFTAs, Oscars, collecting gongs at all the glitziest bashes. And beneath these are the stylists, who do all the *real* work, getting them red-carpet ready and securing their appearances on "best dressed" lists around the world. Sod the little gold trophy—it's making *those* lists that really counts. A stylist like Mona Armstrong can make or break a celebrity with a sheer gown or a statement accessory. Remember when Angelina's leg pose at the Oscars went viral?' I nodded, sagely. 'But can you remember who won any of the awards that year?' I shrugged. My lecturer smiled appreciatively. 'Of course you can't. It was a moment that went down in red-carpet history.' She leaned in conspiratorially. 'But what works for one could be a horrendous fail on the poor cow who can't pull it off. It's a cut-throat world out there and styling underpins it all. Make no mistake, Amber, a celebrity without a stylist is like Kylie Jenner without her pout. We shut the entire shop when Mona comes in to choose pieces for her clients—it's *beyond* fabulous. But don't get carried away, it gets really, really stressful in the run-up to awards season. I ate a cheese baguette once.'

It must have been stressful, because it wasn't hard to guess why Vicky and I had nicknamed Kiki the Stick Insect, or lately just the Stick. I often saw her downing pints of pond-water-looking liquid from recycled water bottles— her famous Super Greens—and the work fridge was always stocked with bags of lettuce and bean sprouts that she snacked on during the day or, more often than not, went off, causing a hideous stench that I would regularly have to clean up. Only once did I see her pick at something vaguely calorific—a lavender macaroon—and that was only because it had been sent in by the fashion editor at *Bazaar* and she wanted to #Instafood it.

Kiki was hardly coming up for air during this particular lesson.

'Seriously, Amber, it's ah-mazing when Mona comes in—she's been dressing the big names like Jennifer Astley and Beau Belle for years. And if they wear an outfit Mona's borrowed from Smith's, when the fash mags come out and we're credited Jas is on cloud nine. It's *sooo* good for business. But it's not only the red-carpet stuff. I mean, it was Mona who introduced the whole gypsy trend we're seeing now.' She fluffed up her billowing sleeves to illustrate the point. 'The second Beau went shopping on Rodeo Drive wearing a peasant skirt and crochet top—literally *all* the high-street stores were knocking out rip-offs within weeks. Mona is *that* powerful.'

I quickly learned that the Stick had a major fashion crush on Mona, and by this particular January day I was well versed in the life of the super-stylist.

* * *

As usual, I had spent most of the morning being bossed around by Kiki, before being directed by Jas to finish off the windows. I loved the narrow wooden 'stage' between the bay windows and the store—a small space that might have felt claustrophobic, but was a beautiful blank canvas to me; somewhere I could create an image of the woman all our customers wanted to be. Dressing the mannequins, I'd follow Jas's chosen 'Look' from the stack of look books the fashion houses provided with each new collection— usually a ring-bound folder containing photos of a series of models posing in a white studio wearing the label's latest designs. Really it was window dressing by numbers, but because we held only edited versions of the collections at Smith's, to my delight, Jas would often let me add personal touches—an edgy accessory or eye-catching shoe—to bring the ensemble to life. We changed the windows on a Monday, once a fortnight, to stop them feeling stale. This week we had refreshed them specifically with Mona in mind—they had to be 'wow'. Jas had instructed me to put a strictly black and white outfit on each of the two mannequins, a look we then made 'pop' with one statement accessory; a bright green leather cuff on one and a stand-out red clutch under the arm of the other.

'Our girls look stunning today!' she declared, before suggesting the footwear I should add to each model's perfectly smooth size seven plastic feet—one was to wear black and the other ivory heels, completing the monochrome vision. As I admired my handiwork from the street outside, I mulled over which pair of shoes should go on which mannequin. *Not bad for a morning's work.*

'Am-ber!' Kiki trilled from the doorway, breaking the spell. 'You forgot to steam the Stella!' *Jesus Christ, does she ever let up?* Three perfectly pressed Stella McCartney jumpsuits later, Jas conducted a final walk-through to ensure everything was just so. And then, decked out ourselves in on-trend outfits (borrowed from the store for the duration of Mona's visit; our slim wages could never afford the real thing), we were ready to welcome fashion royalty.

* * *

Bang on time the assistant director, Rob, arrived. He skidded on the shag-pile and almost slipped over, making me want to giggle.

'Great entrance there, well done, Rob,' he said, quickly composing himself and catching my eye as he laughed it off. My internal laughter then gave way to a fear that the highly polished floor/fluffy rug combo might actually be a potential death trap. *What if Mona breaks her leg?* Rob pushed a strand of floppy brown hair behind his ear. When he came round to shake my hand, I became aware that my palms were sweaty.

'Are you responsible for these gleaming floors?' he quipped.

My cheeks flushed. *Despite wearing new season Jonathan Saunders, I still resemble the resident skivvy. How?* 'Sorry about that.'

'You'd better hope Mona's put the cheese-grater over her soles,' he replied. 'Unlike me.'

I laughed nervously. There was a familiarity about him.

Kiki gave me a withering look. 'That's what people on TV do,' she informed me, loud enough for Rob to hear, 'to stop them slipping on the studio floor.'

'I know,' I lied.

If she was trying to show me up, I didn't really care. I was more interested in Rob taking off his jacket. He pushed up the sleeves of his grey jumper revealing what looked like the beginning of a tattoo on his upper arm.

Rob was the first to arrive of the team of three. The next, sporting a directional dyed red bob and wearing thick, black-rimmed glasses, was introduced as Fran, the director. There was also a long-haired, lanky bloke carrying the camera, who went by the name of Dave. I inwardly christened him Shaggy. I wondered if, like us, Fran and Rob had put on their most fashion-conscious clothes for Mona's benefit, or whether they always looked so media cool. As word went round that 'She' was about to arrive, Rob hurriedly took down our contact details and had us each sign a release form and NDA. I barely read the words; I was too busy concentrating on trying not to do anything embarrassing.

* * *

Today, as ever, you could spot Mona's sunglasses before you saw the rest of her. Huge, round Prada shades, covering at least half of her small, elfin face, came bobbing down the street, swooping towards the store like a large fly. Light chestnut boho waves with streaks of caramel blonde cascaded around her shoulders; now a flash of matte coral lipstick came into view. She was only average height, even in towering heels—in fact she was more shades and curls than actual person—but in the fashion world, she was God. She paused to take in the windows; I felt a prickle of excitement, hoping she liked what she saw. She looked the mannequins up and down, but her sunglasses hid any kind of facial expression. At last, Mona entered our pristine temple of style. As she made her entrance for the camera, Jas, Kiki and I simultaneously clocked a turquoise cocktail ring the size of a golf ball on her petite index finger. Behind me, Kiki let out a gasp.

'YSL, new season,' she whispered, as if we were observing a rare exotic bird.

And then the front door was locked, the shop sign switched to Closed, the French blinds rolled down and we pulled up ringside seats at the Mona Armstrong show. Of course there was no real need to pull down the blinds, to the average person, Mona was just an eccentrically dressed, extremely thin, seemingly ageless woman in OTT sunglasses. But in the world between these four white walls, she was the high priestess.

According to Kiki, my main tasks during this particular visit would be to silently hold clothes for Mona, refrain from taking part in fashion small talk (I wasn't qualified), try to keep off-camera (not photogenic enough, presumably) and above all, concentrate on not tripping up in the stupidly high Nicholas Kirkwoods I'd made the mistake of thinking I could walk in (hello, bunions).

I'd been fully briefed that Mona's long-time assistant, Tamara, would do most of the running around, trying things on, holding items to the light and offering opinions on the season's hottest threads. Blonde and long-limbed, able to pass for a model herself, Tamara was a well-known face on the fashion circuit, too, having been Mona's assistant for several years. She was the only person—other than Jas and Mona—who I had ever seen the Stick try to make an effort for. When Tamara had once retweeted Kiki ('Smith's is now stocking Roksanda! #Ledge'), she'd been bouncing off the walls for days. Today she was more exhilarated than ever about Tamara's visit because apparently there'd been some rumours among the fashion Twitterati that Tamara might be on the verge of setting up on her own—that it was actually *her* who had been dressing some of Mona's regular clients. She had even been snapped spending New Year on board a yacht in the Caribbean with none other than the BAFTA rising star—not to mention former regular client of Mona's—Poppy Drew. Plus, there were hints that Tamara, instead of Mona, would be dressing the actress Jennifer Astley for awards season this year, where she was hotly tipped to win a slew of Best Supporting Actress awards. *But that's just gossip.*

Until today, when Tamara was nowhere to be seen.

Chapter Two

Since Mona entered the store, Jas had been doing most of the talking. They'd begun with the customary detailed appraisal of each other's outfits—the way peers traditionally greet each other in fashion land.

'Mad about the ring…'

'Those shoe-boots…'

'You lucky cow, you've got the Balenciaga leather pants! Isn't the stretch amazing…'

'I must get your colourist's number.'

'Loving the matte nails. Is it gel?'

And so on. Then they finally got down to the juicy stuff.

'No Tamara today, Mona?' Jas asked.

Mona responded by handing her Pradas to Rob, who took them politely. Massaging her temples, she completely ignored the question. The Stick and I tried, unsuccessfully, not to gawp. We felt like we needed to drink up everything about her: her clothes, her shoes, her hair, her skin, which had the kind of pearly sheen that only really expensive make-up could achieve, her whiter-than-white teeth, her bag, her jewellery, the way she moved, her voice. If we weren't so fearful of her, we'd have gone up and given her a good sniff all over, too. There was an intoxicating musky aroma around her, beginning to settle in the air. Everything about Mona was absurdly fascinating.

'Well, just let me and the girls know what we can do,' Jas offered, leading her over to the clothes rails. The Stick gave me a gentle prod in the back, a signal that I should get into position, ready to hold clothes.

As Mona began to rifle through the latest Stella McCartneys, Fran with the bob shouted, 'Action!' Shaggy sprang to life and so did Mona, chatting animatedly to Jasmine. She *really* knew how to turn it on for the cameras.

'It's only Tuesday and this week's already a fucking nightmare, Tamara's gone and left me right up shit creek. The silly bitch handed in her notice this morning.'

From her language, I made the assumption that this was to be a post-watershed pilot. Fran with the bob raised an eyebrow and Rob bit his lip.

'*This* morning. Can you fucking believe it? I go for the bloody Globes tomorrow. That girl's out of her mind if she thinks she'll last two minutes doing awards season solo. Oh wow, look at the Stella jumpsuits, aren't they divine? I'll definitely take a couple of these.'

Mona had no problem with multitasking. Between slagging off Tamara and gushing over the clothes, every so often she pulled out an item from the rail and handed it to me, standing with arms outstretched like a forklift truck, by her side. I wasn't sure if I was actually in shot, though a little part of me hoped I was; just a bit of my dress or, ideally, the beautiful shoes. *Loads to tell Vicky about tonight.*

'But honestly, Jas, what the *hell* am I supposed to do? I've got at least twenty global superstars wanting me to dress them over the next week, and only a few days to sort the whole frigging lot out—I've got photo-calls, cocktail parties at Soho House, premieres—not to mention the awards themselves. She could not have done this at a worse time.'

Jasmine, too cool to play up to the camera or be drawn into slagging anyone off, was trying to offer some comfort, shaking her head and nodding empathically in all the right places, whilst calmly directing Mona back to the clothes and the job in hand.

'You poor love—how will you get through it? Have you seen the new Lanvin?'

'Oh, I'll do it, all right.' Mona looked directly into the camera lens for effect. '*Nothing* comes between me and my superstars. But at this precise moment, it's so unfunny, I actually feel like screaming.'

I glanced over towards the Stick. Brow furrowed, she was totally immersed in Mona's plight, feeling her pain. *Does she know she's folded and refolded that mohair jumper three times?* The *20Twenty* crew huddled around Mona, filming her intently. Fran with the bob was chewing the end of her biro while Rob held a boom mic just above Mona's head.

I wondered if they'd shot the fateful scene with Tamara handing in her notice earlier in the day. *I wouldn't have liked to be in her shoes when she told Mona the news.* Jas began motioning Mona over to her 'Ones to Watch', concern etched across her delicate features.

'What a total nightmare. But surely you have some girls you use in LA, Mona—is there anyone I can have Kiki call for you? Kiki, honey!'

The Stick immediately dropped the jumper and rushed

on-set, almost skidding to a halt on the shag-pile in front of Mona. *Damn—it would have been entertaining to see her take a dive.* Her box-fresh Kirkwoods were clearly as uncomfortable as mine. The camera and boom turned to her. Idly, I wondered if the Stick was Rob's type.

'No, darling—there's no one I can call.' Mona turned away, barely registering Kiki. 'Loving this though—what's the label?'

'Star-Crossed, she's a recent graduate, will show at London Fashion Week,' Jas informed her, pulling a couple of cocktail dresses from the rail.

'Hmm.' She moved on.

Mona then turned her gaze to the front of the store. Kiki retreated, crestfallen, her small-screen debut over before it began.

'That reminds me,' Mona continued, 'the windows. I'm loving the monochrome, but what you've done with the shoes is inspired.'

Jas and Kiki both looked at me, puzzled. We all joined Mona at the side of the bay windows. My cheeks began to heat up as I racked my brains. *What could have happened to the shoes?* The shaggy cameraman headed towards the front of the store, too, Rob lifting cables behind him. Kiki and Fran followed. Surreptitiously, we all strained to see the feet of the two mannequins standing exactly as I'd left them, with their backs to us behind the glass facade. The burning sensation in my cheeks turned into a wave of panic as it hit me like a cold, hard slap in the face—I'd been standing outside, looking at the mannequins from the street, when the Stick had screamed for me to come in and finish steaming the jumpsuits. I'd meant to come back to them, but got distracted by Mona's arrival... *Oh God*... I'd left one white and one black shoe on each mannequin's plastic feet.

I feel sick.

'Which of you is responsible for the mismatched shoes?' Mona asked.

I shuffled uncomfortably, knowing I had nowhere to hide. I wanted to open the door and run far away from here; just keep on running until I found a bush to hide under in Regent's Park, or a cardboard box in an underpass. I wanted to be at my parents' house—better still, my grandma's flat. Somewhere no one would find me. Jas and the Stick both looked in my direction, frowning, willing me to speak, lest Mona should think either of them had messed up the display.

'Come on, don't be shy,' Mona urged, searching our faces.

The camera's big, nosy lens pointed towards us. I hated Shaggy for putting me on the spot like this with his horrible, ugly camera. And I hated Rob and Fran even more, for not stopping him. Eventually I plucked up the courage to speak.

'It was me, Mona, I...'

'The monochrome vibe, it's so fresh, so relevant,' she said. 'But what you've done with the shoes—*j'adore*! You're a genius, girl.'

Is she having a laugh?

Before I could say it was a hideous mistake that I had meant to fix, she was gesturing to the TV crew. 'Have you got this, cameraman?' She ushered Shaggy closer to get a good view of my stunned, blotchy face.

'Babe, it's a brave statement,' she continued, 'but you totally nailed it. The odd shoes grabbed my attention straight away.'

'They did?'

Luckily for me, Mona doesn't listen to other people's doubts.

'And *that's* what this business is all about. You don't gain column inches by blending in with the crowd. You've got to wear a look with conviction, you've got to stand out, kick it up a notch. Mixed up monochrome has a buzz to it—it's the perfect way to inject some attitude into a cocktail look or get noticed on the street. It's cheeky and playful—seriously, it's reinvention at its best. Loving your Kirkwoods, by the way.'

The camera zoomed in on my (matching) pair of too-tight suede and metal heels. They were amazing, all right. Amazing at cutting off the circulation to my toes. I winced.

'Jas, you're a lucky woman to have this talent on your team.'

I still didn't know whether she was being sarcastic or not, when she said: 'I'll take odd pairs of Sandersons, black and white, in all the sizes you've got.'

When I dared to glance in her direction, the Stick looked as though someone had handed her an envelope marked 'Anthrax' and told her to snort it. The camera zoomed in for a close-up of the mixed up shoes on the mannequins and I cringed inside. Then Mona grabbed me by the arm and shoved me into the shot, as well.

'And here is the girl responsible! Kiki, isn't it?'

I smiled awkwardly.

'It's...Amber...' I stuttered.

'Well, what a morning it's been already. It must be time for a coffee break. A big, strong caffè macchiato, that's what I need. You?' She looked at me.

'Sure, I'll go,' I answered, desperate to scurry out of sight and compose myself.

'No, I mean you'll have one, too, right, Amber?'

'You—' Mona looked at the Stick, who skipped forward expectantly.

'You be a darling and run to the Monmouth coffee shop for me and Miss Windows, would you, babe? They do the best caffè macchiato in London and I've been craving one all morning.'

And before Kiki could say, 'But this is a dreadful mistake!', and before Jas could ask her to kindly not wear her borrowed Pucci dress and box-fresh Nicholas Kirkwoods out of the store, she'd been dispatched to a coffee establishment on the other side of Zone One. As she wrapped herself up in a fake fur swiped from a rail by the door, the camera followed her out, witnessing her almost getting tangled up in the French blinds. Meanwhile I remained anchored to Mona's side, her cold fingers still holding my arm in a vice. I battled the urge to ask the Stick to pick me up a croissant while she was at it. None of us had eaten all morning and I was starting to feel faint.

* * *

Mona's sweep of the shop complete, we moved over to the rail I had filled with her chosen pieces. 'Pieces' are what the fash-pack call items of clothing, shoes and accessories, a bit like they're artefacts in a museum.

'Hold it there, babe—you can't shoot the pieces!' Mona turned to Rob, who was helping Shaggy get some close-ups of the designer haul on display.

'Jennifer Astley's Golden Globe–winning gown could be on this rail! We can't let the dress out of the bag. That's enough, let's wrap.'

With the caffeine jump leads not yet connected, she'd lost interest in filming. The crew busied themselves winding up cables, opening flight cases and checking their phones, probably counting down the minutes before they could escape to the pub for a much-needed pint. It was exhausting being in Mona's company. Jas disappeared into her office to prepare a dossier detailing her edit of the store, so we could arrange for items to be couriered to her in the States or packaged up for her to take. For the first time, I was left alone in the court of Mona Armstrong.

'Coffee's taking its time,' she huffed.

I'd almost forgotten about the Stick. I imagined the long queue outside the Monmouth Coffee Company at all times of day. Even if she'd placed the order and had the exact change, with a black cab waiting on double yellows, the macchiato was bound to be stone cold by the time she got back. It was a no-win situation. I suddenly had an overwhelming urge to break the rules and start a conversation with Mona.

'Sounds like you're having a bad day.' *Did I really say that?*

'You can say that twice.' I battled the urge to take her at her word.

Then she sighed. 'You don't happen to know any styling assistants who could start tomorrow, do you?'

A vivid apparition flashed before my eyes: *Me, adjusting the train on Jennifer Astley's diaphanous designer gown as she gets out of a limousine at the foot of the Golden Globes red carpet. The bank of paparazzi awaiting her and the frenzy of flashes when she strikes a perfectly honed pose in front of them,* with just enough leg on display to ensure maximum column inches the next day. *And the Golden Globe for Best Dressed Actress goes to…* Of course I had no actual experience of what this looked like, but I'd seen enough coverage of similar events in the pages of the glossies to have a vague understanding. Then something completely unplanned happened.

'I'm free.'

Crap. Where did that come from?

My heart rate lifted, and I swallowed hard. Mona turned to look at me; I mean *really* look at me, not just my shoes—and she actually seemed to soften. She subtly motioned to Rob and suddenly a light was shining on my face, the boom overhead and the camera lens too close for comfort.

'Do you know how to make a good, strong caffè macchiato?'

'Yes.' *I didn't, but what was this? Not an interview for head Starbucks barista.*

'Can you steam?'

'Yes.'

I didn't think she was talking about milk. Steaming, I did know all about, having lost a colossal number of my life's hours to this hot and stuffy basement, carefully teasing the creases from the latest Cavalli, Chloé and McQueen creations before they made it to the shop floor.

'Can you work the next fortnight straight—that means long days, little sleep and no time off until everything's been returned?'

'Yes, ma'am.' *Why did I say 'yes, ma'am'? Idiot.*

I didn't know if I actually was available, but I would make myself, because I suddenly wanted this…whatever it was…so badly. She lifted a foot and sank her spiky heel into the shag-pile rug we'd found ourselves marooned on, like castaways upon a fluffy island.

'What star sign are you?'

'Gemini.'

'Too good to be true! I love what you did with the shoes back there. It was edgy, it was sharp. I can see you're a risk-taker. You've got flair. Yes, I like you, Amber.' She tucked a stray boho wave behind her ear and looked me straight in the eye once more. 'Surname, poppet?'

The light from the camera was hot as well as bright; it was making my cheeks fizz and my eyes water. I thought of Kiki, obediently trekking back across town in the freezing cold, trying not to spill a drop of Mona's precious coffee. *Perhaps it should be me in that queue; maybe she should be here. I'm out of my depth. No—you can do this, Amber. Just do it!*

'Green. Amber Green.'

Mona looked upwards for a moment, as if she was consulting a higher being. For the first time her face broke into a smile that also engaged her eyes. They were hazel. She was attractive, even under the camera's harsh light. She fiddled with the golf ball ring.

'Amber Green. Love it, babe. Not a bad name…if traffic lights are your thing.'

A hushed snigger went round the TV crew. *Thirteen years of being called Traffic Light at school has made me tougher than this. Thanks once again, parents, it's been character-building.*

'You've clearly had the nous to give yourself a fashion pseudonym,' Mona said, silencing the sniggerers. 'Ralph Lauren wouldn't have got very far if he'd kept the surname Lifshitz, would he, darling?'

I smiled, weakly.

'You're perfect, Amber Green, Traffic Light. I'll pay you the work experience rate of fifty quid a week, plus food and expenses. You can stay in my house in LA for the fortnight,

though we'll be in a suite at the W for most of the time and
out at appointments and events. I'll get your flights. You
have a valid passport, don't you?'

*Fifty quid, is she taking the P? But I like the sound of the
W. I'm pretty sure she means the trendy hotel and not the
loo.* I nodded and mentally pictured the messy state of my
bedroom. I hadn't physically seen my passport for a long
time—I hadn't left the country for over two years. But it
had to be there somewhere. *Absolutely has to be.*

'Good. We're flying from Heathrow Terminal Five tomorrow morning. My PA will give you the details. Write
your number on here.' She thrust a Smith's business card
from a pile next to the candles into my sweaty palm.

'You'd better ask Jas if you can go home and pack.'

'Oh wow—really? Thank you, Mona—thanks *so* much.
I won't let you down! I absolutely promise.' She almost
looked like she wanted to give me a hug.

Should I smile into the camera now? Surely this *is TV
gold!* I suddenly realised what I was doing and stopped. 'Excitement is deeply unsexy,' Mona had recently stated in an
interview with *vogue.com*—an interview Kiki had printed
out and pinned to the office wall. The office Jas was coming out of right now. I'd almost forgotten I already had a
job and a boss—a very nice boss, at that. I averted my eyes,
entrusting Mona to handle the situation.

'Well, babe, seems like good old Amber Green has come
to my rescue.'

'Amber?' Jas turned to me, confusion creasing her face.
Don't blow it now, please, Jas. The camera was still rolling. I suddenly felt guilty for putting her on the spot like
this—not only with Mona, but in front of a TV crew, with
a potential audience of tens of thousands.

'Amber here,' Mona said, 'our traffic warden turned window dresser extraordinaire, Amber has offered to come to LA to help me survive the Globes. She only needs a two-week sabbatical. That's all right with you, isn't it, Jas, babe? There'll be credits aplenty for Smith's with your star pupil out there!'

Jas paused for a moment. I wanted the camera to stop and the rug to swallow me up.

'Of course it is. Amber's a lovely girl and very creative. Mona, you've landed on your feet.' Jas turned to look at me and for the first time ever I sensed a slight look of annoyance spread across her pretty features. 'Just don't have too much fun, okay?'

'Okay.' *Does that mean I'll have a job to come back to?* I daren't ask. Certainly not with this bloody camera in my face.

* * *

And that was it. In less than five minutes I'd gone from shop girl to 'window dresser extraordinaire' to temporary employee of Mona Armstrong: Stylist to the Staaars! The deal was sealed with an air kiss from Mona and then the cameras stopped for the day.

'Nice one,' Rob said, as he gathered their kit together. 'Congrats on the new gig.'

'Thanks... I think,' I blushed, busying myself neatening up the rails as I tried to take it all in.

'We'll see you in LA, then.'

I was holding open the door for the TV crew when a cold, stressed Stick approached balancing a cardboard tray of coffees.

'Hope I didn't miss much,' she said.

There isn't an emoticon to cover it.

Chapter Three

As she sipped her coffee, Mona didn't have to tell us that it was barely warm—we already knew. She sent an equally chilly look in the Stick's direction. I felt sorry for Kiki as she picked at her black painted nails; even her Pucci dress seemed to have lost its playful, voluminous look, and her face had the pained expression of someone whose actual soul had been crushed. Yes, hands up, I'd had nasty thoughts about the Stick from time to time. I'd be lying if I said I hadn't willed heavy, studded bags to fall on her head on more than one occasion. But now I started to feel sorry for her. The hours we'd spent preparing the shop for Mona's arrival suddenly felt like a long time ago—a distant land where expectations were high and fashion-fever reigned; a place where the Stick and I were almost friends.

Prada shades back on and a mirror check as she prepared to leave the store, Mona turned to me one last time: 'Oh, and, Amber? Pack your coolest clothes. Blacks, whites, neutrals are best. I need you to blend into the background.

Directional footwear optional.' She smiled, sunglasses conveniently hiding her facial expression once more, though I would have put money on a wink. 'Think Blake Lively over K. Middy. We're talking Los Angeles, babe, it's a whole different fashion landscape to London. And the weather rarely dips below twenty-five.' The Stick grimaced.

The idea of packing my 'coolest clothes' was already sending me into a panic, as was the weather. *Just what my pasty half-Scottish skin needs.* I doubted I had time to fit in a spray tan. 'There'll be a lot of running around, so bring flats as well as your killer heels.' *'Your killer heels'. Mona Armstrong thinks I'm a stylista who owns killer heels. I've really pulled the cashmere over her eyes.*

I pictured my wardrobe at home, wherein hung a cacophony of Zara, H&M and Topshop, plus some precious vintage finds gleaned from eBay (strictly under Vicky's supervision) and, at the bottom, an overflowing shoe rack stuffed with footwear in all colours and styles, not to mention various states of disrepair. It was a collection that had suited my life perfectly well up until this moment, but I somehow doubted it was up to Mona's standards. Plus the only understanding of 'killer heels' I had right now were the Kirkwoods currently killing my toes.

'But most importantly,' Mona continued, 'don't forget your kit.' The Stick folded her arms tightly, revelling in the knowledge that not only did I not own a kit, I probably didn't even know what one was.

'No, babe, I'm not talking about your gym gear.' Mona smirked, reading my mind. 'You know—the bits and bobs we need to make it all work.'

Hmm. I'd heard Tamara mention 'the kit' on previous visits to the shop, and had regularly noticed her delve into a well-used leopard-print vanity case, and come up bearing bulldog clips to cinch a dress together at the back. I also thought of Jas's bottom drawer in the office: a veritable emporium of tit tape, gaffer tape, Sellotape—every kind of tape known to woman—plus plasters, chicken fillets, cotton buds, Party Feet, pop socks, a sewing kit and a host of other goodies that surely kept the Bond Street branch of Superdrug in business.

'Of course,' I replied, glancing at the Stick. And then Mona was off, big sunglasses, bouncy hair and thin, leather-clad legs springing straight into a taxi.

* * *

Now there were just the three of us, plus Big Al, left in the store. Normally, following such a visit, Jas, the Stick and I would all sort of crumple onto the pouffes, kick off our heels, attack the truffles and champagne and erupt into a fevered discussion of what had just gone on. The Stick would dissect Mona's outfit, generally loving everything about it, and I'd think I *should* love it, but that most of it was plain weird; Jas would debate why she picked some items and not others, and we would all shriek with laughter. Big Al would feign disinterest, but he'd eventually crack, and chip in with a comment like 'What that woman needs is a roast dinner.'

But today, Mona left nothing in her wake but an awkward silence. *And it was all my fault.*

Throughout my final exchange with Mona, I had felt the Stick's eyes drilling holes in the back of my head, correctly sensing she had missed something important while she was queuing for coffee like a work experience flunky. I knew full well it should be her going to LA in the morning. The Stick had the experience, the knowledge, the look—she was born to be Mona's assistant. She idolised the woman. And then there was Jas—my kind boss, put on the spot like that. Left with no option but to step aside and let a member of her staff be poached before her eyes. I began to wonder if it was really worth it, if I was more cut out to be a traffic warden or a teacher after all. If I should do the honourable thing—step aside and offer the job to the Stick or simply tell Mona it was all a horrible mistake and stay at Smith's. But something stopped me. Another voice in my head tried to rationalise: this was the Stick's comeuppance for all the hours I'd spent sweating next to the steamer because *she* didn't want to risk her make-up; for the way she looked at me when I thought that Erdem was the name of a Turkish pop star, rather than the hottest designer on the block. I thought of Jas and her look of confusion when she saw the mismatched shoes on the dummies. She must have known it was an accident, but was too polite to embarrass me while I had the camera eyeballing me. And then I threw it back in her face by moonlighting with Mona. *I'm going to hell, for certain.*

I pulled myself together, stood taller and took a deep breath. *What's done is done.* And besides, perhaps now it was my turn to prove that I could do it, actually; that styling was my calling and Mona the person to nurture my talent; that I could make it in fashion, on my own merit. Yes, I'd show the Stick you don't need to slink around being too hip for Hoxton and live off pond water to get ahead. *Either that, or I'm a fraud—and not only a fraud but a horrible, selfish person.*

If only I'd put opposite shoes on the mannequins on purpose.

It was beginning to sink in that a) I might not have a job to return to, but b) my prospects for the next fortnight were looking up dramatically. I finally had an opportunity to be excited about—I couldn't wait to update my Facebook status. It might even be worth joining LinkedIn! I just had to find myself a kit and pull together a suitcase of cool looks that would get me through a fortnight in the entertainment capital of the world, because *I*, Amber Green of Greater London, was going to Los Angeles in the morning.

If this had been a film, with Jennifer Lawrence playing me, she would have punched the air when my feet, now comfortably clad in Uggs, hit the street outside the boutique that day. However, because this was not the movies, and because Jas had been uncharacteristically cold and the Stick had spent the rest of the day blanking me—bar the occasional tut—the mood was subdued. She broke the silence in the stockroom, as we layered-up for the cold, by taking the unusual step of suggesting we walk to the tube together. Perhaps she wanted to continue blanking me in the outside world, too. Having spent the entire afternoon fastidiously busying myself with my usual shop duties and doing all I could not to look halfway near as excited as I was beginning to feel, I had been planning to bolt bang on six. My phone was burning a hole in my pocket. I was *desperate* to call people, to scream, to see Vicky—to make it all real. The last thing I needed was an uncomfortable three-minute walk to Bond Street tube with a furious Stick.

It soon transpired that far from starting a *Dynasty*-style bitch fight in the middle of South Molton Street, her tactic was indeed to continue ignoring me. Finally, as we turned the corner into Oxford Street, she spoke.

'Bet you've had the best day ever?'

'It's been unusual, that's for sure.'

'So, she just told you you were going to LA, just like that?'

'I think she was just desperate to get someone to replace Tamara.'

'And my name didn't even get mentioned?'

'No. I mean, yes, it got mentioned, but you weren't in the shop.'

'So you went for it while I was out of sight?'

'It wasn't like that, Kiki.'

'Didn't you think you should tell her the shoes were an accident?'

Pass.

'God, this is such a joke!' She spat the words out.

'Listen, Kiki, I don't think it mattered to Mona if it was you or me. She just wanted someone—anyone—to help.'

'Didn't Jas tell her about me? How much more experience I've got? Didn't she put up a fight?'

'Would *you* fight Mona Armstrong?'

'If it was worth fighting for, I would.'

Ouch. I stopped walking. 'Kiki, I hate this. Shall we grab a coffee and talk about it properly?'

Kiki marched on, turning only briefly to shout over her shoulder: 'Coffee? Is that supposed to be funny?'

'Sorry, I forgot. Honestly, Kiki, Jas didn't have a say in it. We both know I'll probably get the sack after a day…'

But Kiki was more than a bit narked. She was angry.

'It's fucking ridiculous, that's what it is. What does she think I am, a bloody skivvy? *You* should have gone for the coffee.'

'Why—because *I* am a skivvy? A pointless skivvy who should have listened to your orders and kept her mouth shut the whole time Mona was in the store?' Now my blood was starting to boil, too. 'Perhaps, Kiki, just perhaps, Mona sent you for her coffee because she, like me, thinks you're not a very nice person. A person who's been so busy putting me down and bossing me around, she's never actually spared a thought for how I might feel—about anything—until I suddenly got something you want. Until now. Well, you know what? Fuck you, Kiki. You're a pathetic, skinny Stick Insect and I'm very happy I won't have to see your thin face, or have to look at your pond water, or clear your stinking lettuce out of the fridge, or steam another piece of fabric because you can't be bothered, because I'll be in LA with Mona Armstrong, styling the stars.' *Hah!* 'Oh, and don't forget, you signed an NDA so none of this can be repeated to anyone. Otherwise you'll be sued. *Hasta la vista*, Stick, I'm off home to pack my killer heels.'

Of course I didn't actually say that. But it was very real in my head. I've never been good at confrontation, so, in real life, I tried to bury the feelings of guilt currently making my stomach churn, and tried a change of tack.

'That guy Rob seemed nice?'

'I preferred the shaggy one.'

Au contraire.

We walked the final few steps in another awkward silence, both ranting inwardly. I decided against asking her opinion of what I should pack or if she had a kit I could borrow. The atmosphere between us was eating me alive, so I fibbed.

'I think I'll get the bus today. I need air.'

'Fair enough.'

She didn't even look me in the eye.

'I guess I'll see you in a couple of weeks, then.'

'Yeah, if Jas will have you back.'

And she was gone, skinny jeans and dip-dyed hair lost in a crowd of commuters, probably heading to a Shoreditch pub to break her NDA and slag me off with some East London hipsters. *I hope the NDA police are sitting at the next table.*

* * *

When I had safely turned off Oxford Street onto Manchester Square—when I could be sure that neither Kiki nor Mona nor any TV cameras were spying on me to see if I was displaying any embarrassing, high-spirited emotions—I did what every twenty-six-year-old in possession of her best job offer ever does: I phoned my mum.

'Are you walking again?' she asked, before I even said hello.

For some reason my mother has an aversion to me walking and talking. Probably because I always seem to phone her when I'm in transit.

'I've just finished work.' I stopped in the street and cupped the phone, to block out some of the traffic noise.

'It'd be nice if you phoned, just for a chat, when you weren't on a noisy street, on your way somewhere, that's all...'

'I know, Mum. Anyway, guess what?'

'You're coming to see us this weekend?'

'No...'

'We're coming to see you this weekend?'

'Afraid not. I've got a new job!'

'That's fantastic news, darling! A proper one?'

'It's in fashion!' Quiet on the end of the line. *An indication that my mother does not view this as news of a proper job.* 'I'm going to be a celebrity stylist. Well, I'm going to be an assistant to a celebrity stylist—and she's *the* celebrity stylist—I'm going to be Mona Armstrong's number two. Well, I think number two.' *Maybe I'm her number ten?* 'I don't actually know what my job title is. It's a two-week thing.'

'I thought for a second you'd decided to do the teacher training course...'

Not again.

'Darling, there's not much security there. Jasmine's happy to let you come back, is she?'

Why can't she just be excited for me?

'I'm flying to LA, tomorrow. For the Golden Globes!'

Another heavy pause.

'Mum? Did you hear that? I'm going to the Golden Globes!'

'Golden Globes, what's that? Some kind of Californian fruit growing contest? Don't tell me it's a beauty contest, you know I...'

'*No*, Mother. It's one of the film industry's biggest awards ceremonies, and I might be dressing some of the winners. I'm probably going to meet Jennifer Astley!'

Was I really saying those magic words?

'Jennifer who?'

Being a lawyer, my mother doesn't pander to the ins and outs of celebrity culture or the awards-season calendar, let alone share my enthusiasm for what dresses the stars might or might not wear during it. Instead, most conversations with her involve her checking I have the relevant paper-work for something.

'Does this Rhona have insurance? You've got travel insurance, have you, sweetheart?'

'Yes, I think I have insurance.'

'*Think*, darling? You need to have it *for sure*.'

'Yes, Mum.'

'And you'll definitely have a job when you get back, will you? Rent doesn't pay itself, and you can't leave poor Victoria in the lurch.' *You'd never have guessed this person had the eccentricity to name her child after a traffic light, would you? Once upon a time my mother must have had a sense of humour.*

'I know, I know, anyway, I need to get myself sorted out. Just wanted to let you know. I'll call from the airport if I have time.'

'Good luck, sweetheart, I'm proud of you. Just be safe, okay?' Though my mother rarely gives me any praise for my achievements—and granted they have been limited so far—for some reason I continue to seek her approval, because somewhere deep down it really matters. I tried to ignore a slight pang in the pit of my stomach. I couldn't face telling her the real circumstances and risk her disappointment in me, too.

'A fortnight you're going for, did you say? That means you'll miss Nora's performance next week,' she continued. 'Well, take care, and beware the Hollywood prima donnas. Remember, this fame thing—it's all smoke and mirrors. Keep your feet on the ground. And please check you've got insurance. Your father will sort it out if you haven't. Promise me, Amber?'

'Promise. Give Nora a squeeze from me. Love you. And Dad.'

Nora is my older sister's overachieving five-year-old, who is already the best in her ballet class and seems to have a recital of some kind almost every week. If we were an American family, she would probably resemble one of those scary over-made-up, disco-dancing, grown-up-looking kids you often see on freaky cable documentaries, their hair pulled back into such a tight bun they can barely blink. Poor Nora. There are already far too many performance photos of her in existence.

'I love you, too, sweetheart. Check your insurance.'

I hung up. Straight after I called Vicky, my flatmate and oldest, bestest friend since we bonded aged five at ballet class.

'I've got a job!'

'What? You've already got a job?'

'A proper one! Well, a temporary one. Actually a two-week one. But a possible career one! You're not going to believe the day I've had. It's been mad.'

It was so great to tell Vic the story—I was like a pressure cooker of exploding excitement, at last able to let it all out. I couldn't stop talking. When I finally paused, out of breath, her response was the one I'd been waiting to hear all day.

'Are you serious? That's bloody amazing, honey! You lucky cow! Oh my God, I'm so jealous I can't bear it. I feel sick! What was she like? Was she not a bitch, then? What was she wearing? Is she pretty? How much better looking than SJP on a scale of one to ten?'

This is why we're best friends.

'She was actually really nice, well, kind of nice, in a stand-offish, scary way, and tiny, so much smaller in the flesh. But actually really pretty. She had on these tight leather leggings and a T-shirt, Chloé, and these amazing black shoe-boots, tons of bracelets. And this ring, it was huge and turquoise, new-season YSL.' Vicky was gob-smacked, taking it all in. For once I sounded like I knew what I was talking about. *Perhaps I can do this after all.*

'And guess where I'm going in the morning?'

'Not Mona's house—don't tell me she's got a miniature dog she wants you to walk?'

'Nope. Well, yes, I am going to Mona's house—but not the one in London, the one in Los Angeles, baby! I'm going to the US of A because *I* am Mona Armstrong's assistant for the Golden bloody Globes!'

I had decided that Los Angeles sounded more grown-up and glamorous than LA. And I couldn't help wanting Vicky to be wowed by my new high-flying fashion status. It was generally her going to cool events and fashion shoots in exotic locations, so for once it was nice to share some fabulous news of my own. Cue screaming.

'Oh my God, it's too much! I'm going to faint!' *I love Vic.* 'Come home immediately—we need to discuss this in great detail.'

'Just getting on the tube. See you in half an hour.'

'Oh, and did you pinch my Mulberry? Either you've got it or we've been burgled, I've been looking for it everywhere.'

'Er, yeah, sorry about that…I needed to look good today. The Stick noticed it.' *Before she wanted to kill me.* 'I'll bring it home safely now.'

As I hung up, my elation was tinged by the return of a deep nagging sensation. I couldn't even admit to Vicky the exact circumstances in which I got my break.

Just before I walked down the escalator at Baker Street, my phone buzzed. Unknown number. *Mona's PA?* I hesitated for a moment and decided to let it ring to answerphone, thinking I'd call back at the other end, when I might be able to detect from her message whether the PA sounded like an uber-bitch or not. And then a much more exciting thought popped into my head. *Maybe it's Rob? He's looked up my number from the NDA. He wants to do some additional film-*

ing with me—take me to Selfridges to choose a few outfits for LA... Too late. Missed Call.

* * *

I got to Kensal Rise quickly. A year of taking the tube twice a day had made me an expert commuter, adept at standing behind the yellow lines on the platform at exactly the right spot to match the doors when the tube arrives, and then standing on the correct side of the carriage to be the first off again. During the journey I mulled over the packing situation. It was a major worry. But Vic would be able to help. She didn't get the fashion assistant position at *Glamour* under false pretences. I have always been in awe of how quickly Vicky can put together an outfit and look like the chicest person in the room. 'Naturally stylish,' Jas regularly comments, surveying her fondly, whenever Vicky comes to meet me from work, and it's been that way since we were at school together; she even made train tracks and a tight perm look good. I don't think anyone has ever said those words about me. I've come to accept that, for me, looking fashionable will be more of an effort. *I hereby vow to make dressing myself part of my job.*

When I reached our flat, circumnavigating the build-up of junk mail and spare rolls of recycling bags in the communal hallway, Vicky was standing in the living room, straining to see over her shoulder into the mirror to admire her near-perfect rear in a pair of eye-wateringly tight pale blue jeans.

'Do they look ridiculous, hon? Can you see my love handles over the top? I fell in love with them in the fashion cupboard, but now I'm worried. I wonder what happens if circulation to your arse actually stops?'

'You get a numb bum. They look amazing, honey, really.

You're probably the only person I know who could get away with jeans that tight. Honestly, you look sensational.'

'You would say that.'

'No, I wouldn't.'

'Oh yeah, you wouldn't. By the way, someone called for you. A man.'

My heart did a little leap.

'I didn't get his name, but he said he was Mona's PA and when he said that I was too dumbstruck and embarrassed to ask for his name again. He sounded *really* camp. He asked me to take down your flight reference number for the morning and to say you're on the 9:45 from Heathrow Terminal Five. Mona will meet you through security. He's texting you her number.'

She stuck a yellow Post-it onto my parka.

'But anyway, I think you deserve a drink, don't you?'

'Too bloody right!'

'And I need to hear more about Mona. Come on, I'm in these things now and I might never get them on again, so let's pop to The Chamberlayne and have one to celebrate. Are you really going tomorrow?'

Part Two:
Los Angeles,
The Golden Globes

Chapter Four

Through scared, aching eyes, I observed my alarm clock the next morning. Six o'clock.

My mouth was dry, my head pounding. I was still wearing my make-up but cuddling a pack of cleansing wipes. For a moment I couldn't remember what I was doing on this strange, unfamiliar planet. And then it all came flashing back: one quick drink at the pub had turned into several drinks and then a bottle of white wine back at ours. It had all culminated in our dizzily turning my bedroom upside down to find my passport and then emptying the entire contents of my wardrobe into a jumble sale heap on my bed. From this fabric mountain, Vic and I lumped all the black things into one pile, white into another, and anything with a vaguely designer-y label—we decided Stella McCartney for Adidas and an Anya Hindmarch protective cotton dust bag counted—into a third, before I passed out in a boob tube, in the middle of it all.

'Is that my case?' Vicky muttered, as I popped my head

around her door and shouted goodbye half an hour later, having lumped it all into the first suitcase I could lay my hands on.

'Sorry, hon. You'll have it back in a fortnight…if I come back. Wish me luck?'

'Luck? You'll need it. Can't wait to hear the stories. Take care. But not too much care. Neck some Nurofen on the way. Love you!'

And I was off—head hurting, stomach rumbling, badly put together, but excited as hell.

* * *

It wasn't hard to spot Mona in the Harrods concession at Terminal Five. She was wrapped in a large, brightly coloured scarf, striking poses in front of a full-length mirror. Two boxes of Marlboro Lights stood to attention in a clear plastic bag by her feet; a Venti Starbucks cup with coral lipstick all over the lid perched on a shelf nearby. *Smoke and mirrors indeed, Mum was right. Make that smoke, mirrors and caffeine.* Mona saw me in the reflection.

'Amber! Babe! I was beginning to get worried. What do you think? The canary yellow or bubble-gum pink? Don't you just love them? They are *so* LA.'

'Oh wow, divine.' *Did I just say 'divine'? Thank God Vicky can't hear me.*

'These little beauties are going to go down a storm for the daytime events. Get on to the Cavalli PR and have them sent over as soon as we land.' *Get on to the Cavalli PR. Have them sent over.* I felt queasy again. I hadn't actually had time to consider the work that was going to be involved with this job: the PRs whose numbers I didn't have, the requests I didn't know how to make, the sending over I didn't know how to go about.

'Right, I'll get on to it straight away.' My efficient tone belied my internal panic.

'I've put you down for the lounge—they *should* let you in. I'll meet you in there when I've finished shopping.'

'Right, boss, I'll see if they've got Wi-Fi so I can make a start.' *Has she noticed I'm wearing yesterday's make-up? My shaky hands?*

'They will, babe. And if I don't come up to the lounge, I'll see you at the gate.'

I hoped she wouldn't come up. What I really needed was some time to get my head together. One person who would definitely know the PR for Cavalli was the Stick, but I couldn't go there, so I texted Vicky as I looked for the lounge: First panic of the day—you don't happen to know the PR for Cavalli, do you? xx

A phone number was buzzed back a minute later, along with the words, Get hold of her Fashion Monitor, babe. It's the Bible. *How I wish Vicky was hiding in my suitcase.*

And then another text: How's your head? Mine's killing! Love ya xxx

I then spent the next thirty minutes in Boots buying Nurofen and Berocca for my hangover, emergency deodorant for my armpits, plus a large ironically garish cosmetics bag which I filled with an assortment of goodies from every aisle—chicken fillets, pop socks, Party Feet, plasters, breath fresheners, bull dog clips, cotton buds, medical tape—as much as I could stuff in.

* * *

When I eventually entered the British Airways Club Lounge, it was like entering a seventh heaven. Smartly dressed travellers sat on swivel stools at high white benches, working on laptops and iPads, and there were dimly lit seating areas with comfy chairs and lamps on coffee tables. I gravitated towards the darkest, most deserted corner I could find. A lady dressed like a pristine air stewardess pointed out the hot and cold buffet and advised me of the full drinks service on offer. Best of all, everything was free! *Had I known about this before, I'd have dragged my sorry self out of bed even earlier.* I headed straight for the brunch buffet and filled up a plate with croissants, scrambled eggs and bacon, all the while looking over my shoulder. The last thing I needed was for Mona to witness me gorging on breakfast like a normal human being. If Vicky had been with me I'm sure we'd have washed it down with a Buck's Fizz, but I decided to stick to a sensible skinny latte.

At last I felt some colour return to my cheeks. After eating, I managed to call a really nice, friendly lady called Jane in the Cavalli press office. She didn't seem pretentious or too fashiony at all, but promised to call their LA office, 'as soon as they wake up', and have a selection of scarves biked over to Mona's suite at the W Hotel in West Hollywood to arrive ahead of us that day. It actually hadn't been as difficult as I thought.

If use of the lounge had gone to my head, I was swiftly parachuted back to reality when we reached the aircraft's door. Of course I was directed to the right and Mona sashayed left, dumping her shopping and Louis Vuitton tote on an air steward, who offered a saccharine smile in response.

'Lovely to see you on board again, Ms Armstrong.'

I'm sure she gave me a knowing look straight after.

* * *

Mona reappeared some time after the meal—a hangover-friendly cheesy pasta. She popped out from behind the coveted curtain, waved a black Juicy cashmere tracksuit–clad arm in my direction, put her palms into a prayer position and then motioned a sleep sign. I mouthed 'Sleep well' back; another sweaty pea-head among the Economy passengers, knowing we were unlikely to get much, if any, shut-eye during the remaining eleven hours to LAX. When she turned back towards the curtain, you couldn't miss the words 'The Stylist' written across the back of her black velour hooded top in Swarovski crystals.

'Should I know who she is?' asked a Northern man sitting next to me, craning his neck for a better look.

No sooner had Mona gone than she reappeared like a magician's glamorous assistant, brandishing a little white tablet which she dramatically thrust into my hand, wafting a large dose of her pheromone-reactive Molecule 01 fragrance through the stale cabin. In a loud whisper, she told me: 'Melatonin, babe. Best sleeping pill there is. Everyone in America uses it. Drop it now and you're guaranteed a few hours.'

Unfurling my fingers, I looked at the small round pill. It didn't look too alarming, but I decided to snap it in half, just in case. I'd always been told it was unwise to accept drugs from relative strangers—especially ones you suspected were of dubious sanity. And then I thought *sod it* and swallowed both halves. After she had left us again, the man next to me shuffled uncomfortably. 'Did you see that camel toe?'

I chuckled. He had a point.

'And that melatonin shit—they don't sell it in the UK, you know. Made from sheep's brains.'

'Too late.'

Sheep's brains or no sheep's brains, I was going to Tinseltown, and there was a guy who bore more than a passing resemblance to Robert Pattinson a few rows in front.

For all the Hermès in Harrods I wouldn't swap places with anyone right now.

The one benefit of having a monstrous hangover on a flight was the ability it conferred to glaze over and, as it turned out, sleep. Maybe it was the melatonin, but I managed to nod off for a few hours. Arriving in LA—Mona in her third outfit of the day, a cool, cream Marni shirt dress and ballet pumps, and me still in my first outfit—skinny jeans, ankle boots, black American Apparel sweater (which Mona eyed disapprovingly and I was paranoid was starting to smell)—we made it through immigration without difficulty. This was 'a bloody miracle', according to Mona, who had given me strict instructions to bat my eyelids, smile and pretend to be dim, should I be asked any difficult questions, like what I was doing in the United States of America. *I wouldn't be lying if I responded, 'I'm not entirely sure'.*

'They nearly *always* question the excess baggage,' she explained, as I pushed a heavy trolley piled high with the rest of her Louis Vuitton luggage, Vicky's battered suitcase, plus two huge, smart, hard black cases full of clothes for the suite, towards the car-rental centre.

* * *

We were soon in the mid-afternoon sunshine, top down on the hired, fashionably eco-conscious Toyota Prius convertible, whizzing up La Cienega and heading towards Mona's second home in the Hollywood Hills. The warm breeze licked at my face and whisked my hair high into a Mr Whippy before throwing it down again to lash against my cheeks. With Vicky's Ray-Bans on—*she won't even know, it's winter at home*—and a slick of lip gloss hastily applied in the airport loo, I was feeling surprisingly good. As we cruised up wide, palm tree–lined roads, a cheesy

Ronald McDonald smile spread right across my face. The sight would have made Mona wince, but she was too busy shouting at the in-car phone, which was failing to acknowledge any of her instructions. I crossed my arms on top of the door, leaned out and breathed it all in. The air smelled sweet and biscuity. *I love it here already.*

A trio of honey-skinned girls, who looked as though they'd stepped straight off the set of the latest Abercrombie & Fitch ad shoot, pulled alongside us in a convertible jeep. I wondered if they were the kind of women I'd soon be hanging out with at the W Hotel. They were intimidatingly pretty, all golden Californian perfection. Wait a minute, wasn't one of them a Kardashian? Could be. Probably is. *I can't wait to tell Vic about this.* I caught myself staring. And then a wave of panic rippled through me: *Will I be able to fit in here?* Suddenly I felt like my teenage self again, the slightly overweight girl with spots and home-dyed hair, denim dungarees and plastic clip-on earrings, who ate her dinner without removing her CD-Man. *I bet none of the Abercrombie girls have had bad hair or been overweight in their lives. I bet they were allowed to get their ears pierced as soon as they could talk.* The car screeched as we sped around a right turn, on a red light.

'Mona! Didn't we just—'

'Oh, sweetheart, you're so funny. This is America, remember? It's perfectly legal to go right on a red.' I sunk back into the seat, not convinced. 'Chill out! No need to call the traffic police, Amber Green.' She laughed to herself and I gripped my seat belt, saying a silent prayer that we would make it to her house alive.

Wiping a bead of sweat from my forehead, another, more pressing thought dawned on me: *I may have packed very badly.* I realised all at once that I was beyond boiling in my outfit. And I had a nasty feeling that, thanks to my hung-over packing, I'd forgotten to chuck the white pile into the suitcase. My heart rate quickened, and my body felt clammier still. This meant I had brought with me an almost exclusively black, winter, working wardrobe—a look better suited to the role of a Black Sabbath roadie about to embark on a tour of Siberia than a cutting-edge stylist preparing for awards season.

I glanced back at the Abercrombie girls. None of them were wearing black. They were wearing spaghetti-strap candy-coloured vest tops and light denim, with delicate, layered gold necklaces to enhance their tans. They looked cool and clean, everything I currently was not.

* * *

Finally, we crossed Sunset Boulevard and followed a winding road, climbing steeply into the hills. The words to 'Sunset Boulevard' played over in my head. The Lord knew I'd listened to the soundtrack enough times, always in the car with Dad tunelessly singing along. Oh, how apt they seemed today.

Sunset Boulevard, twisting boulevard,
Secretive and rich, a little scary.
Sunset Boulevard, tempting boulevard,
Waiting there to swallow the unwary.

Mona began pointing things out: 'That house over there, behind those gates, that's Keanu Reeves's. We used to share a gardener. And that one is Jennifer Aniston's old place, before she moved in with Justin. She hasn't sold yet—maybe she's hedging her bets. Moby's got an architectural house way up there and if you keep going down that road, eventually you reach the Playboy Mansion.' I ooohed and aaahed in all the right places, not even having to feign excitement. It was just like being on a film set as we glided past Mulholland Drive and spied beautiful mansions nestled in the nooks of the winding hillside roads. I imagined Hollywood heavyweights like Sylvester Stallone and Bette Midler tucked away behind the security gates, wearing silk dressing gowns, reading scripts or dictating updates to their autobiographies in sumptuous living rooms.

'Up there—' I craned my neck skywards '—is Madonna's house. I've been to parties there. Insane.'

'What happened?' I attempted to make conversation, but Mona ignored me. I was learning fast that any chit-chat was strictly on her terms. Idly, I wondered how old Mona was and where she was born. I knew so little about this woman currently driving me off into the Hills to stay in her home. I guesstimated mid-to-late forties. Birthplace? I had assumed London, because of her English accent, but now I wasn't entirely sure.

She was on a roll. 'Christina Applegate walks her dog around here every day, and see that tree? That's where Lindsay Lohan crashed her car. And before you ask, no, the Hollywood sign is not near here, it's the other side of Hollywood Heights. So touristy, though—you won't want to do that.' *Oh. I'd been quite looking forward to posting that particular photo of myself on Facebook.*

Eventually we pulled up on Mona's driveway, in front of a magnificent, large Mediterranean-style house with terracotta tiles on its whitewashed walls. It was the kind of house I'd own in my fantasy life. Beneath us was the most incredible view of the sprawling city and the smog cloud above it. It was out of this world. I felt speechless.

'Amazing view, hey, babe?'

I breathed it all in. *Beats the sight of Scrubs Lane from my window at home.*

'It's incredible.'

* * *

Inside Mona's house we were greeted by a zebra skin rug. I hesitated.

'Don't panic, babe, no need to Tweet the WWF, it's fake.'

A wisp of a girl wandered into view. She had long, thin brown hair and was wearing a pale yellow bikini under an oversized white T-shirt with the words 'Relax Don't Do It' emblazoned across the front in shouting black capitals.

'Amber, this is Klara. She's staying here while she takes over the modelling world. Isn't that right, Klara, babe?'

The girl smiled. She was a natural beauty, her face completely bare of make-up. She was younger than me, maybe twenty maximum. And she was thin, so thin. Her pale legs seemed to go on forever. She was like a kind of miniature giraffe.

'Thanks, Mona,' she replied softly, in an English accent, before slinking off again through some large glass doors at the end of the open lounge area onto a patio, and was that a swimming pool behind? *It is!* My insides did the Macarena.

'The great thing about having models as tenants is they hardly eat anything,' Mona revealed, the girl out of earshot as we made our way into the heart of the house, which opened up into a large living area.

'All I do is stock up on peanut butter and rice cakes, leave some fresh coffee and grapes in the fridge and they're happy. They don't even need milk for coffee. Klara's been over from London staying the last six months, on and off, and I've not seen her eat anything but rice cakes and grapes the whole time.'

The girl had slipped some denim shorts over her bony thighs and sauntered back into view. Exotically beautiful, she looked a bit sleepy, dazed, not quite 'with it'. Maybe she had just woken up—I wasn't exactly feeling dynamic myself. Mona beckoned her over.

'Come here, Klara, babe, let Amber see you properly. You're looking gorgeous. Tell us, when are we going to see the new Burberry campaign?'

The girl moved across to the vast open plan kitchen–diner area to the right of the high-ceilinged lounge, and we followed, leaving our suitcases in the hallway. Klara sat on one of the breakfast stools, pulling her long legs up and hugging them into her chest. My eyes darted around the room, taking it all in. It was filled with more shiny white kitchen cabinets than I would ever know how to fill. A thick black marble worktop with inlaid sparkly bits went around in a horseshoe, above which hung three modern white-and-chrome statement light fittings that shed circular shafts of light onto the wide breakfast bar.

Mona followed my line of vision.

'It's filled with Swarovski crystals, babe. One of a kind.'

Klara plucked a grape from a large bowl on the top and began carefully peeling off its skin.

'It's stunning,' I uttered, running my hand across the welcome, cool surface. I wanted to put my flushed cheeks on it, too. Everything was so sparse and clean, I felt like I was messing up the feng shui just by being here.

'Anyway, tell us some gossip, Klara?'

'It's been awesome, Mona,' she replied, barely transferring her attention from the half-bald grape. *She's about to tell us something exciting, but is showing absolutely zero signs of enthusiasm for it—Mona has trained her well.*

'I was shooting with David de la Valle last week—it went on into the night and then we all went to Soho House and had espresso martinis while we watched the sun come up. Leonardo DiCaprio was there.'

'Lovely Leo, I met him once when he was dating that supermodel,' said Mona. 'Did he chat you up?'

'Yeah, we chatted, but he isn't my type. I prefer Harry Styles.'

Leonardo DiCaprio, not your type? Vicky will go nuts! Though I could only assume Klara was more engaging when she was actually *being* chatted up by a Hollywood heartthrob. *Maybe I'll end up bumping into Leo while I'm here.*

Mona cackled with laughter. 'Oh, darling, you'll meet Harry soon enough, I'm sure. Won't she, Amber?' She elbowed me in the ribs.

I smiled awkwardly. I had absolutely no idea how to add to this conversation, my closest previous celebrity encounter having been when Jas offered Orlando Bloom shelter from the paparazzi by letting him into the stockroom. Or there was that time I walked past Helen Mirren on Mount Street. Mona looked at her chunky gold Rolex.

'Maybe you should go unpack and freshen up?' *Oh great, so I do actually smell.*

As I made my way back to my case, I was intercepted by the arrival of another woman, who had let herself into the house. At barely five foot, stocky and Hispanic, she was Klara's diametric opposite.

'Ah, hel-lo, Ana!' Mona shouted, though the woman was barely a few feet away. *Maybe she has a hearing problem.*

'Mona,' came the reply, in a clear American accent. 'How was your flight?'

'Oh, you know, high, long, tedious. This is my new assistant, Amber Green. Like the traffic light.' Klara sniggered. *At least I don't spend my time peeling grapes.*

'No Tamara, then?' Ana asked.

'No.'

'I liked Miss Tamara.'

I liked Ana straight away. She already appeared to be one of the few people who wasn't afraid of Mona.

'Will you show Amber to her room, please?'

* * *

'You work for Mona, then?' I asked, as we made our way up some white stairs leading off the central hallway, Ana insisted on lugging my suitcase despite the fact that she looked older than my mum.

'Yes, I'm her housekeeper,' she replied, a little out of puff.

'How long have you worked here?'

'Fifteen years.'

'Wow, that's a long time.'

'A very, very long time,' she replied wearily. 'When Miss Armstrong was married.'

'Right, of course.'

I suppose she expected me to know this intriguing piece of information already. In fact, I felt a little ashamed that I knew almost nothing about my landlord and boss. I was desperate to hear more, but Ana didn't seem to want to elaborate, and we had reached our destination at the end of a white corridor lined on either side with black-and-white photos of Mona, in various states of gushing ecstasy, with numerous celebrities.

Blake Lively, Jennifer Lawrence, Kristen Stewart, is that Nicole Scherzinger? In another—Jennifer Astley! I made a mental note to come back and study them in detail later on.

* * *

My room—one of five barely used guest rooms, it transpired—was nicer than any hotel I'd ever stayed in. The animal-print theme continued with a faux leopard-skin rug on the floor, and there was a big, soft, cream throw and at least half a dozen cream and caramel scatter cushions on the king-sized bed. There was a large, tasteful black-and-white line drawing of a sitting woman's naked back on one of the walls and a black-and-white photograph of Grace Kelly on another. It was understated, but girly and cool. I loved it instantly. There were two windows in the room, one of which looked out over the driveway and the other the side of the garden, but if I opened it and stuck my neck out, I could just about see twinkling water.

There's a pool! I texted Vicky. But then I deleted it. I didn't want her to think I was showing off. *But wow, this is* The Real Housewives of Beverly Hills *come to life!*

Peering out, I could see Klara, sitting cross-legged on one of the loungers around the swimming pool, tapping at her iPhone. The pool was circular and very inviting. It definitely wasn't the kind for swimming lengths. There were six loungers around it, with black-and-white-striped cushioning over them—one of them with a long, thin wet patch in the middle, presumably where Klara had been basking after a dip. The sun was beating down strongly. I was aching to strip off and get into the water.

'Miss Armstrong will meet you downstairs in twenty minutes,' Ana instructed.

I opened my case and began sorting through the mass of crumpled black clothing within it. I had indeed forgotten the white pile. *You idiot, Amber.* It seemed ironic that I was going to be living for two weeks with one of the world's top stylists and I had absolutely nothing to wear. Maybe

I'd be able to go shopping. I wondered if Mona would ever loan clothing to her staff, like Jas did sometimes, but something made me doubt it. Then I noticed another door leading off the room. I pushed it open and discovered a gleaming, cream en suite bathroom complete with a roll-top bath, a wet shower area and one of those big sinks with a large mirror above it and plenty of space to pleasurably lay out all of your cosmetics, as if you were a professional make-up artist. I started unpacking my case, refolding and hanging up clothes, putting everything into the spacious walk-in closet with far more care than I had taken when packing, and wishing I had a wardrobe on this scale at home. It was practically the size of my entire bedroom. My black capsule collection looked even more pathetic, filling only a tiny area. *Mental note to self: reorganise wardrobe as soon as I get back.*

The quiet was suddenly interrupted by a loud phone conversation going on downstairs on the driveway. It was Mona, and she wasn't happy. I inched closer to the open window.

'Notice period? I'm sorry, darling, but there is no notice period. You never signed a contract. Remember?... Well, expect to hear from my solicitor, too, if you want to take it further...Bring it on...I've got Amber now, she'll do it...You're swiftly losing any chance of a decent reference, Nathan...You've lost the reference...I already have the itinerary.'

And then the conversation came to an abrupt end.

'Fucking prick.'

The front door slammed shut and I heard Mona's heels on the polished white floor indoors. I slid down the wall, coming to rest on my bare heels. I *really* wouldn't want to be on the receiving end of a conversation like that. But before I had time to dwell on it, I was summoned.

'Amber, babe, all unpacked up there? We need to get going!'

I guessed that asking for another ten minutes so I could at least have a 'whore's bath'—what Vicky called a quick, cold top and tail from the sink—wasn't an option.

'I'll be down in two!' I yelled back.

Feeling weak and out of body from the flight, there was nothing I could do but whip off my stale jeans and jumper, put on the one black denim skirt I had managed to pack, a black vest top, black ballet pumps, a heavy application of Mitchum under my arms and fly downstairs.

Chapter Five

'So here's the thing,' Mona said as we sat in the Prius en route to the W Hotel, she in yet another outfit, copper waves tamed in a loose ponytail and a headscarf while she drove. 'You're going to be doing some PA duties for me, too. I had to get rid of Nathan.' She paused. 'He had bad energy.' She put her foot down, accelerating hard, clearly unwilling to divulge any more details about the second member of staff she'd parted company with this week. *Bad energy.* As the breeze lashed my hair against my face, turning it into a tangled mess, I wondered what this actually meant. *Will she think I've got 'bad energy' too?*

'No problem, I've done plenty of PA stuff for Jas,' I offered diligently, with as much good energy as I could muster. It was only a white lie. I had turned into Mona's big-eyed, eager-to-please puppy. Yet I had an overwhelming feeling that I would always be just one accidental widdle on the carpet away from getting the sack myself. *Well, how hard can PA duties actually be?*

'Great. First, I need you to call the TV people. I told you they're coming to the suite to do a bit of follow-up filming for the pilot today.' *Er, no, you didn't. Do you think I'm Derren Brown?*

'They took the plane out this morning, too—the Virgin one, all a bit lastminute.com. But it's a good sign—they must think the network is interested in commissioning the series. Isn't that fabulous?'

I gulped.

'The AD, Bob, was it? The cute one. His number's in my phone, under "TV". I said you'd call when we were on our way.'

She handed her unlocked iPhone to me without taking her eyes off the road, which was lucky because it meant she couldn't see my award-winning impression of Gwyneth Paltrow's face after discovering she's eaten a non-macrobiotic canapé. I wasn't sure what scared me more—the fact that the TV crew was already here, in LA, or that Mona thought Rob was cute. 'What are you waiting for, babe? Give him a call.'

Hastily, I located the number, and it rang, the long, foreign ringtone leaving me in no doubt that he was indeed this side of the Atlantic. My heart started pulsing hard, taking me by surprise.

'Hello, Rob speaking.'

'Oh, hi, Rob—it's, um, Amber here, calling for Mona Armstrong.'

'Hi, Amber, great to speak to you—we were just wondering when Mona would call. Wonder if you're feeling as out of it as I am!'

He instantly put me at ease. I pictured him smiling into the phone.

'Yes, I am pretty tired.' I sideways-glanced at Mona, who flew across an amber light, laughing. 'Amber Green!'

As we sped along a wide six-lane carriageway, glass-fronted shops and parked cars whizzed past. I saw very few actual people on the pavement; it was so different to the packed streets of central London.

'All right, babe, stop flirting,' Mona barked. 'Just let the guy know they should make sure they're with us by at least five, because Beau Belle's due soon after. She'll be perfect for the show.'

I replaced my ear to the phone. 'Mona says, if...'

'It's okay, Amber, I heard. Beau Belle, in the flesh, hey? We'll be with you by five. Get some coffee down you. It's always a killer on the first day, but you'll be fine.'

'See you later, then.'

I handed Mona's iPhone back to her, leaned back into my seat and began mentally listing the things that were wrong with my current situation:

My face looks like Lindsay Lohan's after a bender.
I smell.
I have indeterminate 'energy'.
I'm not sure what I'm meant to be doing at the W Hotel.

And on top of that, my first day at work was about to be recorded on camera by a guy I almost definitely fancied.

Just concentrate on your professional ability, Amber Green. You have a career now, and you can do this. Show her you were worth the gamble. You want this. Focus. But giving myself an internal pep talk was another clear sign I fancied him.

* * *

We pulled up in front of the impressive glass facade of the W Hotel in West Hollywood, the gleaming mirrored walls glinting in the bright sunshine. Mona handed the keys to a waiting valet attendant. Then the boot bounced open, and the bags and hanging clothes cases Ana and I had carefully packed into it were lifted out by a bellboy and loaded onto a trolley. Mona handed him a dollar bill.

'Wow Suite, fast as you can.'

'Certainly, Ms Armstrong. I'll let the front desk know you've arrived.'

'And tell them to send up any parcels—there should be several.'

Like her obedient pet puppy, I followed. We entered the achingly cool foyer. Trendy people stood busily chatting in groups or waiting for others in round seating areas. An organically curved central staircase with a red carpet down its centre swept through the space with impressive elegance. I wanted to stop here for a minute, to take it all in, but we went straight into the lifts. Mona seemed impatient and far too alert—unlike me, she'd obviously had a decent amount of sleep on the plane.

'Your Cavallis should be here by now,' she commented, squeezing out half a smile as we zoomed upwards. *Please, dear Lord, let them be here.* I glanced at my phone—16:35— that meant I had twenty-five minutes, maximum, to make myself look a bit better and to wake up.

'Nathan should have pre-ordered refreshments for the suite, so you can set them out prettily and get the coffee on first of all,' Mona instructed. I wondered if Nathan had ordered her a side dish of cyanide while he was at it. Judging by the phone conversation I'd eavesdropped on, I wouldn't have put it past him.

Our suite was the size of my entire flat. In the sprawling living room, a stylish dove-grey corner sofa and lounge chairs filled one area, above which hung a light installation 'containing 20,000 LEDs' according to the in-room brochure. There were also three free-standing full-length mirrors and a large glass-topped dining table, upon which Mona began methodically setting out an impressive haul of glittering accessories from one of the holdalls, as if she'd robbed the Crown Jewels. There was a large flat-screen TV and an iPod station on one wall; she turned it on and soon Jessie Ware's soothing tones filled the space, a comforting reminder of the music we played in Smith's. All of a sudden it dawned on me that I was a long way from home. There was also a breathtaking outdoor private terrace with an open fireplace and cream patio seating, 'for cigarette breaks and refreshments'. And a compact double bedroom dressed in shades of beige led off from the lounge.

'This will be the changing area,' Mona informed me.

I quickly realised that we were basically turning the space into an elaborate shop fitting room, but with plusher sofas and added Jo Malone candles, which Mona had brought along in her Louis Vuitton.

* * *

Having laid out a table of cups, glasses, bottles of still and sparkling water, two large platters of fruit, a bowl of mixed berries and a plate of fig rolls—a menu she and Nathan had clearly decided was ample sustenance for our clientele, but which I could currently have tipped down my throat in one go—I figured out how to work the Nespresso machine and got busy making my first ever caffè macchiato. My initial attempt was flat, so I kept it for myself and made a second, impressively fluffy, super-strong cup for Mona. It soon transpired that the ability to make good coffee was indeed an integral part of my job. Through the course of the afternoon I learned that Mona was a caffeine addict, and I swiftly became her dealer.

As I re-emerged from the terrace, I saw that Mona had transformed the living area into a haven of shimmering designer wear. The dining table was a magpie's paradise, with sparkling jewellery laid across it in neat columns of necklaces, bracelets and shoulder-grazing earrings—most of them chunky, eye-catching pieces in gold or silver inlaid with twinkling diamonds and elegant semi-precious gems. The opposite end was a treasure trove of clutch bags, from small, hard boxes covered in black and silver crystals, bringing a touch of *Great Gatsby* glamour to evening ensembles, to softer hand-finished half-moons in all colours from navy to ultra-feminine pale peach. Down the middle of the table was a row of evenly spaced sunglasses—or 'pap shields', as Mona referred to them—an essential accessory for our most-photographed visitors. There were big, round Jackie O ones, gold-rimmed aviators and fifties styles that playfully turned up at the corners, all bearing designer names. On a side table, laid out around a large cream lamp, was a symphony of scarves. I breathed a sigh of relief as I noticed the bright Cavalli ones from the airport nestled in the display. *Thank you, Jane from Cavalli. I at least have one fashion PR pal I can count on.* Along the entire length of the room was a row of shoes, all towering heels; some with the instantly recognisable Christian Louboutin red sole, and most in black, nude, silver or gold, so perilously high and delicate they looked like art installations rather than footwear. I was glad I'd brought plasters and Party Feet. Then 'the pièce de résistance' as Mona referred to it: a long clothes rail filled with the most exquisite evening wear I had ever seen. Some gowns were so long they trailed onto the floor;

others screamed for attention with their eye-popping hues or sophisticated detailing. I thought the rails at Smith's were something special, but this was a whole new level of glamour. Each piece struggled to steal the spotlight from the next. I couldn't take them all in fast enough—it was like lifting the lid on a fairy-tale fancy dress box. One dress was so full of elaborate creamy ostrich feathers its plumage rose up above the others, like a sensual showgirl high-kicking onto centre stage. Next to it, a hanger groaned under the weight of a heavy, one-shouldered gown covered in twinkling black sequins: a dress fit for a diva. A stunning emerald beauty threw glitter-ball spots of light onto the ceiling, from the glinting silver jewels hand-sewn onto its neckline. The craftsmanship and love put into each gown was instantly visible.

Amid this cornucopia, there was one that instantly appealed to me; a beautifully romantic, scarlet satin Valentino number, figure-hugging, oozing class. It might as well have had an Oscar pinned to it as an accessory. I ran my hand over the material, cool and silky-smooth to the touch. *I wonder what it feels like to wear a dress like that.*

'Red-carpet evening wear on the left, low-key daywear on the right,' Mona informed me, though I failed to see anything 'low-key' about the entire collection. 'It'll be obvious straight away who's looking for what.'

I really hoped it would. A fug I assumed was jet lag was starting to surround me. I stopped myself thinking that, eight hours ahead of us in the UK, I'd probably be in my cosy bed after an evening on the sofa with Vic, eating pitta and hummus and watching Graham Norton. At five to five, the front desk alerted us that the TV crew were making their way up, so I locked myself in the posh cream marble bathroom and rummaged through the stash of free miniature products, attempting a quick freshen up. I splashed water on my face, rubbed silky moisturiser into my arms, neck and chest—so at least I was vaguely fragrant—and re-scraped my hair back into a ponytail. It would have to do.

* * *

Today's TV crew was similar to the one we'd entertained in Smith's not much more than twenty-four hours ago, only this time, another shaggy-haired cameraman was joining Fran with the bob and Rob. This one was American and called Lyle, but I christened him Shaggy, too. Fran with the bob shook my hand and Rob planted a peck on my cheek.

'Amber, good to see you again.'

It was great to see a friendly face. In a crisp white T-shirt, jeans and Pumas, Rob looked fresh, like he'd actually managed to shower since disembarking the plane. The place where he'd planted the kiss was burning up. He had Mona and I sign more release forms. Then, no sooner had the camera been set up and we'd necked another coffee, there was a ring at the door. *Our suite has its own doorbell!* I opened it to reveal a man mountain, dressed like a nightclub bouncer in a black suit, white shirt and skinny black tie, his hair crew cut, a small earpiece tucked inside his right ear.

'Hey, Mona, good to see you again. I'm here with Miss Belle—should we come in now?' He looked straight through me. I fizzed with excitement, jet lag suddenly forgotten. I was about to meet Beau Belle, star of so many chick flicks. *Vicky would die.*

'Not looking after Miley any more, AJ?'

'No, Trey Jones, but his fiancée, Beau here, has got me run off my feet,' said the Hulk, bending his thick neck to speak into a discreet radio microphone pinned to his collar. 'Just finding out how long filming will take. Keep her close at heel until I say.' *How odd, they're talking about her as if she's a chihuahua.*

'The filming won't take long,' said Mona. 'We'll pick a few pieces together, a few twirls for the camera and we'll wrap. Right, kids?' Rob nodded and Fran with the bob smiled through gritted teeth. It seemed that Mona couldn't help patronising everyone she met.

'Do you have any food? She and Pinky haven't had time to break all day,' said AJ.

'Pinky?' Rob mouthed at Fran, who shrugged in response.

'My assistant, Amber here, has it covered. Water, coffee, fruit, snacks, whatever she—*they*—want.' Mona was in full-on charm mode, although she clearly had no idea about Pinky, either.

AJ spoke into his mic again. 'We're ready. Bring them in.'

* * *

The camera was trained on the door, and I stepped back, hopefully out of shot. As Fran with the bob signalled, 'Action!' a small grunt made all of us look at the floor. A petite, pink micro-pig, dressed in a black leather biker jacket, made its entrance, inquisitively rushing into the room and stopping in the centre of it to check us all out. Its short curly tail lifted eagerly. Mona was trying not to frown, which wasn't all that difficult. I was by now aware that her forehead barely moved.

Vicky would be wetting herself.

'Pinky, baby, wait for Mommy!' a shrill, recognisable voice called out.

And in tottered Beau Belle, an image so familiar from the *Daily Mail Online*, yet strangely different in the flesh—in

fact, she looked like a cartoon character. A torrent of mol-
ten gold curls hung loose around her shoulders, a floppy
black hat perched on top of her head and an oversized black
faux-fur waistcoat hung over pale grey skinny jeans, finished with high, black, suede-fringed ankle boots. Seventies
hippie meets Texan cowgirl, with a sprinkling of Barbie.
She was not unlike a smaller, younger and—we all knew
it—prettier version of Mona. A second bodyguard entered
behind her, rooting himself immediately next to the door.

'Mona, honey! So good to see you!' shrieked Beau, dropping her Burberry Blaze bag on the floor and launching herself into Mona's open arms to exchange air kisses. 'What
do you think of Pinky? Isn't he the cutest? I wanted a Pom-
eranian, but I couldn't get one because of my fur allergy, so
Trey got me the next best thing. Do you love?'

'Adorable!' Mona wasn't good at lying. What her face
couldn't express, her body language screamed as she nervously fixated on the pig's wet snout. Pinky trotted straight
towards Mona's perfectly laid out highway of immaculate
designer heels. She looked at the two beefy guards, jerk-
ing her head towards the pig, but neither seemed bothered
about Pinky. Instinctively, I rushed over to the clothes rail
and scooped the longest gowns off the floor, out of the slobbery snout's reach.

'Perhaps, um, my assistant, Amber, could take little Porky
for a play on the terrace?' Mona suggested, indicating for me
to get the pig outside immediately. Beau turned her attention
to me and looked me up and down, visibly unimpressed.

'Just arrived today,' I muttered, by way of an apology.
'I love pigs.'

Another lie. I had absolutely no experience of pigs, other
than a weakness for the M&S ones called Percy. Picking up

Pinky's lead from the floor, I cringed as I felt the camera follow the pig, my bottom and my pasty legs to the patio before panning back to Mona and Beau. Carefully lifting Pinky onto the clean patio seating next to me, I loosened his studded leather coat and looked into his small, dark, watery eyes.

'Are you thirsty, little piggy?' Admittedly, he was quite cute. And he smelled fresher than I did. 'Want some food? It's not as if anyone else is going to eat much.'

I poured some milk into a saucer and set it down on the floor. The pig began lapping it up enthusiastically. Then I took a couple of fig rolls, broke them in half and put them on another saucer. He chowed them down loudly. I ate one, too. Then another. Then I stabbed a few berries with a fork and quickly scoffed them, as well. I offered a handful of blueberries to Pinky and he ate hungrily, tickling my palm as he bolted them down.

'Aw, Mommy not fed you lunch today?'

'I hope you're not suggesting Beau's neglectful?' a voice boomed above me. AJ was closing the terrace door behind him; a prime example of LA beefcake, completely devoid of a sense of humour.

'Not at all—just making conversation.'

'It's a pig.'

'You're not an animal lover, AJ?'

'Mona's asked for you. I'll take over from here.'

I handed him the lead and headed back inside, where an area had been lit with a bright, free-standing light and the camera was trained on Mona and Beau going through the rail.

'You can afford to go more cocktail for the pre-events,' Mona was advising, holding up a cute on-trend floral cocktail dress from Oscar de la Renta, 'but you still want to make an impact.'

'Hmmm, I know it's very now, but florals are not the new me, Mona, I'm trying to get more serious roles. Do you have anything sexier or edgier, maybe?'

Beau had taken off her hat and fur now and you could see just how slight she was—the human version of her tea-cup pig.

'The camera adds ten pounds, you know—everyone will be thin beyond belief,' Mona had warned me earlier, when I remarked on how miniature all the clothes appeared. 'No one in Hollywood is larger than a size two sample.'

'There's this sexy Dolce & Gabbana,' Mona said, pulling out a glamorous leopard-print, stretch-silk dress. 'I've got the perfect Dolce cuff and clutch to go with it. Trey will go wild!'

'Sold! I love it!' Beau exclaimed, holding it to her chest and turning on that million-dollar smile for the camera.

'Why don't you try it on, along with the Oscar de la Renta, just for comparison? Amber will help you.'

Mona directed her towards the bedroom door and beckoned me over to the accessories table, to load up with suitable 'finishing touches'—a thick, studded gold cuff and matching clutch, plus some black Jimmy Choos with buckles around the ankle and a delicate pair of high gold sandals. I prayed she wouldn't ask me to try them on first, knowing full well that my size seven sausages wouldn't have a hope in hell of squeezing into those delicate beauties. The film crew headed to the terrace for a break and I noticed Rob tickle Pinky under the chin en route, muttering, 'All right, mate?' The movement made the muscles flex in his upper arm. I quickly looked away, scuttling across the living area to the bedroom.

After tentatively knocking on the door, I was ushered in by a semi-naked Beau, the leopard dress at her svelte hips, revealing her ample bust encased in a turquoise lace bra. She had big boobs for a girl so slight; I wondered if they were fake. That was something Vicky would have been able to deduce instantly—one of her favourite hobbies was pointing out boob jobs. Beau wriggled as she pulled the dress up around her shoulders.

'Give me a hand with the zip, would you?'

I struggled slightly to do it up, it was skintight even on her bony frame.

'There we go. Oh wow...'

She surveyed her perfect physique in the wardrobe's floor-to-ceiling mirrors, flicking her luscious locks, and turning left to right and back again. I undid the buckles on the Choos, ready for her petite feet to slip into them like Cinderella. Then a loud twinkling sound emanated from her bag, lying on the hotel bed.

'Chuck me my Burberry, would you, babe?'

I stretched across to retrieve it, thinking how surreal this all was. She delved into the bag to grab her iPhone and looked at it in silence for a moment; then she slumped down and sat on the edge of the bed.

'Shit.' She fixated on the phone, reading the message again, then whispered: 'You absolute shit.' And then she buried her head in her hands and burst into tears. I looked away, feeling uncomfortable. *Has she not got a part? Maybe the casting agents don't think she's cut out for 'edgy' after all?* She began pumping air out of her mouth in short, sharp breaths, like a woman in labour. Perhaps it was helping her fight back the tears. *Has someone died? Talk about #awkward.* Then, phone still in her hand, she appeared to steady herself and stood up decisively, smoothing the dress over her washboard stomach and miniature hips, and resumed admiring herself in the mirror. Seconds later, her phone rang. She lifted it to see the caller's identity, then threw the handset down, hard, on the duvet behind her.

'Fucking asshole!' She hurled herself onto the bed after it, crumpling the dress and letting out a shriek not unlike the sound Pinky might make if you accidentally stood on his trotter. Then she buried her head in the pillow and began to wail.

I looked up from the corner of the room, where I had been pretending to busy myself straightening a curtain. A noise like that meant I couldn't ignore her any longer. Cautiously, I inched closer.

'Um, is everything okay?'

She thumped the duvet. 'No, it is not!' she screeched, turning onto her side to face me, as I stood, hesitantly, by the side of the bed. Her eyes were red, make-up smudged, and the ivory pillowcase now sported two charcoal grey blotches and a dab of cherry lip gloss. Was this a prima donna hissy fit because she was last on the waiting list for the new Chanel bag? Such things did actually happen... A loud thud made us both look at the door.

'Is everything all right in there, Beau?'

Her big blue eyes fixed on my own and, in them, I saw genuine fear. She waved her arm at the door, signalling she didn't want AJ to intervene.

'Yes, we're fine, thanks, AJ!' I shouted back. 'Just a stiff zip!'

'All good!' she seconded. *At least he'd know I hadn't murdered her or anything.*

'Okay, well, we'll see you out here.' I heard him move away.

'Thanks, honey, you're a babe.' Her pretty eyes were wet with tears.

'Is there anything I can do?' I asked.

'I don't think so.' She sniffed.

'Well, if you want to talk about it…' I perched on the edge of the bed. She seemed to want me there.

'Really?' she snivelled, as though no one had ever offered her support before.

'Really. Er—a problem shared…'

I put an uncertain hand onto her thin, childlike shoulder, wondering if there was a law against making physical contact with a vulnerable, crying, miniature celebrity. It wouldn't have surprised me if AJ had her wired.

Chapter Six

We were suddenly interrupted by another knock on the door and Mona's head appeared around it.

'Just me, darlings!' she announced, as she clocked the scene—me looking worried, and Beau dishevelled. 'Jesus, has someone died? Do you hate the dresses, Beau? Seriously, honey, if you don't like the Dolce, there's plenty more on the rails.'

Beau played along brilliantly. 'To be honest, Mona, I'm having a fat day,' she wiped smudged mascara from under her eyes. 'Amber's been trying to talk me into the Dolce & Gabbana, but nothing feels right, you know?' She squeezed a non-existent love handle for added effect. Mona nodded sympathetically.

'Do we *have* to do the filming today?' Beau continued. 'I'm just thinking—if I skip dinner, get a colonic and wear Spanx, it'll look much better in the morning.'

'Little sparrow, there's nothing of you as it is!' Mona said truthfully. 'But I'm not going to make you do anything you don't feel comfortable with. The important thing is that we look after you! The TV people will have to understand.'

I stood up and crept towards the door, guessing that I'd be in the unenviable position of having to tell the *20Twenty* crew they'd made a wasted trip.

'But can Amber stay with me, please?' Beau asked, intercepting me. I was shocked that she had remembered my name. 'I'm feeling a bit sick, too. I just need to sit quietly in here for a little while. With Amber.'

Looking perturbed that Beau had chosen me as her confidante, Mona pursed her lips and forced a smile. 'Sure.'

Left alone in the room once more, Beau was suddenly much more forthcoming.

'The truth is, Amber, I'm being stalked.'

'You're what?'

'Someone, a man, is stalking me.' She gripped my hand. 'And I'm scared.'

She welled up again, her breathing becoming short and irregular. This was either really good acting, or the red blotches and the tears were real—I suddenly felt like we were at a high school pyjama party gone wrong. I dashed to the bathroom to grab her a handful of tissues and took a moment to gather my thoughts. *What am I supposed to do now?* I remembered hearing a story about a stalker being caught hiding on a shelf in Simon Cowell's walk-in wardrobe, and hoped the windows in this suite were locked.

'Maybe we should get AJ after all?' I asked, returning to the room and handing over a stack of tissues. Beau was sitting up on the bed now, her back against the wall, knees tucked into her chest as she clasped a tissue in each hand.

'No need for AJ, I can handle it,' she insisted.

'Might the, um—stalker—be near us now?' I asked. Beau subsided into sniffles.

'It started on Twitter, about a week ago,' she began. 'He was so nice to me at first, this guy, I thought he was a fan, telling me he liked my movies and he thought I was a good actor and pretty and stuff. It was just innocent banter. But then he kept on asking me about Jason—you know, Jason Slater, my co-star in the movie I've just wrapped?'

I nodded. Everyone knew Jason Slater. He was a big-name actor, chiselled, single, with legions of female fans—he'd broken onto the Hollywood scene with a slew of popular rom-coms, and Beau and Jason had co-starred in the soon-to-premiere chick flick *Summer's Not Over*. (The pile of magazines stored under the counter at Smith's, and the Stick's constant drip feed of Hollywood news from various online sources, meant I was well up to speed with my celebrity news.)

'Well, this guy kept asking whether me and Jason were more than work buddies. He just wouldn't let it go,' she explained, blowing her delicate nose.

'Perhaps he's just a troll?' I suggested.

'I thought so, too, but it's got worse than that now,' she said. 'I blocked him, but somehow he got hold of my personal cell number, and he's been texting and phoning me non-stop ever since.'

I sat there, racking my brain. 'Are you sure it's the same person?'

'Positive, because he asks the same thing—always about Jason. The way he keeps going on—it's not right, you know? It's so obvious he's trying to trip me up, trying to get me to say something that isn't true. He's trying to intimidate me, Amber, and I don't know what he'll do next. He's sent me about ten texts already today and I've had as many missed calls.' Her eyes started to well up with emotion again. 'That was him, earlier. He's stalking me and I don't know what to do.'

I thought about the most level-headed person I knew. *What would Jas do in this situation?*

'Do you need me to call anyone?'

'No. There's no one.'

'Your fiancé?'

Beau's intended was the good-looking and highly rated British film director Trey Jones. The couple were regulars on the Hollywood scene and their forthcoming wedding was already creating a buzz in the celebrity world, with rumours that the photography rights had been sold to a glossy magazine in a million-dollar deal.

'Trey? God, no!' She was emphatic, which only made me more perplexed.

'Your publicist?'

I knew about publicists from Smith's. We would occasionally be asked to close the store for a couple of hours if a big American actress wanted to shop in solitude, away from the hoi polloi, and they always came with a publicist in tow. American versions of British PRs, publicists are straight-talking, brash and infinitely scarier than their UK counterparts. Publicists generally get what they want, when they want it, and never return a favour. But today Beau was shunning publicist assistance.

'Honey, I'm just glad my publicist is *not* here.' She picked up her phone again, and reread the stalker's earlier message before turning it off.

'Well—maybe you should go to the police?'

'Never! Oh God, this is a total nightmare!'

I was nonplussed. Who would be stalking Beau and accusing her of being more than friends with Jason Slater?

'Actually, honey, maybe there *is* something you can do for me,' she said finally, looking at me, coyly, with big, puppyish, Princess Diana eyes. *Surely Mona would want me to do anything I can to help…?*

'Just say the word,' I said.

'Can I trust you, Amber? I mean, *really* trust you?' She leaned in close enough for me to smell her delicate, fragrant breath.

'Of course you can.'

She lowered her voice and checked her phone was definitely off.

'I should have been honest with you straight away,' she explained. 'My stalker is actually from the national press. He's a journalist from that shitty gossip website *Starz*. He's been calling me for the past three days non-stop, intimidating me. He's a bully. And now he says they're about to go to press with some photos of me apparently in a "compromising position" with Jason.' She indicated the inverted commas with her fingers.

'He's trying to suggest there's something going on between us, when of course there isn't—we were only filming.'

'If you were filming, can't you just tell him so?' I asked.

'Well, the cameras weren't actually rolling, but we were rehearsing our scenes. You know?'

I wasn't sure I did. 'Does Trey know anything about this?'

'I really love Trey!' she exclaimed. 'He's my fiancé, Amber. We're getting married soon. But this stalking reporter is trying to ruin everything. And it sounds like they're going to print the lies, anyway…'

Tears began to stream down her cheeks, carrying blobs of mascara from her clogged lashes.

'Beau, it's okay, please don't cry. It's going to be okay, you know...' I said. 'Can't you just tell this reporter he's got it wrong? Tell him exactly what you just told me?'

She shook her head in response.

'At least no one is actually trying to kill you,' I continued, trying for cheery. 'I thought for a moment you were going to say there was a crazy man about to jump through the window with a handgun. It's not *that* bad.'

Lightening the mood didn't seem to be working. Now the streams of black tears were joining up into one big river that ran down her neck and drip, drip, dripped its way onto the brand new Dolce & Gabbana dress. *Mona's going to go bananas...* I needed her out of the dress.

I grabbed some more tissues from the en suite and gently tried to dab at the dress. Beau barely noticed—she wasn't interested in clothes any more. Her mind was ticking over, formulating a plan that was inevitably going to involve me.

'So what really needs to happen,' she said after a few minutes, 'is for Trey to know these stupid photos are just me rehearsing with Jason, and nothing more, before they get Tweeted all over the world and picked up by every gossip site under the sun in two days' time. No, I've got to get to him first.'

'Right. I'm sure Trey will completely understand when you explain things to him,' I offered hopefully, and in the face of all the signs. 'No one believes what they read on *Starz*, anyway.'

I didn't think she'd appreciate knowing most of my friends back home were signed up to the *Starz* email alerts, and accepted every single word as gospel.

'Well, what I was thinking was, that that's where you could help, Amber, like you said you would.' She widened her blue eyes; the big, sultry eyes that had led so many co-stars into 'compromising situations'. 'I was thinking that you could just call up Trey, pretend you were one of my producers on *Summer's Not Over*, and tell him that some photos have unfortunately got into the hands of a down-market gossip site, but that you can confirm Jason and I were only rehearsing, so there is nothing to worry about. End of. Right, Amber?'

I remained silent for a moment, while I digested this.

'But, um, but I'm not a producer... I'm Mona's assistant. I'm not sure I'd be very good at pretending I'm someone else—I'm not an actress, like you.'

'But you said you wanted to help?' She had desperation in her eyes.

I felt panicked. *What would Jas do now?*

'Really, Beau,' I pleaded. 'I was always rubbish at drama at school. I never got picked for the school plays. I was always the back end of the donkey in the Nativity. I want to help you, I really do, but I don't think I can do this. What if Trey started asking questions? He might not believe me.'

Right then, we were interrupted by another knock at the door. Mona again—this time shouting through it.

'Are you feeling better, Beau, darling? You've been a very long time. I was beginning to wonder if Amber had fallen asleep on you. She's probably not coping with the jet lag. The TV people have gone now, okay?'

'I'm feeling a little better now, thank you, Mona. We're coming out, literally right now,' Beau clambered off the bed. 'So that's sorted, then, Amber?' She turned to me. 'I'll come back to finish the fitting tomorrow, give you Trey's number and you'll call him. I'll tell you exactly what to say.'

She looked like a different person—certainly not the one who was drowning in tears not more than five minutes ago. She wiped the last traces of mascara stains from her cheeks, added a slick of lip gloss and surveyed herself in the mirror as if nothing had happened. Then she slipped on the Jimmy Choos and swung open the door.

'Ta-da! You know what, I do love the Dolce, Mona. I'll bring my Spanx tomorrow and it'll all be fine.'

I was flabbergasted.

When Beau had changed back into her civvies, Mona promised to call Stefano Gabbana himself to see if she could keep the dress after wearing it for her premiere. Then Beau announced she had to leave, but she'd be back the next day to be filmed as they finished her fitting for the actual Golden Globes. As she made for the door, we all noticed she was missing something—something she had most definitely arrived with—a small grunting pink thing in a leather jacket.

'Ah, Pinky!' she exclaimed, her eyes finding AJ, who was still holding Pinky's lead. 'Amber, babe, you love pigs—how do you fancy Pinky-sitting tonight?' She didn't give me a chance to respond. 'Thanks, babe! I just need a bit of quality time with my fiancé this evening...you know.'

I knew, all right. Beau needed to be on the ball, vetting her phone for calls from the 'stalker'. It had now been thirty hours since my last proper sleep, and London felt a very, very long way away. As AJ put Pinky's lead in my hand, I lacked the energy to do anything about it. Instead, I surrendered myself to whatever a night with a micro-pig might have in store. The look of disdain on Mona's face told me the pig would be staying in my room and nowhere else in her clean, white mansion—I didn't even get a chance to ask what the creature should eat. And I was already dreading the morning and the phone call. This really wasn't the initiation into the Hollywood scene I had been hoping for. I wondered if I should just refuse to be drawn in. *Maybe I should tell Mona about it?*

* * *

'You and Beau seemed to hit it off,' Mona commented frostily as we sped back to her house, Pinky travelling, probably illegally, on my lap. I was gripping him so tightly my knuckles had turned white. One late brake at the traffic lights and we'd have gammon for dinner.

'S'pose so,' I responded, abruptly deciding against telling Mona. I didn't want to appear foolish or out of my depth— for all I knew, this was normal for Hollywood. Besides, Beau had asked me to keep it a secret, and I wasn't sure if I could trust Mona yet. I didn't want to turn it into any more of a drama.

When we got back, Klara was in the kitchen, heating what appeared to be a watery soup of over-cooked vegetables. She barely twitched when she saw Pinky enter the kitchen behind me. *It's a pig in a leather jacket, for God's sake!* I felt exhausted now, off-balance and hardly able to keep my eyes open; I went through the rest of the evening in a daze, picking at the turkey chilli Ana had made for us. I didn't want Mona to think I was a lightweight, but it had been the longest day ever and now I *really* needed my bed. I led Pinky upstairs and used my last shred of energy to text Vicky: Am sharing my bed with Beau Belle's micro-pig. Will call tomorrow. Miss you. A x. Then I turned off my phone and passed out.

* * *

I woke up a few hours later to a loud crash as Pinky over-turned the water bowl I'd left for him on the floor. As it rolled around on the glossy white floorboards and finally came to a halt, I flicked on the bedside light to see him snuffling around the pile of discarded black clothes at the foot of my bed. I didn't get much sleep for the rest of the night. *It turns out pigs are pretty much nocturnal.* My head was spinning with Beau's request and I kept being woken up by Pinky either headbutting the door or scratching at the floorboards as he searched for an escape route. I felt sorry for the little thing. We were both a bit lost in this big, pristine room in a show home high in the Hollywood Hills.

Suddenly a thought occurred to me that made everything seem a little better. *There's a half-eaten family bag of peanut M&Ms in my bag!* Maybe a midnight feast of chocolate would help us both.

I managed to lift Pinky onto my oversized bed and he gobbled the M&Ms right out of my hand. As he slobbered and tickled my palm, I wondered whether Nathan and Tamara had the right idea in quitting. I pictured my own bed in my messy room back in London, where the tapping of water pipes and creaking of radiators regularly kept me awake. At one point in the early hours I actually scooped Pinky's warm body up for a quick snuggle, but he kicked me in the chin. He had powerful trotters for such a dinky animal. *Turns out micro-pigs don't like cuddling, either.*

* * *

At last it was 7:00 a.m. Warm, buttery fingers of sunlight had appeared around the blinds, bathing the room in a golden glow. I thought how pretty it looked as I groggily got out of bed and went to the ample en suite, noticing

Pinky was fast asleep, curled up between two pillows on the floor, the makeshift 'pig bed' I had made for him some time in the early hours. There was something about this bathroom that made me feel as if I was getting a big hug, just by standing in it. Maybe it was the underfloor heating. I stood under the power-shower revelling in the moment. It felt so good, finally, to get properly clean. So good until I remembered what lay in store with Beau today. *Maybe she's had a change of heart overnight?* The thought of seeing her again made me feel sick.

When I made it downstairs to the kitchen, Mona was reading a printed itinerary of our arrangements for the day over a glass of hot water and lemon. The list had presumably been written by Tamara or Nathan before they quit. We would be spending the morning on 'appointments' exactly like the ones Mona had attended at Smith's, so at least I had a rough idea of what to expect.

After leaving the house, we darted around Beverly Hills in the Prius, popping in and out of a stream of glossy boutiques— greeted with air kisses and enthusiastic smiles, browsing, admiring and borrowing, placing orders and loading up the car with yet more clobber for the suite. During car journeys, Mona handed me her iPhone to make calls. To my relief it contained the contact details of all the fashion PRs I could possibly ever need to call, so there was no danger of me having to keep Vicky up all night as I hunted for numbers.

Pinky came everywhere with me as I assumed the role of Mona's mouthpiece, note-taker and sunglasses holder, as well as Beau's pig-sitter.

'He's Beau Belle's, honey, we're on piglet duty as a favour. Isn't he fun?' Mona explained to anyone who would listen, enjoying the opportunity to name-drop and using the term 'we' loosely—she blatantly hadn't come within a trotter's length of little Pinky the whole time.

* * *

Back at the W, the afternoon saw a parade of wealthy-looking girls with smooth Brazilian blow-dries and fresh manicures, clutching python bags and groomed to golden perfection, troop in and flutter out of our suite, buoyed by their appointments with Mona. It was like watching a masterclass in laid-back luxe. Frankly, none of the visitors, with their delicate features, long limbs and good clothes, looked in desperate need of fashion help. Some looked vaguely familiar from bit parts in movies, or photos in magazines of Mona with her crowd. Others just had an air of importance. Perhaps they were up-and-comers, hoping, with Mona's help, to make their mark as a fresh fashion force this awards season. Whoever they were, all were greeted with hugs and yet more air kisses.

Outfits were tried on, accessories were cooed over and selfies were snapped. Superlatives flew around the room, ricocheting off the walls; everything was 'fabulous, amazing, sexy, gorgeous, delightful, darling, pretty, major, stunning, beautiful, to-die-for...' on and on, over and over. There was no need for any other vocabulary, because when you've got perfect genes, let's face it, *everything* looks great. I was the only person looking less than glamorous, having spent the morning rushing around after Mona and Pinky, answering the door, running items to the changing room, keeping everyone hydrated with Fiji water or on the phone to room service requesting an increasingly bizarre assortment of refreshments, ranging from peppermint teas and espressos through to steaming hot mugs of lemon juice with cayenne pepper and maple syrup. Every couple of hours, Mona would mouth her request for a 'little pick-me-up'; my first priority was to keep her caffeine levels at the max. She must have had at least four macchiatos before 3:00 p.m. and we'd only got here at twelve. As well as acting as a waitress, I was also tasked with keeping Mona's database of who was borrowing what, when, and where it needed to be delivered. Mona seemed delighted when I suggested setting up an Excel spreadsheet to keep track of this, instead of the endless Post-it notes she had previously stuck onto her iPad. *What kind of PA was Nathan, anyway?*

Every now and again I had to phone a PR to request a particular dress or accessory in a certain size, and I also had Mona's preferred seamstress—an amenable Mexican woman called Maria—on redial, if a gown needed a hem lifting or a bustier tightening. Couriers came and went, and my black ballet pump–clad feet soon ached from running around opening doors and darting wherever I was needed, which was generally everywhere at once. Every time the doorbell rang, my heart leapt as I wondered if it was Rob returning for more filming, or Beau, back to demand I fulfil my promise. She'd been on my mind all morning, her arrival drawing ever nearer, and I *still* hadn't worked out what to do about it. I was so busy, it was impossible to think straight.

In the bedroom-cum-changing room, I'd never seen so many practically naked, supermodel-like women. Dresses were pulled over heads with impressive dexterity, flashes of athletic, fake-tanned frames with perky, pointy breasts. This was how I imagined the set of a Juergen Teller photoshoot to look, or the scene backstage during London Fashion Week. I suddenly felt self-conscious about what lay beneath my black Zara T-shirt dress.

* * *

Mid-afternoon, we were alerted, via a call from the hotel manager, to the news that a high-profile actress had entered the building via an underground passageway so as not to be seen. She'd booked an emergency appointment with Mona to expunge horrific memories of a gown that drew column inches for all the *wrong* reasons last year.

'Someone really should have told her that see-through is the ultimate no-no on Oscars night,' Mona told me as we straightened things up, having cleared the suite of bodies for this VVIP. 'She hit the jackpot on all the Worst Dressed lists. Should have come to see me then.'

I watched in awe as Mona worked with our 'anonymous' star to select a gown for the Globes and another for the Oscars. In the end they went for a subtle black column gown by Armani Privé and a refined petal-pink creation, to reflect her more gamine personal style, rather than her va-va-voom on-screen roles. The whole experience ensured she left a smiling, more self-assured celebrity. It was fascinating to witness how powerful fashion can be. Mona was saving careers. There was no doubt she had the magic touch. I paid close attention to the way she listened to a problem, turned it on its head, sifted through the clothes on offer, did some temple-rubbing and—bingo!—a sparkling solution. It was undoubtedly a skill and the clients loved it. Mona later explained how she would mentally draw a 'ring of shame' around a celebrity's problem parts, and tackle those first.

'You've got to be ruthless,' she explained. 'Simply erase what you don't want to see by drawing the eye to the best bits.'

I wondered what she'd do to exterminate my own ample bottom. I had become more aware of my shape in the past few hours than I'd ever been before. I'm not big, but I'm not toned, which is hardly surprising considering I can count on one hand the number of times I've ever set foot in a gym. I've always felt lucky to have a size 10 frame, bordering 12 on a fat day. Today, I felt like the Incredible Hulk, and I'd barely eaten anything but berries and M&Ms for forty-eight hours. Mona didn't seem to eat, either—there had been no suggestion of our stopping for lunch. The image I had of Americans chowing down super-sized burgers, dripping with blue cheese and Thousand Island dressing, was very different to the reality I was facing now, where everyone seemed to be a size zero and the word 'food' was an expletive. *Frigging hell, I'm hungry. No wonder I can't formulate a decent plan regarding Beau.*

* * *

Eventually, just before five o'clock, I opened the door to the *20Twenty* crew, and seconds after that AJ arrived with Beau. Rob looked rather distracted and got on with setting up without any small talk. Fran barely acknowledged me as she made a beeline for Mona, describing what they needed from the scene with Beau. Mona, in response, told her how it *would* be. I got the impression they were finding Mona difficult to work with.

Beau almost barged me out of the way to reach Pinky, who was scuttling around happily on the terrace.

'Darling baby! Mommy missed you! Were you good for Mona and Amber? Oh yes, of course you were!'

She popped her head through the glass door. 'Hey, Amber! Come give me a hand.'

A feeling of doom washed over me as I joined Beau in the sunshine.

'Everything okay?' she asked. Ridiculously large sunglasses almost covered her entire face.

'Think so.' I smiled through gritted teeth in response, squinting into the sun and feeling like the bullied girl in the playground.

'I've got it all worked out,' she continued breathlessly, putting an arm around me and glancing over her shoulder to check we were alone. Then she delved into her bag and produced some folded-up paper.

'I've written you a script. You basically call Trey, say you're a producer on *Summer's Not Over* and that Jason and me were just rehearsing our scenes when some pap took the photos. But it's all aboveboard and innocent. Just keep it short and to the point.'

She took a brief moment to study my face. If she sensed I was feeling deeply uneasy about the whole scenario, she ignored it.

'Thanks, honey. One quick call, that's all it'll take.'

She then fixed me with that beguiling gaze and whispered, 'If you do this, I'll never forget it, Amber. I'll make you a success here.'

Bribery. Lovely.

Chapter Seven

I held out the script in front of me. The phone rang and rang. Beau fixed me with the eyes of a puppy watching forgotten sausages burn on a barbecue.

He's not going to pick up. Result!

'Trey speaking.' *Damn.*

'Hello, is that Trey Jones?'

'Yes, who is this?' He was well spoken—I had almost forgotten he was British. That just made me more nervous.

'Mr Jones, my name is Annie, I'm a producer on *Summer's Not Over*, and I've been working with your delightful fiancée. What a charming, talented and devoted young woman she is...' I sideways-glanced at Beau. *This is the biggest load of drivel I have ever read.*

'Ri-ight...' said the unsurprisingly baffled voice on the other end.

'I'm just calling because I wanted to make you aware of a situation my office has heard about today. It, erm, I...'

'Annie, what did you say your surname was?' He sounded worryingly sane.

'My surname?' I repeated, staring pointedly at Beau.

She hurriedly wrote on a piece of paper, 'Liechtenstein'. *Jesus, she could have let me rehearse that in advance.*

'Just call me Annie.' I glowered at her.

'So—how can I help you today? It's just…I'm in a bit of a hurry.'

'Oh, sorry, Mr Jones, you must be very busy.' I scrambled back to the script, my eyes darting over the words to relocate my place. Had this been an acting audition, I would have failed it miserably by now. Only this was much worse than any casting. This was actually happening. In real life. 'It's about a call we had to the office earlier today. It seems that some low-life reporter from that shitty gossip website *Starz* has some photos of your fiancée in what they are referring to as a "compromising position" with her co-star, Jason Slater.'

Beau might as well have been reading the script herself, it was so clearly her voice.

'Hold on, hold it there—is this a prank call?' barked Trey. 'Is Ashton Kutcher or some other joker behind this?' His change of tone startled me. Desperately, I looked at Beau for help.

'What's he saying?' she mouthed, tossing her big glossy mane to one side and shoving an ear close to the phone so that we were both huddled around it.

I put my hand over the receiver. 'He thinks I'm Ashton Kutcher.'

'Duh, that show ended over a million years ago!' She shook her head, totally missing the point. I pulled myself together.

'I'm afraid it's not a prank, Mr Jones, far from it. As I was saying, the website *Starz* has some photos of your fiancée in what they are referring to as a "compromising position" with Jason Slater, but I'm phoning to let you…'

'I'm sorry, I'm *really* not following this.' He cut me off again, his tone authoritative, and verging on angry. 'Would you mind explaining to me, in plain English, what you are trying to suggest here, Miss—Annie?'

I officially want to kill Beau for making me do this.

'Basically, your fiancée has done nothing wrong. She was merely carrying out a rehearsal with Jason when a low-life paparazzo took some photos, and I wanted to offer you my sincere assurance that Beau—and you—have the full support of the studio. Because whatever *Starz* decides to run with, the truth is they were diligently rehearsing their scenes and that's all there is to it.' *'Diligently rehearsing', my soft, white derrière.*

'I'd be interested in seeing these photos—do you have copies of them?' he asked solemnly. 'I'd like to put them into the hands of my lawyer as soon as possible.'

'Your l-lawyer?' As I slowly repeated the words, my voice faltered, and Beau's eyes grew large with alarm.

'No, no, no!' She shook her head wildly and whispered urgently, 'No attorney, Amber!' Frantically, she indicated the slitting of a throat—clearly meant to be mine—with her index finger.

'Your lawyer? That won't be necessary, Mr Jones, we think the situation will blow over quickly enough,' I said, as calmly as possible, channelling my best reassuring producer's voice. 'This is more a courtesy call, just to put you in the picture and to say, you know, go easy on Beau tonight, it's been a tough day. I'm sure she'll tell you all about it later, but she's done absolutely nothing wrong. I just want to make that crystal clear.'

I decided to miss out the last bit of the script, where I was supposed to go on protesting Beau's innocence and flattering her for another minute or so, hammering the point home with all the subtlety of a nuclear rocket.

Mercifully, he seemed to be buying it. 'Well, I'll keep an eye on the *Starz* site and we'll take it from there. I know what these scumbags can be like. I appreciate the call, Annie.'

'My pleasure, Mr Jones.'

Thank God for that. I was ready to hang up.

'Where are you from in the UK, by the way? There aren't many British producers I haven't come across yet.' *No! I wasn't prepared for small talk.*

'London,' I replied, fidgeting to get off the phone.

'Like the rest of us Brits in LA. North or south?'

'North, born and bred.'

'The best side. I'm a Portobello boy.'

'No way—I'm in Kensal Rise!'

For a moment I almost forgot who I was supposed to be—it was so nice to hear mention of home.

'Small world. Will I see you at the Weinstein bash this evening?'

Beau was indicating I should end the call, with another decapitation action.

'Oh, afraid not,' I muttered. 'Early night for me, busy week.'

'Know the feeling,' he said. 'Well, I hope I'll get to meet you some time, Annie. Thanks for the call. Goodbye.'

'Bye, Mr Jones.'

As I hung up—breathing a huge sigh of relief—Beau

launched herself onto me, flinging her arms around my rigid body and hugging me uncomfortably tight.

'You were amazing! You actually sounded like Annie Liechtenstein, too! Well, if she was a Brit, she'd sound just like you.'

'She's not even from the UK?'

I sank down onto the patio sofa, throwing the script down and releasing the phone. My palms were sweaty from grasping it so tightly, and I suddenly really wanted a glass of wine.

'Did he sound okay? He's not going to call anyone, is he?'

'No, he was cool,' I said, trying not to show how exasperated I felt.

From the corner of my eye, I saw Mona approaching. She didn't look happy.

My heart was still racing from the call. Trey had sounded like such a nice, decent man—I felt horrible for having lied to him. *It must have been one of the most bizarre phone calls he's ever received.* Mona pushed the glass door ajar.

'Hate to break up the party, but we've got some styling to do,' she said brusquely, just as Beau's iPhone rang.

'It's Trey. Just let me take this, Mona, and I'll be inside in two minutes, promise.'

Mona gave us a mildly irritated look. I went in and closed the terrace door, not wanting to hear whatever Beau was going to say to him. Anyway, showbiz wedding deal protected. For now.

Back in the suite, Rob caught my eye and came over.

'What was that all about?'

'She's a drama queen, that one,' I said. Half of me hoped he wouldn't ask anything else, although the other half desperately hoped he would.

'Sounds juicy. Anyway, Fran's getting tetchy about filming because we've got some schmoozing to do after this—the Weinstein party—can you get her in so we can crack on with it?'

I looked back towards the terrace, Beau was still there, phone clasped between her cheek and shoulder, giggling and covering it every now and again so no one could possibly hear what she was whispering to her husband-to-be.

Probably pure filth.

Mona, meanwhile, had disappeared from sight.

'Bathroom,' said Fran with the bob, reading my mind. 'Give her a shout, would you. Jesus, it's like herding cats around here.'

I knocked on the bathroom door. 'Everything all right, Mona? They're ready when you are.'

She poked her head around the door and I noticed she'd kicked off her skyscraper Manolo Blahniks.

'Amber, my head's killing me, I need some headache relief. Have you got any paracetamol?'

'Only back at the house,' I replied, cursing myself for not having any in my kit. 'Want me to get you some?'

'I'll get through the filming and then yes, please, there's a CVS pharmacy on the next block. Make a start on the rails with Beau—there's a couple of Roksanda gowns that would be perfect for her. If she wants to make a splash, this will get the fashion press taking note.'

Back in the room I covertly peeked at labels on gowns until I found the two by Roksanda. I didn't want the camera crew to notice that I didn't instantly know my Roksanda from my Roland Mouret. The feeling of being a fraud in this label-obsessed world kept creeping up, but all I could do was ignore it for now. Luckily Beau was oblivious. We both knew she had bigger fish to fry.

'Pleased to see Pinky today?' I asked as she approached, pulling Pinky by his lead, a big smile that screamed 'crisis averted!' spread across her elfin face. Her cheeks were flushed. I imagined some phone sex might have occurred.

'Oh yes! Only he's a bit… I noticed he's got a bit of a gross tummy today, poor thing.'

Sensing Fran and Rob were anxious to start filming, I did what I had seen Mona do countless times by now and led Beau to the rails, pointing out the hot pink Roksanda Ilincic number with big, puffy sleeves. 'Mona was thinking you could start off by trying this,' I offered, noticing that the camera had started rolling and cursing myself for not even touching up my make-up. *Why do I always look like the hired homeless person?*

'Eww—yuck! And not very me.'

'Right, um, so you don't like it?'

'I really want something old Hollywood for the Globes.'

I began riffling through the rail, as I had seen Mona do countless times, my hand soon settling on the beautiful scarlet Valentino gown.

'You can't get more old Hollywood than this,' I said, gently teasing it out and laying it across my arm, presenting it to Beau. Her eyes lit up. *Result!*

'Oh wow—she's amazing! I want to try her!'

It might have seemed slightly odd to refer to a dress as though it were a long-lost girlfriend, but she wasn't the first person I'd heard doing it in LA. Even Mona did it sometimes. Beau reached for the stunning scarlet silk Valentino that had immediately caught my eye while we were setting up.

'It… *She's* beautiful,' I sighed. 'A dream dress. This would look amazing on you. You must try it on.'

I grabbed a pair of diamanté Jimmy Choo sandals and a pretty matching box clutch and led her towards the bedroom-cum-changing room. This time I would wait for her outside; I wasn't stupid enough to risk another confessional. Mona came out of the en suite as we approached the door, still clutching her head.

'Oh. The Valentino. Was the Roksanda not working for you, then?'

She was shooting me daggers; I wasn't sure why.

'Beau thought she'd prefer this.' I smiled awkwardly, painfully aware the camera was still trained on the three of us.

'Yes—I know I'm going to love it, Mona. It's the perfect Golden Globes gown. Out in a sec!'

The camera zoomed in on the items, and then Beau disappeared behind the door. Through gritted teeth, so Rob and Fran couldn't hear, Mona breathed into my neck.

'The Valentino, Amber, if you had bothered to ask, is for Jennifer Astley. It's not on offer for Beau. So you'd better make sure we get it back!'

Shit.

I darted back towards the rails and pulled out another gown, a Marchesa number in a slightly deeper red, still figure-hugging and with a shape that would leave enough cleavage on show to achieve column inches the next morning.

'This one okay?' I asked Mona, who stood with her arms folded, like a teenager in a huff.

'Just get her out of the Valentino. Fast.'

As I headed towards the bedroom, my head was spinning

with reasons I might possibly give for why Beau couldn't be loaned the gown.

It has a big stain down the back.

Valentino himself has requested it be returned because it's faulty.

Michelle Obama wants to auction it for a children's charity.

It's needed to preside over peace talks for the UN.

And then a moment of sanity washed over me.

The truth, Amber. Just tell her the truth. The gown has been promised to Jennifer Astley. Surely she'll understand? My hand was lifted, primed to knock on the bedroom door when it flew open and Beau appeared, looking—it had to be said—every inch the knockout Hollywood starlet in the Valentino. It hugged her curves in all the right places and the slight train at the back made her look sophisticated and chic. In short, it made a brassy bombshell like Beau look like a goddess. The camera crew knew it, too, and as they stepped forward to picture the end result as Beau twirled around, a star in our midst. Even Rob and Fran with the bob were smiling in genuine admiration of the transformation that had occurred. I could envisage her on the red carpet— some dazzling diamond earrings, her hair loosely tousled, scarlet lips—the dress practically styled itself.

'I love her so much, I've never felt so in love with a dress before. She's perfect!'

Her eyes were misted over. She really was in love with it. *Probably more than she loves Trey.* 'And she's even easy to pee in—look, I can just hoist her up and squat!'

She began gathering up the dress. The spell was abruptly broken.

'We get it! No need to demonstrate!' Mona rushed in to

save her dignity. Fran looked pleased; filming was finally livening up. *You can put the girl in a Valentino, but you can't put the Valentino into the girl.*

'Will you thank Mr Valentino personally for me, please, Mona?'

I looked at Mona, wondering what would happen next. I certainly had no idea how to tell Beau that actually, no, she couldn't wear the gown of her dreams after all. Mona didn't strike me as someone to shirk an awkward conversation, but even she looked dumbfounded. She just pushed her hands deeply into the pockets of her silk shirt dress and looked at me. I shifted my weight, uncomfortably. The odd-shoe feeling I'd had in Smith's returned with a vengeance. *Is this a sackable offence?*

'It's just Valentino,' Mona muttered, po-faced, 'no Mister.' Then she seemed to do a volte-face. 'And I'm sure the darling man will be delighted that you can pee easily in his gown. I'll be sure to let him know, after you're a huge triumph in it at the Golden Globes!' She launched herself onto the beaming Beau, throwing her arms around her sparrow-like frame. For a few seconds she completely engulfed her, only pausing briefly to look over her shoulder and check the camera was trained on them as they hugged and kissed.

When it came to keeping celebrity clients happy, there was only one word that applied: a sugar-coated 'Yes!'

At last I released the tension in my shoulders and allowed a sense of pride to wash over me. Mona would never give me the credit for it, but hadn't I just styled my first celebrity? Fran seemed to have read my mind.

'So how does it feel to have selected Beau Belle's Golden Globes outfit?' She stood to the side of the camera, its beating red light letting me know that I was being filmed. Mona suddenly dropped Beau and barged into the shot, placing an arm around my shoulders.

'Exquisite on her, isn't it?' she chimed, pushing a curl behind her ear and looking straight down the lens. 'Valentino is the ultimate awards ceremony designer—the gown screams "screen siren", and I knew straight away that it would be perfect on Beau. She'll be the Belle of the ball! Get it? *Belle* of—'

'Got it, thanks, Mona,' Fran said, a fake smile across her face.

Beau was already out of the dress and heading for the door. *She's not actually going to bother saying goodbye? Charming.* Mona dashed to intercept her.

'Beau, darling, I'm so happy today was a success. You are going to absolutely rock that gown. I knew it would be perfect on you. And will we see you at the party tonight?'

'The Weinstein one? Trey's keen, so we might pop by briefly. But I've got the premiere tomorrow night and I need my beauty sleep. Got to do some wedding planning as well, we've got another meeting with the magazine this week…'

'I was wondering how that was coming along. And what about the bachelorette—have you finalised the venue?'

'Yes, ohmigod, Mona, it's ah-mazing…'

As I strained to overhear their conversation, I became aware that Rob was approaching me.

'Actually, Amber, we couldn't quite pick up your words on that last take—do you mind if we just put this little microphone on you? We'll hear you a lot better. Fran wants to get a quick retake.' He was gesturing towards the open collar on my black dress, and holding up a tiny grey lump of plastic that looked like a bluebottle attached to a black wire.

Instinctively, I stepped backwards as he approached.

'Don't worry, I'm not a micro-pig, I don't bite.'

'I just haven't been mic'd up before—if that's what you call it.' *I sound like an idiot.*

'It takes two seconds and means we can hear you when you speak. Fran wants to get a bit more on why you picked that dress for Beau.'

'Well, if Mona doesn't…' I glanced in her direction, but Mona was still deep in conversation with Beau. They'd moved on to the topic of wedding dresses. 'I guess it's okay.'

Rob came even nearer. As he clipped the tiny microphone onto the collar of my black shirt dress, I became aware that the top of my old grey bra was visible. I cringed. He was so close I could smell him: warm washing powder and a light aftershave. I was afraid to speak for fear that my breath smelled or I'd spit in his ear by accident. I had never felt so aware of my bodily functions. *Please don't do anything weird, body. Please.*

'Perfect, if you just drop this cable through your dress, I'll plug you in.'

I fumbled with the wire, passing it under my dress and out the other end. I was painfully self-conscious. He might as well have asked me to start twerking naked around the room. 'So tell us, Amber, why did you pick the Valentino for Beau?' Fran asked, as a burning sensation spread from my chest to my cheeks. My heart rate was still recovering from Rob's hands being so close to my old bra. Nervously, I spoke to the side of Shaggy's face, just behind the camera, as Rob had instructed.

'I guess it's the ultimate fairy-tale dress. I fell in love with it the moment I saw it—I think any girl would.'

'Do you think red will be a trend on the red carpet this award season?'

This line of questioning is way out of my depth.

'Well, I don't know about that, but I think it's a strong, classic colour that will make Beau stand out from the crowd. The strapless neckline is beautifully elegant and the gown's so well made, she'll feel like a goddess in it.'

'A goddess, I like that. Remind us of your surname, please?'

'It's Green, Amber Green, Mona's assistant.'

Fran looked bemused.

'Yes, like traffic lights,' I qualified, somehow feeling the need to do the job of ridiculing myself for her.

'Well, congrats on adding a punchy red to your name. Now you have the full set—Red Amber Green. That's so funny!'

I smiled, awkwardly. It was the first time I'd seen Fran with the bob actually laugh. But her normally pinched, stern face looked as though it was having problems creasing in the right places. Her mouth was smiling, but somehow her eyes couldn't quite pull it off. I wondered what Vicky's analysis would be. *Heavy Botox, possible fillers, mini facelift?*

'Thanks, all, we're done,' she added, looking as pleased as she was able to look. She clapped her hands together, a signal for the team to begin de-rigging, fast.

'Nice one, Amber, thanks.' Rob smiled. I breathed a sigh of relief as he began helping the cameraman put the equipment back into flight cases.

Finally Mona shut the door behind Beau and summoned me again. But instead of the telling-off I feared, I was given a ten-dollar note and dispatched to the pharmacy for 'drugs'.

Chapter Eight

As I left the hotel to pop to the chemist, Beau was still in the driveway, her perfectly formed butt halfway into a white convertible sports car as a valet held open the door for her. A lucky paparazzo happily chanced upon the scene. The camera flashes alerted everyone in the vicinity that there was a 'famous person' in their midst, and soon a small crowd had gathered to observe the celebrity getting into the car. She lapped up the attention. As she glanced over her shoulder, in full pout-mode for the pap, she spotted me trying to scuttle down the driveway unnoticed.

'Hey, Annie!' Beau screeched. *Drat.*

I pretended not to hear as I felt the hungry eyes of a crowd of tourists instantly turn in my direction. Might they be about to luck out, witness a 'famous person bumps into another famous person' moment? Alas, she's a 'nobody'. They all seemed to realise it at once, heads turning back to Beau in unison.

'No way, *Annie!*' she continued, louder, while the pap

fired off a few more rounds and the bunch of tourists held up their cell phones. *Why is she calling me Annie?*

As I walked in the opposite direction, Beau left the car and lightly jogged towards me, her arms open, ready to welcome me into a big fake hug.

'Oh my God! How cool to bump into you! What are you doing here?'

I looked from Beau to the car and back again. *Oh, bloody hell, she's with Trey.*

I had absolutely nowhere to hide.

'Oh, hi, Beau. I, um, had a meeting here.' *I'm lying again. This is bad energy at its best.*

Beau grabbed my arm and tugged me in the direction of the sports car. The pap snapped us both. I stared at her intently, but she failed to acknowledge the fear on my face.

'You must come meet my Trey. He was just saying he spoke to you on the phone earlier. That's so weird, isn't it? And now you can meet in the flesh. How fun is that?'

About as fun as spending the night with an insomniac micro-pig.

'What a coincidence!' was all I could muster, as she took my hand and led me towards the car. My palm was sweating profusely.

Trey rose out of the driving seat. He was tall, and much better looking than in photos. I immediately realised that showing my face for any length of time was probably not the most sensible thing to do.

'Good to put a face to the name, Miss…Annie,' he said, offering his hand.

'My surname, it's Liechtenstein,' I managed to say, smiling and shaking his hand at the same time. 'But, as I said, call me Annie.'

Now it was Beau's turn to squeeze my elbow for added reassurance.

'I've been thinking about what you said earlier, and we really appreciate the support from the studio, Annie,' Trey continued. 'These gossip sites will run anything. It's good to know you and the studio are above all that.'

'Yes, all the way, Mr Jones,' I said, trying to stop my voice from quivering.

'Well, if you do change your mind about the Weinstein party tonight, maybe we'll see you there for a longer chat.'

'Think I'll give it a miss tonight—scripts to read, you know. Anyway, got to dash. Another meeting! Tally ho!' *I did tell you that acting isn't my forte.*

'You're not walking, are you?' Trey asked, perplexed. Mona had already informed me that no one in LA walks further than the distance from the valet desk to their car door.

'Um, it's a London thing, I guess. Can't help it.'

'A true Londoner! Let us give you a lift, please.'

I looked at the car. It barely had room for two perfectly formed famous people and their queasy micro-pig.

'No, it's fine, I like the exercise.'

Thankfully, they let me get on my way.

* * *

Mona texted as I made my way to the pharmacy: Get me some Touche Éclat too.

The chemist was more like an aircraft hangar than a local shop; a huge warehouse filled with every kind of lotion, potion, upper and downer that a starlet with an addictive personality could possibly blow her trust fund on. There was also a large, desperately tempting aisle stacked with family packs of all kinds of confectionery and enough Red Vine candy sticks to circumnavigate the globe at least ten times.

I returned with three different types of headache tablet for Mona, some Touche Éclat (that I paid for myself, as the petty cash she'd given me barely covered the pills) and an emergency bag of Reese's Pieces. Walking back up the hotel driveway, I was surprised to find Mona packed up for the day and waiting for me at the wheel of the Prius outside the hotel.

'Change of plan, babe. We've been invited to the Weinstein party this evening. Literally *everyone* is going. How fabulous is that!' *Headache appears to have miraculously disappeared, then.*

Before I could scream, 'But one of the biggest directors in Hollywood will be there and he thinks I'm someone else and besides, I don't have anything to wear!' Mona threw me a golden ticket: 'I'll shout you a blow-out and you can borrow one of the Dolce dresses if you like.'

'A blow-out?'

'Oh, sweetie, you're so cute. "Blow-out" is American slang for a blow-dry.' *Dolce dress and I don't have to perform a sexual act for it. Major result!*

* * *

When we got back to the house I logged on to the Mac in Mona's study, which I'd been told was my makeshift office. I wanted to see if those photos of Beau and Jason had made it out into the ether. The web browser had been left open on Mona's Wikipedia entry, where she had clearly been doing some editing. She was now described as 'The world's most famous stylist', which was arguably the truth and listed as 'Age 37', which was definitely not. At least not for seven or so years, I estimated.

I opened a new tab. Sure enough, there on the *Starz* homepage was a large, slightly blurred photo of Beau and Jason, their arms around each other and their lips locked, just inside the entrance to an underground car park. The headline read:

WORLD EXCLUSIVE
BREAKING NEWS!
BEAU'S BIG CLINCH WITH JASON
THE PHOTOS THAT PROVE THINGS
ARE HOTTING UP OFF-SET FOR THE
SUMMER'S NOT OVER *CO-STARS!*

And then in smaller writing underneath:

WHAT WILL TREY SAY?

And in teeny-tiny font, so small you almost needed a magnifying glass to read it, was a line at the end of a piece that said:

*When asked about these exclusive photos, Beau Belle commented, 'We were rehearsing and I have nothing further to say.' Trey Jones was unavailable for comment.

I sat back in the chair. 'Rehearsing', in an underground car park? *Why hide away like that if you're doing nothing wrong?*

I suddenly became of aware of a shape at the doorway and clicked off the site, opening another tab. Klara had appeared from nowhere, draping herself languidly against the door frame. I had noticed that Klara had an exceptional ability to appear silently and sneakily from nowhere, like a ghost. It was unnerving every time.

'How's it going, Klara?'

'Not bad… bored… What are you looking at?' she asked.

'Just catching up on celebrity news, nothing in particular,' I lied.

'Brad and Angelina are meant to be adopting another child, I heard,' she offered.

'Really.'

'I thought you were looking at something to do with Beau Belle. She's one of Mona's clients.' Klara was annoying me now, with her patronising tone. Or maybe I was just feeling tired and irritable.

'Yes, I know. Micro-pig—remember?'

'Why are you Googling her, then?'

'There's some story about her on the *Starz* site,' I conceded, trying to make an effort.

I clicked the *Starz* page open again and Klara leaned over my shoulder for a closer look.

'I know that guy she's filming with. Jason's a major flirt. She been banging him?'

'So they're suggesting,' I said.

'Hmm. He's hot,' she replied. She flicked her hair and slunked off again, vanishing into the shadows in the hallway. It struck me that, for a house painted predominantly white, there was not a lot of light in Mona's home; just a lot of scented candles that Ana would light during the course of the evening. Despite the bright sun outside, it could be a rather dark and haunting place. Klara reappeared at the door.

'Oh, what are you wearing to the Weinstein party this evening?'

'Mona's going to lend me a Dolce & Gabbana dress. Are you coming?'

'Yeah, I'll probably catch a ride with you both. It's at Soho House.'

'Awesome!'

For a moment my guard slipped. I was excited about making it into Soho House, one of the world's most exclusive, covetable, private members' clubs. Vicky and I had twice managed to sneak into the central London branch, but I had never actually been a bona fide invitee. But that was all in the past. Tonight I was to be a guest at Soho House, LA— *the* Soho House. I imagined it was a world where blow-outs, bling, Botox and Hollywood power players reigned supreme. *Thank Christ I'll have swishy hair.* As I regained my composure, I was distracted by my phone ringing.

'Vicky!'

'Babe! Finally! Been thinking about you non-stop,' she squealed down the line. 'You're the talk of my office. Even the Editor wants an update. So come on, spill!'

It was so good to hear her voice.

'Oh, honey, I've missed you so much.' I glanced at Klara, thinking she'd get the hint to slink off and leave me in peace. She didn't. 'It's been unreal. I don't know where to begin really, I can't believe it's only been two days and so much has happened.' I crept past Klara, out of the office and upstairs to my bedroom to speak in private.

'Well, you can start with sleeping with Beau Belle's micro-pig! What the…?'

I heard the TV in the background, Vicky had a habit of turning it on as soon as she got home. I looked at my watch; it must be way after midnight in London.

Still haven't properly got my head around the time difference.

'Oh, Vic, it was the maddest day…'

As I regaled her with the story of Beau's fittings, Pinky's M&Ms dinner, Mona's coffee addiction, the sacked PA, the

gigantic lie, the tiny people, the minders, the gowns, the jewels, the shoes, Klara, my room, the pool—which I still hadn't
even had a chance to dip my little toe in—the housekeeper
and everything in between, I realised that this massively beat
the Groundhog Day of getting up and going to Smith's, five,
sometimes six days a week. Vicky was a fantastic listener—
she laughed, shrieked and made 'Oh my God!' exclamations
in all the right places. She found the Pinky story particularly hilarious; at one point real tears were rolling down my
cheeks, too. I dearly wished she was out here, as well. After
twenty minutes of verbal diarrhoea, I came up for air, having told her everything I could think of, except for the fact
that I missed home and our fridge full of hummus and nail
varnish, and finally asked, 'How are you, anyway?'

'Oh, not bad.'

'Doesn't sound like you, Vic?'

'I'm fine—just tired, I guess. It was a long day—the Editor was in a bad mood, nothing was right—so I had a wine
session with Polly after work. I'm hungover already.'

'Have you got plans for this week?'

'Yes, a couple of things with the work crew, and a launch
party for a new swimwear label tomorrow night—should be fun.'

'No Simon plans?'

Simon had been Vicky's boyfriend for the whole of the past
year. He was a successful freelance film reviewer, perennially
working on his first screenplay, five years older than her. At
first I was impressed she had managed to bag such a clever,
good-looking older man, but he and I had never bonded; I
always felt like the annoying, wallflower friend whenever
Vicky insisted we go out in a three.

'Not yet…you know what Simon's like. He's got a couple
of screenings this week—I might join him at one of those.

Or we might meet after the launch tomorrow. I'll see him on Sunday, if not. What day are you back again?'

'Next Wednesday, 7:00 a.m.' Involuntarily I let out a huge yawn, suddenly aware that I could barely keep my eyes open. Jet lag had caught up with me again.

'You're practically asleep, babe, you go to bed.'

'No time for sleep—I'm going to the Weinstein party with Mona and Klara.'

'Weinstein as in Harvey Weinstein? Bloody hell, that's cool! You'd better not let all this schmoozing go to your head, Miss Green. What are you going to wear?'

'Mona's lending me a dress and shouting me a blow-dry—which is called a blow-out over here, don't you know.'

'Sounds rude. Anyway, all this glamour and blowing is too much for me… I've got to get my head down, I can't afford to be late for work tomorrow. Have fun. Love you.'

'Love you more. Hope work's better tomorrow.'

'Oh, and whatever happens at the party, phone me afterwards. And post a selfie so I can see the blow-out.'

As I said goodbye I rested my head on the pillow and closed my eyes for a second, thinking of the mornings when Vicky and I would buy each other a Diet Coke to drink on the tube to ease our hangovers. It sounded as though she would need one this morning. It all felt so far away.

* * *

Next thing I knew, I was woken up by a loud banging at the door.

'Amber? Amber! You all right in there, *chica*?'

I'd been sleeping with my mouth open, and it had dried out so much, I couldn't speak. I swallowed deeply.

'Ana, I'm fine, sorry, I was asleep…'

As I hoisted myself up onto my elbows, Ana appeared

at the doorway, a patterned Dolce & Gabbana dress over her arm.

'Thank God for that, we thought you had maybe collapsed or something. Mona's ready to go. She wants to know if you've got the dress on yet...'

'What time is it?'

'Nine... The driver's waiting.'

'Oh no! Tell her I'll be literally two minutes...'

* * *

I emerged from the car all flowing, flicky, glossy hair. Clouds parted across the sky in my wake. The sun shone a spotlight over my head. The clip-clop of my towering heels made a satisfying sound as I strode confidently towards the red carpet at the glittering entrance of Soho House. I felt like the most powerful, magnetic woman to stride this Earth. Well, that's how I *wanted* to feel. In reality, I exited the Prius in an underground car park and walked between Mona and Klara towards a small, dimly-lit reception desk, feeling drowsy, hot and uncomfortable, squeezed into the beautiful Dolce & Gabbana dress—unfortunately a small sample size, for my non-sample-size body. My hair was pepped up with a generous spray of dry shampoo. *I hate myself for falling asleep.* Yet, as we gave our names to be ticked off an extensive list, there were still bubbles of excitement in my stomach. I was about to enter the legendary Soho House lifts and an actual top Hollywood event.

Taking in my surroundings, I realised that the underground car park didn't look unlike the one in the paparazzi photos of Beau and Jason 'rehearsing'. In fact, it looked identical. The building at 9200 Sunset Boulevard resembled a nondescript office block from the outside (not the kind of place you would expect to run into Leo DiCaprio), but when we reached the top floor, the Soho House level, its 180-degree views of the city of Los Angeles below took my breath away.

A red carpet led the way towards two huge gold urns, beautiful white roses spilling over the top, marking the entrance to a large entertaining space at the end of a passage. The group of photographers standing at the edge of the carpet knew Mona by name and she lapped up their attention, twisting and turning her slender frame in a jaw-dropping gold and silver short fringed dress, resembling a flapper on heat as they captured her. She looked sensational this evening. *She'd* obviously fitted in a blow-out and applied plenty of Touche Éclat, and there seemed to be no trace of the migraine.

After a minute or two, the paps lost interest and began craning their necks.

'Klara, darling—come join me!' Mona called, her voice raised. 'Hey, guys, get a few shots of this beautiful creature— Klara Sands—the next big thing from London, remember her name, okay!'

I'd never seen Mona as animated as when she was in front of a bank of cameras. She literally sparkled. Klara trotted into the photography area, taking immense care not to roll her ankle in her super-high platform shoes and new season Henry Holland skintight dress, also on loan from Mona for the evening. I was sure that Klara would be checking vogue.com later, to see if her photo had made the grade. I was aware of my exclusion from the photo opp, but I was content with my Z-list status. Especially as the dress was beginning to chafe.

After being guided into the throng by a hostess who looked like a supermodel in a slick white trouser suit, we were given chilled glasses of rosé champagne and I desperately tried to stifle a grin, wishing Vicky was here so we could 'cheers' and appreciate the free fizz together. It tasted delicious.

'Nothing tastes as good as free champagne,' Klara whispered in my ear, reading my mind.

Then I began to take in my surroundings. The room heaved with glamorous guests, dressed in every 1920s fashion item you could possibly imagine: a hypnotic ensemble of beaded drop-waist dresses, fur stoles, peacock feathers, pearls, low backs, high T-bar heels, smooth bobs and chic waves sporting glitzy barrettes. The air was filled with the rich scent of a hundred different fragrances all mixed together to form a strong, heady musk. It was intoxicating. Klara and I looked at each other, in our modern, on-trend designer threads that bore absolutely no semblance to the twenties glamour all around us. We may as well have been two Essex girls gatecrashing a high-society wedding.

'Um, did we miss the dress-code memo?' whispered Klara as we squeezed past a group of men dressed in three-piece suits with pocket squares.

'Thanks for that, Mona,' I muttered, just as my boss air-kissed someone wearing exquisite chandelier earrings who looked vaguely familiar.

'Sensational dress, Mona!'

'Vintage number I've had for forever. Thanks, sweetie!'

Wandering through the party, I witnessed first-hand how having Mona for a boss was a carte blanche into another world. I caught the odd smile of admiration from fashionable women, in recognition of my new season Dolce & Gabbana (poorly though it fitted). I even chinked glasses with one important-looking older man, possibly Harvey Weinstein himself; presumably he'd mistaken me for someone he'd actually invited. I devoured some melt-in-the-mouth king prawn skewers—and turned down a Parmesan pyramid after Mona scoffed: 'Pure cheese in batter? Are you serious?'

I was suddenly snapped from my canapé coma by a crowd-parting moment—a narrow tunnel of empty floor space opened up directly ahead of me, and there at the end of it was Rob, leaning against the bar, it was almost as though he was illuminated.

'Hey, there's Rob!' I exclaimed, embarrassingly enthusiastically.

Fortunately, Mona was busy noticing that her ex-assistant, Tamara, had just arrived at the party with the actress Poppy Drew (an ex-client and, I assumed, the reason for Tamara's sudden departure). The paparazzi went wild for Poppy, lighting up the area for everyone to see. But I was more interested in the pathway towards the bar. Over a finger of melon and prosciutto, Rob's eyes met mine. Jay Gatsby, in his dandy suit with crisp white shirt. *He obviously got the dress code memo.*

'Who's Rob, then?' asked Klara.

'Oh, just someone on the TV crew we've been filming with this week.' I tried to play it down. 'He's the assistant director.' Surely such low status wouldn't be of interest to Klara. She followed my line of vision.

'Why don't we go over?'

'Why don't we have a Parmesan pyramid first?'

I grabbed two from a tray as it whizzed past. Klara gave hers a gentle squeeze, looked at it disdainfully and then passed it back to me. They were warm and gooey and delicious—two of them slipped down far too easily. I had spent most of my time in LA so far feeling hungry. I glanced back up to see if Rob was still looking, but he was now locked in conversation with a very short, very bronzed man.

'Hey, he's with that guy Tim Parker, from breakfast TV.' Klara read my mind.

'Oh yes, I think I recognise him, he does all the red-carpet reports for *Morning Glory* at home.'

'That's him. Mr Perma Tan. I met him once,' Klara continued. 'He's fun. Let's go say hi.'

Before I could protest, she grabbed my wrist and we headed in Rob's direction.

'Hey, Amber—you made it,' Rob said as we approached. 'Have you met Tim before?'

Tim was wearing an ill-fitting purple suit, and a pale lime shirt with pointed collars—more seventies throwback than twenties gent.

'Tim, this is Amber Green, we were filming together earlier today.'

The very bronzed man held out his very orange hand. When he smiled I couldn't help but notice he had the most dazzling bright white teeth I had ever seen. Maybe it was just the contrast with the putty-coloured skin that made them look so radioactive.

'Eh up. Pleasure's all mine,' Tim said, in a strange Midlands-meets-California accent. 'And who's this beauty—I know your face, don't I?'

They both gazed at Klara. To be fair, Klara all dolled up was a mesmerising sight. I felt a horrible twinge of jealousy in the pit of my stomach.

'Klara,' she replied, 'we met at the *American Idol* launch party a few weeks back.'

'That's it. You were with that scary stylist.'

'Mona Armstrong. Yeah, I'm living at her house at the moment while I'm modelling out here.'

'You seem able to handle Mona okay, Amber,' Rob said,

thoughtfully drawing me back into the conversation. 'Tim, Amber is Mona's new assistant.'

I glanced around to check Mona wasn't within earshot.

'I've only been working with her for four days.'

'Brave lass!' said Tango Tim.

'She's all right,' I said, diplomatically, wary of who might be eavesdropping.

'Loving the suit—did you get it made specially?' Klara leaned across and pretended to flick a bit of dust from Rob's lapel. She had him in her sights, I could tell. Were it to come to a showdown, I already knew who would win.

'Luckily our cameraman is into vintage fashion, so he lent me this,' Rob explained, smiling. 'Had to get the trousers taken up at the hotel, but I quite like the old-school look.'

'Suits you, too.' Klara held his gaze for a little too long.

'What do you think, Amber?' he said. 'You're the stylist.' *I'm blushing. I'm blushing and I have absolutely no idea why.*

'We, er, didn't actually realise it was fancy dress. Mona forgot to…'

'Forgot to what, darling?' Mona's voice rang loudly in my ear as she joined our group and fixed me with one of her fearsome stares.

'Forgot to…' I repeated, unsure what would come out of my mouth next.

'Forgot to let you know we'll be back to film again in the morning,' Rob interjected, saving me.

'Yes!' Mona cried. 'Tomorrow's the big day. In fact, girls, that's exactly why we've got to go home now.' She looked over her shoulder as if looking for someone.

Klara and I both turned our heads, following Mona's

gaze, to see Tamara and Poppy Drew staring straight back at us. My heart sank. *But I don't want to go home yet!*

'I think that silly girl has now realised she made a huge mistake,' Mona continued, as we huddled together, our group against Tamara's. 'I've told her I've got Jennifer Astley coming to the suite tomorrow, plus the cameras, and I want to be fresh. We're off.' She made a bad attempt at hiding her horror at the state of Tim Parker, with his Oompa Loompa tan, spray-dyed hair and dangerous teeth. 'Jesus.'

'No, it's Tim, actually.'

I giggled as Mona spun around, anticipating correctly that Klara and I would follow. The beaded fringing on her dress fanned theatrically outwards.

'Girls, let's go. Now, Amber.' We fell into line in her wake, Mona Armstrong's army of two.

'Bye, guys!' Klara called, excited by the drama.

'See you tomorrow,' I said to Rob, gutted that our evening had been cut short. *And* I'd only managed to neck four canapés. 'Nice to meet you, Tim.'

'Au revoir, ladies… Until we meet again!'

'Hopefully never,' Mona replied under her breath. I imagined he was quite possibly the most unstylish person she had ever laid eyes on.

As we made our way back to the entrance, I glanced over my shoulder one final time and noticed Tamara still looking in our direction. For a brief couple of seconds our eyes connected: Mona's old and new assistants. She looked away first to whisper something to Poppy, probably about my too-tight dress. As I turned around again, my heart leapt into my throat—Mona was air-kissing Beau Belle, bright flashes from cameras popping in the air around her like a meteorite shower. And then Mona greeted the man next to her.

Oh shi—it's Trey!

Without thinking about it, I dropped to the floor and froze, like a crouching tiger. Or, in reality, more like a lost frog. A few seconds passed before Klara looked down and saw my frightened eyes looking up into hers.

'What are you doing?'

'My shoe!' I exclaimed, pretending to adjust a non-existent buckle. 'Won't be a sec.'

Shit. Now what? It was an interesting world, down here at the roots of the party, an emporium of well-heeled feet, silky-smooth legs and millions of dollars' worth of fancy frocks. I scanned the area, picking out Mona's sparkling sandals and next to them, a pair of exuberant white platforms that had to be Beau's. Very close to them, some polished brogues probably belonging to Trey. Suddenly, through the forest of legs, a pair of familiar dark eyes stared right into mine: Pinky. His slobbery snout made a beeline for a discarded spring roll on the floor between us—then his lead was yanked and he scuttled off in the direction of the white platforms, his curly tail lifted in the air. I continued fiddling with my shoe a moment longer.

'Amber, seriously, what are you doing down there?'

'Still sorting out my shoe, done in a sec!'

There was no way I could risk Trey calling me Annie in front of Mona and Klara. I had no choice but to sit it out until the coast was clear. But this looked weird, and my thighs were beginning to ache. I slipped one shoe off my foot and held it up for added effect, but not for long enough for Klara to see that there was actually nothing wrong with it.

'Heel's bust. I'm going to the Ladies' to try and repair it. I'll see you back in the car park.'

'Aren't you going to say hi to Beau, seeing as you're best mates with her piggy?' Klara asked, looking irritated.

'Say hi for me. See you in a mo!' I hopped off in the opposite direction, stooped over, so as to keep my face well hidden. I had no idea where the ladies' toilets actually were, but when I reached the windows at the other side of the party, as far from Beau and Trey and the growing crowd around them as I could possibly get, I finally stood up straight, reunited my shoe with the floor and wiggled my foot back into it.

'Breaking in new heels?' asked a male voice next to me.

I turned and looked over the man's shoulder, checking whether Beau and Trey were anywhere nearby. He turned around, too, following my eye line and revealing the back view of his thick, black mop of curly hair and a nicely tanned neck.

'Or maybe avoiding somebody?' This time he also offered a slightly wonky, but attractively broad smile.

'Something like that,' I replied, attempting to smooth down my messed-up hair by pulling it back into a ponytail shape and then letting it fall around my shoulders. As he held out a hand, I found myself sucking in my stomach.

'I'm Liam. And you are…'

I thought for a moment too long. *Amber or Annie?*

'Are you on the run or something?' he asked, looking over his shoulder.

'No, it's all fine now,' I said.

'But you *are* avoiding someone?' He had a lovely American accent.

I laughed nervously. 'I think I've safely avoided them now. Hi, I'm Amber.'

We shook. Electricity crackled.

'Well, Amber, if I need to watch out for an angry ex-boyfriend, just say,' he said, chocolate-brown eyes shining, glancing back again theatrically.

'Don't panic, there's no psycho ex,' I replied. 'Just some-one I wasn't prepared to see this evening, that's all.'

'Sounds intriguing.'

I desperately wanted to carry on chatting, but I was pain-fully aware that Mona and Klara would probably have left the party by now and I didn't want to risk Mona's bad mood if I kept her waiting in the car park. Underground car parks were absolutely not Mona's scene.

'My friends are waiting for me,' I said, reluctantly.

'Leaving already? The party's only just beginning…and you have the most beautiful English accent.'

I blushed. Liam reached into his inside suit pocket and pulled out a business card. Then he asked if he could take down my number. 'Just in case you need to be rescued again.' Gleefully I let him punch it into his phone.

'If you're here in LA for a while, look me up. Maybe we can grab a cocktail together…if you're not still on the run, that is,' he added. *I'm actually being chatted up, at Soho House, by a real-life American!*

'Thanks—that would be lovely.'

Holding the card in the palm of my hand, I closed my fingers tightly around it, squishing it in half. Then I skirted around the edges of the throng back towards the exit, giving the area in the middle a wide berth as a fountain of flash-bulbs exploded once more and I imagined Beau and Trey right in the centre, probably air-kissing Leonardo DiCaprio. When I reached the car park Mona was waiting, beating her thumbs on the wheel. She scowled as I opened the door.

'Sorry, long queue in the Ladies',' I muttered, diving in a millisecond before she slammed her foot down and we sped off. I don't think she'd have worried unduly if I'd been dragged along the concrete. In the back of the car, once I'd regained my breath, I unfurled my fingers from around the crumpled card. I studied the writing on one side of it:

Liam Anderson
Actor
Los Angeles • New York • London

And on the reverse, two mobile phone numbers—one American, one British—and an email address. I slipped it into my clutch bag before Klara could get a look. *Liam Anderson. Should I know that name, or recognise the face?* I pulled out my phone, desperate to Google him. Another text message from Mum was stacked up behind four others asking if I'd arrived okay, if I was getting on with Mona okay, if I was eating okay, and finally, if I was still alive. I quickly typed a response: Sorry mum! It's been mad busy. But everything's fine, having a great time and will call you tomorrow, I promise. Love you A x. She responded straight away: Great, got a pension scheme I need to talk to you about. And Nora was brilliant in her play!

* * *

When we arrived back at Mona's, I was glad of the bag of Reese's Pieces I'd bought in the pharmacy, which became my late dinner. *I really don't understand how Mona and Klara can call three canapés supper.* As I tucked myself into the giant bed just before midnight, I felt disappointed that my first celebrity party had been less roaring, more snoring twenties. Then I studied Liam Anderson's business card again and placed it carefully on the bedside table.

Chapter Nine

By the next morning—the day before the Golden Globes—I'd got into the swing of things. My regime was simple: get up, put on my too-hot black uniform, suffer Mona's disappointment as she scanned my outfit, endure the white-knuckle ride to the suite and assist my boss by drip-feeding her coffee and being on hand with my kit, as LA's hottest women processed through our doors, tried things on and took them off again. The only difference was that today I found myself taking a little longer to apply my make-up. We were going to welcome serious Hollywood royalty in the form of America's sweetheart, actress Jennifer Astley, to the suite today to make her final choice of gown for the awards. Almost as excitingly, I'd woken up to a text message from Liam Anderson: Great to meet you, English girl. See you soon? x

* * *

Unfortunately for Mona, on this particular morning, just as the TV crew started filming, fire alarms began ringing loudly and the whole of the W Hotel was ordered to evacuate, which the whole of the W Hotel obediently did—with the exception of our suite. With no regard for human life, Mona point-blank refused to let us any of us leave the precious merchandise.

'You'll have to break the door down! I'd rather we burned to death than lost all this!' she screeched through the keyhole, as a hotel porter politely attempted to coax us out of the room with news that coffee was being served to the guests assembled outside. Then, when the hotel manager phoned and tried to reason with her, she simply shouted: 'Then we'll all burn down!' and slammed the receiver. Five minutes later, the manager rapped on the door, now accompanied by two security guards.

'Ma'am, if you do not vacate these premises in the next sixty seconds, then I will have no option but to call the Federal police. It's a criminal offence to refuse to evacuate during an emergency procedure.'

Hearing the word 'criminal' thrown into the equation, Mona had a change of heart and conceded that Fran, Rob and Shaggy could leave the suite. But I was ordered to stay put. As the film crew shuffled out, my captor sneakily locked us both in the bedroom, with a suitcase of jewellery, three Chanel bags, a vintage Dior gown, a Fendi fur and all the shoes we could carry, making it crystal clear that should flames engulf the hotel, she would be quite happy to see me perish, alongside tens of thousands of pounds' worth of fashion booty. I had occasionally wondered whether I would ever stare into the cold eyes of death, and this, it seemed, was my answer.

Up in ashes with a designer wardrobe. What a way to go. I wonder if my travel insurance covers this, Mum?

Luckily the alarm ultimately turned out to be a planned fire drill, but Mona's disturbing behaviour gave us all a terrifying insight into her dedication to the cause. If she was trying to achieve legendary status, this was certainly one way to go about it.

'If you ask me, she's uninsured,' Rob observed, when I found him at the Nespresso machine as I prepared a triple-shot caffè macchiato for Mona, and one for me, to help steady our nerves. Rob's words resonated with me long after the alarm had been silenced. I hadn't failed to notice Mona's haphazard filing system in the office at her home—it was basically a lot of unopened envelopes shoved into an old Harvey Nichols Christmas hamper under her desk. But now wasn't the time to broach this with her.

'Did you get all that?' I heard Fran with the bob whisper to Shaggy when Mona was 'taking some air' on the terrace; she was clutching her second triple-shot caffè macchiato with a noticeably shaky hand, following another visit from the manager who had informed her that any further failure to comply with hotel regulations would mean eviction from the suite.

'Best thing we've got yet,' Shaggy replied.

'Totally. I half hoped we'd have to tie gowns together to escape out of the window,' Fran cackled. 'Can you imagine if Jennifer Astley had had to shin it down the side of the building? Priceless!'

I wondered if I should tell Mona that the fire alarm segment was undoubtedly going to make the final edit. She didn't seem to have clocked, but I was beginning to see that the agenda of the *20Twenty* people wasn't the same as hers. Retrieving my phone, I was chuffed to see another text message from Liam. He seemed keen.

Morning, beautiful. How's your day going?

I immediately responded: Hey! All good, busy at work. You? A x

Straight away he replied: Auditions. Pilot season in full flow—up for a flying doctor and a jolly British bobby this morning. Practising my English accent!!

Well, you know where to come if you need any tips!

I'll take you up on that.

Where/when? I shot back, surprised and exhilarated by my directness.

But there the texting session ended. No immediate response. And still no response thirty minutes later. It played on my mind. *Have I messed up my chances? Should I send another text making light of it? No, get a grip. If in doubt, do nothing.* Vicky had told me so countless times as we analysed messages from a succession of guys I had unsuccessfully dated on Tinder.

Fortunately, I didn't have time to dwell on it for long—we were back to business. Anticipation for the Golden Globes was gathering pace and a steady stream of expensive-looking women arrived for their final appointments with Mona, and I was under strict instructions to get them in and out fast so the suite could be cleared in time for Jennifer's arrival. During fittings, my job was primarily to ensure everyone was kept refreshed and that we never ran out of thin slices of fruit and dried goji berries. I'd decided to ditch the fig rolls, because only me and the odd miniature dog seemed to be eating them and—much as I hated myself for becoming susceptible—I was swiftly developing body inadequacy issues, being around all these wafer-thin people all day long.

My other role was to act like a kind of post-office sorting

clerk, ensuring the endless bags of clothes, shoes and accessories were delivered by the couriers to the correct places at the right times and—now that awards season was beginning to get under way with 'pre' parties—there were returns to keep tabs on, as well. Dresses sometimes came back looking like casualties of war, sporting stains from spilt cocktails, occasional cigarette burns, heel-ravaged hemlines and stuck zips. All the promise and excitement they'd once held was gone the moment they'd done their duty and been sent back to us like a dog-eared invitation. But the design houses didn't seem to bat an eyelid. I just had to ensure each gown went back to the correct PR. The part I enjoyed most was my stylist duties, assisting Mona by delving into my kit for anything she might require to make adjustments to outfits, and increasingly trusting me to cinch a dress together at the back or pin a hem myself while a client stood on a stool, so it hung just so. The only thing distracting me today was my phone burning a hole in my pocket. Two hours had passed—still no response from Liam. Even worse, my incessant checking had been noticed by Rob.

'Waiting for a call?' he asked as I pulled out my iPhone, looked at it and replaced it in my back pocket for probably the twentieth time in the last hour. 'Is it Jennifer?'

'No,' I said casually.

'Boyfriend, then?'

My cheeks flushed. 'Sort of.'

'Hope he calls,' he quipped before turning away.

* * *

At 4:00 p.m. there was a buzz in the room as we watched Mona spin into a frenzy in anticipation of Jennifer Astley's arrival. I assisted her straightening hangers, polishing jewels and checking the minibar a million times to ensure we had a huge selection of different types of water, plus a bottle of Perrier-Jouët rosé on ice, to cater for Jennifer's every whim. Bang on time—which I gathered from Mona is rare for most famous people, herself included—Jennifer arrived, exuding star quality. Not in the way Beau did, with her darting, coquettish eyes and false eyelashes so long you could land a private jet on one of them. No, Jennifer's brand of fame was way more established: calm and confident, professional and finessed. Which made her *really* unnerving.

Her rise to superstardom had been steady and consistent, fuelled by a succession of huge box-office hits and an interesting love life involving several A-list relationships, not to mention a stack of industry award nominations. But none of this seemed to have made her self-important. She looked me straight in the eye when she walked in, and held out a soft, tanned, manicured hand.

'Pleased to meet you, I'm Jen.'

Somehow I managed to get out the word, 'Hi' in response. I was spellbound by Jennifer—we all were. She was stunningly beautiful in the flesh, her hair healthy, long and sleek with the glossy swish of an expensive cut and a world-class colourist. It wasn't hard to see why she had fronted marketing campaigns for international beauty giants for almost a decade. Dressed in her civvies—pale blue jeans, white top, flats, cream blazer—she was effortlessly cool, all Californian sophistication. A thoroughbred. She arrived practically alone; no entourage of publicist, manager, PA and bodyguard to speak for her and demand weird drinks, and no miniature pet snapping at her heels—she just came with a make-up artist, introduced as Caroline, who would transform her quickly from fresh-faced almost-normal Jen to the A-list Jennifer Astley we were all so familiar with, ready to head straight off to a pre-Globes party held by a top producer.

'Excuse the state of me, I was rushing to get here from the studio,' she apologised. I became aware that I was actually open-mouthed—I was in the presence of Hollywood royalty, doing a bad impersonation of Nemo.

'Can we get you something to drink, Jennifer?' Mona asked, her hand moving like an electric whisk behind her back, which I took as my cue to stop gawping and look busy. 'A glass of champagne perhaps?' I sprang into action, poised by the door of the minibar.

'Just a little water would be great—thanks so much.'

No mention of room temperature, or whether it has to be lemon-infused, isotonic or coconut. And a thank you!

Then it was time to go through the rails. Jennifer being our biggest celebrity client—and the one the scarlet Valentino gown had been earmarked for—Mona had had me calling around some of the most prestigious design houses before her appointment, and this afternoon we had taken delivery of five incredibly beautiful gowns: two by Armani Privé, one by Alberta Ferretti, an Oscar de la Renta and a stunning ivory silk gown by Dior. Each would complement Jennifer's impeccably classic red-carpet personality. Jennifer barely batted an eye as Fran with the bob practically curtseyed at her feet and asked if they could start filming; she just carried on as if they weren't there. *Even you, Fran, with your bob, are small fry compared to Jen's usual directors.* I noticed Rob seemed as mesmerised by Jennifer as I was. It was impossible not to be.

Though the scarlet Valentino had previously been promised to her, Jennifer didn't show any angst at hearing that it was no longer available, despite Mona blaming it squarely on my shoulders, muttering under her breath that I was her 'new, inexperienced assistant'. Instead she plumped for a cream feather-and-crystal-embellished gown by Oscar de la Renta that showed off her lightly tanned, toned shoulders and back. The dress looked incredible from behind, falling effortlessly into a cascade of wispy feathers. It oozed sophistication.

'It's just right,' she declared, kissing Mona on both cheeks, before disappearing again to take it off. She was our fastest fitting of the week.

Caroline the make-up artist then set to work transforming Jennifer's face into that of a glowing, iridescent goddess. I tried to busy myself neatening the shoe collection while observing every gentle sweep of the make-up artist's brush, hoping I might learn something. In Jennifer's case, less was more. In the blink of a smoky eye, a pearly sheen was dotted across her high cheekbones, a slick of gloss dabbed onto those famously full lips and there she was, dewy Hollywood personified. I was in a Jennifer Astley daze when Rob joined me.

'Pretty cool to be this close to a proper movie star, isn't it?' he whispered.

'Just slightly. And she's so nice.'

'She's just a normal person underneath the sheen, you know. Anyway, you don't strike me as someone who gets star-struck, I saw how you handled Beau Belle.'

'Hmm, she's a different kettle of fish altogether.'

'We're covering the red carpet for Beau's premiere tonight. Should be interesting, with the pap photos doing the rounds at the moment. I'd guess her fiancé will be there, for the big show of "togetherness".'

'Expect so. I'm happy not to have to witness all that, to be honest.'

'You won't be styling her for the carpet? She'll be wearing the Dolce & Gabbana dress...'

He's up on his celebrity gossip and he's remembered she's wearing Dolce. Oh God. Maybe he's gay?

'Mona's going. I don't think she trusts me out in the field just yet.'

'You'd walk it! You handled most of the styling for Beau, anyway. As for the red carpet, just imagine feeding time at a zoo and you won't be far off.' We both turned towards the door as Jennifer prepared to leave.

'Thanks, and see you all again, I hope!' she called, smiling her million-dollar smile and waving in our direction. *Jennifer Astley waved at me. Now this is a moment to bank. I wish I'd asked for a photo.*

'Bye, Jennifer!' Rob called, nudging me.

'Good luck tomorrow!' I added.

'Oh, Amber, she doesn't need luck, silly—she's wearing a lucky dress!' Mona said loudly, keen to have the last word. Then she was gone. I half-expected to see a trail of twinkling fairy dust in her wake. I sighed.

'Wow.'

'She's amazing,' Rob agreed. 'And seriously hot. Right, off to the premiere—catch you tomorrow, for the big day.' *Okay, perhaps he's not gay.*

I could hardly believe it was Golden Globes day.

'We should grab a drink at some point in the evening, when it's calmed down,' he continued.

I stopped dead in my tracks.

'If you're not dashing straight back to London, that is?'

For a moment I was tongue-tied.

'No, I'm here another couple of days before we go back for the BAFTAs. And, yes, a drink—I'd love to!' I'd sounded way too grateful. I busied myself tidying up. Liam *still* hadn't responded to my text. *Maybe Rob feels sorry for me.*

* * *

That evening, when we got back to the house, I was looking forward to a quiet night in: bubble bath, the chance to raid the fridge with Mona out, and overdue phone calls to Vicky and my mum. But all that changed in a heartbeat when Mona informed me she had some last-minute dress drop-offs to do, plus a crisis involving an actress and a crystal clutch, and asked *me* to accompany Beau to the *Summer's Not Over* premiere instead.

'I've got to prioritise the awards,' she said, looking tense. 'Besides, there's no better way to learn than on the job.' She waved me towards the back of a white limousine that was supposed to have been picking *her* up from the house; AJ was already seated inside. All I'd been able to do was grab my kit and head out of the door—I didn't get a chance to change out of my black leggings and T-shirt combo, and I had absolutely no idea what was expected of me. This was not the way I'd envisaged attending my first Hollywood premiere. Holding open the car door, Mona barked my only instructions, like a demented drill sergeant:

'Just keep your kit on you, check the dress is falling correctly and nothing's popping out that shouldn't be popping out. It's simple. Oh, and whatever Beau wants you to do—do it.' AJ rolled his eyes, giving me the impression he'd been here before.

'Hold tight—we can't be late to pick up Her Royal Highness,' he said as I ducked into the limo. Another woman was in there, too. She leaned forward with an outstretched hand, taking care not to let her iPhone, two BlackBerrys and iPad Mini slide off her lap onto the white, carpeted floor.

'Hi, I'm Leslie, Beau's publicist.'

Oh, so you're the person who should have been stopping

*the pap shots see the light of day, instead of letting me do
Beau's dirty work?*

'Nice to meet you, I'm Amber, Mona's assistant.'

'So just one major point for tonight,' Leslie said, displaying innate bossiness. 'Don't let her hem rise. The last thing
we need is to fan the flames after certain images started
doing the rounds—we're filing against *Starz*, by the way.
Beau needs to look demure, elegant and, most importantly,
engaged to be married. Got that, Anna?'

'Got it,' I replied, less concerned that she had already forgotten my name than about the fact that Beau had chosen
a very undemure, skintight, hot-as-you-like, leopard-print
dress for this evening, and that I was suddenly somehow
responsible for helping her look like a Stepford Wife: something I had a pretty keen suspicion she was not going to pull
off. My eyes wandered around the interior of the vehicle.
It was like a room on wheels—there was even a faux walnut coffee table between us. Maybe it wasn't faux. I wondered what all the buttons on the door of the limo actually
did. *Might there be a button for ejecting bossy publicists?*

The limo climbed higher into the Hollywood Hills; it
couldn't have been easy for the driver to manoeuvre a vehicle this length around the narrow, windy roads. It seemed
ridiculous that we needed a car this big for four passengers.
I checked myself: *this is Hollywood and we're going to a
premiere. Of course we do.*

* * *

We stopped outside the tall metal gates of a property not far
from Mona's, but with even better views of the city below.
AJ made a call and the gates slowly glided open. Once
through security, it became apparent that we had entered a
very private, exclusive 'other' world. The building was huge,

modern, with smooth white concrete walls and a panel of floor-to-ceiling glass windows. Perfectly manicured shrubbery and two tall palm trees on the right-hand side of the driveway gave way to the requisite luxury vehicles parked outside—the white convertible sports car from the other day and a large four-by-four with blacked-out windows. We came to a halt behind them. Leslie had clearly been here many times before; she paid no attention to our surroundings, instead punching vigorously at her BlackBerry. I was dying to see beyond the sleek, modernist exterior, where I guessed a land of muted rooms existed, big couches, expensive rugs, crystal chandeliers and pieces of modern art.

'Wait here while I get her,' AJ commanded.

Left alone in the limo with Leslie, who was incessantly typing between huffs and tuts, I pulled out my phone, too. No word back from Liam. I suffered finger spasm and sent him a text. Well, at least I had something interesting to say: At a premiere tonight. What you up to? x

He replied straight away. Hey, beautiful. Learning lines for tomorrow. I'm up for a vampire. What are you wearing?

His comment made my heart speed up a little.

Nothing amazing, I'm styling Beau Belle x, I replied, wishing I'd said, 'a red-hot Dolce number'. *Damn it.*

Tell me how it goes. x

I smiled to myself, deciding not to risk another unanswered text, but leave it at that.

Ten minutes later AJ emerged from the house with a tottering Beau Belle on his arm.

'You move over there, Amber—Beau needs to be on the left side and facing forwards. She gets nauseous otherwise.'

'Amber! I'm so happy you're doing the carpet with me this evening,' Beau gushed, carefully stepping into the vehicle. It definitely wasn't the easiest dress for getting in and out of cars without flashing all your bits. 'Don't tell Mona, but she can be a little cranky at times. And you and I have fun together, don't we?'

'Yeah…we do,' I replied, feigning excitement, as I felt Leslie's sharpened eyes look her client up and down, disapproving of the outfit already. *Well, we did have the fitting before anyone knew Miss Butter-Wouldn't-Melt had been having it off with her co-star.* Keen to keep the subject off Beau's clothes, or lack of them, I asked how Pinky was doing.

'Oh, he's a lot better, thanks, babe. It was weird, he puked up an empty M&Ms packet last night and we never eat M&Ms, especially not the peanut ones, so I don't know where it came from. But he was right as rain afterwards.'

'Oh dear,' I said, looking at the floor.

* * *

When we pulled up outside the Regency Village Theatre in Westwood the crowds were already five deep along either side of the red carpet. As our conspicuous mode of transport drew nearer to an assigned parking bay in front of the velvet rope, a deafening cheer went up from the fans. Beau's fans. I'd almost forgotten what a big name she was out here, although, granted, most of the crowd was made up of spotty, brace-wearing pubescent boys. As the limo door was flung open by a security guard, Beau expertly swung her legs around, knees together but not too together (this was Beau), put her shoulders back and bounced forth from her chariot, one arm lifted into a wave. Her dress instantly lifted to just below her butt-cheeks. *Oops.* The thunderous roar reached a crescendo as a couple of hundred voices chanted her name. I felt a rush of adrenalin power through my veins; I could only imagine how high Beau must have felt knowing all this adoration was for her. AJ jumped out of the car next, closely followed by Leslie, and I took up the rear. Literally. It was becoming clear that Beau's pert little bottom was an unplanned co-star at this premiere, and that keeping it hidden would be my primary role for the evening.

* * *

As things turned out, the Beau and Jason show was so captivating, it was hard to keep my mind on Beau's rising hemline. Only when it appeared to be levitating to a certificate 18 level did I at one point leap forward and gently tease it down again, hopefully out of shot (she was being asked by a German TV crew about her preferred flavour of bratwurst at the time). Beau spent most of her red-carpet performance as a twosome with Jason, and it was clear she was infatuated by him. She hung on his every word and dissolved into flirtatious giggles whenever he showed her particular attention. *If there isn't something going on between them, I'm not a pasty girl from London.* Surely everyone else could see it, too? One interviewer broke with protocol and asked about the recent story concerning the pair's off-screen relationship. Frantically, Beau looked around for Leslie, but her publicist had momentarily vanished.

'I'm engaged!' she protested, thrusting forth the dazzling fifteen-carat diamond rock on her wedding finger, before purring, 'but this one—' she indicated Jason '—was like a *slave driver*, making me rehearse all the time when I should have been ordering my bridal flowers!' Jason's muscles twitched beneath his too-tight white shirt.

'Seriously, though—' she fixed the interviewer with those puppy-dog eyes '—I love my Trey and we're *sooo* excited about the wedding. It's going to be off-the-scale amazing! But I can't say any more, because we've got a magazine deal.' Her eyes shone with excitement.

'I'm going to be pageboy,' added Jason, failing to pull off sarcasm.

'You are?' asked the equally dense interviewer.

'Uh, no. But I'm really excited for Beau and Trey. They are going to be *sooo* happy together,' he said, turning to her and smiling with all the authenticity of a fake Prada handbag.

'That's enough now—subject closed,' interjected Leslie, appearing from nowhere and making a note of the reporter's name so she could ban him from future red-carpet events for breaking the media agreement. I thought about Rob's earlier comment and wondered why Trey wasn't here with Beau, making a show of togetherness. I suddenly felt sorry for him. Surely these fresh premiere photos would stir up the gossip all over again? Looking away from Beau's wandering hem for a moment, and taking in my surroundings, I spotted Tango Tim from *Morning Glory* a few crews down, waiting for his chat with the stars. He looked more orange than ever in the last of the early-evening sun. I scanned the area for Rob; suddenly the top of his head popped up, close to Tim's. On tiptoes, I strained my neck to check it was him. Almost instantly I felt light-headed and my palms became clammy. *Why is it suddenly so insufferably hot?* I tried to loosen the neck of my black T-shirt and gripped a nearby railing with my other hand in an attempt to steady my spinning head. The sensation only intensified and my heart sped up, I could feel it pulsating hard, each beat ricocheting around my body. I took a couple of deep breaths and crouched down; my face felt sweaty now, too. And then nothing.

Chapter Ten

Flickering lights appeared before my eyes, muffled voices at close range got louder, and suddenly a cold, wet sensation made me sit bolt upright.

'She's back with us.'

'Oh, thank God for that.'

'Is she okay? The last thing we need is a lawsuit.'

Three pairs of eyes were staring directly into mine. Another shower of cucumber-scented water sprayed into my face, stinging my eyes and smudging my mascara. As the world came into focus, I registered that the eyes belonged to Tango Tim, Leslie and—*oh no*—Rob. Tim's index finger was poised on a small spray can, about to give me another blast.

'No, I—I'm okay. Thank you.' I quickly sat up on my elbows, a bit bemused, but mostly monstrously embarrassed. Immediately I tried get to my feet, but Rob put a firm hand on my shoulder. 'Just sit here for five minutes. You were only out briefly, but you need to take it easy.' *You were only out briefly? Oh my God, I fainted. At a premiere.*

Thankfully, all three then left me alone to regain my composure as they resumed their responsibilities. I slowly looked around from my seated position, half-on, half-off the red carpet, nestled between two TV crews, and realised that everything looked pretty much as it had done before I blacked out. Beau and Jason were still doing interviews, Leslie was still clutching her three phones and Tango Tim was having more bronzer applied by a make-up artist as he prepared for his interview with the stars, who had inched slightly closer down the media line. *I can't have passed out for more than a few seconds. Thank God for that.* I pulled out my iPhone. One text from Liam and three missed calls from Vicky. It had to be 3:00 a.m. at home, so I discounted Vicky's calls as drunk-dials from her pocket.

How's the premiere? Liam asked, over text. Obviously, I wasn't going to tell him the truth.

Really cool! How's the line-learning?

Fine. I mostly have to rise up and bite people, he replied. Wish I could practise on you though.

Before I could think of a suitably amusing response, Rob reappeared, holding a bag of crisps, a Snickers and a cold can of Pepsi.

'Here, get these down you,' he said. I had never been so grateful to see anything before in my life.

'When was the last time you ate something?' he asked. I thought for a moment. *I can't actually remember the last time I ate much more than a piece of dried fruit or some chocolate. In fact I don't think I've had a proper meal the whole time I've been out here.*

'Yeah, I am pretty hungry.'

'Unfortunately they don't have St John's Ambulance out here, so I nicked them from the production rider. Not the healthiest dinner, but the sugar will help sort you out.'

'Thanks so much. I think I was light-headed.'

'Just because no one eats in this town doesn't mean you shouldn't, too,' he said, wisely.

'I know… and don't worry, it's been humiliating enough.' I opened the crisps and began scoffing them. The Pepsi tasted like amber nectar.

'The beauty of fainting in this kind of situation is that everyone is so wrapped up in getting their two seconds with the stars, they'd barely notice if an alien craft landed and started abducting people,' he said, making me laugh.

'Unless they think someone might get sued,' I added, giving Leslie a reassuring wave. 'Did Beau see me?'

The last thing I needed was for this to get back to Mona. Surely I'd be joining Nathan in the dole queue if it did. Fainting at a premiere was not a good look.

'Seriously? I think you know the answer.'

We both looked over at Beau, who had now perched herself on a high stool, having turned the tables on an interviewer. She was having a ball, clutching the interviewer's microphone and jokily pretending to interview Jason, eagerly watched by three sets of TV cameras, some of which seemed most interested in capturing her ever-lengthening legs. *Shit!*

'Better get back to it.' I smiled, pushing myself up. A bite of Snickers, and the colour had returned to my face. 'I'm fine now, really. It's only my ego that was hurt.'

'See you at the party,' Rob said. Then he winked and added, 'By the canapés.'

* * *

The rest of the red carpet operation went more smoothly—thankfully Leslie didn't bring up the fainting episode, preferring instead to airbrush it from proceedings. Rather like we were all ignoring the blatant flirting going on between Beau and Jason. Tango Tim seemed pleased with his interview—he'd got Beau to reveal not only that her favourite frozen yogurt flavour was blueberry, 'sometimes with a white choc chip topping', but that she and Trey were thinking of adopting a second micro-pig from a sanctuary for abandoned pigs somewhere in Africa, as a sibling for Pinky. Two veritable world exclusives.

Eventually we reached the theatre doors and everyone marched in; Beau and Jason were greeted with a thunderous roar of applause. I then became privy to a secret about film premieres: the big stars rarely actually watch the movie, they do their bit on stage as the film is introduced by the director, then pretend to take their seats as the lights dim, but *really* they get straight back up again and head to their limos for the after-party. There, they schmooze with the film's backers and key sponsors before everyone else arrives to gush about how brilliant the film was—whether it actually was or not—and guzzle the free booze.

The premiere party was being held at Morton's, a hip establishment that once played host to the legendary *Vanity Fair* Oscars party, and it was thrilling to be whizzed straight in with the 'talent'. The main room had been transformed into a high school prom hall, complete with a stage featuring disco lights, a swing band, still in the process of tuning up, and waiting staff dressed in school uniforms.

As I obviously hadn't actually seen the film, Leslie filled me in: 'The final scene—the guy gets the girl, they perform a dance routine at the prom, the whole school is on their feet and no one wants the summer term to end. Hence the name, *Summer's Not Over.*'

The film's title was emblazoned across every available surface, from the twirling 3D projections on the walls and ceiling, to the coasters for the glasses on endless poseur tables, and when I popped open the mini umbrella on my cocktail, there were the words again, smiling back at me in shouty pink capitals.

'Think *Glee* meets *Dirty Dancing* for a new generation,' Leslie enthused, putting her best publicist spin on things. 'It's going to be huge!'

I watched from the sidelines as Beau worked the room, constantly throwing her head back with laughter. At one point, she was all over a man I recognised from the party last night as possibly being movie mogul Harvey Weinstein. Slowly the room began filling up with dressed-to-impress premiere-goers and a sprinkling of celebrities, most of whom had been invited to ensure the party achieved the necessary column inches the next day. I was glad that Mona wasn't here when I saw the photographers go mad for Poppy Drew. It had to be said she looked stunning in a vintage pale blue prom dress, complete with netted skirt, nipped-in waist and a flower in her hair. Tamara had done an excellent job, and she looked like she knew it. Rob arrived with Tim and I felt chuffed when they made a beeline for me and proceeded to assassinate the movie scene by scene as we tucked into the delicious miniature hot dogs and hamburgers now being served. It was great to be amongst company that didn't bristle if I ate more than a mouthful of something containing protein and carbohydrate at the same time.

Still there was no sign of Trey, much to my relief, as I

would struggle to hold a conversation about executive producing *Summer's Not Over*, having not actually seen the film myself and sensing from Leslie's précis that it was destined to be one of the year's biggest flops. Why was it not being released in the summer, anyway? Sometimes, Hollywood was baffling.

* * *

A good two hours into the party, as conversation with Rob and Tim moved effortlessly from one topic to the next, I noticed a kerfuffle going on around the bar.

'Oh, look—there's Mona and Klara.' I spotted them just as Mona clocked me, too.

'Amber, babe!' she called above the throng.

I frantically looked around for Beau, realising I'd been so caught up in conversation I'd totally forgotten I was meant to be working. As if reading my mind, Rob made the sound of a cracking whip.

'The wicked witch is back,' muttered Tim. 'That's the end of your party, then, doll.'

Klara made her way over to us first. She looked particularly pleased to see Rob again. 'Hey, how's it going? Did you get Beau on every Best Dressed list?'

'Hi, Klara, yes, it went well.' I prayed Rob and Tim would keep quiet about the fainting part. Luckily, any appraisal of my performance ended there because Mona was ordering champagne and vodka shots. Apparently she often did this, to give the impression to anyone who cared to look, but mostly Tamara on this occasion, that we were celebrating and having enormous fun. Escorting a waitress precariously balancing a tray containing five full glasses of champagne plus six *Summer's Not Over*–branded shot glasses filled to the brim with pink vodka, Mona was more animated than ever. She even greeted me with a hug.

'You were brilliant, babe, quite simply my little super-star.' She squeezed my rigid body. 'Beau looks divine in that dress and Stefano Gabbana has apparently already been on to Leslie to say she can keep it. Her image has gone every-where, and it's all down to the frock.'

Rob, Tim and I looked at each other, suspecting it was probably rather more than the dress that had garnered Beau so much media coverage this evening.

'Drinks on me… Well, it's a free bar… But here's to you, Amber! Bravo!'

She briefly glanced over to ensure Tamara and Poppy had heard the toast. How could they not? She was shout-ing loud enough. As we all raised our glasses, Mona was already necking her shot, followed by her entire glass of champagne. Because none of us dared do otherwise, we all followed suit, Rob, Tim, Klara and I downing our shots in one. Tim slammed his empty glass on to the table for dra-matic effect, shaking his head and exclaiming: 'Gooood morning, Vietnam!'

The alcohol burned its way down my throat, heating up my insides. I hadn't done shots since I last had a huge night out with Vicky.

'Look at that, they brought one too many.' Mona eyed the remaining glass on the table. *'Saluté!'* And necked it quickly, before swiping another glass of bubbly from a pass-ing waiter.

'Anthony! Wonderful to see you, darling!' And she was off, air-kissing a very good-looking, tall, tanned man with slicked-back hair, who looked as if he might be someone but no one could put their finger on who, and we were all left, our heads gently spinning, in her wake. As a waitress passed, I grabbed another mini hot dog. I *really* didn't want to faint again. But a few drinks felt like a great escape this evening. Better still, Klara seemed to be accepting me as someone it was okay to be seen with—we chatted easily about her day attending castings. Though she was flirting a little with Rob, he didn't seem to be flirting too much back. Tim provided some entertaining stories about his Hollywood interviewees and the inside scoop on what was *really* going on in Tom Cruise's love life. Yes, it was beginning to feel as though I was making some friends out here.

* * *

The startling crash of a champagne flute hitting the floor made us all jump. Partygoers abruptly stopped their conversations. In fact, it was as though all the most glamorous people inhabiting the Earth suddenly ceased what they were doing and turned to look in one direction—at Mona. Then everything went into slow motion as, not more than a few feet away from us, Mona came up for air. Her chest lifted, her head jolted back, and then she violently lurched forwards and heaved, projecting a lumpy pink substance, presumably miniature hot dog mixed with champagne, straight from her mouth onto the beautiful man's pristine, probably Tom Ford, white shirt. Everyone around her stopped what they were doing and stood like statues in a sculpture park. Then there was a mass intake of breath, followed by a chorus of: 'Oh. My. God.' Mona put her hand to her mouth in an effort to stifle a loud hiccup.

'Um, did, er, that just really happen?' Rob, as transfixed as I was by the absurd vision in front of us, whispered in my ear. I felt as though my feet were pinned to the ground. I was temporarily dumbstruck.

'Amber, that really *did* just happen,' he repeated.

'Oh, fuck,' said Klara.

'Brilliant!' squealed Tim, pulling up an invisible chair at the scene unfolding before us.

'I think you need to go and help her. Quickly.' Rob elbowed me in the ribs as people around us began coming to life again, suppressing giggles and starting to whisper. Suddenly the world began spinning on its axis once more. I became aware of cameras flashing around Mona. In desperation, she raised an arm to cover her eyes.

'I think we'd better get her out of here fast,' Rob suggested, taking control of the situation for me. He took my arm and began barging people out of the way as we headed towards my boss. The man who had found himself Mona's spewing target stumbled past us on his way to the gents. A pungent aroma hung in the air as he went by. Suddenly Mona straightened up, bellowing in a slurred voice:

'Where is a manager? I wanna see the GM right now!' More flashbulbs erupted. Recovering from my temporary paralysis, I got hold of myself and rushed forwards, almost gagging as the stench became stronger. I narrowly avoided planting my foot in the puddle of sick around her feet. Thank God I wasn't wearing a borrowed designer dress and ridiculous heels this evening.

'Food poisoning!' she yelled as I put an arm on her back. Rob and I took an elbow each and gently tried to lead her out of the circle that had formed around us. 'You can't get away with serving dodgy frankfurters, you know!'

She wriggled her arm out of mine and limply raised it in a last effort to protest her innocence. As she did so, the colour drained from her face and she sort of crumpled into our arms. Cue more gasps from around the room.

'Mona! What the hell do we do now?' I looked at Rob. Quickly he shoved one of Mona's limp arms around his neck, and I helped him support her weight. Klara rushed forwards, too, picking up Mona's python bag before it could slide into the mess or be snaffled by an opportunist to be sold on eBay. *God, I'm useless in a crisis.* Suddenly AJ appeared from nowhere and swept Mona up in his arms like King Kong with Fay Wray.

'Where am I taking her, Amber?' he asked urgently, his earpiece falling onto his collar. I looked at him, panicking.

'I don't know, AJ… Out of here… Jesus, is she okay?'

'She's just drunk, she'll be fine,' he reassured me. Mona's head flailed to the side and her hair covered her face, at least sparing her the further embarrassment of the room seeing the salmon-coloured dribble spilling from her lips.

'Out the front, I guess, and I'll get a cab?' I offered.

'No, there'll be even more paps. Out the back, follow me,' Rob interjected. He was already ahead of us, leading AJ towards a door at the side of the bar. I took up the rear, suddenly feeling fiercely protective of my humiliated boss. Tamara had pushed her way to the front of the assembled crowd of rubberneckers, her hand over her mouth in disgust. As the crowd parted like a tide to let our sombre procession pass I heard her comment to Poppy, 'The shame… she'll never get over this…'

A fire suddenly raged within me; pumped with adrenalin, I screamed, 'Stop staring—the show's over!' at all the ogling pretty people, who now reminded me of ugly trolls. As my heart raced, Rob turned around and smiled. 'You tell 'em, Amber!' I hoped AJ wouldn't judge me for not knowing how to react earlier on. Thank God he'd been in the room. Did that mean Beau was still here, too? I hoped

for Mona's sake she wasn't—there were bound to be repercussions, perhaps for both of us. But then again, it didn't
really matter. We all knew it wouldn't be long before the
whole of fashion land would be reading all about it, as the
gossip grapevine twined out of these walls and into cyber
space, gathering destructive reach like the famous Californian forest fires. The Tweeters in the room were already
giving their thumbs a workout.

* * *

We watched in silence as AJ called the limo driver round to
the back entrance of Morton's with his one free hand, while
Mona struggled from his other and attempted to stand up
on her own. There she wobbled, pathetic to behold, a fallen
fashionista teetering on her vertiginous heels. I'm certain
we all thought the same thing: *She's not got food poisoning, she's just plain, falling-down, puking drunk.* I hadn't
any idea yet what the ramifications would be, but something told me that tomorrow—Golden Globes day—wasn't
going to be pretty.

Chapter Eleven

Finally, the big day had arrived. Miley Cyrus blasted out from the radio adjacent to my head, sabotaging a vivid dream in which I was tucking into a large plate of roast chicken at my parents' dining table. There were no other family members present, but that hardly mattered—what *was* there mattered: stuffing, perfectly crisp potatoes and parsnips, cauliflower cheese, creamy leeks, honey-roasted carrots and gravy… My mouth watered, just remembering it. *Thanks a lot, Miley. I am honestly starting to believe there's a conspiracy against my eating a hearty meal ever again. Even when I'm asleep.*

Seven a.m., G-Day. It had come around frighteningly fast and I wondered if Mona was feeling as anxious as me. Limply, I silenced the noise—on the surface, it looked like a normal day: morning sunlight streaming through my bedroom window, the gentle ripple of water from the automatic pool cleaner outside, punctuated by the sound of the coffee machine loudly grinding beans in the kitchen. I loved waking up in this spacious, tidy room, and its sounds had already become familiar. But then the memory of last night hit me like a concrete breeze block, making me sit bolt upright. I had almost forgotten my fainting episode, followed by the much larger incident of sick-gate. I threw on a onesie and tried to walk downstairs as quietly as I could, which wasn't easy in flip-flops on varnished floorboards. I became aware that my head was faintly throbbing, a reminder that I'd drunk too much last night. In the kitchen, Ana was wiping the worktop and humming happily. *I wonder if she'd be interested in trading places.*

'Any sign of her yet?' I asked.

Ana shook her head as I poured myself a glass of tap water and downed it in one. 'Darling, by the noises she was making in the night, I don't think we'll be seeing Mona today.'

'But it's the big one—it's Golden Globes day!' I said. 'It's not an option not to see her!'

She didn't seem to grasp the enormity of the situation. 'Oh, it is *normal* to not see her,' she added casually, and carried on humming. *Normal not to see her? What's that supposed to mean?* As if from thin air, Klara made her usual spectral appearance in the doorway, her skin as pale and translucent as moonstone. I hoped we were still friends after our bonding session last night. After AJ had carried Mona from the limo to her bed, Klara and I had sat in the kitchen drinking coffee together before we moved on to white wine, and I almost wanted to kiss her when she produced a large bag of crinkle-cut crisps from a high kitchen cupboard: her secret stash. We were both reeling from what had happened, replaying the moment of doom over and over, and only salty carbs could lessen the trauma. I told her all about the texts from Liam and how Rob rescued me when I'd fainted at the premiere, and she told me all about her near-miss with Leo DiCaprio and a close encounter with David Gandy. And then she opened up about how she was worried about the pressures of modelling and whether she was cut out for it, when she really wanted to reconnect with her friends in London or perhaps take off backpacking around South America. I ended up coming clean about how I'd got the job with Mona by accident and was bluffing my way through it. We had genuinely found some common ground.

* * *

This morning Klara looked as though she hadn't slept much, either, but she carried off dishevelled much better than me, her hair loosely tied back in a ponytail, last night's make-up smudged but passable, wearing leggings and an over-sized T-shirt bearing the slogan 'I'm with the band'. I felt like a tatty old Teletubby sitting next to her in my onesie.

'Do you really think it was food poisoning?' she asked, pouring herself a large glass of Coca-Cola. Despite the hangover, she remained annoyingly graceful. But at last she was starting to put more between her lips than grapes and hot water.

'Maybe.' I shrugged, though I still strongly suspected it wasn't. There was certainly nothing wrong with the ten or so mini hot dogs I had put away during the course of the evening.

'I'll never forget the bad oyster I ate once,' she went on, 'the stuff that came out had the most ran—'

'Okay, Klara, I get the picture! My stomach is rather fragile, too, this morning.'

'Seen Twitter yet?' she asked.

'Not yet. Why, have you?'

She sucked in her cheeks. 'There's a lot going around about Mona this morning.'

'How bad is it?'

'She was trending at one point.'

'Oh God.'

'And there are photos,'

'Shit—how bad?'

'Don't worry, they could be worse, most of them just show the back of her head.'

'Any actual puking ones?'

Klara flicked on her iPhone and began scrolling.

'Not that I've seen so far. She looks really thin in them, so she'll be fine. All Mona cares about is whether she's thin.'

'Well, it's not hard to look thin when you're being carried by a hulk like AJ.'

'You're in a couple, too.'

'What?'

I stood up and leaned over her shoulder, struggling to get a look at the screen.

'You're talking to hot Rob.'

I bristled. I didn't like the idea of Klara calling him hot.

'Do I look thin, too? Actually, don't answer that.'

I gave up squinting at the phone and made my way to Mona's office to power up the iMac.

'Is Rob single?' Klara continued, reverting to type.

'Don't think so,' I pretended, realising that I didn't actually know the answer to her question. Anyway, there were more important things than Rob to dwell on right now. I was very relieved that a quick Google of my name brought up zero entries. Typing in Mona's, however, revealed a very different story—1287 new items on gossip websites, blogs and social networks around the world.

'If it's fame she's after, she's got it,' Klara whispered, pulling up a stool alongside me to read the stories. It was both dreadful and fascinating all at once.

* * *

We were eventually forced to stop scrolling through the endless reports of 'Sick Shame for Celebrity Stylist', when an apparition appeared before us. At least we *hoped* it was an apparition, but then it started making noises and we realised that it was, in fact, real.

'Head... hurts,' uttered the thin, silk kaftan-clad lollipop, clinging onto the door frame as if her life depended on it. The figure, only just discernibly female, resembled what you might expect the aged love-child of Morticia Addams and Keith Richards to look like after spending the night in a coffin. The black kaftan was tied loosely around her waist and she was flashing too much upper leg. Without her usual face of make-up, she looked tired, drawn and—dare I even think it—old. New lines seemed to have appeared around her eyes overnight.

'Good Lord,' sighed Ana, peering at her from the hall-way, looking heavenwards and crossing herself. I fought an urge to do the same.

'Water,' said the figure, from dry, white-rimmed lips. Ana obediently retrieved a cool bottle of Arrowhead, loosened the screw top and placed it in Mona's visibly shaking hand. It seemed safer than passing her anything she was likely to smash. There was a strong smell of stale alcohol around her. Klara and I looked at each other nervously—

neither of us could bear to be first to break the silence. Eventually Mona summoned just enough energy to speak.

'Darlings,' she announced, steadying herself with a small, crinkly hand on either side of the door frame, 'there is only one thing worse than being talked about, and that is *not* being talked about. Surely you know that?' She lurched from the doorway to a leaning position, her right shoulder against the wall. From there, she dragged her tottering, tiny frame along the wall, her kaftan coming more and more undone as she did so. Finally, she glided to a halt within arms-reach of the keyboard and with her index finger, clicked the browser shut. The conversation was closed. Klara took this as her cue to silently disappear from the room, and I hated her all over again for leaving me. Mona turned to face me, shaking her head to get unruly curls out of her face. She looked so different without make-up.

'Big day for you today, Amber, babe,' she said. Her face creased like tissue paper as she offered a smile—well, everywhere but her forehead. I shifted my weight and folded my arms across my waist, gripping my elbows for comfort as I waited for what she was going to say next.

'What a mess, you must be thinking.' She looked down at herself and stifled a laugh. The kaftan gaped a bit more, revealing that she wasn't wearing a bra. 'It's embarrassing.'

'It's fine,' I said, looking at the chipped nail polish on my feet for inspiration.

'I'm not going to be able to prep Jennifer Astley for the red carpet this afternoon—you know it as well as I do,' she said at last. 'This food poisoning has really taken it out of me.' *She's hanging on to her story for dear life.* 'So I'll need you to visit her at the Chateau Marmont for me. It will be fantastic experience for you, Amber, and Jennifer's the easiest A-lister there is.'

A bead of sweat ran down my back. The onesie was hot. *She can't be serious.*

'Ana will call you a taxi, it's only a five-minute drive. Just check she's got everything she needs, and if she wants you to walk the carpet with her.' *Bloody hell, she really is serious.* I chewed my bottom lip.

'Jennifer probably won't want me, though—doesn't she always have you and her make-up artist?' I asked, dreading the response.

Mona winced and put a hand to her temple, shutting her eyes. 'Yes, Caroline will be there, too. You'll be fine.'

'Sure…' I said, already resigned to the fact that it would be futile to show resistance. It wasn't as if Mona had anyone else to turn to. And this was the job I signed up for after all. A vibration in my back pocket alerted me to a text message, and then another and another in quick succession, distracting me momentarily. I itched to take out my phone.

'And then there are the pick-ups from the tailors and gowns from the suite to be dropped off with clients. The list is on my iPad, I'll get it for you in a minute.'

I remembered that I'd carefully listed all the errands to be done today—luckily. I just hadn't anticipated doing them all on my own.

'I guess I'd better get ready. One thing, Mona?'

'What is it?'

Now was as good a time as any. 'Do you have a day dress or a top that isn't black that I could borrow, please? I seem to have packed quite badly, and I'm running out of clothes.'

Come on, it's the least she can do.

She smirked shakily. 'I did wonder. Let's face it, the goth

look was getting embarrassing. You could do with some colour in your cheeks, too.' *Who the hell is she to talk this morning?* 'I'll have Ana get some old things from my wardrobe, and she'll take care of your laundry, too. Ana!' Raising her voice seemed to hurt her head even more. She recoiled, almost melting into the wall.

'Appreciate it, thanks,' I muttered, scuttling out of the room, dying to check my phone before Mona could ask me to do anything else I wasn't qualified to do. 'Hope you feel better.' I had a sense, with Mona, that I was treading on the thinnest of eggshells almost all of the time.

I pulled out my phone in the hallway. It had been throwing a party of its own. Six new text messages: three from Vicky, one from Mum, one from Jasmine and—*yes!*—one from Liam. I read the Liam one first: Morning beautiful x. It made me smile. The guy had only seen me for three minutes, but he already had the ability to make me feel like the most important person in the world. Then I read the messages from the others—news of Mona's eventful evening had of course travelled across the Atlantic, and they all wanted to know if she and I were okay. I compiled one generic response and sent it back to all three.

All fine, Mona still alive but recovering from last night, and I'm styling Jennifer Astley today! Will call after the awards. Love A xx. It would have to do for now

To Liam I responded: And morning to you, handsome x. This was fun.

Vicky replied immediately: Go Am—that's amazing! Will watch E! Love ya xxx ps OMG Mona???!

Jas replied soon after: Please send Mona my love, hope she's ok. J x

And finally Mum: Be careful, the woman's clearly insane x

* * *

As I left the house for the taxi, feeling much cooler than during my whole time in LA because I was now appropriately dressed in a pretty pale peach APC tunic instead of heat-absorbing black, Ana ran out of the house and down the driveway to hand me a torch. *A torch?* I looked at it, puzzled.

'Mona says take it,' she said.

I studied the slim black gadget, completely muddled as to why I would need it. 'Are we expecting a power cut this evening?'

Ana shrugged in response as Mona appeared at the front door; I held the torch up above my head. She cupped her hands around her mouth.

'Secret weapon,' she yelled, mustering her remaining energy. 'To watch Jennifer's train. Use it yourself or give it to Caroline—the torchlight will stop people treading on it. No one wants a tread.' Obediently, I slipped it into my kit.

The taxi whizzed down the hill and along Sunset Boulevard towards the legendary Chateau Marmont Hotel, and I finally allowed myself to feel a ripple of excitement. Here I was, in Hollywood, heading to Jennifer Astley's hotel suite on Golden Globes day, to style her for the red carpet—*this should be someone else*—it was a pinch-yourself moment. Huge billboards flew past, displaying the familiar faces of many of the famous residents of the Hills above me. We passed the luxury Mondrian Hotel on my right, with its larger than life flowerpots at the entrance. Just a few yards further along on the left, we pulled up on a narrow side street, by the entrance to an underground car park. Above us, built on the hillside and rising majestically above Sunset Strip, was the Chateau Marmont, its white, pointed turrets reaching out of the landscape like a castle from a French fairy tale. At the top of a dimly lit flight of stairs, the reception area had the woody hue of authentic antiques mixed with furniture polish and musk-scented candles. Shabby-chic sofas were dotted around, and old-fashioned reading lamps gently glowed on tables. There was a feeling that every chair had at some point welcomed the derrière of an A-lister; this infamous hotel had seen many wild parties, from as far back as the days of Jim Morrison. It was beyond cool to actually be here. I asked for Jennifer's suite and was sent to the penthouse. Even the lift had an old-fashioned French feel; it was a world away from the buzzy foyer and sleek, modern interior of the W.

* * *

Caroline, the make-up artist, answered the door.

'Oh—Amber. We weren't expecting *you*,' she said, in a markedly different tone from that of the friendly make-up artist we had welcomed into *our* hotel suite barely twenty-four hours ago.

'I thought Mona had explained,' I said, rummaging in my bag for my phone and totally failing to find it. 'She's unwell, unfortunately, so she asked me to pop over to check everything's fine with…' I stopped dead as Tamara's head appeared from around the corner.

'You must be Amber,' she said, walking towards the doorway. I had forgotten how pretty she was, with her long, straight Abba blonde hair and legs that went on and on. I had never felt more short and frumpy—and unwanted—in my life.

'Caroline called me in a panic because Jennifer had second thoughts about the Oscar de la Renta,' she explained, a smug smile on her face. Judging by the body language of both of them, there was no way I was going to be let over the threshold. 'She tried Mona, but no response.' She looked at Caroline and rolled her eyes. '*Quelle surprise*, after last night.'

The hotel corridor suddenly felt very cold and unfriendly.

'Of course, I wanted to do anything I could to help dear Jennifer,' Tamara continued. 'I couldn't bear to think of her panicking over her gown. She's a nominee, for goodness' sake!'

An unpleasant sensation of nausea worked its way up from my chest to my neck and stopped, like a golf ball stuck in my throat. I suddenly felt thankful for the fact I hadn't had breakfast.

'Mona's much better now,' I said, weakly. 'Mild case of food poisoning.' I smiled awkwardly at Caroline, who was strenuously avoiding eye contact. And then Jennifer appeared from around the corner. She swept towards me, wearing— no—wait a minute, it can't be… Is it? *Oh Christ. It is.*

She was a vision in red, wearing the same exquisite scarlet Valentino gown that Beau had selected to wear to the Globes. *How could that have happened? I thought it was a one-off?* Her hair was loosely swept over one shoulder. Before I could process what I was seeing, a man built like a bouncer came into view behind her. The suite beyond must have been huge, or else it was a Tardis.

'Bodyguard. Chopard,' Tamara explained, seeing me recoil, wondering if I was about to be arrested for being an unwanted dumpy person at a celebrity's hotel door. I registered the glittering pear-shaped cascade of diamonds hanging from Jennifer's ears and the diamond cuff around her slender wrist.

'You look…incredible,' I whispered, awestruck. And she did. She was Hollywood glamour personified. The problem was, it was exactly the same brand of Hollywood glamour that Beau would be trying to pull off, albeit not quite as well, in approximately—I finally found my phone—five hours' time. The red carpet for the Golden Globes was probably being seen to by its very own grooming team right about now. And I had read enough reports about awards season fashion during my adult life to know that what you must avoid at all costs is a clash of identical gowns. It is fashion suicide. It could even be the death knell of a once glittering career—stealing headlines for *all* the wrong reasons.

'An A-list star must look unique on the red carpet—their credibility depends on it,' Mona had said on our first day in the suite, 'and at no time are the stakes higher than during awards season.'

I started to panic. I was the only person who knew of the potential fashion clash that lay ahead. I had no time to be standing here, watching Jennifer mince up and down the corridor when I knew full well that Beau was probably doing exactly the same dress rehearsal right now, in front of Trey, up in the Hills. I had to act fast.

'Can I have a quick word, please, Tamara?'

Briskly, I told the woman who might well be my nemesis the news that Beau Belle was in possession of the very same red Valentino showstopper, and that she had every intention of wearing it this evening. The golf ball remained lodged in my throat as I finished explaining the situation. How would she react? A tantrum? A screaming fit? A Naomi Campbell–style phone-throw, perhaps? We both knew that in the celebrity hierarchy Jennifer was above Beau, but what about who tried it on first—surely that counted for something?

'Shit!' She sucked in her cheeks and thought for a moment. 'I knew the atelier had sent out two, but I thought both were intended for Jennifer. They sent one to me, thinking I was still working with Mona, and it's always good to have a spare. How did it end up on Beau?' I shuffled guiltily, but remained quiet. 'I think we've no choice but to make Valentino's people aware of the situation and get him to withdraw the dress from Beau. You'll have to tell her,' she continued, her hazel eyes icy cold.

Getting the great man involved seemed a little extreme. I felt certain Mona wouldn't want me penetrating into the realm of the actual designer—that was way beyond my job description.

'Just let me call Beau first,' I pleaded.

I slipped back down the corridor towards the lift, out of Tamara's earshot, to make the call. Thank God, she picked up straight way. I cut to the chase:

'Beau, you know you said if I pretended to be Annie Whatsashitz and spoke to Trey for you, that you'd never forget it and you'd help me?'

'Yeah, babe, what is it?' She seemed to register the panic in my voice. 'Do you want some free tickets to see my movie? I can easily have—'

'No, well, maybe, but it's more urgent, it's about tonight, the Globes and, er…' I hesitated, not even having had time to consider how I was actually going to verbalise the situation. 'It's about the Valentino gown.'

'Oh, Amber, I've been trying to call Mona about it all day. I guess she got my message, then?'

'Your message?' I paused, catching my breath.

Has she heard about last night? Is she sacking us both?

'I'm so sorry about the gown,' she continued. 'I really did genuinely love it and my plan all along was to wear it this evening, but Stefano and Domenico, they've been so kind to me following the premiere last night… I felt I couldn't say no to the gown they've sent me for this evening. Mona will understand—she'll explain to Valentino, won't she?'

I was just about following.

'So, you're not planning to wear the Valentino after all?'

'No, babe—don't hate me.'

If my body was capable of doing a backflip, I'd be doing one.

'The Dolce & Gabbana is so me, it's black, with lace detailing, and figure-hugging. I was thinking I could wear it with one of those fur wraps you had the other day. Trey thinks it's the sexiest thing he's ever seen. We've been playing dress-up all morning.'

'You must wear it!' I said. 'It sounds perfect!'

'Oh, thanks, babe, knew you'd understand. You'll let Mona know for me right?'

'Of course I will.' I wanted to kiss the phone.

'Anyway, what was the thing you wanted help with?'

'Oh, it doesn't matter any more, forget it. I'll drop a couple of fur stoles over to you this afternoon.'

'Love ya, babe.'

'Bye, Beau.'

I ended the call and then, at last, the golf ball felt as though it had dislodged from my throat. And she hadn't even brought up Mona's 'incident'. Fortunately, Beau was so completely wrapped up in herself, she was oblivious to the antics of anyone else. And, come to think it, I couldn't recall seeing her at the premiere party much after the drinks with the crew. Right now, I actually loved her.

I practically skipped back to tell Tamara the good news.

'Sorted,' I said, the second she flung open the door. 'Beau's not going to wear the Valentino.'

'I want to hug you!' she screamed, resisting the urge to

actually hug me. Caroline popped up behind her, sensing correctly that we were all in a much better place.

'I suppose you don't need me any more, then,' I said, after a lustful look at a room service porter laying out some dainty finger sandwiches that Jennifer was unlikely to touch, on a table beyond them.

'Bye!' they both said in unison, the colour back in their cheeks.

'Catch you at one of the parties, maybe,' Tamara suggested, and the French-style wooden door was gently slammed in my face. I called Klara on my way back to the lift.

'What are you doing?'

'Right now? Spying on Mona trying to make herself a macchiato. She's stubbed her toe about five times already just navigating the kitchen and she's been swearing at the coffee machine for the last ten minutes. It's funny. She's got no idea. Mind you, do you know how to work that thing?'

'Where's Ana?'

'Out. Mona sent her to the pharmacy for pills.'

'More pills? I only just picked her up some painkillers, two days ago.'

'Well, she must need some more.' *What's going on with you, Mona?*

'Where are you?'

'At the Chateau Marmont.'

'Bit posh?'

'I'm outside Jennifer Astley's room.'

'Please tell me you've Instagrammed a photo of the door?'

'I'm working. Listen, I've got to be quick, I need your help.'

Pause on the other end.

'Please, Klara. Will you help me?'

'Depends what it is.'

'It's really important, Mona's not working today and there's a ton she's asked me to do.'

Another pause.

'Well, I suppose the sun's gone in.' I guessed she was on a lounger. She shifted herself. 'What's up?'

'You drive, don't you?

'Ye-es…'

'I need you to ask Mona if we can borrow her car. And get the keys to the W suite from her. I need your help with some last-minute errands for the awards.' Adrenalin was beginning to flow through my veins. *Don't let me down, Klara, please.*

'With any more celebs?'

'Well, I need to stop by Beau's,'

'Sounds cool. Have you got tickets to the after-party?'

'Not yet, but I know a man who can get me some. If you help me, I'll sort tickets.'

I had already assumed that Rob and Tim would be going. Hopefully, we could be their plus ones.

'Deal. I'll ask her.'

'Oh, and, Klara?'

'What?'

'Ask Mona for her phone, too. She's already missed some important calls from clients today. Someone's got to save her reputation.'

'Roger that. I'll come and get you at the Chateau in ten.'

I hung up. *Thank you, Klara. Thank you, thank you, thank you.*

Chapter Twelve

Klara and I spent the next two hours zipping between the hotel suite and the grand houses of many of Mona's well-to-do clients, the opening of the Golden Globes red carpet drawing ever closer. Our usual couriers had all been booked up for the day so we had no choice but to do most of the drop-offs ourselves. I soon knew LA based not only on a web of Mona's preferred coffee houses, but by some of the city's most salubrious mansions and fashionable hotel suites, where stars, their publicists, hair and make-up artists, PAs, nutritionists, and other hangers-on, were holed up getting ready for the awards.

Klara was a surprisingly good driver and we operated well together—it was even fun to have her loud rap music blaring as we swerved in and out of driveways and up and down highways across West Hollywood and Beverly Hills. As we returned to the W after dropping a selection of vintage fur stoles at Beau's house, and picking up some last-minute alterations from the tailors, I finally had a moment to look at Mona's iPhone. Sixteen missed calls and fourteen new answerphone messages. I grabbed a pen and the hotel desk-pad and braced myself.

01:46 a.m.: Beep. Mona, hi, it's Sandy here from *Fashion News Daily*—I just wanted a word to clarify a few things about this evening. Can you call me back, please? Number is 310-4256. Thanks.

08:45 a.m.: Beep. Message for Mona Armstrong—it's Sean Drew from *Us* magazine, we're keen to know if you're commenting on your breakdown. I'd be grateful if you could call the office back on 323-4030. We go to press in six hours. Many thanks.

09:04 a.m.: Beep. Mona, hi, babe, it's Caroline here, I'm with Jennifer and we wanted to talk to you about the gown for this evening. Can you call back, please? Thanks, darling.

09:34 a.m.: Beep. Hi, I believe this is Mona Armstrong's number. It's Rochelle from *Starz* here—I'm filing on your sickness and collapsing story at the premiere party last night. I wanted to add an official statement. Can you call me, please? 310-4428.

10:00 a.m.: Beep. Automated message for Miss Mona Armstrong. This is the Long Island Loans Company. You are in serious arrears with your repayments, we have tried unsuccessfully to make contact with you a number of times now. Please call us back urgently to discuss your finances with one of our advisers. 904-4444.

10:15 a.m.: Beep. Mona, Caroline again. Jennifer's getting anxious. Can you please call?

10:21 a.m.: Beep. Hey, Mona! Ohmygod last night was amaz—

10:22 a.m.: Beep. Oops, soz, was too excited! Thank you so much for last night. Love, love, loved the dress. I got on Perez Hilton! And on Fashion Police! Small hiccup about today though, Stefano Gabbana himself called Leslie and they loved me in the dress so much, he wants me to wear Dolce & Gabbana to the Globes, too. How cool is—

10:24 a.m.: Beep. Me again, why do they never leave you enough time to finish a message? Anyway, Stefano himself called—Leslie said he sounds so nice! And he's *sooo* Italian. *Mama mia!* Anyway, he's loaning me this gorgeous black gown. Sure you understand about the Valentino. Love you. Bye! I mean, *ciao*! Speak tom—

11:08 a.m.: Beep. Mona, Caroline. As we can't track you down we've had to get Tamara on board. She's sorting Jen's gown now.

11:48 a.m.: Beep. Hello, it's Maria from the tailors' here, we've got the adjustments for the gowns finished. Please pick up any time.

12:34 p.m.: Beep. Mona, Tamara here, listen, I thought it might be sensible if we spoke. Call me.

01:02 p.m.: Beep. Second message for Mona Armstrong—it's Sean Drew from *Us* again. I wanted to let you know we've spoken to someone who witnessed your breakdown last night, so we're running a story in the next issue. If you would like to comment, please call me on 323-4030. We go to press in two hours. Thank you.

01:57 p.m.: Beep. Mona, Rochelle again from *Starz*. I've tried to contact you several times now with no success, so I'll assume you have no comment on the sickness and collapsing story.

Shit. I rolled my wrist. My arm ached from all the scribbling down of numbers. *Commenting on your breakdown, official statement, story in next week's edition.* No wonder Mona had decided to leave her phone turned off and crawl back under the duvet today. But this was way out of my league. There was one particular message that worried me the most: 'You are in serious arrears with your repayments'. I banked that at the back of my mind to think about later; it was already gone 2:00 p.m. That meant the *Us Weekly* story would be going to press in about half an hour. Klara was in the bedroom, trying on some of the unclaimed dresses; she already had her eye on a slinky yellow Louis Vuitton number, complete with vintage diamond-drop earrings and matching necklace set. She might not be a nominee, or even an actress, but she could certainly look like one.

'Hey, Klara!' I called. 'Need your opinion on something.'

'You still wondering about the Phillip Lim?' she shouted back. 'Just go for it!'

'No, something else. Have you got a second?'

There was a momentary silence, presumably as she un-ravelled herself from the Louis. She padded back into the suite.

'What's the matter? You look like you've seen a ghost.'

'I wish I had. A ton of press have been calling Mona asking for a comment on what happened last night,' I revealed. 'They seem to think she's having a breakdown. I'm wondering if I should call any of them back. Some of them go to print—' I looked at my phone to check the time again '—like, now.'

She scratched her pretty head. 'Hmmm. Did they sound nice?'

'Not really.'

'What was it Mona said this morning?' Klara stopped for a moment. 'That old Hollywood mantra?'

'There's only one thing worse than being talked about...' I replied.

'And that is *not* being talked about,' she finished the sentence for me.

'So maybe we don't do anything? I suppose it's not as if we know what's going on with her, anyway,' I said.

'Alternatively, you could let them know that regurgitated hot dog pink is this season's hottest colour before telling them where to stick it?'

We laughed together.

'But seriously.' I pulled my legs onto the chair and crossed them underneath me. 'You've known her for longer than me, Klara. What do you think's going on with Mona?'

'I make it my business not to know.' She admired the necklace she was still wearing in the mirror. 'Maybe it *was* food poisoning? God, I love this necklace, it totally looks real.'

'Yeah, maybe.'

'Or maybe she's depressed. Remember, everyone's on something out here. Is there anything else we need to do today? It's just that I've been invited to an awards viewing party.'

I decided not to mention the message from the loans company.

'Call me later.'

'Yeah, let me know about the after-party.'

* * *

With Klara off to a party—all dressed up in a borrowed white Roland Mouret number, after changing her mind at the last minute—and Mona's phone eventually calming its incessant bleeping, I got a cab back to the house to watch the main event from the sofa. I hoped Mona might be in a more communicative state now, seeing as it was almost awards time and she had been asleep for most of the day. Returning to the house to watch the awards on TV while I waited for Rob to text about the party felt like something of an anticlimax after the build-up during the week. I wasn't sure what I was going to see on the red carpet, having come to the realisation that basically no one has a clue what anyone is actually going to wear on awards night until the star is physically there, bathed in the glow of a thousand flashes. I wondered if I should go and change out of my dress, just to join in.

As quietly as possible, I turned the key in the lock and crept in, slipping my flats off at the door. The house was eerily silent. I put my head into the kitchen and then the lounge; both rooms were immaculate and empty, just as Ana would have left them, giving me the impression that Mona had not ventured downstairs in a while. I put my head around the doors to the laundry room, cinema room and downstairs bathroom. No sign of Mona anywhere. I tiptoed upstairs towards the master bedroom—fortunately, the door was slightly ajar. Heart pounding, lest she slept with one eye open—*I'm not joking, it's possible*—I slowly nudged open the door to Mona's bedroom and peered round it. The white duvet on her huge emperor-size bed was awash with the flotsam and jetsam of a stylist on the edge—last night's flesh-coloured tights which now resembled the wizened legs of a melted-down model; the python bag with most of its former contents emptied around it; a pile of tissues; a large, half-empty bottle of water; an open box of painkillers; a packet of cigarettes; an iPad with a cracked screen. On one side of the bed was the shape of a small body under the duvet and a mop of curls on the pillow. I placed her iPhone back amongst the wreckage and crept out, sadness in my stomach, resigned to watching the red carpet alone. There seemed little point in a change of clothes, unless Rob got in touch about the after-party or Liam texted again and wanted to meet.

* * *

The build-up on E! was as good as any new feature film— Ryan Seacrest in position on the red carpet at the Beverly Hilton Hotel, Kelly Osbourne primed to discuss the glittering gowns. I suddenly realised I was beginning to feel excited. My heart was actually pounding as the first few C-listers made their way onto the carpet and appeared on-screen, all white teeth, golden tans and blow-out perfection, ready to have their outfits dissected and give their opinion on who would be walking away with a statuette. Then my trance was broken by movement in the doorway: Mona had appeared. Dressed in a grey T-shirt and combat trousers, she was a notch up from the gaping kaftan of this morning, but seriously scruffy for her. She slumped onto the other end of the sofa making a loud, dramatic sigh as she did so.

Ordinarily, I would ask if she needed a coffee. *But not this time.* Instead I sat perfectly still and continued watching. Mona clearly found the lack of attention infuriating. She loudly readjusted her position on the sofa several times.

'Has anyone interesting turned up yet?' she asked, finally, forcing the words out, like a little rich kid in a huff because she didn't get the new Barbie Luxury Yacht for her birthday.

'Kelly Osbourne looks nice.' I didn't move my eyes from the screen. Mona acknowledged Kelly's pretty mint-green Zac Posen gown with an approving grunt.

'So Jennifer didn't need you for the red carpet, I take it?' she asked, after another awkward silence.

'Caroline's with her,' I replied. *Two can play the disgruntled child game.*

'Did Beau get off in the Valentino okay?'

'No, she changed her mind and went for something else.'

'She what?' Mona sat upright now.

'She's wearing Dolce & Gabbana. Stefano gifted it to her.' *Which you would know if you'd been capable of listening to any of your voicemails.*

'But that's not possible—Valentino was aware she would be wearing it.'

'Until Jennifer Astley decided to wear it.'

'Jennifer? But she's in the Oscar de la Renta!'

'Not any more. It's all changed. Tamara dressed her.'

'She—*what?*'

A vein in my neck that I never knew I had suddenly started pulsing.

'Tamara—she dressed Jennifer in the end.' I stayed very

still, waiting for her to throw a fit. Mona had the ability to scare me on a deep, primal level, like spiders.

'That can't have happened,' she said after a long pause, shooting dagger-eyes at me.

'Caroline had been trying to reach you all morning,' I said, voice quivering.

'I can't watch this.' She rose unsteadily from the sofa and stood up, presumably to go upstairs for a showdown with her iPhone, which she clearly hadn't bothered looking at since she'd woken up.

'I had to get Klara to bring me your phone so I could work out what was going on.'

She stared blankly into space. I wondered what was going through her mind.

'But we narrowly avoided both Beau *and* Jennifer wearing the same Valentino this evening,' I said. 'How bad would that be?'

'More importantly, Amber, how bad is this going to look with the designers? When the house of Oscar de la Renta finds out I didn't actually put their gown on Jennifer, and Valentino discovers the mishap with the scarlet gown, they may never lend to me again. I can't have the designers thinking I only actually dressed D-listers for the Golden Globes this year. This is a disaster! How could you have messed it up so catastrophically today?'

Don't bother thanking me, then.

'Well, it's better than a clash, isn't it? The one thing you told me we couldn't have was a clash.' The vein was throbbing so hard now, I thought it might burst. But Mona didn't want to listen any more. Before we had even glimpsed Beau, Jennifer—or any of the D-list stars we *had* managed to successfully dress for this evening—she swept out of the room, loudly slamming the door as she went. Ryan Seacrest's voice continued in the background. 'And the excitement is mount-ing here on the red carpet as we await some of the big stars of the night. It won't be long now before the nomin— Nicole Richie! I see Nicole and she's coming our way! Oh wow… Hey, Nicole! Nicole! Do you look va-va-voom this evening! Tell us about your gown…'

And so it began. The floodgates were suddenly flattened by a celebrity stampede, and I was captivated by the steady parade of stars sweeping down the carpet, one after another, in ascending order of box office pull. It was exhilarating to watch and I felt a ripple of excitement flow through me as Beau Belle arrived on-screen, rocking her fur stole and Dolce & Gabbana gown. She looked a true Hollywood siren, and Trey seemed genuinely proud to be at her side. They made a magnetic couple, laughing and posing as Ryan went through Beau's look and Kelly awarded it a ten out of ten for 'star quality'.

'Hey, Mona!' I shouted, calling into the hallway for her to witness this, just as Beau was lifting up her skirt to show off the glittering Jimmy Choo sandals I had taken to her from the suite. 'Beau looks amazing—she's wearing our ac-cessories!' There was no movement upstairs, but I thought I could hear the muffled sound of another TV playing E! simultaneously—Mona must be watching in her room. I felt a bit forlorn that we couldn't enjoy the frenzy together. And then amongst the final flurry of A-list stars to arrive, Jennifer Astley came into view. I almost didn't recognise her at first because—could it really? *No, wait a minute... Is that definitely her? It is! Oh. My. God. It is!*

'Moooo-na!' I paused the TV and ran into the hallway, just as the door to Mona's room flew open and she bounded down the stairs, taking them two at a time. *Please, please don't let her trip, I can't bear dealing with a night in hospital, too.* Miraculously, she displayed more energy than I'd seen in days.

'She's wearing the Oscar de la Renta!' she cried, throwing her arms around my neck, hugging and kissing my startled face on both cheeks. 'You *were* joking with me, you silly cow! She's wearing the bloody de la Renta!'

All I could do was hug, kiss and high-five her back as we laughed together like schoolgirls. I had absolutely no idea what had gone on behind the heavy closed door of the Chateau Marmont penthouse suite after I had left, but Jennifer was definitely not wearing the scarlet Valentino gown now. Nobody was.

Jennifer's turn on the red carpet was like a faultless, choreographed dance. She knew every pose to pull, her smile was bewitching, and the fans and media went wild for her, the cheers deafening as she lifted a slender arm to wave at her admirers. The dress tightly hugged her every curve, making her body look sensational. I spotted Caroline in the background, torch in hand, stepping forwards every now and again to fluff up the feathers on the small train. It really was an exquisite dress, and it suited her perfectly. But I was more than a little confused about what, in Valentino's name, had happened to his scarlet showstopper? Mona disappeared into the kitchen and returned brandishing a chilled bottle of Perrier-Jouët rosé, two glasses and, to my huge pleasure, a large bag of crisps. *Yes! This is more how I imagined awards night to be.*

'To us!' she exclaimed thrusting a full glass into my hand.

'To us!' I said, as we toasted the gown. We collapsed into

another fit of giggles and backslapping as we spotted a few more of Mona's clients, in dresses *we* had put on them, gliding towards the venue.

* * *

As the drama of the red carpet arrivals came to an end and most of the stars had teetered into the auditorium for the ceremony in their too-high heels, we both sank into the sofa to watch the actual awards. They were almost an anticlimax after the dress parade. It was over halfway through when Jennifer's Best Supporting Actress category was finally up. We both fixated on the screen as the presenter cranked up the tension, taking his time to reveal that the 'Golden Globe for Best Supporting Actress, goes to…Jennifer Astley!'

On our feet again, we shrieked in unison and watched, awestruck, as Jennifer turned to hug the man sitting on her left, before gracefully rising from her seat in the auditorium.

'Hold on a minute—that man—isn't that Beau's fiancé, Trey?'

'You're getting good, honey. Yes, he directed the movie. Look at the exquisite way the dress moves with her body— she made the right choice, babe, no doubt about it.'

'How come he's not sitting with Beau?'

'Oh, she'll be a few rows further back—only the nominees sit at the front tables. It's all about your "movie family" on awards night. Oh, and the earrings, Amber! Look how they catch the light! Divine.'

The camera panned around the elated audience, many of whom were on their feet clapping Jennifer's win, as she elegantly weaved her way to the stage through an assault course of chairs and tables occupied by Hollywood luminaries. All were elated, except for Beau, who the camera picked out looking distinctly unimpressed with the show of affection between her husband-to-be and his leading lady. It really would have been the most catastrophic clanger if they had both been wearing the same gown. Mona held her breath as Jennifer glided up the steps towards the stage, the feathered dress gently rippling as she moved, then sighed with relief as the star was greeted by the hosts.

'She made it, thank God. Remember Jennifer Lawrence's trip up the steps? That would be disaster, for both me and Oscar de la Renta, God rest his soul.'

Jennifer graciously accepted her award, thanking the cast and crew, but most especially the director, Trey Jones, in a well-rehearsed speech. As her eyes glistened with emotion, she then thanked her make-up artist for ensuring she'd worn waterproof mascara tonight. As the crowd made an appreciative, 'Aww', I noticed Mona was on the edge of her seat. Was she waiting to see if Jennifer might extend her thank you list to include her stylist, perhaps? There was to be no special mention tonight. Instead, Jennifer swept off the stage, Golden Globe in hand, million-dollar smile blazing and gown flowing beautifully with every dainty step.

* * *

The rest of the awards came and went and our bottle of champagne was drained. I turned to see that Mona had sunk so deeply into the sofa, it looked like it had swallowed her.

'So, you've done your first ceremony. What do you think?' She turned to me as the credits rolled and the camera filmed a few of the stars entering the after-party.

'I think my nerves are in tatters,' I said. It was true, I felt as though I'd just done four consecutive rides on Oblivion at Alton Towers. 'Is it like this every time?' Maybe that was why Mona had been so unwell last night. Could it have been pre-awards nerves? Perhaps I'd have felt the same if I'd known what we were in for this evening.

'Not easy, is it.' It was a statement, not a question. 'You can never tell what's going to happen until the client is actually there, physically at the event, wearing the clothes. And even then, I've known stars do a quick change in the Ladies' on the way in.' She clearly relished the fact I'd had to learn the hard way.

'It's so difficult to keep track of everything,' I said.

She smiled. 'Missing your old job, babe?'

'This is way more exciting,' I answered truthfully.

I reached into my bag for my phone, looking at it for the first time in hours. A message from Liam, saying that Beau looked great. And also a text from Rob, and it wasn't about filming: So, how was it for you? Got a couple of +1s to the after-party if you and Klara fancy it? x

This definitely warranted a change of clothes, and Mona still owed me a blow-out.

What time and where? x, I replied.

Come to think of it, after today, she owes me a dress loan and a taxi, too.

Chapter Thirteen

As I approached the queue for the *InStyle* and Warner Brothers party at the Beverly Hilton, Klara texted to say she'd been waylaid at Soho House. Apparently a newly single Orlando Bloom had just turned up. Hollywood seemed to be crawling with celebrities this evening—even the atmosphere in the queue was electric.

'Kendall Jenner at a quarter to three,' a wide-eyed partygoer behind me whispered to her friend. She spoke through gritted teeth, barely moving her lips. Apparently that's how you have to talk about megastars in an area where every other person is famous and you're trying not to seem starstruck.

'Tom Hanks left, Charlize Theron just going in,' noted another.

My insides were churning. *Being around stars is such a buzz!* It also helped that, for once, I felt reasonably well put together. Though there hadn't been time for a blow-out, Mona had loaned me a gorgeous little black dress by Bur-

berry and some gold Charlotte Olympia sandals, all infinitely more comfortable than my ensemble from the other
night. I absolutely loved the LBD—it was skintight, but because I'd almost certainly dropped a few pounds over the
past few days due to lack of food, I had to admit I felt great
in it. I texted Rob as I neared the entrance:

Nearly at the front—how do I get in? x

A red carpet and 'step and repeat' boards with various
sponsors logos emblazoned across them stood to the left of
the doors, marking the VIP entrance. Vanessa Hudgens had
just arrived, seamlessly transferring from car to red carpet where a bank of paparazzi were calling her name and
capturing her from every angle, showing off the very low,
bottom-skimming back on her stunning crystal-adorned
gown. It fell into a delicate mini-train at the back, which I
noticed a woman crouched at her heels discreetly tweaking
into place. Must be her stylist. *A comrade!* As she entered
the party, a few more people from the queue of 'normal'
partygoers, in which I stood, hurried up the steps and were
ushered towards the guest-list desk. I frantically searched
for Rob's face amongst the throng inside and seconds later
he appeared, on the other side of the red rope.

'Amber! You're on Tim Parker's list!' he shouted. I felt
his eyes look me up and down appreciatively. *Ooh.* I was
secretly pleased Klara wasn't here to steal my moment with
her attention-grabbing looks and confidence.

'So where's the tan man?' I asked as we got through the
clipboard-wielding door sergeants, who seemed to be taking great pleasure in turning people away.

'You won't believe the number of liggers tonight,' one tutted into a radio handset as I shuffled past. 'We need more security.' I guessed I fell into the 'ligger' category, too. Once in, paper lanterns twinkled and lit the way down to the pool area. The party was warm and inviting, and the soft lighting made everyone look even more beautiful and even more expensive than they already were. Rob looked dashing in black tie.

'You mean Tim? He got a great chat with Keira Knightley on the red carpet,' he said, stopping in a less crowded area, 'so he's happy. He's gone with the editor to knock it into shape for the breakfast show—it's a twenty-four-hour operation out here on awards night.'

'Blimey, that's not much fun,' I said, finding it hard to look him straight in the eye. 'I thought he'd be partying the night away with George Clooney—that's the impression he gives on *Morning Glory.*'

'He wishes! I think he once crashed a party at Madonna's house, along with the rest of the British media, and he once got let into the *Vanity Fair* party by accident because the door Nazi thought he was someone else, but other than that, he struggles as much as the rest of us. Hollywood isn't very accepting of the British media—they think we're all after the dirt.'

'Well, he sorted us out this evening. Thank you, Tim!' I raised my glass to toast our absent friend.

'He has his uses. Why do you think he wears so much fake tan?' Rob smiled, his gaze seeming to settle on me for a little longer than usual. 'It's just to look awake. He's up half the night, sorting out his reports for *Morning Glory.*

Dread to think how pale and knackered he'd be without the old Touche Éclat and St Tropez.'

'You seem to know a lot about make-up.' I smiled.

'Too much working in light entertainment—it's all anyone talks about.'

'Will you have to work through the night, too?' I asked, crossing my fingers.

'Nope. I'm done with the filming. So what you and I really need is—drink. Lots of.'

'Too bloody right!'

Luckily, there were plenty of champagne cocktails to hand. And while sinewy, designer-clad models, celebrities and entertainment executives networked, gossiped and guzzled free Bellinis all around us, Rob and I chatted. Perhaps it was the booze, perhaps it was the fact that Jennifer wore 'our' dress, or perhaps it was just because I was receiving someone's undivided attention; nothing could dampen my high this evening, not even the memory of Mona nearly puking into her bag.

'So, after Mona's, um, what shall we call it, "episode", last night—how has Golden Globes night been for you, Miss Green?'

'Surprisingly fine, in the end,' I replied, noticing Rob smelled more than a little amazing. He still had the clean, washing-powder baseline, but this evening there were subtle notes of cedar wood mixed in. 'Mona was a mess all day, so Klara and I had to do the final drop-offs, and there was a close encounter with a clash of identical gowns, but other than that it was a success. Jennifer Astley wore the Oscar de la Renta we styled her in, so Mona's over the moon. But last night, oh man—it was awful, wasn't it? I've been trying to blank it out.'

Truly, it was great to unload the horror of the previous evening on Rob. 'I really appreciate what you did,' I gushed, after we'd gone through the whole thing, agreeing on how glad we'd both been when AJ swept in and bundled her out. 'Honestly, the way you sprang into action and found us a way out of there—I can't thank you enough.' Cautiously, I touched his arm, just below the biceps.

'It's fine, I didn't really do that much.'

'Oh, believe me, you did—thank you so much. I was a blithering idiot when it happened.'

'You weren't! You told all the gawping crowds to wind their necks in. Not bad considering you'd fainted yourself only a few hours before, remember?' He winked.

I shook my head shamefacedly. 'Yeah—thanks, I've been trying to forget about that.'

'Your secret's safe with me. So you haven't felt faint again?'

'Not at all. It was so embarrassing. I'm not normally a fainting type of girl. Seriously, though, thank you.'

'Stop thanking me, Amber.'

'But I really mean it. And Mona should thank you, too.'

'I only did what anyone else would do.'

'Face it, you're a hero and these Bellinis are delicious.' I lifted another from a tray and swiped a mini-quiche from a passing waiter. I was drinking too fast and I *really* didn't want to do anything embarrassing again.

'Cheers to us!' he said, raising his glass. The drinks were going down well—three gulps and we were on to the next.

'And cheers to Hollywood! We deserve a night out,' I replied.

'Too right. There's been far too much work going on out here.'

'Fancy going to explore?'

My confidence was improving with every sip. We wandered around the first level of the party venue, through little groupings of men in penguin suits and women in incredible gowns talking about the awards, and pausing to gawp every time a major star passed by. It was like Madame Tussauds come to life. Scarlett Johansson brushed past me— stunning, but so much smaller in real life. After a while we found a glass staircase, with candles on every step, leading down to a terrace.

'Ah, the smoking area,' Rob announced. 'The smoking terrace is always where you find the fun people.' We shared a Marlboro Light, which I pretended to enjoy as we continued our conversation.

'Would you want to be a part of this business?' I asked. 'I mean, on the other side of the camera.'

'An ac-tor? Been there,' he replied.

'Really?' I was intrigued.

'Oh yeah, could have been the next Ryan Gosling, if I'd kept it up,' he said, his facial expression deadpan.

'Seriously?'

'Toothpaste ad when I was ten.' He smiled cheesily, flashing his admittedly very straight and white gnashers.

'No way!' I laughed. 'Not the dizzy heights of Colgate?'

'Macleans, actually. My folks dined out on that for at least a decade.'

'Pushy parents?'

'Scarred for life.'

'I need to see some photographic evidence of this!' I delved into my clutch for my phone, ready to Google images but instead noticed a new text from Liam. I quickly scanned it: Hey, sexy, thinking about you xx. My heart raced.

'No need.' Rob gently pushed the phone back into my bag. 'If you look carefully, you'll see a diamond pop in the air every time I smile. Ding! There you go.' He pointed upwards. 'Blink and you'll miss it. I've still got it!' His wide smile was contagious.

I laughed. 'Hey, be careful, someone might be listening in…' I pretended to look around for casting directors. 'You'll get snapped up around here.'

'What—don't tell me Simon Cowell's veneers need a double?'

'I've heard of stranger things…' I giggled.

He looked around and mimed shaking hands with an invisible person. 'Ah, Mr Bruckheimer, enchanted—the new Crest commercial, co-starring Cara Delevingne, you say? Yes, I think my schedule can fit that in…'

I laughed again. Something made me feel like a giggling schoolgirl when I was around Rob.

'Not likely. It was more my mother who had ideas for me,' he continued. 'I just found it torturously embarrassing. When all your mates are getting high scores on Grand Theft Auto and you're being taken to ad castings for antibacterial cleaning products, it doesn't do much for your street cred.'

'Well, at least your parents didn't name you after a traffic light.'

'I did wonder.' He showed off his pearly whites again. 'Did they do it on purpose?'

'They just thought it was quirky. Must have seemed a good idea after too many bottles of wine one evening. Anyway, I'm not a traffic light, I'm the "light of their lives", don't you know.'

'That's one way of looking at it. Got to love parents. So

what about you, Amber Green of the traffic scene? Do you fancy a bit of the Beau Belle lifestyle?'

'Fame? No, I hate being the centre of attention,' I replied.

'Do you, now?' He looked at me. I mean, *really* looked at me, more than he had ever looked at me before. Then a tap on the shoulder jolted me from the spell—I turned, wondering if the waitress had rumbled the fact I'd quite openly had more than my quota of free Bellinis in the last ten minutes.

'Annie! I thought it was you!'

Trey. Help.

'Oh, Trey! Hi!' I sounded way too enthusiastic, my voice too loud, too screechy. 'I didn't expect to see you here.' *And the award for dumbest thing to say to a film director at a film awards party goes to…* 'Let me introduce you to, er, this is Rob, my friend…and colleague. Rob, this is Trey Jones,'

'I know. Wow, awesome, it's great to meet you, Mr Jones. I'm a massive fan of your work.' Rob shook his hand eagerly.

'Call me Trey, and the pleasure's mine,' Trey replied. 'Great party, hey?'

I imagined this was like every second night out for him.

'Yes, amazing Bellinis!' I yelled, suddenly aware of all the people around us. The fun smokers were now staring smokers. *Where did all these people come from?*

'Is Beau with you?' I asked.

'Yeah.' He gestured over his shoulder and I realised exactly why it was so crowded all of a sudden. In the white fur stole, brandishing a long black cigarette holder, working the figure-hugging Dolce & Gabbana gown with a diamond choker shining so bright it made my eyes squint, she looked like Marilyn Monroe. People with big smiles, enormous hair and animated faces swarmed around her like bees around their queen.

'So how do you know, Annie?' Trey turned to Rob.

'Amber? We're working together at the moment,' he replied, innocently.

I squirmed and my palms suddenly felt sticky. My feet wanted to leave this spot immediately. *Why isn't Beau rushing over to help me out?*

I playfully nudged Rob in the ribs.

'Ahem, Annie. Yes, a new project I've got on the go.' I avoided meeting Rob's gaze. 'And talking of which, we were just about to take a quick conference call about it. I'm so sorry, Trey, but I've got to drag Rob off quickly. Are you here all evening? We'll be back!'

And I put my hand firmly onto Rob's arm and yanked him away, leaving a bemused Trey in our wake.

'Hey, missy, hold up a minute,' Rob said as I charged through the crowd and back up the glass stairs towards the crowded bar area, concentrating hard on not slipping over, and simultaneously looking for a spot where we'd be well out of Trey's sight. 'A "new project"—what's that all about? And I thought you'd want to say hello to Beau?'

'Just not right now,' I stammered.

'I didn't realise you were on first-name terms with Trey Jones.'

'I'm not,' I sighed. 'Well, I am—but the wrong first name, as you might have noticed.'

'Annie... I thought he'd made a mistake. No one in LA remembers anyone's name unless they need something from them—and he can probably afford to buy his own suits. What's that about, then?'

I paused to think for a second, worry etched across my face. I really needed some fresh air. And some proper food.

'Can we get out of here for a bit?'

* * *

Over a basket of chicken and mugs of hot coffee in a diner a block away, I explained the situation with Beau and Trey. In the cold light of day—well, evening—describing how I'd pretended to be someone called Annie Liechtenstein to provide Beau with an alibi for her almost certain infidelity sounded like the script for a low-budget film. Finally I paused for air and a slurp of coffee, and—*is he laughing at me?*

'I'm sorry, Annie, I mean, Amber. It's just—kind of funny, don't you think?'

'Funny?' I was infuriated. *This is my work! My livelihood.*

He apologised again. 'But just think, Amber—if Beau and Trey don't make it down the aisle, you're probably first in line to get the pig.' He burst out laughing again, almost sending a mouthful of cappuccino over his chicken bones. 'I'm sorry, but it is…just a tiny bit funny.' He gestured a tiny measure with his thumb and forefinger and looked up at me mock-apprehensively. 'Just a weeny bit, Amber. Annie?'

He was right—this week had become more than a bit ridiculous, and he was the only person out here who could make me see it. I decided to tell him everything. All about working at Smith's, how I accidentally got offered this job, my cobbled-together kit, rushing out here without really having a clue, Mona's erratic behaviour, the message from the loans company on her phone, the hamper of unopened bills in her office and the constant feeling that I was within a whisker of getting the sack the whole time. When I put it all together, it did sound pretty entertaining. In a black-comedy way.

'So the boyfriend's pining for you back home in London, then?' Rob asked, just as a waitress landed the most delicious-smelling hot brownie with vanilla ice cream between us. My cheeks coloured as I wondered whether to come clean and explain there was no boyfriend.

'Actually I live with Vicky—my best friend stroke house mate.' I stared into my mug. 'But, we're not, um—' I went red instantly. *Meep.*

'Special friends?' Rob smiled.

'Yeah, I mean, no.'

'I didn't think you were a lesbian, Amber,' he said, smirking, 'Not that I have any problem with lesbians. Did the mystery caller ever get in touch the other day, by the way?' I was surprised he remembered.

I shrugged, thinking about the text from Liam again. 'It's nothing.'

'You've got the guys queuing up,' he teased. 'But I saw the way you were looking at Trey Jones this evening.'

'Trey? He's a good-looking guy, but no, he's engaged. Although like you said, whether they'll make it up the aisle is another thing,'

'You really think he'll break it off?'

'If he's got any sense. She's so clearly playing him. Oh, and did I tell you why Pinky was less than perky in the suite the other day?' I was really loosening up now. 'He ate an empty M&Ms packet on my watch. I could have *killed* him!' Now I was laughing, too, proper from-the-belly laughter that made my eyes water.

He spluttered. 'This is too much! You're lucky animal welfare aren't after you...'

'Anyway, enough about me—what about you? Trey or Jennifer?'

'You think I'm gay?' He giggled again. 'Sorry to disappoint, but Jennifer all the way.'

The waitress broke the conversation by asking if we wanted to pay. Instead, we ordered more coffee. I felt so comfortable in his company, and it was great to speak to someone on my wavelength—someone who didn't take this town and what we were doing in it too seriously. Later, as we became aware of tables being wiped and chairs stacked around us, Rob announced: 'Don't know about you, but I'm not ready for bed yet.' I was comforted by his dependable London accent. 'Why don't we pop back into the party for a quick drink, seeing as we're so near? It's bound to be still going and if we bump into Pinky and Perky—' as he had now nicknamed Beau and Trey '—I'll play along, I promise. I'm an ac-tor, remember?' We both cracked up again. He insisted on paying for the food, and I pulled out my phone to check the time: 1:10 a.m. I knew there would be a ton of clothes returns to get through tomorrow, and negotiating Mona's mood was a headache at the best of times. There were calls to make, cases to pack, errands to run ahead of the flight back to London. All the gloss of the past few days was rubbing off rapidly, but my drunkenness had been replaced by a caffeine buzz and as there was definitely going to be a crash sooner or later, one more cocktail wouldn't hurt.

'Are you trying to get me into trouble tonight?'

'All the celebs will have gone by now, anyway,' he reasoned. 'Come on, I don't want to go home yet, so you're not going, either.'

I gathered up my handbag and we strolled back down the

street. Once inside the party again, we headed straight for the now almost deserted smoking terrace and sat on a bench looking out over the half-asleep city below. The crowds had vastly thinned out, suggesting, as Rob had predicted, that all the celebrities had left the building. A row of tall, thin palm trees stood proudly in the foreground, silhouetted in front of the impressive vista. As the lights of Los Angeles glimmered beneath us, I didn't want our evening to end. When the breeze cooled, Rob rested his jacket around my shoulders.

'You've got very twinkly eyes this evening, Miss Green,' he said, during a natural pause in conversation. Our arms were lightly touching, and I could feel the heat from his body on my bare skin.

'Perhaps they're just glazing over—I'm so tired.' I suddenly felt self-conscious and pulled my arm away from his. 'I can't actually believe how much has happened this week.'

I became aware that my heart was beating fast.

'You're right,' he said after a pause, looking away. 'I'm shattered, too. We'd better make a move. Taxi for twinkly eyes.' He stood up. 'I guess this means I'll see you back in London.'

Along with the other remaining guests, who were now admitting defeat and going to bed, we were ushered from the venue by a waitress who probably had an after-after-party to get to. When we reached the street Rob gave me a friendly kiss on both cheeks, and closed the door on my cab back to Mona's.

'Safe travels—and don't let that madwoman get you down!' he said through the open window as I was driven off. As the taxi sped along a dual carriageway heading for the Hills, I was still chuckling to myself about how crazy the past few days had been. I was already looking forward to seeing Rob back in London; he had made the whole thing fun again. And at least I wasn't sharing my bed with a micro-pig.

As I slipped off my heels at the front door, ready to sneak in without being heard, my phone lit up. Message from Rob:

Sleep well, twinkles x

I read it over and over.

Chapter Fourteen

All the lights in the house were off, so I crept straight up-stairs, assuming Mona was asleep and Klara still partying. Perhaps she was sitting on Orlando Bloom's lap by now. I took my make-up off, still thinking about the text from Rob, brushed my teeth thinking of it some more and then reread the message several hundred times when I got into bed, just to check I hadn't misread it in any way. I then spent an in-ordinate amount of time concocting a response. I deliber-ated several responses, ranging from: 'You too, A x' (too blunt); 'Hey green eyes, I had a great evening x' (too much); to 'You made them twinkle x' (too soppy).

I finally settled on: Sweet dreams, see you soon x (friendly and alluding to meeting up again). Sent. Then I immedi-ately panicked that the 'Sweet dreams' part was too girly and the 'See you soon' too presumptuous. Perhaps I should have not replied at all? *Christ, why isn't there a twenty-four-hour helpline for text etiquette?* I looked at the radio alarm. Just gone 2:00 a.m. in LA meant soon after 10:00 a.m. in London. Vicky would be up.

'A-ha, it's the talk of the town. Had almost forgotten the sound of your voice,' she answered.

'Hey, Vixter, can you speak?'

'Sure, if you don't mind me sounding out of breath. And no, not for any dirty reason—I wish! I'm late for work and got the hangover from hell, hence making a bad attempt at jogging to the tube. If I stop talking it's because I've passed out. How were the awards? Isn't it the middle of the night over there?'

'Yes, I drank too much coffee. It was crazy. Literally no one has a clue what anyone is going to wear until they are standing there on the red carpet being interviewed about it.'

'Jennifer Astley looked amazing…she's going to be on our Best Dressed list.'

'Fantastic! Thanks, hon, I'll tell Mona. We were so happy she wore that gown, but it was a close call.'

'So Mona's still alive after the other night? There've been all kinds of things written about her…'

'I know, I saw some of it and then couldn't look any more. I can't work her out, Vicky, she's so lovely sometimes, and then she's so out of control at others. Maybe it *was* food poisoning that made her collapse.'

'Why, what else could it be?'

'I don't know…drink problem, addiction to painkillers, depression, she's hiding something, I'm sure of it. Anyway, why are you so hungover?'

'Oh, you know, I met up with Chloe and one drink led to another…'

'No Simon Sunday?'

'No, hoping to see him later. Anyway, why are you still up so late? Don't tell me you've been partying with Jen and you're calling to tell me I'm dumped because she's your NBF?'

'Ha, no way! I drank too much coffee…'

'*Coffee?* I thought it was Dom Pérignon all the way for you out there?'

'Well, it was, but then Rob and I went to get some food and had a stupid amount of caffeine, so now I can't sleep.'

'Rob? And why don't I know about him?'

'He's assistant director for the TV pilot they're making. He's a sweetheart…'

'*And*…have you kissed his sweet face off?' It sounded as though she'd stopped attempting to jog.

'No! It's not like that.'

'Well, next time I want a snog, so make sure you keep me posted. Listen, hate to cut you off but I've got to go, I'm at the tube now and I'm already late.'

'Love you, honey.'

'When do you get back?'

'I land Wednesday at seven. Can't wait to see you.'

'Until then, *amigo*. Love ya more. And kiss Rob!'

I hung up. There hadn't been enough time to tell her about the texts from Liam. He'd sent one text late in the evening, asking if I was having a good time, but it had gone unanswered—I'd been busy. He was my most likely chance of a snog out here but it was beginning to bug me that he hadn't actually asked me out. I could barely remember what he looked like or the sound of his voice. In fact, the more I tried to conjure his features, the more blurred he became. I read Rob's text a few more times until I eventually fell asleep, phone next to me just in case Liam decided to actually ring. *Pathetic, I know.*

Next morning, my phone showed one new message from Liam, asking how my 'pretty self' was feeling. *If only he could see how un-pretty I look right now.* But no matter how bad the hangover, it was never a chore to wake up in this beautiful bedroom—and this was my second-to-last morning of doing so. It was nearly time to leave LA, and I had no idea if I would ever be back. I had a few days left working for Mona in London, as she prepped for the BAFTAs, before I was going back to Smith's.

I was dreading the shop already. It felt like the start of a new term at school, as though I could barely remember the person I was when I left, and I didn't even have a new pencil case to show for it. My eyes had been opened to a new world over here, and I didn't want to slip straight back into my old one—besides, I didn't even know if I had a job to return to. I was nervous about seeing Jas again, but the thought of seeing the Stick made me physically shudder. Without a doubt she would have spent a lot of time plotting how bad she was going to make my life.

As I opened my bedroom door to head downstairs, I accidentally trod on a small box lying on the floor. A piece of folded-up paper lay next to it. At first I thought some jewellery from the suite must have fallen out of a bag somewhere along the way and Ana had put it there for me, but when I opened the paper it said, in swirly handwriting: 'You're a stylist now. M x'. I undid the box, and inside was a sweet little gold necklace with the letter 'S' on it. *S for Stylist.* I warmed the metal between my fingers, a huge smile on my face. It was classic Mona—she pushed me to the edge of despair, but gave enough to make me come running back. Unclasping the delicate gold catch, I put it on immediately, and admired myself in the bathroom mirror. It really was adorable. I read the note again, and then noticed something scribbled on the other side: 'Does have to be returned when the PR asks for it, but yours to borrow until then'. *Ah well. It's the thought that counts.*

* * *

'Thank you, darling, you're so *organised*,' Mona said as I ended the call to British Airways, having confirmed our return flights to London. Compared with Mona, I suppose I *was* organised to a degree—you only had to look at the state of her filing and the whole array of hotel desk pads and Post-it notes she used as diaries to realise the concept was entirely foreign to her. And, this morning, she couldn't find her wallet.

'I'm sure I left it in the suite—it's bound to be there, it was such a rush to leave for the premiere party and I've barely left the house since. Unless someone swiped it when I was, um, incapacitated.' She tipped out the python bag to check for the umpteenth time that it wasn't in there. Meanwhile, I had to pay for our flights, which weren't cheap considering the last minute–ness of it all and the fact Mona refused to fly in any class inferior to Club.

'And if it's not in the suite tomorrow, I'll call the bank,' she continued, still rifling through travel-sized beauty products, hair clips, bangles, cigarette packets and other bits and bobs from the bag. 'At the same time, I'll add the flights onto your wages for the two weeks.'

'No problem,' I said, trying to sound more confident than I was about wiping out my entire overdraft. My rent was due at home at the end of next week, and I certainly didn't have enough to cover both. It had been a hectic morning, coordinating couriers to criss-cross through Beverly Hills, collecting gowns from clients and returning them to PRs or the W Hotel, where we'd finish the returns process before packing up and flying home to London. I wondered if it was time to broach the loans company message on Mona's answerphone, but another text from Liam put paid to that. He'd been texting me audition updates all morning.

'Jesus, it's like Kim and Kanye over there,' Mona said, mistakenly assuming I was reading a message from Rob. Having slept off her twenty-four-hour 'food poisoning' attack, she was, thankfully, now back to her punchy self. She seemed pleased I'd had a night out, and even more impressed that I'd spent it partying with someone as 'cute' as Rob. Her outlook was further improved when Caroline called to explain what had happened with Jennifer's gown yesterday. Mona put her on speakerphone in the office.

'Honestly, Mona, it was beyond stressful,' Caroline said. 'The driver had arrived and we were all set. She looked incredible in the Valentino, and I mean absolutely stunning. We were all ready to go and then Tamara popped a bottle of champagne so we could all toast Jen's big night, but she was standing too close and the fucking fizz went right down Jennifer's front.'

I whipped my hand to my mouth and pressed down hard, afraid that loud, hysterical laughter might burst out. Mona gritted her teeth, seemingly also trying to stifle a snort.

'All over her front, it flew. Totally ruined the gown, and you know as well as I do there is *no way* you take a hairdryer to a fabric that delicate. Thank God Amber had left us with the Oscar de la Renta, because I don't know what we would have done otherwise.'

'Oh, babe, that is awful! Tamara *never* should have done such a thing.' Mona was enjoying the chance to lay in to her ex-assistant. 'It's in every rule book—don't pop a cork close to a star, let alone a star in a Valentino gown. Jesus Christ, what was she *thinking*?'

'I know—and believe me, she won't be coming close to Jen in a gown again. Or Jen in anything, for that matter,' Caroline continued. 'She was livid, and you know Jen—she's *so nice*. But we're so grateful to Amber—she handled the situation with such grace yesterday, and we're so thankful she had the foresight to leave the de la Renta, just in case. She's a clever chick. Organised, too.' I smiled with pride. Mona turned and gave me a wink, clocking that I was wearing the necklace. I stroked the smooth letter. *My lucky talisman?*

* * *

Next morning, I arrived at LAX feeling all kinds of fabulous, pulling a large suitcase of dazzling fashion around the Tom Bradley International Terminal. Although no one who saw me would suspect it, the case was pulsating with a smorgasbord of silk, lace, satin and sequin-adorned gowns, crystal-encrusted shoes, exotic handbags and some seriously heavy-duty jewellery. Mona had sashayed off to check herself in at the Club desk, leaving me alone to negotiate the trauma of whether my huge cargo was over the twenty-three kilo allowance for World Traveller passengers.

Approaching the bag drop area, I suddenly felt irrationally nervous—my palms became sweaty and my eyes darted around the check-in desks like an illegal immigrant making a bid for a better life as I tried to identify who looked like the friendliest steward. The warning signs on each desk left no doubt that there would be excess charges if luggage was over the allowance, and I had no idea what mine weighed. If I had to pay for the excess my card would almost certainly be declined, and, of course, Mona was nowhere to be seen. *There's nothing I can take out of this case. It all has to come with me.* In my panicked state, I decided that if I *was* over the limit, I'd have no choice but to take some stuff out and wear it. The embellished Dolce & Gabbana and Chanel bags, a textured-leather Burberry jacket and the Cavalli jewellery were probably the heaviest items. Yes, I was fully prepared to resemble Elizabeth Taylor risen from the dead on board this flight, if necessity demanded. It was ironic really, considering the weight would be exactly the same on board the plane, but this was no time for clever remarks about airport baggage policies. I held my breath as the case was weighed and let it out slowly in relief as the nice woman on the desk slapped on a big, eye-catching orange 'HEAVY' sticker and pushed it through. As it disappeared into darkness on the conveyor belt, I prayed we would be safely reunited on the other side. *Is Mona insured?* I decided not to dwell on the thought as the case vanished into the ether. *Thank God my mother isn't here.*

* * *

Despite my increasingly stiff neck, a puncture in my scratchy neck pillow and the man next to me constantly flopping his head onto my shoulder, the flight passed reasonably quickly. Three mini-bottles of white wine and one of Mona's horse-tranquilliser tablets helped me to achieve a few hours of broken sleep. When I woke, we were flying over the Thames—it snaked through the toy town beneath us like a long grey worm. The *EastEnders* theme tune played in my head and a warm feeling rippled through me. *Home, sweet home.* I'd be reunited with Vicky in a matter of hours and there was so much to discuss. I planned to see Mum and Dad tomorrow, and, if I asked really nicely and gave them some duty-free gin, they might cook a roast in the evening and I would savour every single mouthful, in between filling them in on my glamorous working holiday that might one day turn into a lucrative career. Mona certainly seemed to enjoy a high-flying lifestyle. Anyway, let's face it, it was the *only* career development I'd had in a long while. Just as the seat-belt sign went on Mona appeared, her timing impeccable.

'Get any sleep, babe?' she asked. A black satin eye mask rested on top of her head, her lipstick was freshly applied—presumably because you never knew *who* you might bump into, wandering through Club en route to the cheap seats—and there was the usual strong waft of her pheromone-reactive scent.

'A little. You?'

'Eight hours—don't you just love it when that happens?' I grunted, as did most of the cattle-class passengers around me. 'Just wanted to give you a heads-up that tomorrow's going to be busy,' she continued. 'I caught up on a few emails and Wonderland Artists Agency have been in touch. Clive needs some help with an artist—an image change.' She looked around the cabin, giving my fellow passengers a blatant once-over to deduce whether any of them were cool enough to care about what she was about to say. I leaned in closer as Mona whispered loudly, 'It's Miss P. She's not cutting it in the charts since she won the show, and a new look is all part of the overhaul to turn her into a credible actress. She needs to go to the BAFTAs and make a splash.'

An air hostess appeared behind Mona: 'Excuse me, ma'am, but you need to return to your seat now please.'

'Just a second.' Mona flicked her away with a brusque hand gesture.

'Ms Armstrong, the pilot has put on the seat-belt sign, so you must—'

'There's a studio booked on Sunday for a styling session ahead of the awards,' Mona continued, ignoring the steward completely, 'so we'll need to do the ring rounds tomorrow. We'll call some designers and pop to Selfridges to pick up some bits. No rest for the wicked!'

'Ms Armstrong, I need you to return to your seat right now,' said the air hostess with increasing sternness. 'Please don't make me ask you again.'

Sixty pairs of tired, bloodshot eyes stared at Mona, who briefly held the hostess's stony glare before realising there was little point in resisting. I'd already learned that the one thing Mona hated more than a badly made caffè macchiato was authority, especially wielded by someone sporting green eyeliner and wearing top-to-toe uniform polyester. As she was frogmarched down the plane, the Swarovski crystals on the back of her tracksuit caught the early-morning sun above the clouds, sending shafts of light around the cabin. My foggy brain tried to process what she had just said.

I knew instantly who Clive was—a well-known music mogul and host of a highly successful TV music reality show—and Miss P was his winner and prodigy from last year. But… Miss P, a serious actress? It seemed unlikely. She had failed to set the music world alight so far and the BAFTAs was a serious event; not somewhere you'd expect to find a failed music reality show contestant. More pressing than that, though, all I could immediately think was: *Bang goes my roast dinner.*

Part Three: London, The BAFTAs

Chapter Fifteen

'Vicky!

'Vicky!' I had been yelling through the letter box for the past five minutes.

'Viiic-ky! Pleeease wake up, it's bloody freezing out here!' I'd almost forgotten how cold it was back home, and I was still dressed for LA. It was bright, though—the sky was almost cloudless—and the street had the crisp, metallic, unmistakable taste of London. *I love this city.* I hammered on the door again, harder. It was Wednesday, it was nearly 8:30 a.m.; she should be awake by now. She should be getting ready for work. Naturally, my phone had no power and I had buried my door keys somewhere within her giant suitcase, which I sure as hell wasn't going to risk opening in the middle of the pavement at this time of the morning on a Kensal Rise backstreet. An opportunist would be peddling the lot on Portobello Market before you could say, 'Call the fashion police.'

'Vic? It's not a nutter, it's me. It's Amber! Open up!'

After what seemed an age a groggy Vicky came to the door. Her hair was a mess, and she looked a bit like a cave-woman.

'You look as rough as I feel.'

'Hungover, okay. Why so early? Thought your plane got in at seven,' she said, wiping her sleep-filled eyes with the back of a finger and blinking like a newborn bat that had accidentally rolled out of its nest and into the sun.

'Yes, seven in the morning. I've come straight from the airport,' I gave her dishevelled appearance the once-over again. 'I probably smell as bad as you do.'

The pile of letters, unwanted leaflets and junk mail littering the communal hallway seemed even higher than when I'd left. I was suddenly seeing my life through new eyes. Vicky was barefoot, wearing her American Apparel tracksuit bottoms and a baggy white T-shirt. Halfway up our dusty stairs that hadn't seen a Hoover in the whole two years we'd lived here—in fact, it was only just possible to tell the carpet had once been pink—she turned and looked at me as though she wanted to say something and then decided against it. She looked like she still had last night's make-up on, but she still looked pretty—something only Vicky could get away with.

'Bad hangover?' I asked, despite the answer being plain as the day.

'Bleurgh,' she confirmed. 'But so good to see your face, I've missed you so much. I can't believe it's only been just over a week—it feels like forever. Come here.' She stopped on the mini-landing and turned around, arms open. I dragged the heavy suitcase up behind me and set it down as she reached around my shoulders and engulfed me in a big, warm, slightly smelly bear hug.

'Love you, honey,' I said.

'Love you, too. Best friends forever.' She paused. 'Um…' Her hand rested on our shabby front door. I noticed it was being held ajar by an Adidas trainer. It had a serious hinge on it, that door; I'd lost count of the number of times one of us had been locked out when it slammed shut. She lowered her voice to a quiet whisper. 'There, um, don't kill me, because my head can't take it, but there, er, there might be someone else in here.' She pulled a cringe expression and studied my face.

'*Might?* Or definitely is?' I said, clocking that the trainer in the doorway looked too big for Vicky's size-five feet.

'Er, pretty definitely.'

'How come something tells me you're not going to say you bought us a kitten?'

'I wish that was it,' she replied. 'But I didn't think you liked kittens. We could still get one if you like—you know I'd love one. But this thing, it's, um, *he's*, quite a lot bigger than a kitten.' My jaw dropped open. 'And before you say it—it's not Simon.'

Something had already told me it wasn't Simon. Vicky was never this unkempt around Simon.

'Vicky! You minx! What the—' She shhhed me down to a quiet whisper again. 'And on a school night?'

'I had a few drinks with work people in Soho, and then a few of us ended up in The Shadow Lounge. It was such a laugh. And Jim from the art desk was there…and some of the guys in the club thought he was gay and were pestering him, so, well, we kind of snogged to show he wasn't.' She gripped my hand and came closer. I could smell the alcohol, still. 'And it felt so good, we kind of carried on snogging, and he ended up here…'

'Not *the* sexy Jim? The one you've mentioned before?'

'Yes, he's *really* sexy, Am.' She knocked the shoe out of the way and poked her head around the door, just in case a half-naked sexy Jim was lurking in earshot. 'But I didn't actually mean for him to end up here. We shared a cab and then I remembered I had a bottle of fizz in the fridge.'

'Ahem—don't you mean *I* had a bottle of fizz in the fridge?'

'Oh God, yes, probably, sorry, babe, I'll get you another one. But it went down so well—and he's such a great kisser.' *If I'd had a pound for every time I've heard Vicky say those immortal words.*

'And now you're wearing his T-shirt.'

'It smells so nice—he's the one who wears that aftershave I love!' She held it out to me invitingly and I backed away.

'No, thanks. So it's the aftershave's fault?'

'Totally, the aftershave and the cocktails, along with everyone in Shadow Lounge,'

'I think it was also a full moon?' I added.

'Yes! Did you see it from the plane?' We both giggled and she smiled her big contagious smile. 'That, plus the fact you basically have to be borderline alcoholic to be single.' She wiped at the smudged mascara again.

'But you're not single—*are you*?' I replied, confused. 'What about Simon?'

She looked over her shoulder to check we weren't being overheard.

'It's been the week from hell. He basically blew me out last Tuesday when I wanted to see him after the launch party—said I was too drunk—and then he wasn't around on Wednesday, didn't call me back all day, and on Thursday he was too busy to have the headspace to think about anything other than a new film segment he's trying to get on the radio. And then he didn't seem to want to make plans for our normal Sunday session—and he cancelled the other night, hence… Oh, I don't know, Am, he's either met someone else or he's gone off me. He's made it pretty clear, wouldn't you say? I guess I wanted to press the self-destruct button last night. I did try to call you about it…' She finally stopped for air, worry etched across her pretty brow. I remembered the three missed calls on my phone just after I'd fainted at the premiere. That last sentence hurt.

'Honey, I'm sorry, I was so caught up in everything over there—I thought you'd pocket-dialled me because it was so late. I was actually trying to pull myself together after having a minor fainting episode at Beau Belle's premiere, and then I guess I forgot, I'm sorry.'

'A "minor fainting episode", at a premiere?' She sniggered loudly. 'Amber, I do love you—we've got sooo much to catch up on!' We both laughed. 'I could *really* do without having to go to work today. I just want to drink tea and eat toast with you.'

'Give us another hug.'

There was something about my best friend that meant however stinky and messy she was, however annoyed I might be that she and a random bloke had drunk the bottle of Verve Clicquot I'd been saving for a special occasion; however heinous it was, I couldn't be angry with her for long. And anyway, I'd never particularly liked Simon. To him, I was the shop girl who wasn't worth a proper conversation because I didn't know much about the works of Pedro Almodovar or the existential qualities of *American Beauty. Ha! If only he knew about my burgeoning friendship with Trey Jones, that would have him taking notice.* And though she had never actually admitted it, I sensed this bloke, who was meant to be Vicky's boyfriend, seemed to make her feel insecure, too. I'd previously put it down to the age-old tension between best friend and best friend's boyfriend, but perhaps now was the time to finally tell Vicky what I thought of know-it-all Simon, the Barry Norman wannabe who took himself way too seriously and was nowhere near good enough for my best mate. Just then, a clattering noise came from inside the flat.

'Must be the kitten knocking over a vase,' I said, and we both creased up.

After some slightly awkward chit-chat with Jim from the art desk (who was definitely sexier than Simon, but not as good-looking as Liam, or Rob, come to think of it), plus a big mug of tea, I made it into my bedroom. I heaved the suitcase onto my still-unmade bed and emptied it. Within seconds, it looked as though a bomb had gone off in Harvey Nics. Having seen sexy Jim off with a snog and strict instructions to go to work perpetuating the story that she was suffering from food poisoning and wouldn't be in today, Vicky joined me. Laying her eyes on the treasures before us, she was actually lost for words. Only momentarily, because she was soon screaming, 'Let's play dress-up!', before coming up with the genius idea that we should go out for brunch wearing some of my haul. We both knew, of course, that it was actually a load of expensive clothes belonging to a series of PR companies, not mine (or, come to think of it, Mona's) at all. However...

* * *

We headed out of the flat looking like a cross between Eddy and Patsy from *Ab Fab* and two actual fashion editors during London Fashion Week. I was wearing a black Stella McCartney jumpsuit, accessorised with some gigantic Cavalli jewellery, including a panther bracelet and necklace set that I had taken more than a small shine to in real life, a Pucci scarf over my head and some sky-high Saint Laurent two-tone ankle boots. Vicky opted for a high-fashion hooker look: a Burberry oxblood-latex trench coat over a tiny body-con dress and some round Chanel sunglasses, even though there was hardly any sun, finished off with a killer pair of metallic gold Alexander McQueen stiletto boots. In other words, we looked ridiculous. We decided to go to the Electric Diner for brunch. Snuggled in the heart of Portobello Road, next to the Electric Cinema, this was probably the place that would be most accepting of our outfits.

Brunch somehow demanded to be washed down with a Bloody Mary, and somehow one turned into three Bloody Marys, just to get the level of hot spice right, and that was followed by a tipsy stroll around the antique markets where I bought a maraca and Vicky bought a vintage gold necklace, and then we ended up in the Portobello Gold having a bottle of red wine and two bowls of nuts for lunch. All in all, minus the crazy clothes, it was a pretty typical Portobello day for us. I told her all about Rob and how that last night in LA was one of my best nights ever.

'Have you stalked Rob on Facebook yet?' she enquired.

When I said no, Vicky looked aghast.

'Well, I did look, but his profile is locked and I didn't want to seem like an *actual* stalker,' I admitted.

'But you *must* stalk him—it's a given. Send him a friend request!' I fiddled with the stem of my wine glass. 'I know your password, I'll do it myself otherwise.'

'You know my password? That's a violation of my privacy!'

'Privacy? But you are not permitted to have a life that is

private from me, Amber Green—especially in situations when you're really not helping yourself.'

'And how exactly am I not helping myself?'

'Well, do you know if he has a girlfriend? That's the first thing you'd find out on Facebook.'

'I don't care if he has a girlfriend!' I exclaimed. 'Anyway, he hasn't mentioned anyone, I think it would have come up.' It hadn't really crossed my mind that Rob might have a girl-friend—he hadn't given that impression. *Besides, it wasn't any of my business, anyway.*

We turned our attention to Sunday Simon and LA Liam. Throughout the day Liam continued to update me with a series of text messages, each one I read to Vicky.

'He's *so* into you,' she enthused.

'But why hasn't he actually asked me out?'

She shrugged. 'Why don't *you* ask him on a date?'

'But I can barely remember what he looks like.'

'Maybe you can at least use him to get Rob's attention. You blatantly fancy this Rob and once a guy thinks he could lose you, he soon ups his game.'

'Vicky, I don't fancy Rob!'

'Whatever.'

She was having none of it. Regardless, we both decided that Vicky was much better off without stupid Simon, and though sexy Jim from the art desk probably wasn't going to be suitable long-term, he was a fantastic distraction for now, helping to create some interest at work and fuzz the edges of the break-up. Then the conversation moved on to Mona.

'She's just so hard to work out, the way she blows hot and cold,' I explained. 'Like—she gave me this gold necklace to wear after the Globes, which was so lovely and thought-ful, but she's so out of control at other times, getting sick in the middle of a huge industry event and then turning her phone off on the day of the awards. I mean, you can't do that, can you?'

'Clearly you can if you're Mona Armstrong.'

'It's like there's something else going on. I found a stack of unopened bills in her office and there was a message from a loans company on her phone the other day. Add that to the puking and the not showing up, and it's like she's avoiding facing up to something.'

'She sounds stressed out. Maybe she's in debt? Or having a breakdown? People have breakdowns as often as getting their roots done over there. It's la-la land, remember?'

'But she's got mansion houses in LA and London, she travels Club Class, she only wears designer clothes, her make-up bag alone is worth more than my entire belongings. She's like a celebrity herself… It doesn't make sense.'

I suddenly remembered the state of my own bank account and my looming rent. Mona had made no mention of when I'd actually see the funds in my account and I'd have to broach the subject with Vicky soon.

'Have you tried to ask her about it?'

I rolled my eyes.

'It would be scary,' Vicky continued. 'But maybe she'll open up to you.'

'I'm not so sure. I'm just the lowly—highly sackable—assistant. Likely soon to be joining the pile of former assistants.'

'More like the assistant who has saved her butt numerous times in just over a week.' She gave me a look. 'Does she have any good girlfriends or a boyfriend you could speak to, in confidence?'

'That's the other thing. I don't think she actually has anyone—other than her housekeeper and a bunch of celebrities, who certainly weren't there for her when she nearly puked in her bag. I think she must be lonely, too. And she's kind of asexual. I can't imagine her with a man, or a woman, for that matter.'

'Well, then, there's only one person for it—you.'

I shrank back into my seat. 'I'll try to broach it this week, while we're in London. Everything feels more normal over here.'

Vicky high-fived me across the table. After a brief silence, she asked me: 'Do you think you'd ever want to live in LA?' Her question was impressively nonchalant, but I could tell she'd been working up to it. She stared at me in a moment of sobriety.

'Nah. Everyone's too self-obsessed,' I replied quickly, and saw Vicky visibly relax. I had told her what she wanted to hear—and I was pretty sure it was the truth. I paused briefly to consider what I'd do if Mona offered me a permanent job, which would need me to be based in LA. My mind wandered: me, Liam, sunshine, a Cadillac, the Pacific Coast Highway. Who knew what the future might hold.

'Anyway, I'd better get back,' I said, breaking off the daydream. I had momentarily forgotten about the outfits we were wearing, and suddenly felt ridiculous amongst the appropriately dressed after-work drinkers. 'I've got all this to pack up again before the morning—we've got to prep for Miss P tomorrow.'

'You're styling Miss P? I thought she'd disappeared!'

'Mona's planning to bring her back with a fashion bang at the BAFTAs.'

'Awesome! I wouldn't mind being *your* assistant one day, Amber Green—stylist to the staaaars! One for the road?'

Four for the road later, I finally staggered into my freezing cold bed, feet once again aching from being squashed into ill-fitting shoes. Needing some attention, I texted Liam to let him know I was home safely, as requested. He replied: I wish my head was resting on your pillow too x. Hazily I Instagrammed the pillow, tagging him in it. Naturally, I spent a good fifteen minutes styling it, lighting a candle on my bedside table, making a delicate head-shaped indentation and setting it up so the light fell on it in the right way and it looked as enticing as any pillow could.

I'd like to meet that pillow x, came the immediate response, giving me goosebumps. I went to sleep wondering if he ever would.

* * *

Next morning I was rudely awoken by my phone ringing. *Rob—he had to be back in the UK by now? LA Liam? Shit, I still haven't called Mum.* No—Mona. 'Meet me near Selfridges at 10:00 a.m. I'm seeing the personal shopper to get the bits for Miss P.' No chance to get over my jet lag today, let alone make it out to Zone Five on the tube to see my folks or sleep off this hangover. Aargh, my head! *When will I learn that spending time with Vicky, even for brunch, never turns out to be just a simple outing involving eggs and coffee? It always turns into something we later refer to as 'messy'.* My head was killing me, far worse than any hangover I'd had in…let's see…just over a week, since I last went out with Vicky.

In the shower, my thoughts returned to LA Liam. Communications with him had crossed the Atlantic and we'd swapped surely a hundred messages. I reflected on his American accent. He did have an American accent, didn't he? Somehow I couldn't quite hear it in my head. I mulled over his mega-watt smile, curly hair and the way he'd made my heart race that night at Soho House, but the more I thought about it, the more cloudy the image became in my mind. Like a misted, sepia photograph of a celluloid heart-throb, he was in danger of becoming a movie-perfect moment forever lost in time. Yet over the past week he had forged his way into my world.

* * *

Even in the busy surroundings of Starbucks on Oxford Street, Mona was easy to spot. Dark glasses, a tumble of chocolate curls with highlights like caramel ribbons, skin-tight leather leggings, a cotton tee, her favourite Isabel Marant leather jacket and Jimmy Choo biker boots. A big, impossible-to-miss cherry-tomato Anya Hindmarch tote was plonked on the table in front of her, along with two Venti cups of strong caffè macchiato—enough to power a small school. She was talking loudly on the phone, but that didn't stop her standing up to aggressively wave me over, a jangle of bangles making customers turn. *Uh-oh, she doesn't look happy.* Mona didn't blend in, even amongst cosmopolitan London shoppers.

'Fear not, Clive, I hear you loud and clear,' she was saying. 'What she needs is a "wow" moment. Miss P *will* make an impact at the BAFTAs. She'll be the front page of all the red tops on Monday morning. I'll make sure of it.'

Two girls sitting at the table next to Mona tried and failed to discreetly take her photo, and she shot them a dirty look. Perhaps the jet lag had caught up with her after all. I had forgotten Mona was probably more famous in London than she was in LA, thanks to the buzz about the pilot show and the fashion blogging scene. She seemed somewhat stressed.

'You're late,' she stated before I'd reached the table, loud enough for the adjacent customers to know I was being told off by my boss.

When I reached the table and sat down, she ushered me in close, casting more dirty looks at the two girls who were now desperately trying not to laugh. I was pretty sure a badly taken snap of Mona had already made its way onto Instagram.

'What I'm thinking is a gown with guts, preferably sheer cutaway panels revealing just enough side boob and side bum to get people talking,' she announced, causing a businessman on a neighbouring table to look over his copy of the *Times*. 'We need some serious flesh on display to secure the front pages.' She stretched out her arm to reveal a very new-looking, chunky rose-gold Michael Kors watch. 'Shit, Amber! Now you've made me late for the appointment.'

I was still taking in the side-boob-and-side-bum brief—or rather, lack of briefs—as she stood up. I had a flashback to Rita Ora once flinging off her undies to pull off the see-through side bum look at an Oscars after-party. It was definitely daring. 'Do you think Miss P will be up for it?' I asked nervously, picturing the five-foot-three singer, with legs half the length of Rita's.

'She'll have to be. That's why they've asked me to do it—I get results.' She produced her iPad from the tote and handed it over. 'You hold the fort here, catch up on returns and manage appointments for the BAFTAs, and I'll be back in an hour.'

'You got it, boss.'

The girls on the next table had stopped bothering to hide their iPhones now, and snapped away, recording Mona's look from behind as she sashayed out of the cafe, sunglasses on, persona firmly in place.

'So cool,' said one.

'Total bitch, though,' said the other. A part of me wanted to pull up a chair at their table and let it all out.

* * *

As I waited for Mona to emerge from Selfridges, weighed down with eye-popping gowns, my mobile phone rang on my makeshift Starbucks desk. Instead of an irate PR chasing the return of their precious gown or questioning why it had come back hacked off below the thigh—Mona had told me that Beau once took a pair of scissors to an Armani because she wanted it to look 'sexier' halfway through a party, much to the dismay of the designer—I almost choked on my second coffee when I saw LA Liam's name lit up. He had actually called! *That means his voice is at the other end. And I am expected to speak to him.* It was such a shock, I bottled picking up, but listened to his voicemail three times in a row. He sounded slightly husky, American all right and mischievous, sexy. LA Liam had arrived in London, too. And he wanted to meet up. A cool half hour later—it was painful to wait that long, but I didn't want to appear over-keen—I rang him back. And half an hour after that, he was sitting opposite me in Starbucks.

'My very own Eliza Doolittle,' he said, pulling up a seat. 'You look so...*English* today.'

My mind boggled—was this a compliment? Judging by the fact he was leaning so close he could almost certainly smell my coffee breath, I supposed it was.

'Hello, Henry 'iggins,' I replied, blushing. He looked puzzled, clearly his understanding of *My Fair Lady* only stretched to Eliza.

'What a great coincidence—fate has brought us together.' He smiled. His black hair so naturally thick and unruly, it was a battle to keep it out of his face. My American Poldark. *Wait until I tell Vicky about this!* He tucked a curl behind his ear and leaned in closer. He had devastating brown eyes with eyelashes that reminded me of a baby camel. He was so exotic-looking, almost the exact opposite of Rob with his pretty-boy features—or Henry Higgins, for that matter. I felt like I was starring in my own rom-com, he being the hottest holiday romance ever. All we needed were some piña coladas and a palm tree. I wished the iPhone girls were still here to record this: me being wooed by a bona fide American hottie.

'Anyway, what brings you to London?'

'Flew in late last night,' he said, stretching his arms across the table. His body language was all over me. 'You know, few BAFTA parties, more auditions—I'm up for Gillian Anderson's surgeon in a new miniseries. But anyway, that's boring—'

He reached for my hands. Before I knew it he was lacing his fingers with mine. I suddenly felt painfully self-aware. PDAs with a virtual, albeit fit, stranger in the middle of the morning in a crowded Starbucks was alien terrain for me. Yet it was thrilling. A girl on the next table seemed to have clocked Liam; his good looks certainly stood out in a crowd. Or perhaps she had actually seen some of the obscure TV dramas and low-budget films he was listed as having bit-roles in on IMDb. I let my fingers be wiggled by his, desperately trying to shed my self-consciousness. An inner voice urged me to live in the moment; throw caution to the wind—think more like Vicky than myself. What was it she said? 'When one man wants you, others do, too.'

I found myself staring at his full lips, wondering what it would be like to kiss them. And then he lunged forwards. We were like two tortoise heads popping out of their shells, stopping just shy of knocking noses. He hooked one hand firmly around the back of my head and pulled my stunned face really close, right across the middle of the table. He was staring at my parted lips. I could feel his breath on them. *My God, he's masterful.* I felt like a wobbly marshmallow in his hands.

'I've been thinking about kissing you from the moment we met,' he said, brown eyes shining with lust as they fixed on my now quivering lips.

And before I could decide how to react, or had a second to wish I'd sucked a mint, it was happening. We were kissing.

His tongue was hard, urgent, investigative. There was a sound as our teeth clashed. I wanted to laugh but instead he held my head in place, working his tongue deeper, silencing me. Granted, it had been a while since I'd had a proper snog, but I didn't remember it being quite as aggressive as this. The experience was beginning to feel more like a dental procedure than a kiss as his tongue explored my mouth.

'You taste so good, Amber,' he said, pausing momentarily to stare at my glistening lips once more.

After another minute or so of tongue warfare, I slowly moved my head back, and gently pulled his hand down from its vice-like grip of my neck. He slumped back into his chair. When I dared to look up again, I was staring into the green eyes of Rob, who looked equally shocked.

'God, so sorry, I, um, Mona said you were working in here and so we—' Over his shoulder were Fran and Shaggy. Both seemed to be trying not to laugh.

The TV crew saw me having the worst kiss I've ever had. So did most of Starbucks. Please, dear God, what have I done to deserve this?

Liam noticed we had company.

'All right, mate?' Rob said awkwardly.

Liam barely registered him, clearly unfazed that we'd been caught mid–bad kiss by some people I knew. *Or maybe he doesn't think the kiss was bad?* I didn't know which was worse. Instead, he was eyeballing the serving counter towards the front of Starbucks.

'Don't know about you, Eliza, but I'm ravenous. If I don't get something inside me I might end up eating you again.' He winked.

Rob raised an eyebrow.

I felt myself turn scarlet.

'Um, yes. I mean no, not had lunch yet, I'll grab us a baguette each, if you like?' Being Mona's assistant had turned me into acting like everyone's assistant, but I really wanted to get away from Terminator Tongue.

'I'll go. What can I get you?' he insisted.

I thought for all of two seconds. 'BLT, please.' I suddenly felt starving. Perhaps some stodge would give me the energy to get through whatever the next part of the day would have in store. Nothing was predictable when it came to Mona and I needed to know why the camera crew was here.

'A whole one?' He looked shocked. 'Gluttony is one of seven deadly sins, you know. I thought you'd be watching your weight. Whatever.' And he headed off towards the counter.

I gasped. *Did he actually say that? I'm gluttonous for wanting a sandwich for lunch?* Fury flashed before my eyes. *Bloody LA and its starving hungry people.* Rob heard, too, but he looked away, seemingly embarrassed at having seen me full-on pashing with a guy who had now pretty much told me I was fat.

Fran pushed in front of Rob. 'So, I take it Mona hasn't mentioned the filming. Again?' She rolled her eyes.

'Um, no,' I muttered, so utterly sick and tired of having the wrong answer. 'She's in Selfridges at the moment, if you want to find her there.'

I was still digesting the gluttony comment and more than anything I just wanted them all to leave me alone.

'That's not a bad idea,' Rob said, after a pause, sensing my mood. 'Let's do the background stuff outside Selfridges and try to hook up with Mona later or tomorrow.' He had offered me a lifeline and I was grateful. Fran turned on her heel to leave, huffing as LA Liam knocked her arm on his return to the table. He chucked a BLT across it towards me.

'What time will you finish work, babe?' he asked.

'Never,' I replied, truthfully. 'I'm working for Mona 24/7 at the moment. Until we get the BAFTAs out of the way, at least.'

'Catch you *mañana* then, baby girl. I'll text you,' he said, before picking up his jacket and swaggering off. *Baby girl? Just don't expect a reply.*

And in a heartbeat I was alone again, reeling. Well, alone bar all the people around me gawping.

* * *

I had managed to demolish the BLT—every lip-smacking mouthful of it—before Mona returned, on a fashion high after nabbing half of Selfridges' best second-floor offerings. She didn't seem bothered when I told her filming was off, instead—to my glee—she suggested we call it a day.

I didn't have any urge to call LA Liam, instead I erased him completely from my phone and rushed home to tell Vicky all the cringe-worthy details. *Life's too short for a second bad kiss.*

* * *

During the two days before the BAFTAs and our makeover of Miss P, I continued to assist Mona, meeting her in a variety of coffee establishments around town. As she ummed and aahed over which gown and accessories to put on the aspiring star, and we attended appointments at shops and PR offices for her other BAFTA clients, I incessantly checked her email inbox. She was fretting hugely about whether Jennifer Astley was going to call: the scarlet Valentino still needed to be seen on someone this awards season, and Beau Belle had decided not to make the trip from LA with Trey, so we were holding out for Jen, as was Valentino's office, who was ringing for updates on a twice-daily basis. Mona's mood swings were as erratic as ever. She would flit from 'lovely boss', offering to take me for a mani-pedi once we'd got this round of fittings over, to 'bitch boss from hell', tearing a strip off me in front of clients if I used my initiative, and then fail to turn up to some of our appointments, so I had to blindly take them alone. One afternoon she shrieked at me in public when I ordered her a Grande Starbucks instead of a Venti. This particular afternoon, she'd been an hour late to meet me outside Bond Street tube station. I hadn't been wearing enough layers and my fingers had almost turned blue. There was no hint of an apology.

'Would it be easier to do some meetings at your house?' I asked, when my lips had thawed. She ignored the question completely.

As we walked in silence towards Smith's for our appointment with Jas, I wondered where Mona actually lived in London. So far, there had been no mention of where she was based over here. But more pressing was my fear about what kind of reception awaited me at Smith's—especially from the Stick.

As we turned onto South Molton Street, I felt a tap on my shoulder.

'Ladies!' It was Rob. The sight of him in the middle of a London Street made me jump. He looked really handsome in a black polo neck and thick grey winter coat. 'You've got a pace on you today.' The tip of his nose was red.

'Rob!' I felt my cheeks match the colour of his nose.

'I didn't realise we were meant to be filming this afternoon?' Mona scowled at me, pre-emptively angry. Had I somehow failed to pick up a message?

'We're not, don't panic.' Rob smiled. 'Though I wanted to ask if we could do a few more scenes in Smith's this week—Fran thought it would be good to get you talking about the BAFTAs and Oscars. What do you reckon?'

'Fine with me, if Jas is okay with it,' Mona replied.

'We can ask her today,' I suggested. 'That's where we're going now.'

'Great. Just let me know.' He pulled up his collar, clapped his hands together and shifted his weight from foot to foot in an effort to keep warm; he looked like he wanted to say something else. I prayed he wouldn't ask me about Liam in front of Mona. I wanted to forget the whole sorry thing. 'What are you doing after the appointment, Amber?' he asked finally. 'Might you have five minutes for a quick drink, or a coffee? I need to ask you something.'

Mona elbowed me really obviously. I turned to my boss, whose mood appeared to have warmed.

'I suppose she's allowed a break sometimes,' she said. 'We'll be done at Smith's in a couple of hours.' It was pretty clear that Rob was one of the few people who could get what he wanted from Mona; his good looks definitely helped.

'Great. I'll meet you in Pret by the tube, five-ish?'

'See you there.' And he turned back up the street.

'He's into you,' Mona stated. I was uncomfortably aware that Rob was definitely still within earshot.

'He's not. He's just being friendly.'

As we approached Smith's, a sinking feeling began to develop in my stomach. Mona seemed distracted, too. She started dragging her heels, and we finally came to a standstill two shops down from the boutique, where she put a hand on my wrist.

'Listen, Amber, there's something I wanted to ask before we go in.' She turned to face me. Sometimes I literally had no clue what was going to come out of her mouth, and this was one of those times.

'Your job,' she began; her tone was stern. *She's firing me!* She paused for dramatic effect. 'I know it was meant to be a fortnight, but I'd really love you to stay on and help me through the BAFTAs and Oscars. It's only another couple of weeks.' She looked at me with something like desperation in her eyes, and I breathed out, overwhelmed with relief. 'What do you say?' She gave me what was meant to be a reassuring smile. 'I was thinking we could let Jas know this morning.'

'Wow, I'm really grateful for this,' I began, unsure where my sentence was going to end. 'I wasn't sure if you thought I was doing a good job or not.' I smiled awkwardly, and Mona squeezed my wrist. *She won't actually say it, but I guess this is her way of telling me I'm doing something right.* 'If I did take it, do you think Jas will mind?'

'Jas will want you to be happy,' she said, without a second thought.

I did some quick analysis in my head.

Plus sides: the past week has been a blast; I got to meet Jennifer Astley; I occasionally get to wear incredi-

ble dresses; there might not be much food, but there is free champagne.

Minuses: my boss seems to be on the verge of a breakdown; I may completely burn my bridges at Smith's; I've got rent due and no idea when I'm getting paid; I'm not sure I'm cut out for the world of size-zero people; I don't want to run into LA Liam ever, ever again.

'Do you mind if I think about it?' I answered at last. 'Just a few hours, I need to see what Jas says and I should probably call my mum.' That reminded me. 'What, er, would the terms be?' Vicky would understandably kill me if I couldn't cover my rent this month, and it would be the first question on my mother's lips. 'And the money for the flights?'

'Well, I'm sure I could let you keep the Burberry you looked so cute in the other night.' She ignored my question and did a jazz-hands gesture before motioning towards the 'S' necklace. 'A stylist has got to look the part.' Hmm. That dress was the most beautiful thing I'd ever worn. *Maybe I can eBay it. Or maybe she's just awkward about discussing financial matters in the middle of the street?*

'Let's see what kind of mood Jas is in, and I promise I'll give you an answer by the end of the day, okay?' I offered.

'Deal.' She lifted her collar and put on her sunglasses, ready to enter the store.

Chapter Sixteen

Once inside, the atmosphere in Smith's wasn't as frosty as I'd feared, although it felt odd to be on the 'other side' of the appointment. The Stick barely made eye contact with me—though I did spy her giving my outfit the once-over and she no doubt felt relieved I was still in my standard uniform of AllSaints parka, skinny Topshop jeans and black Zara jumper. Jas, however, was much warmer, greeting me with a chic kiss on each cheek, and Big Al was reassuringly oblivious to awkwardness.

'So, have you met Al Pacino yet?' he asked, following me down to the stockroom, where I had been invited for a sneaky peek at some of the new collections.

'Afraid not, but I'll get you his autograph if I do.'

'You look thin. You haven't gone all Hollywood anorexic on us, have you?' He scanned me in a protective-dad way.

'The people out there definitely don't like wine and chips as much as I do,' I replied. 'But don't worry, I've just been running around a lot. I'm not about to waste away.'

'I should hope not.' He smiled. 'Any plans to go back out?'

'Hmm, that's the big question,' I replied.

'The madwoman's trying to lure you into working for her permanently, then? Jas thinks you're back here from Monday, you know, she was talking about the windows earlier—wants you to work your magic.'

'Mona wants to extend things—not permanently, but just so I can help her out for the Oscars, too.' I was glad to share the secret with someone. 'But I don't know—it's a bit nuts working for her, to be honest.'

'You don't say.' He rolled his eyes. 'You didn't seriously think it wouldn't be, did you? Sharp tool like you, Amber Green?'

I chuckled. 'I don't know what I thought. But the question is, can I handle any more?'

I sat on an unopened box in the stockroom, not feeling like rushing back upstairs yet.

'Cuppa?'

'Ooh, yeah—builder's, please.'

'I might be able to stretch to a Hobnob, too, if you're lucky.' He smiled and moved skilfully between the boxes stacked in small piles around the floor. But before he disappeared behind the screen in front of the makeshift kitchenette, he stopped, resting an arm on top of the wobbly divider. From here, he looked around the windowless room, taking it all in: the half-opened boxes and rails of clothes still covered in protective polythene wrappers; the wall of shoeboxes stacked on top of each other like oversized bricks. The low ceiling and lack of windows made it feel oppressive. The hours I'd spent unpacking clothes and steaming them down here came flooding back. Alan let out a sigh.

'I'm in this room hours at a time, six days a week,' he

said at last. 'I know every crack on the walls, all the areas of peeling paint that need touching up. I've changed every frigging light bulb, several times over. I open boxes after deliveries—and then when they're empty I flat-pack them and put them with all the other boxes I've flat-packed, out the back. I do it over and over again, week after week.' I kept quiet. 'There's got to be more adventure to be had from life than this. Don't you think, kid?'

I didn't need to answer. Alan had given me everything I needed to make my decision.

* * *

Back upstairs, I could tell by her slightly agitated tone that Mona was itching for her mid-afternoon caffè macchiato. Remembering what happened last time, I offered to run and fetch it. Just as I flung my coat and scarf back on, the Stick finally acknowledged my presence.

'Wait a sec,' she called, 'I'll come with you.' She pulled a cashmere cape over her head and turned to Jas. 'If you're okay here for ten minutes?'

'You can grab me a copy of *Drapers* while you're out,' Jas replied.

Bewildered, I held open the door and we walked down South Molton Street side by side. I was blowed if I was going to break the ice after the way she'd seen me off when we last walked up this street together, so for a while we strolled in silence.

'So, how's it been?' she asked finally, itching to pump me for information as we turned onto Brook Street. But her demeanour remained as ice-cold as the temperature.

'Good, but pretty full-on,' I replied, unsure how much to give away. The last thing we needed was for her to be blogging or Tweeting my gossip from 'a source inside Mona's camp'. 'The Globes were a success, and Jennifer Astley is lovely.'

'Everyone's been talking about Mona's breakdown at the party,' she scoffed, clearly pleased to have the opportunity to pick a hole.

'It wasn't as bad as it sounded,' I shot back. Well, it was partially true. *The puke missed the bag, didn't it?* 'Mona's asked me to stay on with her,' I added. It just came out. The Stick silently digested what I'd said, while I convinced myself that I might as well be upfront about the fact I was unlikely to be back in Smith's on Monday morning. Her expression suddenly changed, the chilled attitude replaced by curiosity.

'So what are you going to do?'

'I'm not sure yet. I'll probably do it, but I want to talk it over with Jas first.' We ordered the coffees in Caffè Nero and waited for them together, both lost in our own thoughts. I wondered what she was plotting. The Stick was always plotting. She picked at her matte black nails.

'What do *you* think I should do?' I asked a few minutes later, as we left the cafe and headed back towards the shop, the Stick staring intently into the white, plastic lid on top of her coffee.

'Do whatever you feel is right.' Then she stopped and turned to me. 'I just have to say, what you did to me wasn't fair, Amber. The shoes in the window were blatantly a mistake. And you don't care about fashion like I do. You don't even own a McQueen skull scarf, for God's sake. You should have stepped aside and offered me the job. I taught you everything you know about fashion.'

For a few seconds, nagging guilt washed through me. *Maybe I should just step aside now?* But something made me resist. Besides, Vicky had got me into fashion way before I even met the Stick.

'The shoes weren't a mistake, actually,' I said. My skin prickled, but didn't give anything away. 'Listen, if Mona needs an extra pair of hands while we're in London, I'll put your name forward,' I offered. 'That's the best I can do.'

'How generous,' she huffed, before pulling up her hood, signalling she didn't want to discuss it any more.

Thankfully we had picked the closest coffee place to the shop, so we didn't have to endure any more time in each other's company and I didn't have to tell any more lies. Kiki stopped by the newsagent to pick up Jas's magazine.

'I'll see you back, can't give Mona tepid coffee.'

* * *

As I entered Smith's, Mona and Jas came up from conversation. I noticed the full rail between them; there were some very sheer gowns I assumed had been selected for Miss P.

'Loving this, Amber,' Mona said, holding up a daring, barely there black creation that had more cutaway panels than actual fabric—only a couple of swirls covered the essential areas.

'Mona's just been telling me how brilliant you were with Jennifer Astley last weekend,' Jas said, ever the thoughtful boss.

'It was luck, really.' I smiled, secretly wishing the Stick was hearing this.

'Anyway, haven't you got a date to be getting to, babe?' Mona said, winking at Jas. 'Love bloomed in LA for this one, you know.'

I squirmed. Jas laughed in disbelief. 'For Amber? Well, I never. I thought you looked glowing!'

'Oh, she's glowing all right,' Mona added, elbowing me.

This was like being humiliated by two extremely well-dressed, crazy aunts.

'You go meet lover boy,' Mona ordered, now holding the door open for me.

'He's not my—well, as I haven't taken my coat off yet...' I smiled. I was itching to get going.

'Meet me in Soho House later on, I'll text when I'm there,' she continued. 'Bye now. Go!'

Just as I looped my scarf around my neck again, the Stick came back through the open door.

'I'll call you, Jas,' I promised, and left them to it, my heart racing at the prospect of meeting Rob and clearing things up over Liam. Discussing Mona's offer with Jas would just have to wait.

* * *

There he was, in the window of Pret A Manger. I took a few paces back, snatching a look at my reflection in a shop window and hurriedly running my fingers through my hair to swish it up. It was really good to see him again, just the two of us. I'd known Rob for less than a fortnight, but being in LA together made it feel that we'd shared so much. Spotting me, he seemed a little agitated, jumping off a stool and dusting some bits of croissant off the one next to him, before motioning for me to sit down. I felt fresh embarrassment for the bad kiss he'd witnessed.

'I ordered us both a hot chocolate, hope that's okay.' He nudged a paper cup towards me. This wasn't exactly the most thrilling location for our reunion, but it would do. 'And thanks for this,' he said, as though I was doing him a big favour just by turning up. His tone puzzled me slightly.

'It's fine, it's great to see you. Thanks for the drink.' I thought of the twinkles text again. I wondered if he remembered that evening as vividly as I did. It seemed funny that out there we were drinking Bellinis at amazing parties and here we were, back in the real world, sipping hot chocolate in Pret.

'It won't take long,' he continued, his voice faltering. 'It's just that I wanted to get your opinion, your being a stylist and everything.' He delved into his pocket for something. Why was he acting so nervy? He was making me feel on edge, too.

'Don't tell me you've been hitting the Primark sales,' I teased. 'Have you bought some really bad-taste jumpers you want me to tell you have to go back?'

'Ha—not quite.'

'A bargain's not a bargain if you don't actually like it in the first place,' I said.

I caught sight of a slightly crumpled pale turquoise bag peeking out of his deep coat pocket. Typical boy—not wanting to be seen carrying around anything so dainty and pretty. Some shop bags are almost as precious as their contents, and this was one of them. Yes, this bag was easily recognisable by its colour alone. It was a Tiffany bag, the holy grail of special-occasion jewellery. I watched in confusion as he hurriedly untied the pretty matching ribbon and pulled out a small box from inside. *Why is he showing me a beautiful little Tiffany box? He's not proposing to me in Pret, is he? He saw me snogging another guy and now he wants to put a ring on my finger? Surely not.* I felt breathless, slightly panicked, yet strangely elated at the same time.

He looked around to check we weren't being overlooked, and then he slowly, carefully, teased open the box. There, between us, twinkling brightly as the shop lights caught its perfectly cut edges, was the most beautiful sparkling diamond engagement ring I had ever seen in my life—well, ever since my sister showed me hers seven years ago and it reduced me to tears. The brilliant stone was cradled in a tapered platinum band. It was exquisite in its simplicity. A huge lump rose to my throat. I felt sick.

'Wow,' was all I could muster. Then I looked up at him, and in a heartbeat I realised that he was definitely not proposing to me.

'So you like it?' he asked, his expression intensely earnest. My stomach flipped as he searched my face for a response.

'You mean, will *she* like it?' I said, trying as hard as I could to stop my voice from trembling.

'Well, yes, that's the idea.' His shoulders dropped. 'I'm not proposing to a man, Amber. I thought we'd cleared that up.'

I made a pathetic attempt at a grin.

'She'll love it,' I finally managed to gasp, in as normal a voice as I could muster, trying to pretend that I didn't really want to get off this chair and run away. *How could I have not known he has a girlfriend—a serious girlfriend that he's planning to propose to? How could I have been so stupid? So* bloody *stupid?*

'It's not too simple?' he asked. 'Or too obvious? I felt like such a cliché in there.'

'Not at all. It's beautiful—a classic.' I looked at it again. The sick feeling had returned with a vengeance. My physical response startled me. This was the kind of ring I would choose for myself, if I was ever able to. Half of me wanted to swipe it out of its stupid, perfect little box and throw it across Pret. Perhaps a homeless person would find it—

someone who *really* needed it. Tears began to build up behind my eyes. I excused myself for the loo.

As I washed my hands I took a moment to stare at my pathetic, crestfallen face in the mirror—it was one of those fake mirrors that made your head appear contorted. Holding my hands to my cheeks, I looked a bit like Edvard Munch's *The Scream*, and screaming was exactly what I felt like doing. I wondered why they put these unhelpful fake mirrors in public toilets. To stop suicide attempts?

It hit me all at once: I felt strongly for this guy, this bloke I'd only known for a short space of time but with whom I'd shared so much. Vicky could see it, even someone as self-obsessed as Mona could see it. So why couldn't I? I guess a little part of me had hoped that he might make a move on me; tell me that I was the person he'd been searching for and create a Hollywood-style happy ending for us. Of course I would have reciprocated if he'd tried to kiss me on that terrace on Golden Globes night. But no, the Tinseltown fairy tale was well and truly shattered into a billion little pieces now.

Things started falling into place; *Rob was just being friendly when he invited me out on Globes night. He'd never really answered the 'girlfriend' question, so I couldn't complain he'd led me on. The 'twinkles' text was just his way of being matey. And when he saw me with Liam in Starbucks? It didn't bother him in that way at all. He probably found it as funny as Fran and Shaggy clearly did. In fact he probably thinks that's how I normally kiss!* I felt such a gargantuan fool for letting a little part of myself dare to imagine I might mean anything more to Rob. It felt as though I'd taken a bullet to the heart.

I shook my head and the ugly reflection did the same.

Why are you so rubbish with boys, Amber Green? A 'car crash' when it comes to relationships, as Vicky had once helpfully pointed out, congratulating herself on yet another name-based pun at my expense. But the label had stuck in my mind. It was no coincidence my mother bought me a double electric blanket for Christmas, considerately pointing out that it was 'perfect for you, Amber, because it has an energy-saving facility—you can turn one side off'. *Thanks, Mum. I'm destined to sleep in a single bed forever.*

I'd been in the loo for five minutes now and the last thing I wanted was to give Rob the impression something was wrong, or that I had a dicky tummy. I took a deep breath and mentally pulled myself together. *I'm going to go out there and congratulate him properly, like a good 'mate' should.* I even spared a thought for whether Hallmark made cards to mark this kind of occasion—'Good luck with the proposal! Hope she says no!' I wondered what Rob's imminent fiancée might be like—was she Cambridge-educated, fashionable, blessed with a cute button nose, dainty feet and a high metabolism? I decided my best tactic was to act not bothered.

* * *

'So how are the BAFTAs shaping up?' he asked when I returned, seemingly also keen to change the subject, and thank God he didn't move it onto Liam.

'Quiet,' I said. 'I'm a bit worried about it, but Mona seems confident things always happen at the last minute.' I'd wondered if we were feeling the repercussions of sick-gate— if the stylist had become more infamous than her clothes. 'Anyway, I've got to go and meet her at Soho House now. She's just asked me to work with her until after the Oscars.'

'Do it! I'll be out there, too, we'll have some fun,' he said, eyes shining—the eyes that I had a crushing feeling I was falling in love with. 'If you thought the Globes were mad, you ain't seen nothing yet.'

'Will you be filming Mona still?' I asked, knowing my boss was unlikely to give me any details until the last minute.

'It's up for discussion.' Rob fiddled with the rim of his cardboard cup. 'I'll be with Tim, mostly. But it'll be much more fun working with her again if you're there—you made it all happen in LA.' He was beginning to relax into the old Rob again—I didn't like the nervous, nearly engaged version. But the thought of LA already felt infinitely less fun knowing that Rob would be there, clearly marked 'taken'. LA Liam was a poor substitute, though I did momentarily wonder if it was possible to find previously deleted contacts on an iPhone. *Perhaps the distraction will do me good.* Then a hideous thought crept into my mind. *Next, Rob will be asking for my advice about what he should wear to get married. Even worse, maybe* she'll *be in LA, too, the Tiffany ring on her slender finger, smiling smugly, like the luckiest girl on the fucking planet.* I definitely wasn't going to send him a friend request now. It would be far, far too painful.

'Anyway, when are you planning to do the deed?' I asked, trying my best to look sincere.

'Not sure—when the time feels right. I might wait a few weeks. We'll see. So you've got to keep it a secret, okay?'

'Safe with me!' I faked a smile and put my scarf on again. I needed fresh air.

* * *

As I walked to Soho House to meet Mona, I called my mum, desperate to hear a comforting voice.

'Darling! Dad and I were just talking about you, in fact—hold on a minute—Richard!' I had to move the phone away from my ear. I'd forgotten what a piercingly loud shout my mother had.

'Amber?' Dad picked up another receiver. I hated three-way calls.

'Hi, Dad.'

'I'm still here, too!'

'Hi, Mum.'

'We were wondering if you'd got back safely, and what was going on with that Rhona woman?'

'It's Mona.'

'Nora's concert was so sweet last night—honestly, your sister and I could barely hold it together when she did her solo!'

'Like gibbering wrecks they were, snivelling into their sleeves,' Dad laughed. 'But anyway, tell us about your trip. Did you meet Michael Caine? He won something, didn't he?'

'He did indeed, Dad, good skills, but no, afraid I didn't get to meet him. I didn't actually go to the awards—we watched them on TV.'

'You flew all the way to Los Angeles to watch an awards ceremony on television?' Mum sounded flabbergasted. 'I've told the whole of the firm you were there!'

'What Mona does is more behind-the-scenes—dressing people for the red carpet,' I explained. There was silence on the other end while they took this in.

'Can't they dress themselves?' Dad asked eventually. 'Honestly, do these people have someone to do everything for them? Do they never have to think for themselves?'

'I don't expect you to get it, Dad, but there's a lot more to it than putting someone's head through a jumper.'

'Yes, Richard, it's *high fashion*,' said Mum.

'But it went really well, and Mona's asked me to stay on

with her for a bit longer to help her through the BAFTAs and the Oscars, too.'

The conversation swung to the inevitable. 'Well, I hope she's paying you handsomely for all this jetting about?'

'Not sure yet—I'm about to meet her to talk through the logistics.'

'Well, don't sell yourself short, girl, or she'll have me to answer to.'

'Okay, Mum, I'll let you know. Listen, I'd better go, I'm nearly there.'

'All right, darling, but when will we see you?'

'Hopefully this week, once the BAFTAs are over, I'll come round. Can we have a roast?'

'I'll get your dad on to it.' The words felt as good as a hug.

'Amazing, love you.'

'Love you, too,' they both said in unison.

'Oh and Nora's got a recital next Wednesday, perhaps you'll make it this time?' Mum added.

'I'll try. Bye.'

* * *

When I reached Soho House, I felt frozen to the bone. The Christmas glitz had been stripped from the streets, and now it was just cold, grey and on the verge of snowing. Only this wouldn't be the lovely fluffy white stuff that falls in the countryside—it would be the London snow that turns into grey sludge as soon as it lands, bringing the public transport system to an immediate halt. Snow doesn't have any benefits at all in London, unless, of course, you live near Primrose Hill and have time to Instagram photos of yourself making snow angels all day long. It was getting colder, seemingly by the second. The thought of the warm LA breeze was definitely appealing.

Mona had secured a spot in the Circle Bar and there were two glasses of champagne on the table in front of her, one nearly drained. A candle burned enticingly. It was cosy, warm and conducive to celebration.

'So, how was cute Rob, babe—has he made a lunge for you yet?' she asked, direct as usual, as I pulled off my layers and laid them down on an empty part of the bench seat next to us. I felt glad that she hadn't witnessed the lunge event a couple of days ago. I'd never live it down.

'Not exactly,' I said, reaching for my drink. Alcohol was exactly what I needed right now.

'Well, have you lunged for him, then?'

'Not after today,' I sighed, necking a healthy glug.

'Don't tell me he's gay—what a waste!'

'Worse,' I replied. 'He's about to get engaged. He showed me the Tiffany ring he's bought her.'

'Tiffany? For the love of Lanvin, how obvious,' she scoffed. 'The poor girl.' Sometimes I had to love Mona. On this occasion she managed to say exactly what I needed to hear. A waitress passed and Mona ordered a bottle of champagne.

'I thought we'd celebrate tonight,' she declared, taking me aback.

'Did Jennifer come good for the BAFTAs?'

'She did indeed.' She smiled, as the waitress plonked two fresh glasses on the table. 'Caroline called this afternoon. She's flying in tomorrow and wants to wear the Valentino, easy-peasy. I've said you'll swing by the Dorchester on Sunday morning to see what we can do accessories-wise.'

'This is great news!' It also meant that there would surely be cash coming in—money was playing heavily on my mind. 'But what about Miss P? I thought you needed me to assist with her on Sunday?'

'Leave her to me,' she instructed. 'Anyway—there's something else we need to toast this evening.' Bang on cue, the waitress filled our glasses with fizzing cold champagne. I lifted mine in anticipation. 'I had a little chat with Jas, after you left,' she continued. 'And she said she'd be more than happy for you to continue on with me for the next few weeks. It'll all be done in just over a fortnight and you can go back to your little London life. Isn't that great news?'

I was horrified she'd gone behind my back. I didn't know what to say as she lifted her glass to meet mine. I felt furious she'd taken the decision for me, leaving me with no control over my own life. *What if I'd decided against it? And what about my money?*

'But I thought we were going to talk about it some more?' I said, feeling my cheeks sizzle. I hated confrontation, especially with someone as up and down as Mona.

'What more is there to discuss?' She wasn't having any of it. 'Come on, Amber, babe, it's a no-brainer. And forget Rob. You'll feel better after another glass.'

Chapter Seventeen

We sat together, feeling worlds apart. Mona was gazing around the room, picking at her fingernails, fiddling with her zips, chatting about the upholstery on the seats; anything but invite questions about my wages. She made eye contact occasionally, to check whether I was looking at her pretending not to look at me. But tonight I didn't feel like being a total pushover. The knock I'd taken from Rob had given me the guts to stand up for myself—not to let ambiguity rule the day. If only I'd known he had a girlfriend, I could probably have stopped myself from feeling so hurt. Vicky was right, I should have stalked him on Facebook. Besides, my rent was a pressing issue and I needed to know where I stood.

'So about the money for the flights—are you okay to transfer it first thing tomorrow, please, Mona?' For once I resisted the urge to fill the awkward hush hanging in the air between us as I waited for a response.

'I found my purse,' she replied at last. 'It must have fallen out of my bag during the premiere party.' *The 'sick party', how could I forget?*

'Great, so we're set? And for the new job, will I be paid more than the work experience rate of fifty pounds a week? My rent is due now, and I can't ask my flatmate to sub me. It would be humiliating to have to ask my parents.' *Stay firm, Amber.*

'I'll see what I can do,' she replied eventually, and gazed in the opposite direction, her eyes hunting for the waitress. Silence descended again. But I was ready to boil over now.

'I'm sorry, Mona,' I began, voice trembling, 'but you've already accepted a job on my behalf—a job that will turn my life upside down for the next few weeks. I've had to fork out for flights I can't afford, plus I haven't received the pay owed to me for the last fortnight. The least you can do is transfer my money in the morning, like you said you would.' I took another large gulp of champagne. She just sat there, motionless. *Why is she being so evasive?* I was enraged.

'Is there any problem with paying me?' I pressed. 'I think I deserve to know if there is.'

Still no response. *I have to finish what I've started now, I've got no choice.*

'I've seen the pile of unopened bills in your office, you know. And I heard the message from the loans company.' Mona's face did not reveal a flicker of acknowledgement. I necked another mouthful, finishing off my glass. If she didn't say something soon, I was preparing to storm out. But first, buoyed by the alcohol, it was time to pull out the big guns. 'My mother's a lawyer, you know.'

Finally, a glimmer of vulnerability: 'How did you hear about the loan?' she asked, her tone calm, measured.

'Your phone, on the day of the Globes. I had to listen

to your messages so I could sort out Jennifer and get the gowns to the right clients, because you were…recovering. Remember?'

A solitary tear formed in one of her eyes and hovered there for a few seconds. I stayed very still, physically almost unable to move. Then I handed her a napkin from the table and she dabbed at the corners of her eyes, embarrassed.

'It's okay,' I offered, a pang of guilt shooting through me for having caused a grown woman to weep in the middle of Soho House. 'If there's a problem, perhaps I can help you with it? I am your assistant after all.'

'I've not talked about this before,' she muttered, her bottom lip beginning to tremble. 'It's hard.'

'I'm happy to listen.' I shuffled a bit closer.

As a group of men entered the bar, looking in our direction, Mona reached into her bag for her sunglasses. I noticed actual big, hot tears falling from Mona Armstrong's eyes and plopping onto her leather jacket. She wasn't made of steel after all.

Is she having a breakdown before my eyes? Oh, how I wished I had one of Beau's scripts for what to say. I shuffled up the bench seat, leaning in, wondering whether to put my arm around her, as I naturally would if I saw anyone other than Mona so upset. I grabbed another napkin. The tears were really falling now and I suddenly saw her in a completely different way. She looked so defenceless.

'Jesus, you must think I'm going down the Britney Spears path,' she scoffed at last, pulling back her hair and sitting up straighter. Crying wasn't in line with Mona's image.

Tentatively, I placed a hand on her arm. 'Nah, you're much cooler than Britney ever was.'

She made a feeble attempt to laugh, before sighing. 'I *was*.'

'Then what happened?' I asked, softly.

'Oh, Amber, you're so young. You won't understand.'

'Try me,' I said.

Her breathing was erratic, like a child who's cried for too long. I could almost hear her brain turning over as she internally debated whether to unlock the door. In the silence, I tried a different tack.

'Maybe there are things I could help you with?' I said, trying to sound more upbeat. She slipped her feet in and out, out and in of her Chanel ballet pumps, balancing one shoe on her big toe. We both looked at it sticking out from under the table.

'Like the box of paperwork under the desk in LA?' I said, instantly panicking that I'd overstepped the line. She didn't respond. 'My mum—she's a lawyer, you know,' I said again, but this time with a different motive. 'If you need legal advice, maybe she could help?'

'Oh, it's all bullshit!' she cried, sending the shoe falling to the ground.

'Everything okay here?' A waitress approached. 'Another drink, maybe?'

'Two double vodka tonics,' Mona said. The canyon reappeared between us as we waited for them to arrive.

'Sometimes,' she began, 'I just want to be your age again, rest my head on someone's shoulder and let them make some decisions for once—let them open the bills, pull the clothes, suck up to the celebrities and designers, and deal with it all. I keep telling myself it'll get easier, and the money will start rolling in, but then another red carpet, another premiere, another awards season, another year passes—and what do I have to show for it?' She looked at my blank face. 'I'll tell you what I have,' she continued, 'endless bouquets of beautiful fucking flowers, designer handbags, enough scented candles to open a small concession in Harrods and some dresses even Anna Wintour would sell her children for. But what about the cold, hard cash? The stuff that will actually stop the bailiffs and the loans companies from calling?' I let out a sigh. Vicky had been right.

'I'm broke, Amber—isn't it clear to see? If I had my way right now, I'd go to sleep and never wake up. I'm buried alive in bills and unpaid loans, and I don't have the energy for it any more.' She held her head in her hands and started crying again. 'And I don't know what to do.'

I placed a cautious hand on top of her mound of curls. She came up for a second to throw down her sunglasses and then hid her face in her folded arms on top of the table. She stayed there, sobbing, for a few moments. The bartender gave us a strange look. My mind was racing.

'But what about the clients—Beau, Jennifer? They pay you, right?'

She lifted herself up and replaced her shades, before anyone else noticed her eye make-up had made a bid for freedom. 'Oh, their management or the film companies pay some of my expenses—the odd flight, hotel bill and the like—but most of them think the honour of my being able to say they're my clients is payment enough. It's crass to discuss money in the circles I move in. Everybody thinks everyone else is swimming in it, but the designer clothes on my back mean jack shit.'

I exhaled loudly. I had to admit I had Mona down as someone 'swimming in it', too. Didn't you have to be, to live in a Hollywood mansion with a pool?

'But your house in LA—it must be worth a fortune?' I said.

'My divorce,' she scoffed, without taking her eyes off her

nearly drained glass. 'Only thing the bastard gave me was to live rent-free, with a housekeeper, in that prison. He owns it, Ana keeps it clean and tidy, and I'll never make a penny from it. But at least I have a roof over my head. At least I'm not completely destitute. Wonderful!' She clapped her hands together sarcastically. The house wasn't exactly somewhere I'd describe as a prison, but this wasn't the time to argue.

'Can he help you at all?' I asked.

She puffed out her cheeks. 'We haven't spoken in ten years and I'm not about to start.'

'What about Clive?' I asked, shocked by what I was hearing.

'Clive sent me this charming watch, but can I use it to pay your wages? No pawnshop wants this season's Michael Kors ladies' timepiece until it's become an antique. It's a frigging joke!' She snorted into the napkin and then looked me straight in the eye. 'I'm counting my last shekels, Amber. I'm bankrupt.'

Bankrupt. The word sounded so scary and final. It also meant I was unlikely to see a refund for the flights or the money to pay my rent until it was sorted out.

'Listen, I'm not an accountant, but I think I might be able to help you,' I suggested. Even I knew that a situation involving bailiffs, loans companies and bankruptcy was not something that would go away of its own accord, and the last thing Mona needed was for this to become news in itself. I was starting to feel sorry for her—she seemed so completely alone. 'We'll make sure we go through every single bill in the basket in LA—we'll do it together. It might even be—fun?' That last comment caused both of us to titter slightly hysterically. 'Well, it won't be fun, but it's necessary,' I corrected myself. 'And in the meantime, why don't we take some of your most amazing gifted clothes—' her eyebrows shot up in alarm '—the ones that you hardly ever wear, I mean, to one of those designer sale shops? They'll think Christmas has come round again, and you'll make a tidy sum. That will help tide us over through the BAFTAs, anyway.' I pulled a notepad from my bag. Surely a list would sort out everything. 'Here, let's make a note of everything you could sell.'

'We'll have to go to my lock-up,' Mona snivelled, wiping at a clump of mascara that had settled beneath her right eye. I sucked the top of the pen. *We must be talking a treasure trove if she needs a whole lock-up for her discarded designer wardrobe.*

'Fine. Do you have the key?' She nodded in response. 'Great, we can do that tomorrow and then focus on the BAFTAs on Sunday.'

She seemed a bit perkier after we had made a rough list of the bits she could bear parting with. Three classic Chanel handbags would easily set us up for the immediate future and there were dresses by Zac Posen, Azzedine Alaia, Hervé Léger and Christian Dior—all unworn—a Balmain wool cape, plus a couple of Bvlgari bangles that came to mind, all off the top of her head. I was confident we wouldn't go short.

The throng around the bar had thinned as it approached midnight, and with Mona all cried out and drunk, and my eyelids barely able to hold themselves open, I asked for the bill and put it on my card. By some miracle it didn't get declined. I hadn't quite worked out what we'd do if it did. I decided to use the last of the cash in my purse to put Mona into a taxi.

'Where to?' asked the driver. I realised I didn't have a clue where she lived.

'Mona—your address?' I repeated, loudly, praying she wouldn't pass out.

'Travelodge,' she slurred, almost lying flat across the back seat. 'Barking.'

I put the forty pounds remaining in my purse into the driver's palm before begging him to get her home for not a penny more, and shut the passenger door. Then I pulled my scarf up around my ears for the frosty walk to the tube. If I hurried, I'd make the last train. *Mona, living at a Travelodge, in Barking?* Nothing more could shock me this evening.

When I got home the flat was silent and Vicky's bedroom door closed, indicating she was either asleep or entertaining. I pressed my ear to the door and was relieved to hear her quietly snoring. I'd been half-expecting to find her with her head in a bag of chips, just back from another drinking session somewhere in central London. It had crossed my mind to call her on the way home and I would have, had I not been so exhausted by the evening's revelations and desperate to be reunited with my bed. I hadn't failed to notice that Vicky had been either tipsy or full-blown drunk almost every evening since I could pretty much remember. But who was I to talk? *Jesus, what a day.*

* * *

Next morning I was woken by the sound of a mug of tea being clunked down on my bedside table, loud enough to wake a sleeping log. Bleary-eyed, I looked up to see Vicky, hair in a topknot, bright-eyed and bushy-tailed.

'Left you as long as I could, but it's nearly ten and I know you've got the Miss P fitting today,' she said, looking way too together for my foggy brain to deal with. 'I didn't want you to oversleep, because you're doing this job for the both of us, remember?'

'I am? What day is it?' I croaked.

'Saturday, honey. Do you want some eggs?'

'Saturday,' I repeated, looking at her, uncharacteristically smart for a Saturday, in a structured black dress and the chunky gold choker she'd bought the other day. 'You look amazing—but why so posh? Are you due in court for something?'

'Silly! I'm coming with you to see Miss P.' She smiled. 'Oh, please let me, it's the weekend and I'm dying to meet Mona. I thought I'd better look the part,' she begged, registering my confused expression.

The memory of last night began flooding back. It made me feel even more queasy. I reached for my phone. One new message, and it was from Rob. I pushed myself up, fumbling to squish the pillows behind my back.

'Do you think she'll rate my dress?' Vicky was far too alert this morning. I think I preferred her hungover. 'It's by a hot new designer, Star-Crossed, a graduate—we're featuring her in this month's mag. I thought Mona might be interested.' I recognised the name from Smith's and Jas's 'ones to watch' rail, but right now I was distracted.

'Rob's going to propose to his girlfriend,' I sighed.

'He *what*?'

'Long story, but let's just say yesterday was a nightmare, and I'm an idiot for not realising he's taken.'

I tried to focus on the phone and Rob's message: So how did it go with Mona—are you coming back to LA? x

I flung the phone on top of the duvet.

'I'm totally over men, too,' Vicky said, thankfully not reminding me of the fact I should have stalked him on Facebook and that she had guessed I fancied him before I'd admitted it to myself. 'Anyway—eggs?'

'Yes, please.'

She left the room and I wiped the sleep from my eyes. I didn't actually know what I was meant to be doing today, but my vague memory was that we were putting Miss P's styling session off until tomorrow and instead going to Mona's lock-up to sell some of her clothes for cash. The BAFTAs were little more than twenty-four hours away, though, so we didn't have much time. I called Mona to check and the phone rang out. It really didn't help that my head, yet again, felt like it was in a vice. *Another thing I had Mona to thank for.*

'So, why are you off men, too?' I asked, as I sat at the kitchen table waiting for Vicky to present me with breakfast: two slices of thick-cut granary toast, topped with smoked salmon and a heap of creamy scrambled eggs, with two paracetamol tablets on the side. I eyed it suspiciously. This was unlike Vicky. 'Ten out of ten for presentation, but what have I done to deserve this?' I asked, necking the pills.

'I had an epiphany last night,' Vicky said, sprinkling parsley over our plates. 'As a result, I've decided to stop drinking for a while. It was making everything cloudy and I was doing things the sober me wouldn't do.' She registered the concern on my face. 'It's cool, I'm cool, I just need to focus on other things for a bit. You know?'

I nodded solemnly, wondering if Simon's comments about her being 'too drunk' had anything to do with it.

'I'm proud of you, I mean that,' I said, horribly aware of my own splitting headache. 'Cheers to that, my friend!' I held up my mug and we chinked.

* * *

True to her word for once, Mona soon sent an email containing the address of a Big Yellow Self Storage Company depot in Kennington. I took this as a positive sign, but decided to take Vicky along, too, for backup (and because she begged me). I could see that cajoling Mona into parting with some of her best-loved fashion items might be harder work in the cold light of day—and perhaps she wouldn't sack me if we had company. But she had shown such vulnerability last night, I felt she needed me now. And, strangely, I wanted to help. Though crestfallen having to change out of the fashion-forward LBD for our trip to the lock-up, Vicky was buzzing about the opportunity to hang out with my much-fabled boss. She alerted her followers on a number of social networks that she was spending the day with 'fashion royalty'.

Miraculously, Mona was pleasant all afternoon. It seemed that last night had actually brought us closer. She greeted Vicky warmly, making her entire year by commenting on how much she loved her vintage biker jacket, before throwing herself into the unpacking of boxes and suitcases containing her wardrobe overspill. She had even dressed appropriately, and the jeans, pumps and baggy Acne sweat-shirt really suited her; she looked prettier, more human. For three hours solid we worked, taking our orders from Mona about which box to put where and giving her a few moments alone when she came across a suitcase containing her Galliano wedding dress, made for her by the young up-and-coming designer eighteen years ago. She didn't even pause to scream for a macchiato (though I had already cased out the storage company's refreshment offerings and ruled out anything as suitable for Mona, except for the chewing gum).

'She's so sweet!' Vicky gushed, when we were left on our own. 'I don't know what you've been complaining about.'

'Sweet' was a word I never would have used to describe Mona ordinarily, but it really seemed as though she'd turned into a different person overnight; she appeared relieved to be doing something to help herself and got into the spirit of turning her niche wardrobe to her financial advantage.

As the three of us worked on unpacking cases, we were soon surrounded by teetering piles of expensive shoes; a rack of jaw-dropping; barely worn designer gowns, coats and tops; and a box overflowing with some incredible costume jewels. Some of it had clearly been residing here, in a dusty storage container, for years. Both of us were enthralled by the stories accompanying some of the items— like the pillar-box-red vintage Yves Saint Laurent suit Mona was allowed to keep after wearing it to the wedding of Liza Minnelli and David Gest, the pale blue Christian Dior gown she was given by the design house following success at the Oscars with Charlize Theron, and a joyful silk floral Cavalli maxi, gifted to her to wear on one of the infamous trips aboard Roberto's yacht in Cannes. Every dress held an enchanting 'Cinderella' tale, captivating to hear.

* * *

As the end of the day approached, Mona's final selection bagged up, Vicky had to exert all her mental strength not to offer Mona her life's savings for a quarter of it. Leaving Mona to lock up, Vicky and I peeled off to drop three hefty suitcases of her former belongings at a luxury designer seconds shop on the New Kings Road, figuring we'd get the best prices in an upmarket area. Mona had sensibly decided it wasn't advisable for her to come along, too, in case the shop assistant leaked the story to a gossip site.

The assistant gasped when she laid eyes on our wares, and immediately called for her manager, who very nearly had a coronary on seeing a haul of this quality. We were almost rendered speechless ourselves when they offered us the grand total of four thousand, three hundred and eighty

English pounds in cash for the whole lot. I was sure they must have been quietly congratulating themselves on driving the bargain of the century, but it sounded like a good enough deal to us and would more than cover the money Mona owed me, plus our expenses for the next week; maybe more, if I was careful with the budget. Besides, we didn't have time to peddle the goods around town. There was also something profoundly rewarding about knowing this sumptuous, dazzling designer gear, that had long since lost its shine for Mona, was waiting to be discovered and transformed into the treasure that someone had been unwittingly searching for their entire life.

Chapter Eighteen

The morning of the BAFTAs arrived, and the weather was terrible. Rain and wind thundered against my bedroom window, making it rattle loudly, and infiltrating an anxiety dream in which I was about to jump off Roberto Cavalli's yacht in the middle of a stormy sea, with no life jacket, only a faux-fur gilet. I was mightily relieved to wake up marooned only on my bed in the middle of my messy bedroom. The weather outside was the kind of grim greyness set to last the entire day. It was the worst kind of red-carpet weather you could imagine. You could almost hear all the specially flown-in Americans sighing in their hotel suites: *Typical British weather.*

* * *

Mona rang at 10:00 a.m. At least her name came up, but the caller was a heavy breather.

'Who is this?' I demanded briskly, following several seconds of wheezing, spluttering and deep breathing on the other end. For one moment my muzzy brain thought that it might be LA Liam trying out a werewolf impersonation for his next audition. A few seconds later I heard a voice that sounded like Mona, but a Mona half-submerged in water with a clothes peg on her nose:

'It's Mona, babe.'

'Mona, it doesn't sound like you at all—are you okay?' *Stupid question.*

'Not really,' she said. She sounded completely blocked up. 'I had the hot sweats in the night and then some unpleasant bowel movements, then I was sick. Ouch!' There was a noise sounding like a limb knocking into something. 'I'm lying down on the bathroom floor. I'm not in a good way, Amber.' More coughing and sniffing to emphasise the point. 'I've got the Norovirus. Must have picked it up in that grotty lock-up. You pick up all kinds of things in horrible places like that. That's why I've avoided it for so long.'

'Have you seen anyone about it?' I probed.

'Doctor's here right now...' Cue a rustling sound. 'Yes, thank you, Doctor—complete bed rest, yes, whatever it takes...' Sometimes you couldn't make her up.

'Do you want me to speak to the doctor?' I offered.

'There's no time, babe—the BAFTAs are tonight.'

'I'm fully aware of that, Mona.' *What the hell is she playing at?*

'Jennifer will be expecting you at the Dorchester, I need you to go and do the BAFTAs with her, Amber. She's wearing the Valentino—she has it with her.' *Yes, thanks to me retrieving the duplicate gown from Beau and having it sent to Caroline for Jennifer.* 'But she needs you there, too, for final tweaks. I've used some of the cash to send a car to pick you up and take you straight there. Maybe your flatmate—what's her name?—could help you. She seemed a capable girl.'

After our trip to the New Kings Road I'd taken the funds owed to me, and given Mona the rest. *Aargh, I hate myself for being so stupid.*

'But what about Miss P? Who's going to style her big moment?' I could feel the all-too-familiar sensation of my stress levels rising. 'I thought we were going to manage them together?' It all felt out of control and on such an important day. *Why is Mona doing this?* I just couldn't fathom what was going on in her head.

'Don't worry about Miss P, I had the gowns sent over to her hotel from Smith's yesterday—her management team will all be there, too. Perhaps you could just pop in on her when you've set up Jennifer?'

'But who's doing the fitting?'

'I don't know yet—leave it with me, just make sure Jen looks incredible. My reputation depends on it. There are plenty of suitable accessories in your suitcase.'

'Do I have a choice?' And before I could proclaim that I wanted to pack in this stupid job and open a coffee stall on a beach in a remote part of Mexico—or Margate, anywhere would do; Lord knows I could make a good caffè macchiato by now—she was gone.

I slowly walked back into the lounge, some new lines no doubt already etched on my face. *I'm too young to be ageing this fast.*

'Mona, I take it?' Vicky could tell from my expression.

'Reckons she's got the Norovirus. Pah! She must think I'm a total idiot.' I folded my arms. 'She wants me to style Jennifer Astley today. Once again she's royally dumped me in it, right at the last minute.'

'But that's great news!' Vicky's face lit up. *She doesn't seem to get it.*

'Er, no—it's really not. She also wants me to pop in on Miss P and I can't be in two places at once. Plus, she's got all the money from the exchange shop. Aargh, Mona! I've never known someone so unreliable. I don't know how she still has a career.'

Vicky grinned. 'She has really amazing assistants, that's how. I'm free today. No Sunday Simon has advantages already, I'll help you—it's going to be amazing, dahling!'

The doorbell went. As Vicky flew downstairs, I paced around trying to calm down and formulate a plan. First up, I supposed I had better get dressed—wearing my big bed T-shirt and old ski socks was not conducive to productivity. Secondly, I would sort through the case and pick out some bits to take to Jennifer. At least the gown was a definite; I just had to take accessories and make sure no one was allowed within a mile of her if they were holding any kind of liquid.

Vicky was almost out of breath when she reappeared clasping an open brown envelope.

'It was a driver, he dropped this off from Mona—it's full of cash. Says he's gone to fill up and will be back in half an hour to take us to the Dorchester. Come on, girl, we've got a date with Jennifer Astley. I can't believe I just said that! Man, today's going to be more fun than I've had in ages!' And she skipped off to her room.

* * *

After showering, I changed into my grey Hudson skinny jeans, a black sweater and comfy Uggs, adding a Kenneth Jay Lane gold tiger cuff borrowed from the case at the last moment. We were meeting a Hollywood superstar after all.

Then I went through the case, whipping out all the gowns and leaving a sizeable selection of shoes, bags, jewellery and some spare lingerie—there were plenty of options to set off the Valentino. Vicky emerged, wearing the same black dress she'd had on yesterday. She gave me a twirl.

'Okay, okay, you look amazing—are you trying to show me up in front of my client?' I felt a twinge of jealousy. The Star-Crossed dress had a statement gold zip at the back and a small, flattering peplum; the vintage necklace from the market went with it perfectly.

'May as well see if Jennifer appreciates it,' she sighed, 'seeing as Mona probably never will.' She smoothed the material over her enviable curves. *Damn my gorgeous flat-mate.* But there was no time for me to swap clothes because in the street below, a car horn sounded.

* * *

When we reached the heavy revolving doors of the Dorchester, there was already a pen of autograph hunters behind railings next to the driveway, ready and waiting to pounce on any emerging megastars. This hotel was a firm favourite with the A-list for the BAFTAs and especially the Americans, who loved its 'quaint' British decor, reminiscent of the 1930s, but boasting all the trappings of a modern, five-star hotel in the heart of Mayfair. The reception was bustling with people checking in, waiting for taxis, looking out for people—or pretending to, while they surreptitiously played 'spot a celebrity'. Bellboys in traditional bottle green uniforms weaved between them, artfully dodging bodies, their trollies stacked with expensive luggage. I spotted Caroline to the side of the lobby waiting for us, wheeled the case towards her and set it down. Vicky hung back. I noticed she hadn't bothered wearing a coat today, despite the weather, so her dress got maximum attention.

'Amber! We're *so* pleased you're here.' Caroline greeted me warmly, both hands clamping on to my arms and a kiss on each cheek. How different to the frosty reception at the Chateau last week. She looked straight through Vicky back towards the doors. 'Where's Mona?'

'Oh. I thought she told you?' I frowned, trying not to look as though I was about to lie. 'She's been struck down with the Norovirus.'

Caroline's expression was blank. 'Norovirus? Is there something wrong with her computer?'

'It's like a serious flu thing,' I explained.'She's bed-bound, on doctor's orders.' Caroline's expression turned to grave concern. 'Oh, it's okay—I mean, she's not going to die or anything. But she can't do anything today, apparently.'

Vicky piped up from over my shoulder: 'Think flu with added sickness and squits.' Caroline registered her for the first time, and gave her a look usually reserved for a bad smell. It clearly wasn't elegant to use a word like 'squits' when standing one degree of separation from the Holly-wood A-list.

'This is Vicky,' I said, by way of an apology. 'She works at *Glamour* magazine and is giving me a hand today. Mona suggested it, seeing as she's unwell. Don't worry, we're both feeling fine, we're not infected.'

Smiling, Vicky offered her hand to Caroline. 'It's lovely to meet you.'

Caroline declined the hand, but clocked Vicky's appearance. 'Gorgeous dress.' She reached forwards to touch the peplum fabric. 'Is it Victoria Beckham?'

'Actually, no, it's by a new designer—Star-Crossed.' It

was incredible to witness how a simple garment could break down barriers.

'Beautifully made, very chic,' said Caroline. 'Anyway, ladies, Jen's in the Harlequin Suite, so we'd best head up—time is ticking.' We set off towards the lifts. 'Oh, meant to check—how's the weather doing out there?' She paused momentarily, neck stretched towards the entrance.

'Still hideous.' We watched the latest flurry of guests being led safely inside under big green Dorchester umbrellas.

'Shitty British weather,' she muttered.

* * *

We were let into the suite by a woman called Nicole, who introduced herself as Jen's publicist. She only had to look for a second too long at my Uggs for me to take the hint that shoes were to be left by the door. Vicky looked peeved to have to remove her stratospheric Steve Madden heels, worn especially to set off the dress. As I resisted the urge to do a running skid along the stately walnut floor, I was glad that for once I wasn't wearing socks with holes in them. A floral scent filled the air and the suite was bathed in a gold, buttery glow from stylish lamps. I peered around some double doors leading to an elegant lounge area, but I couldn't see Jennifer. Vicky quietly followed me, occasionally nudging a finger into my back, presumably to draw attention to the fact that she was as wowed by the place as I was.

Nicole ushered us into the dining room where, under a beautiful crystal chandelier, a round walnut table was awash with every piece of make-up you could possibly imagine. It was as though the entire Mac counter in Selfridges had been transported here and laid out by someone with an extreme case of OCD. On one side were more brushes than

Leonardo da Vinci probably got through in his entire career; next to them was a row of foundations, powders and all kinds of concealer, and beneath that a line of eyeshadows, neatly presented in ascending order from nudes to browns to metallics and pearls. There were at least six different types of mascara, a host of eyeliners and brow definers and a whole other section of lipsticks, cheek stains and powders, plus more tubes of primer and iridescent lotions than the world's most decorated drag queen could possibly know what to do with. In one corner of the room a manicurist was quietly packing up her kit, presumably having just worked her magic on Jen's digits. Next to her, a miniature hair salon had been set up, complete with its own collection of brushes, straighteners and tongs and a free-standing full-length mirror. It was quite unbelievable that all this was needed for just one face.

'This is Caroline's kit,' Nicole explained, as if reading my mind. 'She works from the same palette each time, so they know exactly what they're doing.' *So all this stuff is actually needed?* She gently pulled the French doors together and ushered us in close.

'Here's the thing,' she began, giving me a foreboding sense that once again I was about to be told something I did not want to hear. 'The weather's diabolical out there and, as a result, Jennifer's not feeling the Valentino any more. It's too much of a risk. The fabric is so delicate, it'll only take one wayward drop of rain or splash-back to spoil the look of it completely. She can't be photographed with a sodden hemline or wet patches—it'll ruin everything. And I have to say, I completely agree with her. Remember the year the rain caused the BAFTAs carpet to foam up? It was a skating rink out there. I know, because I was the person patting Kate Winslet dry in photos across the world's media the next morning. And I, for one, don't want to be dealing with a disaster like that again.'

Caroline joined us and nodded in agreement. They both looked at my case. 'Well, let's get her open and see what you have that's more suitable. You brought a steamer, didn't you?'

* * *

Vicky gave a weak smile and looked at the floor. I stared at the case and then back at Vicky. We both knew that the case held no designer gowns, only a myriad of shimmering, sparkling accessories—a magpie's heaven—to set off, beautifully, a certain Valentino gown; a gown that, once again, seemed unlikely to grace the world's stage. *If I were that dress I'd be getting a massive complex right about now.* I took a deep breath and decided to come clean.

'I hear what you're saying but, the thing is, Nicole, I didn't—'

Before I could finish my sentence, Jennifer appeared, making us all stop in our tracks. She wafted into the room with her trademark air of calm—the kind of aura that only the biggest, best celebrities emanate. She was wearing a delicate cream silk dressing gown belted around her waspy waist. She barely looked up—she was blowing on her freshly manicured nails. Her hair had been styled into a neat updo that accentuated her delicate features. As the fingernail-waving subsided, she stopped in front of us. 'How are we getting on, girls?'

'Great!' I said, more loudly than was appropriate.

'Weather's still abysmal, I see.' She moved towards the French doors in the lounge area and we all gravitated into the living room behind her. It was a very pretty suite, light and airy with buttercup-yellow upholstery on ladylike day chairs, a large cream sofa and a white leather pouffe. Minimalist but feminine—a reflection of Jennifer's own clean aesthetic. She stood at the windows, the outline of her slender, willowy frame silhouetted through the gown, every bit as beautiful off-screen as on it. Without turning around, Jennifer spoke again: 'I gather Mona is sick, poor bird.'

'Hmm,' I said in response.

'So I guess Nicole and Caroline have told you I'm worried about the Valentino?' Jennifer continued. Big drops of rain lashed against the window and we all watched as a lone jogger, soaked to the skin in soggy training gear, persevered against the elements in Hyde Park beyond. 'I mean, look— that rain is not going anywhere.' She had a point. 'So, what other pieces do you have for me to try?' She looked at the Cartier watch on her slender wrist. 'Bearing in mind I have to be on the carpet in a few hours.'

'Well,' I began, my voice trembling slightly. 'The thing is, um, I haven't actually… I mean, I was, or rather Mona told me, you were definitely sold on the Valentino. So…' At that moment, Vicky, who had so far remained mute, took it upon herself to step forwards.

'Hi, Jennifer, I mean, Miss Astley,' she said, almost falling into a curtsey at her feet. I looked at my best friend, horrified. *What is she doing?* It had taken us forty minutes in the cab to get from home to the hotel and there wasn't time, let alone a budget, to visit any shops to pick up more dresses—that Jennifer might not like, anyway. *Please, Vicky, I beg you, don't make this worse for me.* Vicky sounded infinitely more confident than I felt.

'I'm Victoria. I'm assisting Amber today,' she said, shooting me a glance that screamed 'Keep your trap shut and let me handle this.'

'And, er, I know it's a little unusual, but we thought it was an idea for me to model this alternative option for you.' She looked down at her dress and smoothed it over her hips. I eyed her in absolute horror. And then she slowly twirled around 360 degrees, gently holding on to the edges of the peplum for added effect. We all watched her and, I had to admit, the dress looked sensational on Vicky's svelte frame—her figure was not unlike Jennifer's, now I came to think of it. Jennifer, Caroline and Nicole all folded their arms.

'It's not Burberry, Roland Mouret, Victoria Beckham, or any designer you will have heard of,' Vicky continued, before anyone could ask. 'But, here in London, we consider ourselves fashion-forward—we like to be trendsetters on the red carpet—and, in all honesty, Amber, myself and—' her voice faltered, but she held it together '—Mona, we all thought you couldn't do better than to wear an emerging London label like Star-Crossed to the awards tonight.' She stopped and stood there, like a model striking a pose on the runway. We all looked her up and down again.

I felt as though a blood vessel might be about to burst on the side of my head. You couldn't deny it was an exquisitely tailored dress, clingy in all the right places; it was sexy but demure, too, hanging just below the knee. It was classic, but with subtle details to create some interest. And best of all, the black crepe fabric would be sure to withstand the most torrential downpour the heavens could throw. There would be no foam or water damage with this little baby. Still nobody said anything.

'I've brought a wide selection of the most stunning accessories to set it off perfectly,' I offered, feeling the need to fill the silence and support my friend. After all, Vicky had provided my *only* life raft. 'I think we should keep it all British—perhaps some gem earrings to add a pop of colour, and a playful Lulu Guinness clutch perhaps. We've some stunning Nicholas Kirkwood sandals—so many options, in fact...' We both stood before the trio, wide-eyed, like two young birds trying not to fall out of the nest. Jennifer's eyes were still glued to Vicky. All of us held our breath.

'Do you know what,' Jennifer began, her expression softening ever so slightly, 'it's not something I would have immediately been drawn to, but I hear exactly what you're saying. London *is* a very different fashion landscape to Los Angeles. Isn't that right, Caroline?'

Caroline stepped forward and spoke: 'And the dress is stunning, I noticed it when I first saw you. I think the girls are onto something, Jen—the British are so patriotic, they love nothing more than shouting about their own. I think it would go down well if you were to wear an emerging Brit to the BAFTAs.' *Go, Caroline! That's three against one.*

We fixed on Nicole, who was standing very still, a finger on her lips as she took her turn to appraise the dress. My phone vibrated from inside my pocket, distracting me. I ignored it, but it rang back immediately. A text from Rob followed: In reception, let me know when's good to come up? x. *In reception?* My eyes nearly popped out of my skull. *Has he tracked me down and come to tell me that the engagement ring was a terrible mistake and he and whatever-her-name-is have split up because he's realised he's fallen in love with me...?* Another text: PS. Fran's getting impatient!

Great. Mona had gone and arranged for the film crew to

come and not bothered to tell me—or, more importantly, to tell them filming was off because she was 'sick'.

'What's up?' Vicky whispered, noticing the panic working its way across my already stressed-out face.

'Even from her sickbed, Mona's managed to cock things up,' I whispered back. 'Rob's downstairs, with the bloody film crew.'

Finally Nicole gave her seal of approval to the dress on Vicky's back. 'I think it could work, too,' she said, stepping forwards to rub some of the peplum fabric between her fingers. 'And this means you could save the Valentino for the big one, Jen. The Oscars are infinitely more dressy than the BAFTAs. And the weather will be better.'

'It will work beautifully with the updo, as well,' Caroline added, gently spraying down a stray strand of hair with the large can of Elnett permanently in her hand.

And so it was decided. Vicky would offer up the actual clothes on her back in the name of saving Jennifer Astley's red-carpet moment.

Then there was a knock at the door.

Chapter Nineteen

I felt a hot flush flow through my body. Standing behind the door was Rob, Fran with the bob and Shaggy, two cases of camera equipment in his hands.

'I've been trying to call, thought you must have your phone on silent,' Rob said. Damn him for being so good-looking, and damn my flushed cheeks.

'Hold on,' I whispered loudly, 'it's just, Mona didn't tell me any filming was planned for today, plus she's not actually here, so we weren't expecting you. And I'm not sure there's going to be time.'

'Psst, Amber!' Vicky's head popped around the bathroom door in the hallway, making the four of us look in her direction. At the end of her bare arm, held in a pincer grip, was the black dress. 'Can you take it to Jennifer, please? I'm kind of—not very *decent* right now.'

'What's going on?' asked Fran, her foot in the door. 'Seems like the perfect opportunity to shoot some footage.'

'Oh—hi,' said Vicky from behind the bathroom door,

as she clocked Rob for the first time and clearly liked what she saw. She offered a limp wave with a bare arm, no doubt practically naked from the neck down. Suddenly Fran was barging past me, into the suite. Thankfully, Nicole came scuttling down the corridor to intercept her before she got anywhere near Jennifer.

'Hey, hey, lady! What're you doing in here? This is a private suite.'

I swallowed a dry lump of nothing and whisked the dress from Vicky to take it to Jennifer. I really did not want this caught on camera. When I returned from presenting her with a dress still warm from Vicky's body, Nicole had exercised her pushy publicist powers to the full and the camera crew were back out in the corridor, chain pulled against the slightly ajar door to keep them at bay. Shaggy was sitting on the floor, Rob was pacing and Fran was furiously holding her phone to her ear—no doubt trying to contact Mona.

'This is so unprofessional,' she muttered as I removed the chain to speak to her, like a prison guard. 'Rob said everything was set with Mona—and now we've wasted nearly two hours getting here and waiting around for nothing.'

'Listen, Jennifer just wants to get ready in peace this afternoon, as there's not much time. But I could ask Mona if you can pop in on Miss P, who we're also styling for the awards? I'm heading there after this and it's only round the corner.' It was the best I could offer, and I didn't want to land Rob in trouble for the mix-up. She and Rob glanced at each other.

'Sounds good, Amber, let's do it,' he said. 'We've got the van out front, so we can all go together?'

'Give me ten minutes to finish up with Jennifer and call Mona and I'll be out. See you downstairs.'

Returning to the lounge, I tried Mona's mobile but it went straight to answerphone—*quelle surprise*. My eye was drawn to the pouffe where a copy of *Heat* sat, Beau Belle's name and face jumping out from the top right-hand corner in a bright pink, shouty font. As I covertly read the headline: 'Beau Belle and Trey Jones latest: Is the wedding off?', I was relieved to find Caroline and Nicole making appreciative noises at Jennifer, who was admiring herself in the full-length mirror positioned close to the natural light.

'Wow,' said Nicole.

'You look beautiful,' Caroline agreed.

'It fits like a glove,' sighed Jennifer, contentedly.

I stepped forwards to do the stylist thing, remembering everything I had seen Mona do, securing a delicate clasp above the zip, gently tucking in the label and fluffing out the peplum. Without time to lay out all the accessories and shoes in their perfect columns as we had done in LA, I had set the case down on the floor. I knelt down next to it and began pulling pieces out like a children's entertainer with a suitcase full of props. Luckily I had brought plenty of options. I fished out a pair of black pointed high courts with a thin gold heel by Nicholas Kirkwood.

'He's the man of the moment in the British shoe scene,' I said, glad I could impart something that made me sound more experienced than I was. 'Or if you want to make more of a statement, which I think you can with this dress, these are *really* special.' I held up another pair of Kirkwoods, a pair of laser-cut black sandals with iridescent appliqué.

'Ooh, love those!' Caroline enthused, reaching forwards to take one from my hand, while I searched for its partner. 'Chic but edgy—these are *so* you, Jen.'

Jennifer perched on the sofa to try them on. I felt my

palms grow clammy with excitement, as she stood up and moved towards the mirror. They were spot on.

'Stunning!' she declared. 'And I can actually walk in them. What about jewellery?' I was one step ahead now, sifting through the carefully packaged boxes and little bags, passing over some pretty designs by Oscar de la Renta and Carolina Bucci because they didn't have the British association, and finally settling on a python cuff by Burberry. I felt like a presenter on QVC as I showed it to Jennifer.

'Love it!' she exclaimed, stealing the piece from my hands.

Caroline helped her put it on and we all gazed at the vision of hip home-grown style before us. She looked classy and chic—the embodiment of her signature style—but it was also an outfit that packed a punch and would not fall foul of any flooding.

'And then we just need to keep the clutch simple and cool,' I added, relieved to be on the home straight as I pulled out a silver purse by Anya Hindmarch. 'Voila.'

I handed it to Jennifer, who held it expertly, striking a well-honed pose in front of the mirror once more.

'Perfect. Thank you so much, Amber.' She turned and gave me a kiss, in the air just above each cheek, which I took to mean she was pleased. I breathed out a sigh of relief.

'Right, time for some touch-ups,' declared Nicole, clapping her hands together, as Jennifer was whisked off into the makeshift beauty salon by Caroline. 'And, Amber, you'll be on the carpet, won't you? Just to ensure everything's in place? I'm going to be super-busy handling the media and it's Caroline's wedding anniversary today, so she can't hang around.'

I hesitated and looked down at my jeans, inappropriately dressed yet again for a glamorous event. 'Of course—whatever I can do to help.'

'Great, come and jump in the car with us—we'll be ready to leave at five-thirty.'

'See you then.'

As I repacked the suitcase and zipped it up, I pinched the copy of *Heat* and stuffed it in, too. It didn't seem like Jennifer's kind of reading material and I was desperate to know what was going on with Beau. And then it suddenly occurred to me that I hadn't seen Vicky in a while.

Lurking in the corridor just outside the bathroom was Vicky, looking like a posh flasher in a white towelling Dorchester dressing gown and her Steve Maddens. I couldn't help but giggle.

'Well, what else was I supposed to do?' she said, through gritted teeth and a fake grin as Nicole crossed the corridor and did a double take.

'Keep your gob shut and pretend it's all part of the plan,' I muttered, giving Nicole a wave. *All fine here!* 'And a bloody great plan it was. You saved me today, honey. Big time. Seriously, thank you so, so much.'

'You owe me one.' She softened.

'I owe you times a million and I know it. I would say I'll get you a drink, if you were drinking. Do you want to wear my coat?'

* * *

'I can't believe we're smuggling you out of the Dorchester in a stolen bathrobe,' I whispered as Vicky legged it out of the lift back into reception and we scarpered through one of the side doors to a few raised eyebrows, but mainly unnoticed, thanks to the arrival of Joan Collins out front. With just over an hour before the public pens would be filled to capacity and the BAFTAs red carpet at the Royal Opera House in Covent Garden declared open, we all jumped in the production van and darted round the corner to pop in on Miss P.

* * *

Inside a discreet apartment-block entrance, a block down from the Grosvenor House Hotel, was a rabbit warren of corridors and sleek black doors to expensive suites, used mostly for short-term lets to the wealthy. I rang the doorbell, feeling like a travelling salesman with my trusty suitcase beside me. Vicky had started to shiver and I wondered how I was going to explain her lack of clothes to Miss P's management team within. Heavy dubstep was blaring from a sound system and a cool-looking girl barely out of her teens, with short neon-pink hair, opened the door.

'Hi,' I shouted above the racket. 'I'm Amber, assistant to Mona Armstrong.'

The girl looked at me blankly. *Is she stoned?*

'Miss P's stylist?' I shouted.

'Yeah?' replied the girl, sucking in her cheeks, one of which was pierced.

'I've come to see that everything's okay.'

'Okay? With what?' she replied. *It would help if you turned the sound down.*

'The dress! Has Miss P chosen her dress from the selection we sent over?'

Fran made an impatient tut behind me. The girl opened the door a little wider and I clocked a familiar bottle of green pond water on a sideboard just inside. It was busy in there, more like a Brits after-party than preparation for the BAFTAs.

'Someone's here for the stylist!' she called out over her

shoulder, begrudgingly ushering us in. A few people turned around, and at the end of a large room I got a glimpse of Miss P, in a *very* revealing dress. She looked even shorter than I'd imagined. From within the room, between a multitude of people standing around, a familiar face began making its way towards me. *No, it can't be.*

'Bloody hell, isn't that the Stick?' said Vicky, chin on my shoulder, trying to hide her outfit. The Stick strutted towards me as if she owned the place; she was more elaborately dressed than the talent, clearly in her element. *Aren't those the Balenciaga spiked heels she'd been coveting in Smith's? And the next season Marc Jacobs I spied in the stockroom?*

'Oh my God, what *is* she wearing?' the Stick said, staring at Vicky's spa guest-cum-hooker outfit. Defiantly, Vicky pulled on her towelling belt and stood up straighter.

'More to the point—what are you doing here?' I asked.

'Mona asked me, and I was happy to help,' she replied, all sweetness and light. 'I might have known it wasn't you who put me forward.'

* * *

'Kiki's here!' I shouted into the phone, far enough down the corridor to be able to hear myself think.

'I had no choice,' Mona blasted back, with the venom usually reserved for her sacked members of staff—a select rank it suddenly seemed very appealing to join. 'You're looking after Jennifer, so I had to ask Jas to loan me Kiki for the day. It was my only option. It's Sunday—she didn't mind.' *I'm not worried about Jas's staffing issues.*

'Fine,' I muttered into the phone, loud enough for the Stick to hear, 'I'll leave it to her, then. To be honest, I've had enough for today.' I was incredulous. After the revelation at Soho House and now today, I was sick of Mona's games. And there seemed to be no trace of the Norovirus in her voice now. *Maybe the Stick is more suited to this life, anyway. Perhaps we should trade places after all.* I really wasn't sure about the idea of a barely there side-boob gown on Miss P, anyway. It just didn't seem respectful at a prestigious awards ceremony like the BAFTAs.

'Oh, and don't let the film crew anywhere near our clients today,' Mona barked down the phone.

'Bit late, Mona, they're already here.' I glanced over my shoulder at Fran's pinched face.

'Well, get them out. Clive will go nuts if Miss P appears on any show other than his own. Seriously, Amber, use your brain.'

The Stick approached and stopped right in front of my face: 'Listen, hate to do this to you, but management is getting twitchy about too many hangers-on in the suite.' She ran a hand through her freshly blow-dried hair, Marc Jacobs bangles rattling next to my ear. 'So I think it's best if you leave.' She looked across at our motley crew, just as I noticed Shaggy holding his camera, red light blinking, indicating he was filming us. 'All of you.'

The gormless girl with the pink hair was still holding the door open.

'The dress fits okay?' I asked, peering inside, clinging on to a shred of professionalism.

'Yes, I've got it all sorted—she looks *in*-cred. Going to blow the boring gowns out of the water—just you wait.'

Defeated, I put my arm through Vicky's, turned on my Uggs and stormed down the corridor, our entourage of Fran, Rob and Shaggy in tow.

'Bitch,' mumbled Vicky as we left.

Outside the apartment block, Vicky belted the dressing

gown even tighter and pulled its shallow collar up around her ears, though it did little to protect her from the biting cold.

'Well, she seemed pleased to see us,' she said.

'What a cow,' I muttered. 'But I can't be bothered to let her get to me any more.'

'That's the spirit,' said Vicky, digging me in the ribs. 'At least you weren't the one looking like a dick in a dressing gown. It's difficult to be hard when you're wearing fluffy white towelling.'

'Hear, hear,' agreed Rob, joining our group. 'The not letting her get to you bit, I mean. I'm loving the outfit—is it Helmut Lang?' he asked Vicky.

'No, cheeky, Dorchester Collection, actually,' she replied, smiling.

Fran with the bob rolled her eyes. 'Well, if we're not going to be getting anything done today, I'm off,' she declared, to our relief.

'Sounds like pub-o'clock,' said Shaggy, putting the cases back into the van. 'Leave you with the wheels.' He handed the keys to Rob.

'Catch you all tomorrow, then,' Rob said. Despite myself, I was pleased the others were leaving.

'This is Rob from the documentary, as you might have guessed,' I said, turning to Vicky. It felt as though I should make a proper introduction. 'And, Rob—Vicky, my flat-mate.'

'I've heard lots about you,' he said. 'But I didn't hear about your unusual taste in clothes…'

Although the teasing was light-hearted, something felt different between Rob and me today, as though there was a chasm between us. A chasm with a diamond engagement ring at the foot of it. *I wish I didn't find him so attractive.* My emotions for him were running out of control. I looked at my phone. Only thirty minutes to go until Jennifer needed to leave the Dorchester.

'I'd better get back to the hotel,' I said. 'Any chance I can leave this case in your van?'

Rob nodded. 'Of course.'

'Er, and how exactly am I meant to get home? I'm not getting on the tube dressed like the Big Lebowski. I might see someone I know. Anyway, I've left my Oyster card at home,' whined Vicky.

'I'd drop you if I wasn't running late myself,' Rob said. 'I'm doing the red carpet for the breakfast show and we should be setting up now.'

'Here, take some of Mona's cash for a taxi.' I handed her two twenties.

'Thanks, Mum.'

'Don't spend it all at once. I'll be home in time to watch the awards on TV with you. Actually, here's another thirty, grab a bottle of fizz and some crisps on your way. Oh, sorry, you're not drinking…'

'I think I'll make an allowance, after today.'

Rob flagged her down a black cab and we waved as she whizzed off, hand raised, waving sedately like the Queen.

'Jump in, Amber, I'll drop you back up the road, it's on my way,' Rob offered.

* * *

'Vicky seems fun,' he said as we pulled into the traffic.

'Yeah, she's great. She saved my bacon today—it's rarely dull with us two.'

'I got that impression. So what's up with Mona, then?'

'Don't ask. I'm over it, to be honest,' I moaned. 'She's

just so unreliable, I don't think I can handle the Oscars, too. I'm thinking of quitting.'

'No! You can't, Amber—you're not a quitter. Anyway, you're the one holding it all together for Mona—it's clear to see in the footage we've shot. That's if any of it actually sees the light of day,' he said, solemnly.

'What? Are they thinking of axing the pilot?' Mona would go crazy.

'Listen, I'm not meant to say anything.'

'Come on, it's only me—I won't say anything to Mona.'

'Fran just doesn't think it's working—and your boss's lack of communication isn't really helping.'

'Tell me about it. Maybe it's no bad thing. You know I'm not exactly loving the filming part.' I fiddled with the tiger bracelet. 'I discovered Mona's totally broke, too,' I grumbled, 'so I'm not even sure I'll get paid this week.'

'Can't you get your lover boy to help tide you over?' he asked, throwing me a sideways glance as we turned onto Park Lane. His sudden reference to the Starbucks 'incident' took me by surprise.

'Er, you mean Liam, I presume. I think it's safe to say we are definitely *not* an item. Not that we ever really were.'

'Really? Didn't seem like that the other day.'

My cheeks prickled and I was cringing for England inside. 'I'm sorry you had to see that. Let's just say it was the beginning and the end.'

'He wasn't exactly the world's greatest charmer.' Rob smiled.

I remembered the BLT comment. 'No. Anyway, can we change the subject, please?'

'Well, then, you'll be wanting to cheer yourself up by joining me at the Grosvenor Hotel for a few free drinks at the BAFTAs dinner tonight, I'll be there with *my* crazy boss, the perma-tanned one.' He looked at me for a moment, completely unable to read the lust in my eyes. 'Oh, come on, Amber, don't lose your sense of humour! We're doomed if we can't have a laugh.' Finally, he made my face crack into a small smile as he pulled over on the Dorchester driveway.

'I think I'll watch it from home, with Vicky,' I said. There seemed little point in socialising with Rob—it was only going to cut me deeper. 'Or we might go to the pub. Anyway, you'd better get to the red carpet.'

He glanced at his watch. 'You're right, I need to split.'

'Thanks for the lift. And good luck with Tango Tim.'

'Send Jen my love!'

Chapter Twenty

Jennifer looked stunning that night. The effect was of a city-slick goddess, and despite the rain and cold, the crowds erupted when she stepped from our plush Audi onto the flashbulb-lined carpet in front of the Royal Opera House. Some of the girls from *Downton Abbey* swanned past us. Damian Lewis arrived at the same time, and the public pen burst into chorus.

'Damian! Damian! Jennifer! Jennifer!' Flash. Flash. Flash.

There was very little I needed to do to assist Jennifer, I only stepped forwards once, to puff up the peplum as she faced the main bank of paparazzi, but other than that I stayed on the sidelines and admired the way the dress held its structure. I was pleased I'd cheese-grated the soles of her shoes—they weren't going anywhere this evening, despite how slippery it looked. I wondered if Mona was watching the arrivals from home, her mouth open in shock, trying to work out where Jennifer's dress could possibly have come from. It gave me a faint feeling of satisfaction.

Anne Hathaway arrived on the red carpet and greeted Jennifer like a long-lost friend. *Flash! Flash! Flash!* And then George Clooney! They embraced, and a blaze of lights erupted all around. Then George led Jennifer by the hand over to a group of fans on one side and they spent a few minutes signing autographs and posing for camera phones together, laughing and joking. The attendants with their big clear plastic umbrellas had a job keeping up with them. Thanks to Vicky's quick thinking, Jennifer didn't have to be concerned about the weather at all; her dress was robust and easy to move in, unlike another poor actress, whose ill-advised pale blue silk creation had unfortunate damp patches, which looked like sweat marks, all over it. She cursed her stylist as she dodged puddles as though her life depended upon it. Nicole was right—the Valentino would undoubtedly have been a risk.

As we reached the TV pen I spotted Tim, and just behind him, Rob, headset on, a loop of wires in his hand.

'Hey, Amber!' Tim called, waving. The London weather wasn't doing anything for his fake tan. 'Come and say hi!' He beckoned me over. 'Loving Jen's frock—but can you get her to come and speak to us?' There was desperation in his eyes. 'I'm dying to get a chat with Astley and Clooney for the show. It would make my whole piece.'

I looked around for Nicole and found her gently guiding Jennifer by the elbow through a line of print journalists, Dictaphones outstretched as they shouted a barrage of questions about her outfit and her chance of winning this evening, each desperate to out-scoop the others by getting a millisecond longer of her time.

'I'll try—but it's Nicole, her publicist, you really need,' I said, gesturing over my shoulder. At last I was beginning to feel like I knew some of the players in this world. As I turned back to say hi to Rob, I was startled by a hand on my shoulder. My heart leapt. It was Trey Jones.

'We meet again, Annie!' he exclaimed. I felt his eyes wander down to the ground, noting my grubby Uggs and jeans. 'Does it feel good to be home?' He looked really dashing this evening. I assessed the situation for a moment before replying: 'Sure does, Trey. I'm not stopping tonight though, hence the warm clothes. Brrr! Just popped by to say hello to a few—' Then we were interrupted by the appearance of a shocking vision in front of us. As far as I was concerned, the timing couldn't have been better—it took Trey's attention right off me.

* * *

The vision was Miss P. The pop star and one-time reality show winner, now relegated to the ranks of the Z-list, had made her entrance amongst the thesps, and the paparazzi were going wild. To call her outfit eye-popping would be an understatement. And where was her stylist? The Stick was nowhere to be seen, and I was certainly not getting involved in the disaster unravelling before my eyes. In a dress that left nothing to the imagination, she posed happily for the cameras. *Flash! Flash! Flash!* More than a bit of side boob—and side bum—was on show. The paparazzi couldn't lap it up fast enough. *What kind of fairground mirror was she looking in before she left this evening?* Some of the actors around us turned to gawp; they clearly had no idea who she was or what she was doing here, infiltrating their industry bash and lowering the tone in her tawdry costume.

Thankfully, Jennifer was deep in conversation in front of a Sky News camera, next to which stood Tim, *Morning Glory* microphone poised ready for his 'exclusive'. Jennifer was near enough to the entrance of the Opera House now, away from the harshest of the elements. I looked around and saw Trey safely in conversation with someone else. It seemed like a good time to make my quiet exit.

* * *

Vicky and I watched the awards together from the sofa in our pyjamas, with a living room coffee-table picnic and glasses of Cava for me, orange juice for her. It was infinitely more comfortable than watching the Globes with Mona, and we both leapt with genuine joy as Jennifer scooped her second Best Supporting Actress gong of awards season. Thankfully, she made it onto the stage with no stumbling on the steps. *And relax.* At around ten-thirty, when Vicky was beginning to doze off and I was debating whether to grab an early night, too, my phone rang. Rob. My hand hovered over it. *What's the point in meeting up?* He rang again, straight away. When it stopped I immediately sent a polite text, saying I was out with friends. *Maybe he'll think I'm out with a bloke.* He texted back immediately:

Where r u? You left your suitcase in the van, was thinking I could drop it off, grab a quick drink? I shook Vicky's arm in a panic.

'Rob wants to meet me!' She jolted into life. 'What shall I say?'

Two weak thumbs in the air.

'Meet him—yes?' I checked.

'Why not,' she said, dozily.

'Really?'

'As long as you don't need me to come…' She reshuffled into a foetal position, stretching the dressing gown over her toes.

'I've told him I'm out, though,' I said, feeling a bit stupid that I couldn't work out what to do on my own.

'So meet him out,' she muttered. 'You can borrow my heels. What are you waiting for?'

Another text from Rob: Am about to leave the Grosvenor—let me know.

I responded fast, knowing I'd probably change my mind again if I didn't: See you at The Chamberlayne, Kensal Rise, in 20?

Great.

I leapt into action: splashed water on my face, brushed my teeth, pilfered Vicky's Steve Maddens, dry-shampooed my hair, put the jeans, black jumper and Kenneth Jay Lane bangle back on and set about re-applying my make-up. I didn't want to look like I'd made too much of an effort, but I made the biggest effort I could in just under ten minutes. Just before I left the flat I swigged a large gulp of Cava from the bottle for Dutch courage, whispered 'Love you' at Vicky, who was gently snoring, and quietly closed the front door. Thankfully, I'd drunk enough to bolster my confidence, but not enough to feel drunk.

* * *

When I reached the pub, Rob was parking outside.

'Sorry, didn't meant to drag you away from anyone,' he said, coming round the van and greeting me with a peck on the cheek.

'Oh, it's fine, Vicky wanted to go home, anyway,' I lied. 'And Mona will go nuts if anything happened to the case. Anyway, how was it for you?'

'Same old,' he replied, smiling. 'The dinner was amazing, must have cost a fortune—there were themed tables for all the nominated films. I stole this for you.' From behind his back he produced a square place mat with a still of Jennifer from Trey's film on the front.

'Awesome! But am I going to get arrested for having this?' I pretended to look concerned.

'I'm sure it can be added on to your sentence for robbing a dressing gown from the Dorchester,' he joked. 'Don't worry, everyone nicks them.'

'I'm touched. Thanks.'

We made our way into the pub and sat on two empty stools at the bar. It was warm and cosy—not too busy, not too empty.

'Your Jennifer's lovely, isn't she?' he said.

'She is, and I'm sure most of the male—and female—population of the world would agree with you.'

'She gave Tim a full five-minute chat. He was over the moon. And she *loves* you—was full of praise for her stylist and how she was proud to be dressed top-to-toe by Brits.'

I smiled. *Thank you, Jennifer.*

'More than could be said for Miss P,' he went on. 'She clearly thinks she's bigger than all the Hollywood stars put together—flew past the entire TV section and straight into the auditorium. Everyone was slagging her off. That outfit was horrific!'

I shrugged. 'Well, I did try to save her.'

'Bet you're glad you had nothing to do with that, as it turned out...'

The camp-as-a-row-of-tents Italian bar manager interrupted us, greeting me warmly: '*Ciao, bella* Amber! Always good to see you, looking *bellissima* as usual.' He reached across the bar to cup my face in his hands and kissed me on both cheeks.

'The usual for you, *bella*? And what can I get your handsome friend?' He winked. I wasn't quite sure what my usual was going to be, having drunk pretty much every type of spirit behind this bar with Vicky at one time or another. But I appreciated his familiarity; it was making me look good.

'Yes please, Nico—and for my friend?' I emphasised the 'friend' as I turned to Rob.

'Just a pint of lager shandy for me please, mate. Unfortunately I'm driving.'

Thankfully a large glass of pinot grigio was placed in front of me, rather than a Jäger bomb. I took a moment to steady my hand before raising it. *Damn, I feel so nervous around him.* Fancying Rob was becoming all-consuming. I enjoyed his company so much and then felt totally bereft every time I remembered he was taken. I tortured myself with an image of his soon-to-be-fiancée. It made me sad, so I tried desperately hard not to overthink it. Which of course made me think about it the entire time.

'Great that Jennifer won again,' Rob continued, fortunately oblivious to the thoughts inside my head. 'I mean, for you as well as her.'

'Did I tell you the story behind Vicky's dressing gown?'

* * *

'…and so, we ended up hitch-hiking all the way home from Gibraltar,' Rob said, lifting another tequila shot and cheersing with me and Nico. After which we all rammed yet another chunk of lemon into our mouths and stuck our tongues out with a roar.

'Right, that one is *definitely* the last,' I hiccupped, wiping my mouth. I noticed Rob's eyes had glazed over.

'Oh man, I love tequila,' he slurred, tipping the shot glass so the last drops fell onto his tongue. After one tequila shot on the house, we had moved on to a whole string of them, each telling a 'truth' about ourselves that had to outdo the one before.

'I do believe you're drunk, Mister— Oh my God, I don't even know your surname!' I declared, trying to sound less drunk than I was.

'The name's Walker,' he slurred, 'Rob Walker.'

'Mr Walker. Funny, you don't look like a Walker.'

'And what does a Mr Walker look like, if you don't mind me asking?'

'He wears tweed trousers tucked into thick socks and hiking boots.' I laughed.

The hours had melted away and, thanks to my good friend alcohol convincing Rob to leave the van parked outside overnight, we'd been chatting and joking as easily as that night in LA. The bar crowd had thinned out to one rowdy group at a table in the corner and us. Nico's special lock-in playlist, consisting of pop classics from Kylie, Prince and Daft Punk, was turned up loud, sparking a spontaneous disco party from the rowdies. But just as I was considering jumping off my stool, grabbing Rob's hand and joining them in some moves, he sprang out of his seat to take a phone call outside. Nico and I stretched our arms over our heads and I chair-danced as we shouted the lyrics at each other, giggling loudly between each chorus.

'She's up all night 'til the sun,
I'm up all night to get some,
She's up all night for good fun,
I'm up all night to get lucky!'

The group seemed to be enjoying it; they were on their feet throwing shapes on the makeshift dance floor, which only encouraged Nico and I to get louder with each verse. It was so good we had to play it twice. My heart was beating hard in my chest. The pub seemed to get very hot. Each time I paused to catch my breath, the walls seemed to keep moving. As the song came to an end for the third time, Rob returned, plonking himself back down on the stool.

'Been told to get home by the fiancée?' I asked, out of breath from all the excitement. 'Does she hate me for keeping you out so late?'

'Umm—not exactly.' He smiled, awkwardly.

'Uh-oh, sounds like someone's been told off,' I laboured on, pulling an exaggerated sad face. 'Got you under the thumb before you're even married?' Talking was making everything spin.

'She's abroad right now,' he replied, not looking at me. He seemed to have instantly sobered up. 'So we only get to speak at odd times of the day.'

'Abroad! Ooh la la!' I immediately despised myself for the spiteful tone, but I couldn't help it. It was the demon booze talking.

'She's in Bangkok,' he said, recoiling slightly. Nico backed away to prepare a tray of shots for the table, clearly sensing that the atmosphere between us had changed.

'Sorry. Must. Not. Shout,' I stage-whispered, my finger across my lips. I leaned forwards, closer to his face. 'Work or pleasure?' I hissed, my tequila breath ruffling his hair.

'Work. She's in travel PR, visiting some hotel clients.'

'Oooh, nice work if you can get it. Doesn't *she* have a name?'

'Yeah, she does. Listen, I should—'

'So will you propose when she gets back?' I cut in. 'I mean—you must be planning the big moment?'

'Maybe,' he replied stiffly, clearly wanting to get the hell away from the nasty, nosy woman who was talking way too close to his face. 'We'll see.'

'Doesn't sound very romantic to me. Where's the romance in that?' I stage-whispered, shuffling to the back of my stool.

Rob muttered something about eating someone's face off in Starbucks not being very romantic, either, and then the conversation went dead. Neither of us said anything for the longest time. Rob stared into the dregs of his pint and I drained my glass of wine and shouted above 'All Night Long' for another.

'All okay?' Nico mouthed, as he set it down.

'Fine,' I replied, taking a large glug without really knowing if anything, including my sanity, was anywhere near fine. All I knew for certain was that my head was spinning out of control and that if I had so much as another sniff of wine I would probably be sick. I needed to get off this waltzer. I reached down to pull my phone out of my bag and tried to focus on the time. When I finally managed to punch in the pin and my vision straightened for long enough, I thought it said 01:35. Though it could have been 03:51. *Bleurgh.*

'I guess I'd better get a cab ordered,' Rob said, turning to Nico.

'*Si, signor,* if the night really must end—where to?' *How does Nico always manage to stay so sober? How come Rob doesn't seem drunk any more? How come I...* I became aware that I had fallen off my stool onto the floor. After that I can't remember much more than feeling very relieved to be in my bed.

Chapter Twenty-One

I woke face down with a horrible dryness in my mouth, stomach cramps and sweaty hair. It couldn't be that early, because I'd forgotten to close the curtains and it was light outside. I moved my neck left to right, and wiggled my fingers and toes, just to check everything was working. This was something. As I hauled myself onto my back, my head felt like it was having trouble keeping upright. I didn't want to think too much about last night right now, but, from what I dared to recall, even though I had acted like a total cow, Rob had delivered me to my front door—*Shit, the suitcase!* I flew out of bed, narrowly missing Vicky's shoes, and ran downstairs, the door slamming shut behind me. My whole body ached. The suitcase was there, at the bottom of the stairs by the main front door, alongside my open handbag. *Thank God.* I must have been too drunk to carry them up. *Jesus, you stupid idiot, Amber Green.* Luckily the tenants of the downstairs flat were decent people; people who had correctly assumed that one of the drunk girls upstairs was too lazy to carry up her bags last night. A quick inspection revealed my purse, credit cards, the placemat Rob had given me and all the crap I carried around was all still in the bag.

'What time is it?' I asked, huskily, as Vicky opened the door, Dorchester dressing gown on, damp hair in a topknot, and a piece of toast and Marmite in her hand. She looked disgustingly fresh.

'Seen this?' she said, ignoring my question and holding up the *Sun* in the other hand. 'Miss P made the papers, all right.'

I set the suitcase down. The exertion of making my feeble body haul it upstairs had made a bead of sweat trickle down the side of my face. I took the paper in my clammy hand, and there was Miss P, front-page news—a full-body shot down the paper's entire length.

'Oh Lord...' I stared at it for a good ten seconds, taking in the full horror, suddenly properly awake. 'Oh my God. She's flashing more than a bit of side boob,' I finally uttered. She was indeed—she was flashing two whole full-frontal nipples and more. It was too much even for the *Sun*, whose design department had compassionately covered her modesty in three places with BAFTA statuettes. 'How the hell did the Stick let that happen? How could she have sent her out like that and not seen the dress move and go totally see-through under the flashbulbs?

'Mona's going to go mental. So is Clive... And Miss P, she'll be devastated. This is humiliating for her.'

'And for the Stick... You've got to admit though, it serves her right.' Vicky led the way into the kitchen. 'She was a complete bitch to you yesterday and you were only trying to help. She brought it on herself. Tea?'

I stared, bewildered, at the photo again. There was absolutely no good way of looking at it—it was a total fashion disaster. But a bit of me couldn't help feeling for Kiki. It had been Mona's decision to put a barely there dress on a star who didn't have the lengthy limbs to pull it off. It would be a tall order for Miranda Kerr to work a gown like that. *And she looks drop-dead amazing in everything.*

'Meanwhile, over on vogue.com this morning,' Vicky continued, shovelling another bite of toast into her mouth and turning her iPad to face me, 'have a gander at this.' I peered at the screen and read the words aloud:

'"Hollywood siren Jennifer Astley wows at the BAFTAs, wearing hip new British label Star-Crossed. Her structured LBD is from the up-and-coming designer's first collection and, teamed with an eye-catching Burberry cuff, it proved an instant classic on the red carpet, showing that cocktail can be every inch as chic as couture. Jennifer continued to fly the flag for British fashion by teaming the look with sexy Nicholas Kirkwood heels and an Anya Hindmarch clutch, as she scooped her second gong of awards season for Best Supporting Actress."' I paused to catch my breath. Vicky looked as delighted as I was.

'Oh wow! This is amazing, Vic, and she's wearing *your* dress, can you believe it?'

'Alice from Star-Crossed has already been on this morning—she's over the moon.' Vicky beamed. 'She's already said Jen can keep the dress and offered us pieces from her collection as a thank you. But there's more, hon—look at the photos again.'

I focused back on the screen. It had to be said that Jen totally rocked the outfit. There was a stunning sequence of shots of her hugging Anne Hathaway and posing with George Clooney, with whom she made a *very* gorgeous pairing. There were also a few shots of her with Trey; they looked good together, too—I could see Beau being furious about that. And then I noticed a little white circle over one of the images, highlighting a figure crouched just behind Jennifer, part hidden in shadows. There was a caption next to it with the headline: 'Who's that girl?'

'Ohmigod, it's me!' I looked up at Vicky, grinning like the Cheshire cat. 'That's me, behind Jennifer, I just wanted to check she wasn't finding it too slippery in the shoes.'

Vicky read out the rest of the caption: "'Jennifer's long-time stylist, Mona Armstrong, 47, has not been seen with her leading lady so far this awards season; yet while one star fades, fashion always makes space for the new. This is *Vogue*'s second sighting of the petite brunette stylist who now appears to be working her magic on Jennifer. Watch this space—we hope to hunt her down and bring you more soon." *Vogue* wants to "hunt you down", honey! Can you fucking believe it?'

I was gobsmacked. 'And they called me "petite"!'

'And Mona's forty-seven—she's not going to like that.'

There was only one thing for it. 'Can we just scream, please? Aaaaargh!' We lunged for each other and jumped up and down, hugging like loonies.

* * *

'I'm leaving for LA earlier than I thought,' Mona said later that morning, phoning from the lounge at Heathrow. 'I'm sorting the clothes for Beau's bachelorette party and I thought I'd get ahead with Oscars prep. Seeing as you're the talk of fucking London and Clive's blanking me, I need to get out of town for a bit. Why don't you take a couple of days off and just come over on the night of the Oscars to help me with the returns? You should have enough money in

the kitty to pay for your flight. Economy flight, of course.'
She sounded really prickly, and this was her first reference
to my BAFTAs triumph with Jennifer. She hadn't been in
touch at all the previous evening (I'd been trying to block
out the fact that Miss P was anything to do with either of us).

'Sure,' I replied, as casually as possible. 'Will you style
Jennifer, then? She still has the Valentino—I guess she'll
bring it back with her.'

'Too right I will,' she sneered.

'Fine, I'll see you in LA on Sunday, then.'

She grunted in response and hung up.

'You know, I'm tempted to just not turn up at all,' I said
to Vicky, stuffing a fork-full of French fries into my mouth.
Vicky had taken the day off work and I'd taken her to the
Electric Brasserie for a celebratory lunch to say thank-you;
the kitty was paying because we felt as though we'd earned
it. 'After all, she's done it enough times to me. Why am I
always the person picking up the pieces?'

'Listen, *we* know who's doing all the work and, thanks
to a super-sleuth at *Vogue*, the rest of the world soon will,
too,' Vicky said. 'This could be the start of a new career.
You'd be mad not to do the Oscars. I mean, it's the *Oscars*,
honey! If you don't go, I will—I'd quit my job tomorrow for
an opportunity like that.' She had a point. 'Anyway, you've
completely forgotten to update me about the most important
thing. How was it with Rob last night?'

Over two more skinny lattes and an extra side of fries
I told her the sorry story. Rob hadn't been in touch this
morning, so I knew I'd totally messed up, and I could kiss
goodbye to any flimsy hope of him not proposing to his
girlfriend. *He's probably practising on one knee right now.*

'I don't know what came over me.' I cringed. 'I guess it

had been building up in my head and then booze made it all spill out. I was such a stupid cow.'

'Sounds like he was just as drunk,' Vicky sympathised, 'and at the end of the day, he's a bloke and blokes don't think about things as much as we do. He probably can't remember, anyway.'

'Hmm, I wish,' I muttered, stirring my latte for the hundredth time. 'From now on, please tell me to shut up if I talk about him ever again. It's pointless.'

* * *

Mona's sudden departure did at least give me time to see my parents. When I arrived at the front door, Mum flung her arms around me like I'd just been handed over by terrorists.

'Darling! I can't tell you how great it is to see your face!' *Has she been on the sherry?* 'I was in the hairdresser's, reading one of those gossip mags and there was a story about that mad Rhona. "High fashion?" the hairdresser said. "That woman is just high!" What's going on? She sounds horrific!'

'It's Mona, Mum. And it's been an *interesting* experience, yes,' I conceded, flinging my coat over the banisters. 'But, as you can see, I'm fine and Mona will be fine, too. It's just a crazy time of year for her.' I was glad I'd worn a dress—things always appeared better to my mother if I was in a dress. *Jeez, it's almost as cold as outside in here.*

'You've not got the heating on, then?'

'You're not in LA any more, darling. You're thin!' She took a step back, to survey me properly.

'It's only been two weeks, Mum.'

'A lot can happen in a fortnight, evidently.'

'Anyway, what's baking?' I changed the subject, inhaling the familiar sweet smell of home. I peered into the living room to check whether, just perhaps, the coffee table was laden with freshly baked afternoon tea goods made especially for my arrival. Instead, the answer came flying around the corner in the form of Nora, running towards me, sticky fingers outstretched and a partially licked spatula in one hand.

'Nana!' she squealed, jumping into my arms and smearing cake mixture in my freshly washed hair. She was high on beaten-together butter, sugar and eggs. Nora's inability to say 'Amber' when she was first able to talk meant she'd called me 'Nana', and it stuck—which has done wonders for my image as the young, cool auntie.

'Grannie's got you working in the kitchen again, I see?' I said, rolling my eyes at Mum in mock revulsion at the child labour. I'd only been in the house for two minutes and Mum was already talking me through the recital I had missed. Sometimes I wondered if she was more interested in Nora's life than mine. Her voice sort of buzzed away in the background as Nora lost interest in baking and pestered me to read her a story.

'I'm sorry, *again*, that I couldn't make it,' I moaned, noticing there was a new picture up. An original artwork by Nora. *I hate myself for feeling jealous of a five-year-old.*

'Was your mobile not working properly while you were away?'

'Hmm?'

'Just a quick call, now and again, so we know you're okay.'

'I'm sorry.' *I know I've been rubbish.* 'It was just so busy, I hardly had any time to myself.'

'Even a text.'

Okay, I get the picture. I could feel my mood changing, but I knew better than to start an argument, so I sulked instead, like a twenty-something teenager. But before the full effect of the sulk could be felt, my phone rang. Mona. I debated not answering. *This is meant to be my day off.* After some rushed pleasantries, she cut to the chase, putting on a disturbingly friendly voice.

'The kitty, babe—I left you with most of the money, didn't I.' It wasn't a question.

'Well,' I replied slowly, mentally doing the sums, and concluding that this wasn't quite true.

'Just need you to transfer me a few hundred dollars so I can pick up some last-minute bits for Jennifer for the Oscars. Can you do that today, please?'

I thought about it for all of one second. 'I'm sorry, Mona, but I can't. I need the money to get me out to LA. There's barely enough.' It wasn't a total lie; we had left yet another flight booking to the last minute, so it wouldn't be cheap, and I needed to ensure there was enough for taxis and to pay my paltry wage. I'd only managed to cover this month's rent by the skin of my teeth, and the bills would need paying when I got back.

'You're no better than the rest of them,' she spat, hanging up. A sourness hung in the air after she'd gone.

'Everything okay?' Mum asked suspiciously.

'It's fine.' I hated the fact that even though she was thousands of miles away in another country, Mona had managed to spoil my mood, highlighting to Mum that everything really was not fine. I sat down and accepted another cup of tea and an undercooked fairy cake, and then, over three further cups and I lost count of how many cakes, I confided in Mum about Mona, her erratic behaviour and the small issue of her bankruptcy.

'Sounds like she needs an accountant as soon as possible,'

Mum advised gravely. 'Problems like this don't go away, and I wouldn't bet she's paid all her taxes, either.'

'What she needs is a chat with someone like you.' I stared into my tea. Mum had a way of putting everything into order so that you felt it could all be worked out. But it was a lot to ask. She sucked in her cheeks and thought for a moment, tapping her fingernails on the table. 'I'm stacked up as it is,' she said at last, breathing out heavily. 'And bankruptcy isn't my area. But—and only because you're my daughter and I care about you getting paid—I'd be willing to have an off-the-record chat with her, to offer some advice, if you think it would help. I know a few good accountants, including one in Los Angeles, who specialises in this kind of thing. I suppose I could recommend someone to get her moving in the right direction.'

'Mum, I love you.' I jumped up and flung my arms around her.

Part Four:
Los Angeles,
The Oscars

Chapter Twenty-Two

I pulled my suitcase off the carousel. *Last on, first off—a result. It makes me so happy when this happens.* En route to Customs I trundled past a fully made-up Poppy Drew. She semi-smiled in recognition, and then looked me up and down in disapproval—I was still wearing my onesie from the flight. *Am I bovvered?* I wanted to sneer back, but instead I semi-smiled in return. There seemed little point changing clothes when I'd had absolutely no sleep on the plane and would now be getting straight into a taxi and then my bed in Mona's house. It wasn't as if the paps, always posted in the LAX arrivals hall, were interested in me. I switched on my phone, and almost immediately it sprang to life, trilling from inside my onesie pocket: Caroline.

Why is she calling me? Mona should have told her I wasn't working today. All the prep was done and tonight was Mona's night with Jennifer; she'd rammed it down my throat enough times, and I was happy to let her get on with it. It would be mid-afternoon by the time I'd got back to Mona's house, so I planned to sneak in, heat up some of Ana's turkey chilli and watch the awards from the sofa before confronting the post-Oscars returns madness in the morning.

My phone stopped ringing, only to start again seconds later. *It will be a mistake to answer it.* Seconds after that it rang again. This time it was Mona's house number. It had to be Mona or Klara. But why would Mona call from the house instead of her mobile? My finger hovered over the answer button. *Maybe it's Ana and she's phoning to see if I want any food leaving out. Mmm…fresh guacamole.* Ill-advisedly, I picked up. It was Klara.

'Thank God, Amber! I've been trying to get you for the last half an hour. It didn't say the plane was delayed?'

'No, I've just been getting through immigration—you know how long it can take. I've only just got my case. What's up?'

'It's Caroline from Jennifer Astley's team—she's been calling the house non-stop. She can't get hold of Mona and they're with Jennifer prepping for the Oscars. She's freaking out, and thought you might know where she is. Please can you call her? Honestly, she's going nuts.' A wave of nausea swept through my body.

* * *

'It's Mona,' Caroline said, sending panic coursing through my veins. 'I can't believe we gave her another chance. We felt sorry for her—food poisoning was unlucky and then being struck down by the thingy-virus, well, that was unfortunate—but now she's gone totally AWOL. On Oscars day! We've been ringing off the hook for hours.'

I was momentarily lost for words. *What the hell is going on?* 'But I spoke to her just before I boarded,' I said. 'She told me everything was under control. She sounded excited about Jennifer wearing the Valentino. She mentioned something about lingerie, but that should have been sorted hours ago.'

'Mona was meant to be picking up some chicken fillets and extra underwear for Jennifer, but it's been four hours since we last heard from her. Nothing. We're worried. We're not just worried, we're freaking out. Do you think she could have been in an accident?' The panicky feeling was turning back into nausea. 'Jen's waiting at her hotel, she's in a bungalow at the Chateau Marmont, and she needs one of you there,' Caroline pleaded. 'She's got to leave for the Oscars in one hour. Please, Amber, I'm literally begging you. This is the biggest night of her entire career. Of her life. Of all of our lives, for Christ's sakes! *Please* come and help us.'

'Hold on,' I said, my head reeling. Surely someone would have heard if anything really bad had happened? 'I'll keep trying her, too. There's got to be a simple explanation, maybe, maybe she's just run out of juice and she'll turn up any second?'

'Please, Amber, call me back straight away. I mean it.'

When I finally looked up I found myself staring into the cold, hard eyes of a customs officer, asking me for the second time where I had travelled from today. For a few long seconds I couldn't actually remember. I half-hoped he'd drag me aside for further questioning, forcing me to escape the soap opera my life had become. With no response from Mona's number when I tried it several times in a row, and nothing on email, instant messenger or any form of social media, I found myself getting into a taxi and burning up La Cienega to the Chateau Marmont, to help Jennifer into the Valentino gown. Wearing my onesie.

It felt like Groundhog Day as Nicole came to the door of the penthouse suite, her face a scary shade of stern.

'Your boss...' She shook her head. 'I swear to you, she is never going to work in this town—or any other town, come to think of it—after today. It's totally unprofessional. Has she no idea how important today is to Jennifer? To all of us? It would be a joke, if only it was the slightest bit funny.' Then she noticed my outfit, and pulled a face like she'd eaten something rotten.

'I agree with you, Nicole,' I said, trying to keep my temper under control. I didn't want to get into an argument, but I couldn't let her walk all over me for something that was not at all my fault. I'd just about had it with Mona and her dramas, too. 'With all due respect, I wasn't meant to be working today, so I'm only here—straight off a flight, as you may have noticed—to help you. Now, if you don't mind, I'm just going to get changed and then I don't think we've got a lot of time.' I stormed past her, dragging my suitcase and trying my damnedest to look both dignified and pissed off, wearing a slightly smelly onesie.

* * *

I set the suitcase down on the bathroom floor. Funny, the zips were in a different position to how I remembered them. As I peeled them open, a cold panicky sensation washed through me. I flipped open the top and the horrible truth hit me straight away. *This is not my suitcase. Shit shit shit!* I slammed the foam lid down and bit my lip so hard I almost drew blood. Then I tried to calm myself and opened it again. *Perhaps I'm hallucinating.* I peeked inside. It still wasn't my case. *Could today get any worse?* My mind raced. There was no way I had time to get back to the airport in hope that my case was still there for a straight swap. Now

I had to add calling Lost Luggage to my ever-expanding 'to do' list. *Maybe there's something in here I can borrow, anyway...just for a couple of hours...* I checked that the door was locked, and began peeling off the top layer of items—a blanket, a baby's changing mat, more blankets. *Surely there are some clothes in here? What kind of person travels without clothes?* I finally reached some garments, but when I pulled them out they were all miniature—a host of onesies, vests and other outfits in a range of sizes suitable from newborn to age five. Everything was more than twenty years too small for me. I looked at the luggage tag: behind clear plastic was a business card: Sarah-Louise Moore, Head Buyer, Mothercare. I slumped back onto my heels and breathed out deeply. I looked down at myself, at my outfit that was, ironically, basically a giant Babygro. *Looks like you and me are together for the long haul.* I decided to hold my head high and make like it was all planned.

* * *

Thankfully the weather conditions outside were LA perfect and the strapless, scarlet Valentino gown looked breathtaking on Jennifer. She had been gifted some incredible sparkling Christian Louboutin heels, and any crisis over suitable lingerie seemed to have gone away. The PR from Chopard had sent over a pair of stunning white-gold, twelve-carat diamond-drop earrings and two vintage diamond bracelets, complete with their own bodyguard, to accessorise it. A security guard was positioned in the hallway outside Jennifer's bedroom, looking like an Oscar nominee himself in an immaculate black suit. Jennifer's hair was in a beautiful, soft updo, a diamond clip, also from the fabled jewellery house, glinting at the back. Everything about her look was a notch higher in the glamour stakes than it had been for the BAFTAs and Golden Globes. She was Hollywood romance personified.

With still no news from Mona, we finally left the Chateau for the short drive to the Dolby Theatre in Hollywood. As we neared the foot of the red carpet, fashionably late (but not too late, so Jennifer was sure to arrive in the throng of the excitement along with the night's other big names), we joined a long queue of limos with blacked-out windows. The roar of the crowds grew louder as we crept closer to the venue. I wondered who was in the cars in front and behind us. Brad and Angelina, perhaps? Catherine and Michael? The atmosphere in the car was tense. We were all lost in our own worlds, concentrating on the job we each had to do on Hollywood's biggest night; plus I had the additional worry about my lost suitcase and how I was going to explain to Mona that thousands of pounds worth of borrowed shoes and accessories were currently missing without trace. *If Mona is still alive that is.*

Sensing the unease among us, Caroline flicked on the TV in the back of the limo so we could watch the red-carpet arrivals whilst we queued. Ryan Seacrest, all tanned face and cheesy grin, enthusiastically addressed us: 'Tonight, back by popular demand, E! has our 360-degree fashion camera here on the red carpet to give you a detailed view of all the grand fête fashions from the star-studded red carpet. E! is here to bring you every buzzworthy moment!' His head kept twitching, eyes excitedly darting around the setting behind him, awash with instantly recognisable faces. 'And I can see some of this evening's nominees for the big categories arriving now—don't go anywhere!' he shrieked. I swallowed hard. *Talk about pressure.*

* * *

When at last we reached the entrance; the car doors were suddenly flung open and men in black suits helped us out. The roar of the crowds reverberated around my head and my heart pounded harder. The scale of it all was so much bigger than I had imagined. It was like a giant film set, complete with lighting rigs, stadium-style stands for the public and the widest red carpet I'd ever seen, buzzing with the ultimate cast. We all hung back so that Jennifer could make her entrance. One long leg after the other unfurled from the limo, and she rose up like an Amazonian goddess. Her crystal-adorned sandals—complete with a personal message of good luck from the designer on the soles—sparkled in the early-evening sunshine. The air turned electric as she raised a hand and waved at her fans. Her name was chanted by the public, twenty people deep:

'Jennifer! Jennifer! We love you!'

The security guard was next out of the car, followed by Nicole and Caroline. Finally I emerged, taking up the rear and hoping for anonymity in my baggy onesie. Unfortunately, against all the glamour around me, I hardly blended in. A rush of adrenalin propelled me to straighten her skirt where it met the ground, and then I dashed to the safety of the sidelines where I crouched down beneath the autograph hunters, my eyes trained on Jennifer. All around me the public shrieked for her attention. *The screams are so much louder over here.* Nicole was leading her gently towards the first set of paparazzi, the security guard never more than a few paces behind them. I watched in awe from the shadows as the dazzling dress put in an Oscar-worthy performance of its own. This was exactly what Valentino must have imagined as he designed it.

She made her way towards the TV crews, and I automatically strained to see Rob's face among them. The line was infinitely more crowded, and twice as long as it had been in London. My eyes skimmed over the logos of CNN, Sky, Fox News, ABC, and E!, but I couldn't see Rob or Tim in the jumble of wires, cameras and bodies. As Jennifer moved on to the main bank of paparazzi I stepped forwards again, briefly, to gently pull down the delicate layers of pure silk organza. The tiny, shimmering beads and sequins sewn into the gown glinted exquisitely. She looked like a fairy-tale princess. As I stepped back to admire my handiwork, I noticed Trey and Beau, arm in arm, approaching Jennifer. It had to be said that Beau looked smouldering in a shimmering low-cut silver Dolce & Gabbana gown with floral embellishments. I recognised it from the rails in our suite at the W Hotel—Mona must have given it to her before she went missing. Beau winked at me in recognition; as I backed off I prayed Trey hadn't noticed me, too. *That batty British producer—in her Uggs at the BAFTAs and now in a grubby onesie at the Oscars.* But he seemed transfixed by Jennifer, a vision of ethereal beauty.

'You look incredible,' he whispered, squeezing her arm, as Beau cattily surveyed her outfit and latched on to him even more tightly. 'Tonight's the big one, good luck!'

'Hey, Jennifer! Trey! We've come all the way from London—can we get ten seconds about the movie, for the BBC?' A microphone was thrust between them.

'Go on, then, as you have *such* a charming accent,' Jennifer replied, threading her arm through Trey's and gently peeling him away from his disgruntled fiancée.

Ducking out of sight, I moved back to the sidelines, and was shocked to see Beau follow.

'Amber, babe! *So* good to see you! What's with the one-sie? I mean, I *love* the statement, but—aren't you hot?'

'Don't ask.' I shrugged. 'Mona's gone missing and I had to go straight from the airport to Jennifer.'

Beau motioned towards a larger than life gleaming gold Oscar statue, intimating that we should stand in its shadow, half hidden, lest I tarnish her image with my shoddy appearance.

'Missing? Where is she?' she stage-whispered.

'Good question. Call me if you find out.'

'*She* wore my Valentino, then.' She looked over her shoulder and gazed at Jennifer, her nemesis. 'It looks—okay.' She sighed. 'Anyway, babe, I'm so glad I ran into you—I've been wanting to ask you something.' She looked around to check no one was close enough to overhear. Not easy on the world's stage like this. I felt my body go rigid as I remembered what happened last time Beau needed a favour.

'I wanted to ask if you would style me for my wedding day?' she asked, speaking behind her hand. 'We brought the date forward and I *really* need to look amazing. I've chosen the dress, I just need you there to do me up, tweak the bridesmaids and check my garter doesn't slip—the usual stuff. I can't do it without you. Besides, it'll be fun! Pinky can't wait to see you! Dolce & Gabbana have made him a tiny white tuxedo—it's *sooo* cute. Please say yes—*please*?' There was desperation in her eyes.

'But what about—'

'Mona? Oh, she'll be there, too, natch, but you know what she's like—I can't rely on her. You saw her at my premiere party, you've read all the stories. I've invited her to my bachelorette, but I'm nervous about the wedding, and the magazine is, too. And I saw what you did for Jennifer in London—she rocked it. The venue's in Hawaii, the Four Seasons. Oh my God, Amber, it's incred—total tropical paradise—everyone says "Aloha!" everywhere you go, it's *so cool*!' She paused to study my face. I was teetering. 'But there's not much time. I really need you on board. *Mona* needs you on board. We *all* need you. Oh, go on, Amber, please?' She fixed me with those puppy-dog eyes. *'Pleeease?'*

I glanced back towards Jennifer and Trey, who were now talking animatedly into a CNN microphone.

'But what about Trey? He thinks I'm someone else, Beau—Annie, your producer, remember? How am I going to explain that?'

'Oh, don't worry about him. You can be at the wedding as Annie—I wasn't planning on inviting the real one, she's a bitch—and every now and again you can just pop to check I haven't got the dress tucked in my panties. Trey won't notice a thing. He'll be too wowed by how amazing I look. I'll make sure you're invisible to him, I promise.' I undid the onesie zip a bit further—Jesus, it was hot. Trey turned around briefly to check on Beau's whereabouts. She clocked him and blew a kiss, just as I darted out of sight behind a handily placed large gentleman. *Harvey what's-his-name again?*

'But, Beau, I hate lying—you know I hated it in the first place.'

'Listen, I'll get you Club Class flights, an ocean-view suite—I'll cover all your expenses.' She was speaking quickly now, keen to wrap things up, and she wasn't taking no for an answer.

'When is it, anyway?'

'Next week.'

'Next *week*?' *Talk about putting me on the spot.*

'Trey wanted to bring it forward, to stop all the stupid

rumours and we didn't want the magazine to pull the deal, so...'

'I'll be back in London in my old job then, Beau, I won't be working for Mona any more. I...'

From the corner of my eye I noticed Trey turn around again, eyes scanning the red carpet to spot his wife-to-be amongst the growing throng of famous people. We were out of time—I couldn't face pretending to be Annie in front of him again.

'I can't do it, Beau. I'm sorry.' I was painfully aware that this was probably the first time in her entire pampered life anyone had ever said 'no' to her.

'Suit yourself.' She raised her chin in the air and spun on her spiked heel. 'Don't say I didn't give you an amazing opportunity.'

'I'm sorry,' I called after her. *But for once I have to do something for myself.* I had to know when to leave the party before I became a casualty, too. Besides, I couldn't handle another fiasco with Mona—she'd have to find herself another crutch. I watched Beau rejoin Trey, hiding any sign of disappointment, all smiles for the flashing cameras. And then I scuttled off to lie in wait for Jennifer behind another huge golden man, feeling quietly confident I had done the right thing.

The paps flinched as I darted past. Even they had noticed my ridiculous outfit. *Is this this year's red carpet fashion turkey; the Bjork in a swan dress?* But then they carried on jostling for the best spot before the inevitable moment when all the major stars walked past at once and it was a mad scramble, each paparazzo driven by the possibility that one exclusive could set them up for early retirement: a 'Julia Roberts with hairy armpits' moment. I waited beside the railings, my kit poised ready to offer anything Jennifer might need before she entered the ceremony. At one point Nicole came over and asked for my spare permanent marker for Jennifer to sign autographs.

It was intoxicating observing the steady parade of big names glide past me, offering plenty of photo-perfect moments en route to the entrance to the theatre, embracing each other along the way, and stopping to talk to some of the younger nominees in their fancy ball gowns, just as wowed by the whole surreal experience as I was. No matter how many times you do it, the red carpet at a major event is such a buzz. My phone vibrated in my pocket. I hoped it might be Rob. Or the airline calling about my case. Rob's friendly face would be welcome right about now, if he forgave me for my drunken tirade in London. He would be bound to see the funny side of my ridiculous appearance.

Instead it was a text from Mona: Are you with Jennifer?

No explanation of where she was, or anything else. I was livid. It was tempting to reply 'No,' followed by 'I quit', but there was little point. Instead I replaced the phone in my pocket. *I'll deal with her later.*

* * *

With Jennifer safely deposited outside the grand art deco facade of the theatre ready to make her entrance, Caroline and I shared a cab back to the Chateau to retrieve our things, relieved and happy that the carpet had gone smoothly. I called the airline and was emailed a lost-luggage form to fill out; meanwhile, I was informed that someone would be round to return Sarah-Louise Moore of Mothercare's suitcase to its rightful owner. Somehow this all made me feel like a thief. When I eventually arrived at Mona's, the jet lag was really starting to take hold. The exhilaration of the evening was wearing off, my eyelids felt heavy and my mood was suddenly flat. Even the mansion didn't look as spectacular as it had the first time I'd laid eyes on it, barely a fortnight before. Ana met me at the door, tea towel in hand.

'Any sign of Miss Armstrong?' she asked, concern etched across her face.

'One text,' I replied. 'She's not dead, but I don't know any more than that.'

'Nothing here,' Klara said. 'We even called a few hospitals, just in case, but nothing.'

I pulled out my phone, realising I hadn't checked it in a while. I had three missed calls from Mona, soon after the text.

'She's been ringing,' I informed the others and almost immediately, it vibrated again. Mona's name flashed up. I shouted into the phone: 'Where on earth have—'

A male voice interrupted me. 'Is this Miss Amber Green?' He sounded serious.

'Yes, it is.'

'My name is Officer Lyle, from the LAPD in Beverly Hills. I'm calling about Ms Armstrong—yours was the last-dialled number in her cell and she thought you would be the best person for us to contact.'

'The police?' I whispered, stumbling backwards to sit on a chair. Ana and Klara stared at me wide-eyed, then huddled close.

'We have Ms Armstrong here with us. She's been detained, following an incident this afternoon.'

'Detained?' I looked at Ana and Klara in disbelief.

'That's right, ma'am—she was shoplifting,' the officer continued.

'*Shoplifting?*' I repeated the word aloud, as if repeating

it might make it go away. Ana put one hand to her mouth and crossed herself with the other.

'She was caught by the in-store detective outside Barney's Co-op, Rodeo Drive, at approximately midday.'

'So, what's happening to her?' I asked after a lengthy pause. Jet lag wasn't helping me process the situation.

'She'll be released from our custody with a ticking off this time, but she's lucky. Barney's have decided not to press charges because she has no other theft-related conviction— but things won't look so good if it happens again. She had some expensive items on her person.'

'What were they?'

'Five hundred dollars' worth of silk lingerie and hosiery,' the officer informed me. 'Plus some silicone bra inserts, and something called "Tit tape". You can pay for them in cash or with any major credit card. Ms Armstrong said that you could make this happen for her.'

Frantically, I gestured for Klara to pass my bag and I rummaged through it to find the brown envelope containing what was left of my portion of the kitty. There had been roughly £500 in cash, which luckily I'd changed into US dollars at the airport. It was just enough to cover the loot, and taxis to and from the police station.

'I'll be down within the hour,' I replied.

'Thank you for your co-operation, ma'am.'

An image of Mona's mugshot making an appearance on E! News this evening flashed into my head. If her career wasn't already over, it would be after that.

* * *

We sat in silence for the first five minutes of the journey back to the house. The roads were deserted, the city felt like a ghost town—everyone was either at the Oscars or glued to the ceremony at a viewing party. It would be nearing Jennifer's moment now and I was itching to watch the TV, which only compounded my frustration with Mona. When I'd got there, Mona hadn't been in a forthcoming mood. A bashful 'Does Jennifer know about this?' was all she said at the station, and since then she had avoided eye contact entirely. Beverly Hills whizzed past the window as I sat quietly fuming next to her. After noticeably staring into his rear-view mirror more times than was necessary to check the empty lanes behind us, the driver eventually broke the silence: 'Hey, that's it! Ma'am, aren't you—'

'No!' she snapped, slamming the privacy window shut, sinking down and pulling her collars up. We were over half-way home when she finally spoke again.

'So, did she wear the Valentino?' Through big sunglasses I could just make out her eyes, they were focused on the horizon.

'She did, and it looked incredible,' I replied, coolly.

'At least that's one person who doesn't hate me,' she said, presumably referring to the designer. Then there was another lengthy pause, before she sighed. 'It's been complete humiliation today.'

'For you?' I scoffed. 'Wasn't I the idiot wearing a onesie at the Oscars?'

For once she hadn't even seemed to register my clothing, she was so wrapped up in herself.

'Full-body search to find the lingerie and implants,' she continued, bottom lip quivering. 'I shouldn't have had to be in that position. Why didn't you transfer me the money, like I asked?'

'So it's *my* fault you got frisked by the LAPD?' I turned to face her, fury in my eyes and adrenalin pumping through my veins. 'I hardly had enough to get myself over here—flights aren't free for assistants, you know.'

'I had no choice, Amber—Jennifer was waiting for me.' Her voice began to tremble. *She's trying to justify shoplifting now?* I doubted this would stand up if it ever went to court.

'You could have asked her to pay for her own underwear, or called some in?'

'It doesn't work like that, dear. Not on Oscars day, when everyone's panicking. Besides, it's not as if a star like Jennifer carries cash to sub her penniless stylist.' She paused for a breath as we both considered this.

'I could have left you in there,' I muttered, not quietly enough.

'Perhaps you should have,' she spat.

'Oh, for God's sake—you're hardly Nelson Mandela!' I folded my arms and waited, unsure where any of this was going. Finally, as our surroundings began to look more familiar, she took a deep breath and spoke: 'Anyway, I had a chance to do some thinking when I was…in the cell.' She turned towards me, and her features appeared to soften. There was a hint of a smile. 'Oh, don't look so terrified, babe! There's no drink or drugs problem. I don't need rehab, if that's what you're thinking.' She raised a sardonic eyebrow. 'Not yet, anyway. But I've made a decision—I'm going to get my accounts in shape. I mean it this time.' She scoured my face for a reaction. I bit my bottom lip.

Against my better judgement, I still clung to an unlikely fantasy that Mona would come round and finally, really, do something about all this mess. Her eyes still on me, she continued: 'When they said you were coming to get me out, I was so thankful, Amber. Not just because there was money left in the kitty, but because you were there for me. I realised there wasn't actually anyone else to call—I couldn't think of a single person. None of the famous people I know would be seen dead walking into a Beverly Hills police station in the middle of the afternoon—let alone Oscars afternoon—to bail me out.'

'It was pretty hard to top,' I said, determinedly, when she appeared to have finished. 'You landed me in it. Jennifer, Nicole, Caroline—they were all going mad. It was bloody lucky I was on the afternoon flight, otherwise I'd have missed the awards, too. And Ana and Klara were so worried—they were phoning around hospitals looking for you. So don't tell me no one cares.'

She bowed her head. 'They were?' She suddenly looked like a child.

'There is someone who could maybe help you get your accounts in order,' I offered, after a sufficient pause, 'my mum.' Mona let out a grunt. 'Before you dismiss it, she's a hotshot lawyer and she has contacts out here. She's offered to talk to you, offer some advice. For free.'

Mona rested her head back against the seat and closed her eyes. 'Sweet of you,' she finally said.

* * *

When we reached the house she headed straight upstairs to her room, presumably to turn on the TV to discover, as I soon did, too, that Jennifer had made it an awards-season hat-trick, triumphing at the Oscars and sealing her place in the Hollywood hall of fame with a beautifully choreographed, tearful acceptance speech. I celebrated alone with a glass of flat champagne from the fridge and the news from Ana that an airline representative had picked up the Mothercare woman's suitcase and mine was still safely at the airport. I couldn't face a trip there to collect it now—I'd send a courier for it tomorrow and wing it until then. Besides, I consoled myself with the realisation that the one benefit of spending the past twenty-four hours in a onesie was that I was ready to roll straight into bed.

As I nodded off, I was jolted awake by a text from Rob. Despite everything, my heart leapt. *Has he forgiven my drunken fiancée-slagging?* I read the message with one eye. No mention of fiancée-gate. Phew. He was wondering if I fancied a run in the morning.

A run? Are you joking? I texted back. *Maybe this is his way of punishing me for being an arse.*

I'm serious—Runyon Canyon.

A run in a canyon? No thanks. *Stay firm, Amber, he's taken, so what is the point of humiliating yourself further.*

It's an LA rite of passage. You'll be thanking me afterwards.

I'm pretty sure I won't. Sounds hideous. Plus I don't have any running gear.

Borrow some.

Do you seriously think Mona runs?

Excuses. I'll pick you up at 8 a.m.

8 a.m.?

No reply. I supposed the run thing was happening. And I supposed I still needed Rob in my life for professional reasons, so I resolved to start afresh, try desperately hard to push all filthy thoughts to one side and see him as a mate.

Chapter Twenty-Three

Early the next morning, happy to be hangover-free, unlike the rest of Hollywood, I decided to enlist Klara in the hunt for some sportswear that would:

1. Enable me to look vaguely attractive in front of Rob.

2. Give the impression I was reasonably fit.

3. Cope with the tricky terrain of a canyon.

My situation was greatly helped by the fact that Klara, the dirty stop-out, had not returned all night. Rummaging through her wardrobe, I found a pair of leather-look leggings, some cream Isabel Marant wedge sneakers, and her big 'Relax Don't Do It' T-shirt. The irony wasn't lost on me. They would have to do.

* * *

Rob arrived early. 'You're running in those?' he looked at the shoes.

'They're trainers, and more to the point they're all I've got,' I replied, admiring them. And then we were off, puffing next to each other as we climbed higher and higher into the Hollywood Hills until we reached a dirt track signifying the start of 'Runyon Canyon'.

'You spot actors every time you're up here, normally,' Rob explained, barely breaking a sweat and, thankfully, without showing a whiff of ill feeling towards me. *Maybe he was drunker than I thought that night.* 'Unlikely today, though, being the morning after the Oscars.'

'Sensible people are probably having a lie-in,' I panted, desperately trying to regulate my breathing. It was already getting hot.

'Only mad dogs and English ladies in silly shoes would go out for a run.' He nudged me playfully as we started a slight ascent. I noticed the wedges were already covered in a layer of brown dust. Meanwhile, Rob had clocked the pained expression on my face.

'Think of the good it's doing,' he encouraged, 'getting the toxins out and oxygen flowing. Do you ever run at home?'

I was having to concentrate very hard on the rocky gravel path. As it turned out, wedge trainers are almost impossible to run in. I side-glanced at him, 'What do *you* think?' He chuckled in response. 'It was these or flip-flops. Anyway, I wanted to apologise to you.' A film of sweat was developing across my face and I was starting to lag behind.

He glanced back. 'Why?'

'I was a total idiot to you in London, after the BAFTAs. I'm really sorry.'

'Don't be. You weren't an idiot at all.' He considerately slowed the pace to a brisk walk—a huge relief, as I was developing a stitch.

'I was. I got too drunk and I don't really remember everything I was saying, but I woke up feeling horrible. I know it was bad,' I panted, catching him up and trying not to sprain my ankle. He had stopped by the side of the path to survey the scenery beneath us. I dropped my hands to my knees. My inappropriate push-up bra was digging into my ribs, and my knickers were in my bum.

'Look at this view. It's worth the climb, right?'

I looked out over the flat, sprawling city: row after row of low-rise grey buildings and long straight roads in a grid pattern, dotted with tall skyscrapers on the horizon. Above it all, a light, hazy smog was being slowly burned away by the morning sun. It looked calm down there, as though the whole of LA was just coming round, nursing a collective hangover after the excitement of the night before. We stood there, next to each other, for a few moments of quiet as we admired the view. *Why do I always find myself in perfect snogging settings with Rob?* I physically ached to be held in his arms; for him to tell me he was falling in love, too.

'It's a concrete jungle, but it's beautiful.' He sighed, finally. 'I love this time of the morning.'

'Could you live here?' I asked, allowing myself to contemplate what it might be like if this was our daily run, together, in another life, where I was wearing suitable shoes and displaying a washboard stomach. Oh, and Rob wasn't engaged to someone else.

'Maybe,' he sighed, wistfully. 'But it won't happen now.'

'Why not? You've got loads of work out here.' I paused. 'And a soon-to-be fiancée who likes travelling. The world's your oyster, surely?'

He hesitated, as if mulling over whether to tell me something. He paused for the longest time. At last he spoke: 'It's not a very baby-friendly city.' He stretched his arms back behind him and clasped his hands to distract attention from the bomb he'd just dropped. I caught my breath. Slowly, I turned to face him. 'You have—*a baby*?' I raised an eyebrow. *How many secrets can one guy have? How can I be so dumb as to not have known this?*

'There's one on the way.' He kicked a small rock over the edge. We both watched it go, and heard it bounce once, twice, three times before it stopped.

'You're not kidding, are you?'

'Nope.' He dropped his hands and dug his heel into the soft rubble at our feet.

'That's big news. When is it due?'

'I'm not sure. Listen, I wasn't going to tell you, but the truth is I can't think of anything else and I feel I can trust you, Amber. Can I?'

He had no idea how hard this was to hear. 'Of course,' I put a hand on his shoulder and swallowed hard. 'We're mates.'

'Let's walk and talk,' he said. I too was glad of the distraction. As Rob talked, I tried to take it all in, pretending he wasn't cutting me deeper and deeper with every word. Everything began to make sense as he described how his girlfriend of only six months, Emily, had told him the news that her period was late—*two whole weeks late*—during her work trip. Rob, being the gentleman he was, had decided to do the right thing—get a ring and propose to her on her return, when they'd done the pregnancy test together. The whole thing made me feel sick to the core. Getting engaged was one thing, but a baby? There was no going back from that.

'You don't sound too overjoyed about it,' I said, when he finished. He'd barely looked up from the path the whole time.

He shrugged. 'We've not been together that long. I suppose I hadn't imagined becoming a dad just yet—we hadn't had *that* conversation, you know? But I've always thought I would have children, at some point. Maybe now is that point. Got to man up, I guess.' He half smiled although his body language told a whole different story. We walked in silence for a while, leaving the canyon path for the safety of tarmac roads. My calves could finally relax, but my mind was now in overdrive.

'Once it sinks in, I bet you'll be really excited,' I said at last. 'You'll make a great dad. You've already "manned up"—whatever that's supposed to mean.'

'Jog the last bit?' He picked up the pace, running backwards facing me and forcing a weak smile. The sun backlit his movie-star physique. *God, he looks handsome, even more so when he's sweaty and mixed up.* Compared to this news, the thought of him buying the engagement ring seemed so small. I could feel tears rushing to my eyes. I breathed deeply and forced a weak smile back.

'If you insist, Mr Motivator.'

When we reached the house again, he hugged me close on the doorstep. He felt hot and comforting. He smelled of warm washing powder and fresh sweat. I could have stood there, holding him, inhaling him, for ages.

'Sorry if that got a bit heavy,' he said, pulling away. 'Thanks for being a great mate.' *Mate. I hate that word so much.*

'Any time.' I raised a forced smile of my own.

'I'll be back later, to say goodbye before you fly,' he continued. 'Fran's keen to see Mona about the pilot.'

I cleared my throat. 'Great—see you then.' Then he was off, jogging down the street and straight to his car without looking back. I stood there, rooted to the spot, watching as he drove off. I didn't want to move, because in the warm, still air that enveloped me I could still just about smell him. I stood there for a minute or so, my arms folded over my chest, aching for another cuddle like that. I realised it was the first hug I'd had from a man in months—maybe a year. LA Liam hadn't even tried to cuddle me when we had the bad kiss. *How tragic.* I replayed the safe, happy feeling the hug gave me over in my mind, fearing it would never happen again. Then my brain caught up, remembering that there was really nothing safe or happy about it at all, because he was going to marry someone else. Someone who was having his baby. *His baby! Could I have picked a worse person to fall in love with?* As his car vanished around the corner at the foot of the hill, I visualised it coming back, reversing up the street at high speed so that he could carry me off like a caveman and tell me it was all a twisted joke, just his warped sense of humour; that there was no fiancée, no baby. I'd forgive him in a second before kissing his gorgeous face off.

* * *

As I entered the house, Mona was marching downstairs, wearing a white silk blouse tucked into a tight black leather pencil skirt, and heels, her hair in a neat bun on top of her head, chunky gold chain around her neck, red nails. Pristine and ready for business. But, as it turned out, not for a meeting with an accountant.

'Fran from *20Twenty* called this morning,' she declared, bright and breezy. 'They're coming over to show us an edit of the pilot. Isn't that fabulous?' She clapped her hands together, as if the memory of yesterday and her time at the cop shop had been completely wiped. 'Ana's setting up the living room and she's going to make popcorn.' She stopped in front of the big hallway mirror to admire her reflection. She'd trowelled on make-up this morning and it certainly didn't look as though she'd lost much sleep last night. Eventually she took in my appearance, fixating on the dusty Marants.

'Jesus.' She looked me up and down. 'What the hell have *you* been doing?'

'Exercising,' I replied, smugly.

'In *those* shoes?'

When she had finished briefing me on the returns to be processed and ticked me off for nearly mislaying a suitcase full of borrowed accessories, which a courier was now on its way to pick up from Lost and Found at LAX, thank goodness, I found myself alone in the office, surveying the aftermath of yesterday's antics.

While the internet was awash with Oscars gossip, and Jennifer's gown made all the Best Dressed lists, fashion blogs were also buzzing with the story of Mona's arrest, and increased speculation about the downward spiral of the 'wayward stylist'. The least flattering of all paparazzi photos of Mona were plastered across gossip sites to illustrate the point. They even knew about the stolen chicken fillets, which, coupled with the rest of her recent behaviour, created a seriously bleak picture. On the *Starz* website, a 'source' was quoted, revealing the lack of remorse she'd shown as she escaped with a ticking off and a fine. It had to have been leaked by our cabbie. My phone was full of text messages; Nicole and Caroline had called and people at home had seen the stories, too. In fact, it seemed as though only Mona was living in a bubble, fingers in her ears, going 'la, la, la'. On the surface, at least.

Are you okay? We're worried about you, darling, Mum texted.

Don't be. I'll be home tomorrow x, I replied.

Tried to call her about the accountant, but no response, she texted back. It didn't surprise me at all.

Text from Vicky: Mona—shoplifting!?! And will you be back for Tuesday? xx

Jas: Is Mona okay? Are you? x

I shut my phone down. Maybe, if I ignored the outside world, too, the Mona problem would simply go away. I only had twenty-four hours to get through, sorting out the returns, and then I was free.

* * *

Fran and Rob arrived and set about linking their laptop to the big TV. Mona had asked Klara and Ana to join us— she'd even mentioned it to the pool cleaner—anything to maximise the audience for her star turn. Klara had rocked up from her twenty-four-hour Oscars bender not long before; she clattered through the front door, slightly dishevelled, with a mischievous smile on her face. She looked as though she'd just rolled out of someone's bed.

'Okay?' I mouthed. She winked in response, confirming my suspicion, not even clocking that I was wearing her clothes. As Ana passed round bowls of warm popcorn, Klara appeared to drift off, her eyes glazing over as her mind wandered, presumably back to an X-rated scene from the night before. The only thing pulling her out of it was some text tennis, presumably with last night's conquest, as there was a soppy grin on her face with every beep from her phone.

As the TV screen came to life, the volume grew loud and we all giggled as Miss P's new single pumped out during the opening credits—a hint of the flashing incident that was surely to come. Then the camera panned across rails of glamorous gowns and rows of shoes, peered inside a treasure chest of gleaming jewels and came to rest on an image of Mona, dressed in her trademark leather leggings and tank top. Stacks of bangles on her arm, iPad on her lap and phone to her ear, she looked every inch the workaholic international super-stylist. Mona dragged her chair closer, eyes glued to the screen—captivated by her own image. The opening scenes showed her at the first appointment in Smith's, rifling through the racks with Jas. I squirmed when the camera caught my flushed cheeks. Mona described Tamara leaving her 'right up shit creek. The silly bitch handed in her notice this morning. I go for the bloody Globes tomorrow! Oh, I'll do it, all right.' She peered menacingly into the camera lens. '*Nothing* comes between me and my superstars.' *How incongruous her words seemed now.* And there I was, a rabbit in the headlights, barely able to walk in my borrowed shoes as I was plucked from obscurity to become Mona's assistant. You couldn't help but notice the scowl across Kiki's face.

'Look at you! So cute!' Mona turned and squeezed my knee. I realised I was clutching the sides of my face tightly, my eyes half-closed in a giant cringe as the camera zoomed in on my blotchy red face while the mix-up over the monochrome shoes in the shop window played out. Then we were magically transported to LA. 'The land of palm trees, limos, A-list stars and the start of awards season,' intoned the narrator, who sounded suspiciously like Fran and not Joanna Lumley, who had been promised at one point. The W suite looked like a dazzling boudoir, awash with the finest fashions in Tinseltown. In came Pinky, and in tottered Beau Belle, looking even more like a mad, pneumatic Barbie than she did in the flesh. Pinky's miniature leather jacket looked ridiculous—it was as though someone had pressed the 'exaggerate' button, but it was all painfully true. There was a comedy moment when Pinky took a shine to a pair of glittery Jimmy Choos, nuzzling them gently with his snout until Mona kicked him off with more than a little force. The moment she saw the camera on her, she smiled broadly and bent down to pat the pig, 'Dear Porky, there's a good boy!'

Then the mood of the programme seemed to change. The narrator cut in to explain that while Mona was feeling unwell in the bathroom, it fell to her new assistant, Amber Green, to finish the dress fittings with Beau. There I was, in my gothic black shirt dress, make-up forgotten, the beginnings of sweat patches under my arms and wearing a strained expression, presenting the scarlet Valentino dress to Beau. When she returned from trying it on we all sighed collectively, then stifled our giggles as she exclaimed: 'And she's even easy to pee in!' And then I was on camera, full frame, discussing the Valentino gown: 'It's the ultimate fairy-tale dress. I fell in love with it the moment I saw it—I think any girl would.' As I continued to answer Fran's questions, I was surprised by how authoritative I sounded. Mona started to get twitchy.

'A little too much Amber in that scene, don't you think, Fran?' she announced, twisting around. Fran kept her eyes silently trained on the TV, which was now showing Mona holding us hostage during the fire alarm at the W.

Next we were whisked off to the red carpet on Golden Globes night. I hadn't even registered that Rob was filming for the pilot as well as the breakfast show that evening. I breathed a sigh of relief that my fainting episode at the premiere the night before had not been captured. Instead, the story focused on the fact that Beau had gone for Dolce & Gabbana over the Valentino and Jennifer Astley had opted for the Oscar de la Renta, despite Mona being nowhere to be seen, as she was 'recovering from a bout of food poisoning picked up at a premiere party the evening before'.

The film continued at a cracking pace, criss-crossing the Atlantic and chronicling Mona's escalating blunders as she failed to style her biggest client on the most important nights of her career. A dressing-gown-clad Vicky made a hilarious cameo, her startled face darting in and out of Jennifer's bathroom at the Dorchester as I tried to stop Fran shoving a microphone into my face through the doorway, I looked a bit like Jack Nicholson in *The Shining*. It was so embarrassing I wanted to laugh hysterically—either that or bawl. *And I've signed* several *release forms for all of this. There's no way out.* I glanced over towards Rob, who had his head in his hands, too.

But my starring moment really came on the BAFTAs red carpet, when images of Jennifer in her fashion-forward British ensemble made all the Best Dressed lists around the world. The camera had caught me crouched at the side of the carpet, watching every move like her shadow. A strange grunting noise emanated from Mona as some swirling newspaper and social media cuttings showed the contrast between the international coverage of Jennifer's sartorial success and Miss P's indecent exposure on the red carpet.

'Should never have got that Kiki girl involved,' Mona muttered frostily, shunning all responsibility. But when the narrator informed viewers that Mona was once again absent from the red carpet, this time due to contracting the Norovirus, she really lost the plot.

'You've got it all wrong, you know.' She stood up, blocking the front of the screen. 'Why aren't you showing the appointments to stores, the calls, the hundreds of emails—

the *stress* I'm under during awards season? Whoever edited this *pathetic* piece of film has no idea.'

We all sank back into our seats, afraid to speak.

'It's not over yet,' said Fran bravely.

The filming then turned to a collection of short vignettes to camera from some of Mona's clients and contacts. Jas talked with great warmth about Mona's flair for making the most high-fashion trends accessible to the general public purely through celebrity placement.

'Thank you, Jasmine. See that? A class act,' Mona said approvingly, turning round to ensure we'd all taken it in. Then it was Jennifer Astley's turn to speak to the camera, giving another Oscar-worthy performance, her face drawn with concern:

'Dear Mona, I'm worried about you. If you let me in, I can help you. I know an amazing spiritual guru who deals with reversing bad energy. I'd love to put you in touch. You'll get through this, Mona, and be stronger for it. You can do this.' She looked earnestly into the camera. 'You're so lucky to have found an assistant like Amber. She's one in a million—an awesome stylist with an incredible eye for detail. She saved my awards season. Thank you, Amber.' And she blew a kiss out of the screen. But it didn't give me the warm feeling that she intended.

'Oh, how cosy,' spat Mona. '*Saved* my awards season? Do me a favour!' She turned to look at me, scowling. I felt hideously conspicuous; my cheeks reddened and I wanted to melt into the chair. 'How could you do this to me?' she continued. I looked around for support, but everyone else seemed to be looking at the floor, their fingernails, a lampshade—anything but me. 'You, whose life I transformed. You couldn't wait to steal the spotlight from me, could you?'

My mind raced with all the things I wanted to say back. I'd often imagined the moment when I would give Mona a piece of my mind; tell her how selfish she was, how everyone was sick of her irrational behaviour. But now the moment had arrived, I didn't have the energy to do it. So I said nothing. Instead, stray, angry tears began falling from my eyes. I tried desperately to wipe them away with my sleeve before anyone noticed, but it was a losing battle. More than anything, I wanted to run out of the house, down the street and get as far away as I could from this poisonous woman, these mad people and this horribly self-indulgent world.

The pilot continued to play, showing Miss P, looking no better than a Soho hooker, with tears streaming down her face as she was led away from the BAFTAs after-party, supported by Clive. 'How could you let this happen, Mona?' He scowled into the camera. 'Total balls-up. Last time I count on you to do anything.' Things didn't get any better as the footage drew closer to the Oscars and the narrator told the sorry story of Mona's arrest for shoplifting. And then Tamara's face appeared. 'I tried to help you so many times, Mona, but frankly, I got sick of doing all the work. You were never around!'

'This is a witch hunt!' Mona screamed, drowning out the voice of her former assistant. She was really on the warpath now, standing up in front of us all, eyes narrow. 'Why are you *all* trying to ruin me? What did I do to you?'

'I had to tell the true story, Mona,' Fran reasoned with her. 'I've only shown what I saw. We agreed to make a documentary, not a work of fiction, remember?' Her words hung in the air long after their sound had melted away.

'Well, it's defamation of character.' Mona's voice finally cut into the silence. 'I'm going to call my lawyer.'

'How can it be defamation, Mona?' Fran snapped, also on her feet. *Oh God.* The last time I'd seen two women so close to physically fighting was over a reduced Chloé bag during the Boxing Day sale at Smith's. 'I saw it all first-hand— *everything* is caught on camera, these are first person accounts, and it's all been legalled. You signed the release forms for all of this, and besides, you can't afford a lawyer!'

It was the final straw. Mona had had enough. She fled the room as quickly as her tight pencil skirt would allow, looking like a famished penguin trying to chase a fish across a frozen lake. Perhaps she was in a hurry to hide her tears; perhaps she really meant to call a lawyer. *Please say she's not going to ring my mum.* Somewhere upstairs, a door slammed loudly. The five of us were left shell-shocked. I found the only dry patch on my jumper sleeve and wiped my nose.

'Wow,' Rob sighed at last, looking around.

'She should have seen it coming,' Fran said defiantly, turning off the screen. 'I mean, what did she think we were going to show, *Little House on the Prairie*?'

'Coffee?' asked Ana.

'I'll show myself out,' Fran said, heading for the door, 'Are you coming, Rob?'

'I'll catch you up at the hotel,' he replied, hanging back.

'This has done nothing for my hangover,' announced Klara, pushing her extra big sunglasses back onto her face and skulking out of the room.

Rob and I were suddenly alone. There was what seemed like an endless silence.

'Well, that was intense,' he said at last. 'I honestly didn't know Fran was going to make it *that* harsh.' He bowed his head.

'To be honest, I'm glad,' I confessed. My tears had almost dried now, my breathing more steady. With my finger I wiped a landslip of mascara from under my eyes. 'Let's see if any of it will make a difference.'

'I won't be holding my breath.' He squeezed my shoulder. 'You okay?'

'She's just so evil sometimes,' I said.

'She's a class-A bitch, Amber. She's out of control. She shouldn't have spoken to you like that. What now?' Rob asked, as I mentally pulled myself together. 'Perhaps a glittering arrival at an ashram? Big sunglasses, silk dressing gown and a carefully managed press conference where she makes a tearful pledge to sort herself out and dedicate her life to helping others?' He smiled wryly.

I tried to smile back. 'Perhaps we *should* stage an intervention? Isn't that what people do for wayward stars?'

'You're not serious?' He was looking at me like I was mad. *Perhaps I am.*

'Well, obviously it's the last thing I feel like doing. Anyway, she doesn't need an ashram—or rehab—she told me that herself yesterday. It might help her reputation right now, though. Have you seen the internet? She's become a joke.'

'What Mona needs is to stop being so lazy. Jennifer's right—you saved her awards season and she knows it. You put gowns on backs while she was hungover, pulling a sickie or busy nicking things. She deserved to see the truth today. The only person who can help Mona Armstrong is herself.'

We were interrupted by the doorbell—a courier, and he wasn't delivering my suitcase, but the biggest white box I'd ever seen. I was pretty sure Mona hadn't ordered a new fridge-freezer, and even if she had, I doubted it would have come packaged with a big elaborate bow on the top. Rob leapt up to help Ana and together they set it down on the kitchen top. The box was big enough to make a house for Klara.

'For Mona,' Ana informed us. 'Another gift, happens every year after the Oscars.'

'Should be addressed to you,' Rob muttered under his breath, as we walked back into the living room together.

'Don't feel sorry for me,' I said, turning to face him. 'I'll be fine. I'm really tired, but I'm going home tomorrow, and soon this will all be a distant memory.' I felt uncomfortable— I couldn't get this morning's conversation off my mind. But half of me also wanted to pull him in for another hug. I'd never needed one so badly.

'Anyway,' Rob said, retrieving his bag from the other side of the room, 'I may have just been upstaged by the world's biggest box, but there's something I wanted to give you before you go.' He lifted out a small cream paper box.

'What's that?' I asked, my heart already sinking. *A matching pair of earrings to go with the diamond ring for your baby-mother? Could today get any more depressing?*

He smiled at me. 'Open it.'

Inside, wrapped up in tissue paper, was a tiny silver chain with the word 'Hollywood' hanging across it. I lifted it out.

I held it in my palm, my fingers curled around it.

'Fran chose it,' he said, suddenly embarrassed. 'I just wanted to say thanks for your advice. It's been great working with you these last few weeks, I've had so much fun, and I, well, we, saw it soon after you'd helped me with the ring, and I...' He trailed off. *Is he blushing, too?* 'I thought of your "S" necklace and how it was only on loan from Mona.'

I was flabbergasted that a guy could be so thoughtful. I looked at it again. 'It's so pretty. I love it. Thank you.'

It was time to take off the 'S', anyway. I'd never felt completely comfortable with my borrowed piece of jewellery—it had started to feel more like a ball and chain than a fashion accessory. This meant so much more. He might not be my boyfriend or have any intention of becoming my boyfriend in the future, but perhaps it didn't matter. Maybe I *could* be Rob's friend instead. It felt really nice that he'd got me something so thoughtful, for no particular reason. In my limited experience, actual boyfriends rarely did that.

'Hopefully see you in London soon,' he said, shuffling now, slightly embarrassed. 'I very much doubt the Mona Armstrong show is going to get commissioned after this, so at least we might be able to go out and talk about something else.'

'I'd love that,' I replied, sort of meaning it. 'Good luck, with—everything. You'll be great.'

And then, before things could get any more awkward in this house today, we were saved by a courier arriving with my suitcase. As he closed the door, my entire world felt emptier.

* * *

Thankfully, there was plenty to busy myself with for the rest of the day. I unloaded my suitcase of its shimmering wares and sorted out the last of the Oscars returns, dealing with a potentially sticky moment regarding a misplaced pair of Jimmy Choos, which thankfully turned up in the ladies' loos at Cecconi's. Then I had a hot bath and packed up the bits and pieces in my room. Mona surfaced only once, to inspect the big white box. Cautiously I joined her in the kitchen, curious about the contents. After endless sheets of tissue paper had been cast aside, inside was a stunning, pillar-box-red studded tote. My Smith's training meant I knew this bag was worth well over a thousand pounds.

'It's from Valentino,' she announced curtly, pushing it towards where I stood across the breakfast bar. 'Have it.'

'I couldn't, Mona. He sent it to you.' I pushed it back.

'I insist,' she retorted, nudging it towards me once more. It had to be the most stunning bag I'd ever laid eyes on.

'I don't want it!' I exclaimed, my voice much louder than I had intended. Ana at once scurried out of the room, and Klara poked her head round the corner before quickly retracting it.

'Why are you so ungrateful and so angry, Amber?' Mona's strident tone made me see red.

'I'm angry because of the way you treated me earlier, Mona,' I fumed, 'in front of everyone. But not only about earlier, since you ask. I'm also angry about the countless times I've had to make excuses and pick up the pieces for you in the last few weeks. You've spent most of the time treating me like a speck of dirt on your clothes. And then you wonder why *I'm* ungrateful?' Fury was taking me over.

'You're overreacting. I just thought the bag would be a nice treat.' She began moodily stuffing tissue paper back into the box.

'Can't you see, Mona? You're doing *exactly* what everybody does to you. You're trying to buy me with free gifts, and you know what? I don't want your freebies. I don't even want this job any more. I've had enough of this superficial world and I can't wait to get home tomorrow and leave it all behind.' I could feel a prickly sensation building up behind my eyes again, but this time I wouldn't let the tears break through.

As Mona quietly replaced the lid on the box, I fought an overwhelming urge to punch it off the table. But then I paused, a thought occurring to me.

'Actually, you know what, seeing as you insist, I *will* take the bag.' She looked up, confused. 'But not for myself—I want to give it to Ana. It seems to me that Ana is the most loyal person you have in your life, and *she* definitely deserves a treat.'

'Fine. Whatever,' she conceded, pushing the box towards me once more.

And that was as close as I was going to get to an apology.

* * *

The following morning Mona breezed into the kitchen, dressed in a powder-rose blouse, canary-yellow capri pants and kitten heels. There was a touch of 1950s Portofino about her. She plonked her big white Louis Vuitton tote, personalised with her initials, onto the kitchen counter. *No wonder she didn't want the Valentino.*

'Thought we could grab a taxi to the airport together, babe,' she said, grabbing the counter for support while she polished her heel with a wet finger.

I was confused. 'Where are you off to?'

'Beau's bachelorette. Ten girls on tour—it's going to be insane!'

It was tempting to mention the conversation I'd had with Beau at the Oscars, but I stayed quiet—that would only rub more salt into open wounds.

'Are you allowed to fly when you've been recently detained for shoplifting?'

'Oh, it's only a hop and a skip to Cabo,' she replied, all smiles.

'A hop and a skip across the border to Mexico,' I muttered.

'I didn't get charged, you know, Amber.'

I ignored that last comment. *Leave it, Amber. She is no*

longer your problem. The cab was due in thirty minutes, so I returned to my room for a final check—there was only my hand luggage to pick up. I carefully placed the 'S' necklace on the dressing table for Mona to discover.

I peered out of the window to see Klara in the garden, sunning herself on her favourite lounger as usual. There was something cathartic about the scene—it reminded me of the first time I'd looked out of this window, excitedly spotting the pool—which I *still* hadn't even trailed a hand through. Then a man strolled out to join her, naked from the waist up. He had a large tattoo across his back. *Hmm, fit body— no wonder she's been smiling so much.* He bent down for a kiss and then sat on the end of her lounger; Klara sat up on her elbows as he quickly closed in for another, more lingering kiss. They looked besotted. I leaned closer to the glass. There was the back of a thick, black mop of curly hair and a long, tanned neck. *I recognise that mop.* They began kissing, heads bobbing together, his hands holding her cheeks in a firm grip. And then the penny dropped. *I recognise that head hold. Hang on, I know that kiss. Jesus, it's LA Liam!* I moved away from the window and sat on the edge of the bed, wanting to laugh. *The auditioning actor with a text obsession and terrible lip service. She must have met him at Soho House, too—the place was practically her second home. No wonder she was texting away so furiously yesterday. Their fast fingers are made for each other. Of all the people in Hollywood...* Well, at least he'd found a compatible kisser in Klara. I smiled, deciding that rather than interrupt—though it would be funny to see his face—I'd call Klara to say goodbye from the other side of the Atlantic.

Downstairs, I located Ana in the laundry room, busily

transferring the contents of her battered tan shopper into the gleaming Valentino tote.

'Amber, it is *so beautiful*! Thank you very much,' she cooed.

'Stunning, isn't it?' I stroked the smooth, cool skin. 'Red suits you.'

'We'll miss you.' She reached to take my hand.

'I'll miss you, too.' I leaned in and gave her a hug. 'Look after her, hey? Well—as much as anyone can.'

She rolled her eyes. 'After fifteen years, I know her pretty well...'

Then a car horn outside signalled it was time to go.

* * *

We didn't say much to each other during the journey to LAX. Mona was too busy covering her face with a scarf, in case the cab driver happened to recognise her and alert the gossip sites that Mona Armstrong was on the move.

We entered the departures hall, and as I scanned the screens for my check-in desk, she turned to me.

'Thank Christ awards season's over, hey, babe?'

We both smiled, awkwardly.

'Don't think I could handle another one,' I said, truthfully.

'Maybe I'll see you at Smith's some time.'

'I guess, if Jas has me back. And, Mona—I really hope you get everything worked out.'

At last she smiled. 'Bye, Amber.' We began to turn away from each other. 'Oh, Amber...' I glanced around. 'You were my best assistant yet. Thank you. For everything.'

We walked off in opposite directions, but after a few paces I turned back to look at her one final time. I watched her hurry towards the check-in desk, blow-out bouncing, bangles jangling, heels clip-clopping and manicured hand soon to be brandishing another first-class boarding pass to another glamorous destination, paid for by someone else; no spending money in her pocket, and all her troubles packed up in a Louis Vuitton bag. I had to drink her in, just like I did in Smith's the first time I laid eyes on Mona Armstrong. I wondered if I would ever see her in the flesh again.

Chapter Twenty-Four

I pulled my suitcase off the carousel, triple-checking it was definitely mine. Satisfied, I opened the zips and pulled out my winter coat; it was going to be freezing on the other side of the Heathrow arrivals hall. The benefit of having barely worn any of the clothes in my suitcase this entire trip was that my washing load would be significantly reduced when I got home. Travelling light had actually been quite liberating. *Have onesie, will travel!* I chuckled to myself. There was just about enough left in the kitty to treat myself to a taxi all the way home, and it seemed a neat way of drawing a line under my time as Mona's assistant. As we whizzed along grey, frosty roads, being back on home turf made me want to burst with happiness. My phone buzzed. Text message from Rob.

Hope you got back ok. R x. I read it twice and deleted it. Magic FM was playing on the radio and I would be seeing Vicky soon. *Life is good.*

* * *

When I reached the flat, it was dark and empty. Vicky must have gone to work already. A horrible jet-laggy tiredness descended, so I headed straight for my cold bed and immediately fell asleep for a few hours. When I woke up, I rang Vicky. It took three calls for her to finally pick up.

'You're back, then,' she said coolly.

'Yeah, just had a few hours' kip. Wondering what you're doing later, if you fancy grabbing some food together and catching up? I've got so much to tell you—LA was bonkers!'

'Maybe. Not sure what I'm doing yet.' Her voice sounded flatter than my plane-seat hair.

'You okay?'

'Fine.'

'You don't sound it. Vicky, what's wrong?'

She huffed loudly. 'You don't know?'

'Well, I can't read your mind. What is it, honey?'

'I guess you'd be a bit pissed off, too, if your so-called best mate completely forgot your birthday.'

I took a deep breath, totally floored. My mind raced.

'Oh, honey—it was yesterday!' *How could I have been such a bad friend?* I stumbled back and sat on the edge of the bed. 'That's why you asked if I'd be back on Tuesday. Oh God, Vix, I'm so sorry. It's been a mad few days, I got swept up in all the dramas with Mona—it was worse than ever. I feel awful. Please let me make it up to you.' Silence.

'Vicky, please?'

'I can't talk at work.' That was a lie—she'd regularly spent over an hour chatting to me from inside the fashion cupboard. She had to be really furious.

'Did you have a good birthday though…?'

Eventually: 'Yeah, it was fun, I went out with the work lot. Ended up crashing at Jim's again. Anyway, better go, some of us have to pay rent by doing a *normal* job, and it's busy today.' *Ouch.*

'You'll be home after work, will you?'

'Maybe. I'm not sure yet.' And she hung up.

I lay back on the bed. *You stupid, selfish idiot, Amber.* My phone buzzed into life again. Vicky calling me back? No, an answerphone message:

'Amber, it's Beau, I'm in Cabo at my bachelorette and something really bad has happened. Please call me back. Please.' She sounded serious. *Has something happened to Mona again? Not my problem. Not...my...problem. This is just what I've been trying to escape.* But, after pondering it over a cup of builder's and two more missed calls from Beau, curiosity got the better of me.

'Thank God, Amber, I was desperate to speak to you.'

'What time is it there—must be the middle of the night?'

'It's late, but I can't sleep and I didn't know who else to call. Mona has been a complete nightmare. She hit the tequila on the flight from LA and got us thrown out of the restaurant this evening, she was so drunk. Amber, she's out of control. And she messed up the bachelorette outfits, too. We were meant to be Playboy bunnies with Pinky as our Hugh Hefner and she didn't even bring him a red silk smoking jacket. I mean, how could he be Hef without a smoking jacket? What kind of stylist could mess *that* up?'

I was suddenly immensely glad to be five and a half thousand miles away. I could feel what was coming, and it was much easier to say no to someone—Hollywood star or otherwise—over the phone. 'And now I'm so worried about my wedding I can't sleep a wink knowing that she's going to screw that up, too. There is so much resting on this magazine deal—I just can't do it without a stylist. I really need your help, Amber.'

I breathed out heavily. 'Please, Amber,' Beau begged, her voice beginning to crack, 'I *need* to be styled by you for my wedding—you're the best, and you were my first choice, anyway.' She paused to compose herself.

'Beau,' I reasoned, 'I'm back in London now—I can't just—'

'Oh, please don't ruin my wedding, Amber!'

'Don't cry, Beau…' I tried to soothe her. 'Where's Mona now?'

'We got her into bed at the hotel, but all she really cares about is whether the paps caught her drunk at the restaurant. All the girls think she'll be reported, and then the cops could give her an electronic tag. How's she going to wear Louboutins with a big black plastic thing clunking around her ankle? But, more to the point, it leaves *me* in the horrendous position of getting married in three days' time without knowing if Mona will make it to Hawaii, and, if she does, whether she'll be in a fit state to style me, anyway.' She started to snivel again. 'Amber, I really need you in Hawaii—you're the only one who can handle Mona.'

'But what about the Annie situation? How will we stop Mona blowing my cover to Trey?' There was silence on the end of the line while she mulled it over.

'It won't be that hard,' she finally replied. 'You know what it's like at a wedding—the guys do their thing, us girls will do ours. We'll just stop them from being near you at the same time. It won't be hard.'

I tried to think the scenario through. It wasn't easy, especially as I was still reeling from being a totally shit friend to the most important person in my life.

'Anyway, Jason will be there, too, and he knows about the Annie thing—he'll help keep your cover. It'll be fun!'

'Jason will be there, too?'

'Of course, babe, it would be rude not to invite him.'

Oh God. This didn't sit well with me at all. But a bigger, more important realisation was beginning to dawn on me.

'You did say you'd get my flights, right? In Club? Plus a suite with sea views?' If I was going to ask Jas for another few days off work, it had to be worth my while.

'Of course,' she simpered. 'Whatever it takes.'

'And could I bring a friend—you know, to share the suite and help me?'

'Your boyfriend, you mean?'

'No, I don't have a boyfriend. It would be my best friend—a girl.'

'Of course. In fact, that's perfect! I did mention Annie's a lesbian, didn't I?' Her mood appeared to brighten.

I smiled to myself. *You couldn't make this up.* 'You didn't, but if my friend can come, we're agreed.'

'You got it.'

'Okay… It's a deal. I'll do it. But just this once, *only* because it's your wedding. When do we need to be there?'

'Yay! Love you more than Pinky! Thank you, Amber! I mean, Annie. I won't forget this. It'll be so much fun! I'll get all the details to you later today.'

* * *

Late afternoon, two e-ticket numbers for Club Class flights in two days' time, all the way to Kona, Hawaii, were emailed to me by Beau's PA. I texted Vicky immediately:

I really need to see you, honey, please. I want to make it up. Can you meet me in The Chamberlayne after work? I've something for you xxx

After a cool sixty minutes, she appeared to thaw. OK. See you then.

That left me just enough time to buy two fake Hawaiian flower garlands from a fancy dress shop on Portobello Road—I thought grass skirts were a step too far, given the wintry weather—and the ingredients for Vicky's favourite bangers-and-mash dinner, with an expensive bottle of red for supper back at the flat. Surely she'd be able to take a few days off work at short notice? If anyone was worth a once-in-a-lifetime, all-expenses-paid trip to Hawaii, she was.

Part Five:
Hawaii,
The Wedding

Chapter Twenty-Five

The air was hot and humid, filled with the sweet scent of hibiscus, in the outdoor arrivals area at Kona Airport on Hawaii's Big Island. It was dark, we were both overtired and nursing monster hangovers—it's impossible to say no to a steady stream of free champagne and red wine when travelling in Club—and Vicky and I had the giggles, big time.

'Aloha! Miss Annie Liechtenstein and partner? Please, let me take your luggage,' said a porter from the prestigious Four Seasons Resort. When we arrived at the entrance to the hotel—by air-conditioned car, complete with bottled water and cool flannels—garlands of beautiful, fresh pink orchids were placed around our necks. Beau was right, it was like landing in paradise. We were so woozy from the two flights from London via LA that it was surreal to find ourselves now standing in a stunning open foyer, decorated in an upmarket traditional Polynesian style with wooden tables, comfortable chairs and fragrant white orchids. The light rustle of palm trees and the soft sound of a ukulele player entertaining late-night revellers somewhere in the distance permeated the warm air. If you listened really carefully you could just about hear the rolling waves of the Pacific Ocean far beyond. Everything about it was totally worth the journey, even for our whistle-stop trip.

'So who do we check in as—you're Annie at the moment, right?' Vicky whispered in my ear as we approached the reception desk.

'Beau told me Annie for anything official,' I muttered, mentally practising my pseudonym for the next couple of days: *Lick-ten-stein, Lick-ten-stein. Hello, my name is Annie Liechtenstein.* I really hadn't nailed my backstory.

'When do we have to start acting like we're a couple?' Vicky was trying hard to stop her wobbling voice from turning into full-scale hysterics.

'Hopefully everyone's in bed already,' I said, through gritted teeth. 'Don't put me off!'

A waiter presented us each with a chilled glass of passion fruit Bellini, delivered on a silver tray. Just what I needed to steady my nerves.

'Aloha!' he chimed. 'Welcome to the Four Seasons, we *really* hope you'll enjoy your stay.'

'Aloha! Don't mind if I do.' Vicky downed a large gulp to stifle any involuntary outbursts of laughter. *How we're going to hold it together for these next two nights, I just don't know.*

* * *

As we took our room key and turned to follow our porter, another vehicle glided to a halt in the driveway. Three figures got out of the car, which had a boot full of cases, and we could hear that they had British accents, too. Though the lighting was muted, I'd recognise that voice anywhere. I gripped Vicky's arm, my heart racing.

'Amber?' Rob called. 'No way! Didn't realise you were doing the wedding with Mona—I would have called. This is great!' He dropped the two flight cases in his hands and walked towards us. 'Vicky, too—nice one! How did you wangle that?'

'Rob!' I looked at him, his face all lit up and welcoming. This was the best—and worst—surprise ever.

'What's the plan, then?' demanded Fran with the bob, stepping in front of him, instantly in work mode. A feeling of doom descended upon me as I imagined how Mona was likely to react to the documentary crew's reappearance.

'Why are you here, guys? Does Mona know?'

'Mona invited us. Wanted to see if we could turn the pilot around with this job. The production company have agreed to give it one last shot—so it better be good,' said Fran ominously, marching into the hotel.

As the reception staff looked on, I pulled Rob to one side. 'By the way, I'm Annie in front of most of the guests for this trip. Remember, to help out Beau?'

'You don't make things easy for yourself, do you?' he chuckled. 'Of course—Annie it is.'

'And, um, Vicky is Victoria—my "partner".'

He sniggered. 'As in, your "civil partner"?' I nodded, mutely. 'Awesome. I love this trip already! You make a beautiful couple. Production meeting after breakfast, then?'

'I'll let Mona know.' I fiddled with my orchid garland anxiously. The butterflies in my stomach were already throwing a party and we'd barely arrived.

Thankfully, a porter came to our rescue, and led Vicky and I off to a white golf buggy. We were soon following a pathway lit with tiki torches to our bungalow, an elegant two-room suite, almost hidden by lush tropical flora and fauna. During the short five-minute journey our driver must have said 'Aloha!' at least seven times, each with the same level of enthusiasm, to every passing staff-member and guest. But I could barely concentrate on anything, other than the fact that Rob was here. I wasn't over him at all. Vicky read my mind.

'It'll be fine,' she promised, squeezing my knee.

* * *

As is the law on entering the best hotel suite you have ever set foot in, we immediately set about exploring—bouncing on the super-king beds, stroking the bamboo headboards, checking out the fully stocked minibar and nearly passing out at the huge bathroom, complete with outdoor shower for bathing under the stars. But when we flung open the balcony doors in the living room area, we were both finally rendered speechless. Beyond our balcony, not more than a stone's throw across a strip of perfectly raked sand, was the ocean, gently lapping at the shoreline. A full moon sent a magical beam of light across the beautiful, rippling expanse. We breathed it all in deeply, and felt our shoulders drop.

'Pinch me, please,' I uttered.

'Sod Rob, I think you might actually fall in love with me here, Amber Green,' Vicky teased. 'Anyway, this view alone is the best birthday present ever. Thank you so much.' She pulled me in and planted a kiss on my cheek.

'You're right. Sod Rob—he didn't look very handsome today, anyway. It's handling Mona I'm most worried about. But, whatever happens, we've got to make the most of being in this amazing place.'

That meant no unpacking, just getting some proper sleep

in our luxury beds. The long journey had left us both shattered, and I'd noticed crusty red-wine stains decorating my lips.

* * *

The only thing that could top our arrival in paradise, under the cover of nightfall, was waking up and seeing it all over again, bathed in early-morning sunlight. After a deep sleep I emerged to find Vicky on the balcony already, Instagramming the hell out of everything.

'Shit! Careful!' I rushed to pull down her arm. 'You've not put anything up, have you?'

'No, but I've sent one Tweet. What's the panic?' My palms were sweating, and not because of the humidity.

'I forgot to say—Beau and Trey have a deal with a magazine, and no one can know the wedding's happening here. It's got to stay exclusive. Beau called me about it just before we left—sorry, I meant to tell you. It's really important. If you take it down fast, hopefully no one will have seen anything.'

Vicky fiddled with her iPhone, holding it up and waving it around.

'Damn reception, it's really in and out here.'

'What did it say?' I was beginning to feel panicky.

'That I'm here at the Four Seasons, Haulalai,' she muttered, sheepishly, '...for a celebrity wedding... Shit, sorry, hon, I didn't know.'

'But you didn't mention Beau's name, right?'

'No. And it's not like I've got millions of followers—I'm sure no one's picked it up. Ah, that's it. Deleted.'

The phone in the room buzzed into life, making both of us jump. Nervously, I dashed over. 'A-Annie speaking?'

'Amber, it's Beau. Aloha! Welcome to paradise—isn't this the most amazing place you've ever seen?'

'Certainly is! Have you seen Mona yet?'

'Only briefly—she arrived really early this morning in a foul mood after spending three hours being questioned before she could get through passport control. Must be something to do with the shoplifting or the Cabo episode. I give up. Anyway, she was asking after you, and I said it'd be best if she met you at my villa after the brunch.'

'Brunch—great! We're starving.'

'It's at the main beach restaurant in ten minutes, and then it'll be time to start making everyone over. We've got so much to do and not much time. You okay to come to brunch and then my suite? It'll be only us girls—and Mona and Pinky of course—I'm staying in the Presidential Villa. And one other thing—I, um, there's been a change to the wedding gown. I brought two of them out with me, because you can never be sure if your suitcase is going to make it, and I couldn't risk getting married in my birthday suit. I was going to wear a Vera Wang, but then Dolce & Gabbana came through with the most incredible custom-made dress for me. It's covered in crystals with a sexy fishtail and a veil with a really long train. I look like a mermaid in it—it's perfect for Hawaii, you're going to die! And I was thinking we could build on the mermaid theme by adding some shells and pearls onto the bridesmaid dresses.'

I took this in. 'Does, um, Mona know about the theme yet? It sounds like quite a lot to do on your actual wedding day, Beau…'

'I thought we could tell her together.' *She's as scared of her as I am.* 'Oh, Amber, I'm so in love with the idea. Think

Birth of Venus meets Hawaii. How cool?' Hmm. Beau had the most un-Botticelli body imaginable.

'Awesome!' *Well, what else can I say?* 'I'm just a bit concerned about where we'll get the shells and pearls from though—where's the nearest town to here?'

Her voice broke into a raucous laugh. 'Oh, Amber! You're so funny sometimes. Look where you are! We're on a beach, for Christ sakes—just send your wife-stroke-assistant out to pick up some shells, the more authentic the better, and my mom's got a long pearl necklace she's donated as my "something old" so we can dismantle that and sew them on. I mentioned the idea to the editor at the magazine and they're going crazy for it: they're working on finding a giant shell for Trey and I to stand in when we have our photos taken! I know it's a lot to pull together, but it'll be fun!' Beau's catchphrase was really starting to grate on me.

'You're the bride. See you at brunch, and then let's do this!' Resistance was futile, so I mustered all the American enthusiasm I could before replacing the handset, slamming my fist against the duvet and crumpling into a heap on the bed as I relayed it all to Vicky—including the part about Mona already being in a foul mood. Vicky, obviously, found it hilarious. Then I remembered an important question I'd forgotten to ask, so I quickly called Beau back: 'Other than Mona, is there anyone here who will know I'm not actually Annie Leichtenstein? I mean, you said Jason Slater would be here—is that still...?' Vicky's eyes lit up. I braced myself.

'Of course, Amber! Durr! But don't worry, he's in on the Annie thing, so he'll keep it up in front of Trey. He's an actor after all.'

I laughed nervously. 'Okay, if you're sure.'

She paused. 'He's a good guy, you know—he's been a rock to me.'

'I believe you,' I found myself saying, with no conviction.

* * *

Trey and Beau stood greeting guests at the entrance to the ocean-facing restaurant. Beau looked stunning in a sheer peach flowing gown with a high slit showing off her golden tan and revealing her slender body, barely covered in what looked like a Missoni string-bikini, underneath. I began to feel self-conscious in my cut-off denim shorts, white vest top and Havaianas—my idea of beach cool was clearly not on the same level as hers. The assembled party of guests before us was something to behold. Women dressed up in finely embroidered kaftans in coral colours. Wealthy-looking girls in animal print silks and hippy-chic crochet dresses, worn casually over expensive bikinis to show off their model-perfect limbs, their faces hidden behind over-sized sunglasses and big, floppy beach hats. Vicky was going to have her work cut out telling apart the fake from the natural boobs gathered before us.

The men were mostly in preppy pastel colours, linen trousers or Ralph Lauren shorts with open white shirts, re-vealing tanned chests and admirable pecs. A concoction of flowery summer perfumes, mixed with the sweet scent of coconut sunscreen, hung in the air. I recognised sev-eral faces from TV and film appearances and one guy in a straw fedora and Ray-Bans had a definite resemblance to Justin Timberlake.

'It's not, *is it*?' Vicky nudged me, thinking the exact same thing. But I'd just noticed Jason Slater in one corner, biceps bulging in a white string vest, as he bent down from a bar stool, apparently putting something into a pouch around

Pinky's neck. Finally he patted the little pig on its derrière, and it was whisked back to Beau by an excitable young guest far more interested in playing with a micro-pig than mixing with any of the beautiful people. Jason had a shifty look in his eye, for sure—but I parked that for now.

* * *

'You should have seen Pinky's passport photo—so cute!' Beau cooed, as the little animal started licking my feet in recognition.

'Dear Annie, welcome! I see that someone's obviously taken a shine to you!' Trey greeted me with a kiss on each cheek, like a long-lost comrade. I felt a twinge of guilt at how friendly he was.

'It's so great to have a fellow Brit here. Beau and I are over the moon you could find the time to join us—aren't we, baby?'

Beau smiled. 'Sure are—*and* they've flown in from freezing London.'

'Filming at Shepperton Studios,' I offered, awkwardly, 'with Scorsese.' *What am I saying?*

'Ha—I know only too well what those gruelling production schedules are like.' Trey smiled. 'And you must be Victoria?' Trey seemed impressed that I had bagged such a pretty wife. Vicky offered her hand. 'Welcome. I hope you both have an incredible time here in Hawaii.' He gestured to the postcard-perfect vista before us.

'Thanks so much, Trey—it's an honour to be here, for both of us,' I cooed, having instructed Vicky to smile sweetly and leave all the talking to me.

* * *

After a buffet of tropical fruit, pancakes and eggs done every which way, plus some strained conversations with guests keen to know how I enjoyed working with Beau and Jason on *Summer's Not Over*—which I still hadn't actually seen—and limited chat about what I was doing with Scorsese, Vicky and I excused ourselves and headed over to Beau's villa. Mona opened the door, dressed in an OTT, long, wafting zebra-print kaftan, hair loosely tousled around her shoulders and at least twenty bangles jangling loudly on each arm. She had rings on almost every finger.

'Babe! I've been calling you all morning!' She greeted me with open arms, which was suspicious.

'The reception's terrible,' I muttered, as I felt her eyes scan my clothes and then settle, much more approvingly, on Vicky's outfit—a tropical Mary Katrantzou floral-print dress. 'Well, anyway. Beau tells me she wanted to treat you both, and I'm thrilled you offered to dress the bridesmaids.' We both smiled in response.

Inside, the suite was a hive of activity. It quickly became clear Beau had omitted mentioning that instead of your average two or three bridesmaids, she had opted for *ten*, whose styling Mona had delegated solely to me. The motley gaggle of attendants ranged from a tiara-wearing baby in the arms of a woman who was presumably Beau's mother, looking like an almost identical, if slightly wizened, Dolly Parton–esque version of Beau; four little girls currently running in circles around the suite, having just coated their pretty aquamarine Chantilly lace–netted dresses in chocolate; three hefty blondes introduced as Beau's old school friends from Ohio; and somewhere in the middle her younger sister Bethany, currently going through a goth stage, complete with long, dyed, black-and-purple hair. It was her baby their mother was holding. Plus Beau's PA, Krystal, who was still in her pyjamas and looking as if she was close to a nervous breakdown, struggling to calm a hyper Pinky whilst juggling two phones. None of the assembled wedding party looked particularly as though they wanted to be turned into mermaids for the day.

Putting thoughts of the bridesmaids to one side for a moment, I joined Mona in Beau's bedroom for a quick production meeting with Fran and Rob. The atmosphere was already tense. Judging by Fran's body language—arms crossed tightly, furrowed brow—the meeting had ended before it began, with Mona back on her old, unhelpful form.

The light was pulsing on Shaggy's camera, and Mona's stress levels seemed to be rising as she struggled to get to grips with Beau's stunning Dolce & Gabbana wedding dress, currently standing to attention on a dressmaker's dummy in the centre of the airy room.

'The chest needs letting out—she's only grown a cup size in the last week,' Mona grumbled, picking violently at the fastenings. Fran looked like she was enjoying seeing her struggle.

'Need a hand?' I offered.

'No, no! I've got it,' Mona spat, smiling through gritted teeth, just as a tiny silver clasp pinged off the dress and was instantly lost on the floor. '*Bloody* thing.'

I ducked out of shot, deciding instead to give Beau's Louboutin sandals a gentle polish before I got to work with the bridesmaids. I positioned myself close to the tall balcony doors, allowing the soft, warm sea breeze to wash over me as I worked. It was definitely preferable to be dealing with Mona in this picturesque setting than in the freezing cold or stifling heat. *And this really is the last time I'll ever have to do it.*

'Hey, Victoria, right? Annie's other half?' My ears

pricked up. Trey was talking to Vicky no more than a few metres away from me, beyond Beau's balcony on the sandy beach. I kept my head down, lest he saw me crouched inside the room, looking distinctly more like a stylist than a film producer. *Please don't screw this up, Vicky.*

'Oh, yes—hi, Trey,' she exclaimed, taken aback. Trey looked at the pile of shells she was currently collecting in her hat.

'I see you're enjoying being beside the sea.' He smiled. 'Collecting a few mementos?'

'Something like that,' she answered, scooping up a little clam shell and gently placing it next to the others. Beau's imagined limitless perfect Hawaiian shells decorating the beach didn't seem to have materialised. 'To add to my shell collection.' *Shell collection? What is she on about?* 'And you?'

'Just getting a bit of air. You know, doing the groom thing and clearing my head, working on some ideas for my speech.'

'I bet you'll be a natural, being a hotshot director and everything,' Vicky said.

'So, tell me, how long have you and Annie been an item?' he asked. Vicky frantically glanced around, which I took as my cue to go and rescue her. Leapfrogging over the balcony edge, I scuttled behind some bushes and from there, casually strolled out and joined their group, winding my arm around Vicky's waist.

'Hey, what are you two gossiping about?' I asked.

'Just getting to know your shell-enthusiast other half,' Trey replied. He nudged my arm. 'Us Brits have got to stick together! I hope you'll be joining me in some serious dance-floor action later this evening. None of this LA "got to get my beauty sleep" stuff, please!'

'That's a deal,' Vicky replied, and the two shook hands.

Then a flashing light and a series of clicks made us all stop dead and turn towards a large palm tree a few metres down the beach. In the blink of an eye a shadowy figure, his face covered by a camera lens almost the size of the tree trunk, darted out of sight.

'Oh, Jesus. The paps are onto us,' Trey exclaimed, withdrawing his hand from Vicky's. 'And it probably looks like we've just shaken on some kind of dodgy deal.'

'But this is a private resort,' I said, astonished. 'We can just call security and get him escorted off, can't we?'

'You're joking, aren't you?' Trey replied. 'You've evidently not filmed in Hawaii before, Annie—all the beaches are public, so that scumbag has as much right to be on this sand as you and I. Fucking hell, this is the last thing we need. I really thought we'd got away with it. If I find out anyone's leaked the venue, I'll...'

I looked at Vicky, her face ashen, fear in her eyes. My heart began to beat erratically as Trey tapped furiously at his phone. *Is he calling the Twitter police? Will he be able to find out?*

'AJ, get Bill and Jonah down to the beach, we've been rumbled.'

Some flashes in the opposite direction suddenly erupted and another paparazzo, more brazen than the first, stepped out into the bright sunshine and began clicking away. He didn't even bother pretending to hide.

'Let's get off the beach—they can't touch us on the other side of the path,' Trey instructed, and we scrambled back to the safety of manicured Four Seasons turf. 'How the hell are we going to have this wedding now? The beach will be swarming with paps within the hour.' Trey's mood had done a U-turn, and I couldn't blame him. Behind us, two huge Polynesian guys, presumably the security, Bill and Jonah, stood, each marking a pap, blocking their view and ready to challenge them if they tried to get another clean shot of the hacked-off groom. AJ joined us. I'd almost forgotten what a massive hulk he was.

'Amber.' He nodded in recognition. I squirmed. *Don't blow my cover now, please, AJ.* Thankfully Trey was too distracted to notice.

'No way we can have the wedding on the beach now, with these assholes around—there will be tenfold this number in an hour or two, believe me,' AJ said, optimistically. 'And there's no point calling the cops. Absolutely jack shit we can do about it.' He folded his huge arms.

'I know, mate, I know. Any ideas where we can move it to?'

'Not really—the whole point of this place is the beach.' He scratched his head. AJ was definitely one of those 'we're all doomed' type of people.

'Isn't there a tropical garden, or some kind of function room we can move the ceremony to?' Trey looked desperate.

'I'll ask the wedding planner, but the marquee tent is in the garden, and I don't think there's anywhere else. And it won't be anything like the beach.'

'Damn it! Beau will be devastated. And what am I going to tell the magazine? We need to get those beach pictures, AJ.' Trey kicked a sunlounger and then set it straight again. He wasn't normally one for losing his cool in public. Vicky remained painfully quiet at my side. As my mind ticked over, my cheeks blazed in the sun, though it was less to do with wearing zero SPF and more the fact that in less than 140 characters, Vicky had quite possibly blown a 'world exclusive'.

* * *

Trey insisted on breaking the news to Beau. Through a crack in the door—in case he accidentally saw her wedding dress or caught a glimpse of the production line behind her attempting to sew pearls onto aquamarine netting and cover chocolate stains with shells—he spoke calmly and slowly to his wife-to-be:

'Listen, baby-cakes, don't panic, but there's been a bit of a change of plan.' Her already big blue eyes grew wider. 'There are paps all over the beach, baby, and unfortunately we can't just get them kicked off. So AJ has taken the decision not to go ahead with the wedding on the beach as originally planned.'

'But, baby, I don't understand?' She struggled to keep her voice even. 'We can't not have the wedding on the beach— the beach is the whole reason we're in Hawaii. And what about the photos on the giant shell? We can't do that by a swimming pool, it'll look tacky. Oh, baby, please tell me I'm dreaming?' Manically, she began pinching her arm. 'Oh my God, I'm *not* dreaming.' Suddenly Mona appeared behind her at the doorway, swiftly followed by ten brides-maids and a tearful mother of the bride, who all clustered around Beau with panic written across their faces. As the door opened, Pinky promptly made a run for it, dashing between Trey's legs and out of the suite.

'Pinky!' Beau screamed urgently. 'Get him, Amber— Annie! Quickly!' Instinctively I dived for the little tyke, pulling him back and scooping him up as he squealed loudly in my arms. There was a momentary pause as we all took in the miniature pig's specially customised tiny ivory tuxedo, complete with bow-tie collar and, attached to this, an ivory silk purse embroidered with the letters 'B' and 'T' in aquamarine crystals, soon to contain the wedding rings.

'Baby, baby—shhh, shhh.' Trey leaned in close, as the gap in the door narrowed again.

'It's bad luck to see the dress—he must not see the dress!' Mona instructed from behind Beau.

Trey reached for Beau's tiny hand and guided it through the opening, tenderly lacing her fingers with his.

'It *has* to be on the beach, baby,' she pleaded, her eyes shining, on the brink of tears. 'I can't bear it otherwise. Seriously, baby—no beach, no wedding.'

'Well, then, we're going to have to come up with a plan,' said Trey, with awe-inspiring patience.

'I think I'm going to be sick,' Beau declared suddenly, whipping her hand from his and disappearing into the suite. Mona and the ten bridesmaids followed, while the mother of the bride tried to slam the door in Trey's face. He pushed against it.

'Baby Belle! I can't bear to—'

'Let me.' I barged past Trey, dumping Pinky into Krystal's open arms and elbowing half-naked bridesmaids and netted dresses out of the way to get to the front of the line.

* * *

I locked the door of the ornate marble bathroom behind us and knelt down to hold back Beau's hair, gently rubbing her back as she threw up in the toilet bowl.

'You okay?' I asked as she finally rested on her heels, wiping her mouth with toilet paper.

'Better now,' she said, weakly. 'That's the second time I've vommed today.'

'Pre-wedding nerves?'

'I guess so,' she confessed, smiling wanly, eyes watery and skin pale despite several coats of fake tan. A loud knocking at the door startled us both.

'Beau!' It was Mona. 'Darling Beau, let me in!' We looked at each other.

'She's been knocking back the Buck's Fizz since she arrived,' Beau said. 'And she's more interested in her TV show and getting in the magazine photos than sorting out my dress. Look, it still doesn't fit.' She pulled out a pin from the corsetry under her arm, and the dress immediately gaped. The knocking came again, louder.

'I've got an idea… A really good one!' Mona sounded excited. I wasn't sure whether an excited Mona was preferable to a foul or even an elusive one, but Beau and I exchanged a look, and I reluctantly got up and let her in. The magazine photographer's camera flashed in my face making me lift my hand to cover my eyes.

'Great—you're here, too,' she said. 'Mind if the photographer gets this, as well?'

'Yes, I do!' screamed Beau from the floor behind me, with such vehemence that the photographer immediately backed off. The bathroom suddenly felt claustrophobic with Mona in it, too. I sat on the edge of the bath and Beau propped herself up against it, her legs stretched out on the cool floor in front of her.

'Oh, Beau, it's terrible luck about the paps,' Mona began. 'But someone's got to think quickly—I've got a plan. You said you brought the Vera Wang dress, too, right?'

'Uh-huh,' she nodded.

'Amber's about the same size as you…give or take,' she continued, mentally sizing me up and smiling sweetly. My back stiffened. 'I think we should put Amber in the Wang and set up a fake photo shoot down one end of the beach to distract all the paps, while you and Trey come out down the other end and have the ceremony. By the time the paps realise Amber's not you, you'll be officially married. Genius, hey? My God, I amaze myself sometimes.' She turned towards the door. 'Are you sure we can't let the cameras in?'

There was what seemed like an endless silence as Beau and I digested the idea.

'Couple of major flaws here, Mona,' I eventually declared, in desperation. 'One, I'm twice the size of Beau, not to mention brunette. I'll never get into that dress. And two, even if I did, no one would think I was Beau.'

'Oh, Amber.' Beau used my body to push herself up onto her feet, sickness seemingly forgotten. 'I think this is a great idea! I don't know, we're not that dissimilar.' She steered my head towards hers and pointed to the mirror, where our differences became even more obvious. 'And the good news is I didn't get the Wang taken in yet, because I've, um, filled out a little lately.' She cupped an ample D-cup in her hand. 'It'll fit you—I know it. And if it doesn't, we'll just take it out a bit.'

I went through the idea again, imagining how it might all look. But however I tried to picture this ridiculous scenario, I came out looking like an idiot. *Brilliant.*

'What if the paps aren't fooled?' I protested. 'These people are professionals. And besides, who'll be my groom?' They both ignored me.

'Oh, Mona, you're a genius! And, Amber, I knew you had to be here today—you were *meant* to save my wedding!' Beau, now smiling brightly, threw her arms around our necks. 'Oh no—hold on a minute.' She chucked up in the toilet once more.

* * *

We emerged from the bathroom to find Fran, Rob and Shaggy, camera blinking, poised by the door, the magazine photographer shooting away just behind them.

'What's the plan, then, Mona?' Fran asked, shoving a furry microphone in her face. Mona was only too delighted to fill them in on her brilliant idea, only now there was an additional twist:

'As for the groom—it makes sense if my *assistant*—' she exaggerated 'assistant' '—Amber here, ties the knot with you, Rob, don't you think?'

Rob instantaneously coughed, nearly choking on a sip of Coke. *I know, mate, this is not in my job description, either.* The cameras turned to take in the look of crushing embarrassment on both of our faces.

Chapter Twenty-Six

'How do I look?' Beau asked, twirling slowly in the living area, as we all gathered to admire her. The magazine photographer set about capturing her from every angle.

'Incredible,' Mona said. And Beau genuinely did look breathtaking. Shaggy's camera swooped around her Dolce & Gabbana fishtail ivory gown, hugging her curves to perfection. Delicate crystal embellishments glinted in the sunshine, and the long train created the drama of an Italian bride meets Hawaiian goddess. Mona, it had to be admitted, had done a good job, thanks to one of Beau's bridesmaids turning out to be a half-decent seamstress. Even the ten bridesmaids looked adorable. The pretty pearls and a few shells stitched into the netting gave a subtle nod to the mermaid theme, and strangely enough it all hung together.

'And how do *I* look?' I asked, sarcastically, stepping through the door of the guest bedroom wearing the Vera Wang. My hair and make-up were in the exact same style as Beau's, though an inordinate amount of dry shampoo made my updo look more white and powdery than Beau's brassy blonde. It was as good as we could do.

'Squashed!' Mona said, cackling to herself. I felt the whole room take in the huge tulle-skirted princess gown with its tight bodice and long veil.

'Thanks for that, Mona.' I scowled. *I'm so over pretending to be nice to her.* 'I may not be able breathe properly, but I think I can just about walk.' I tentatively lifted the gown and placed one heel-clad foot in front of the other. The shoes were at least a size too small, as well.

'My God, lock up your sons!' gushed Vicky, hand over her mouth. 'Seriously, Amber, you look damn hot as a bride! You're working it, girlfriend!' She rushed forwards to take a photo on her iPhone.

'No Instagramming! Not yet, anyway!' I called. *Flash! Flash!* The official photographer started going for me, too.

I caught a glimpse of my reflection in the balcony doors and for a second allowed myself the fantasy that this was *my* wedding day. Though the dress was way more flamboyant than anything I could imagine myself choosing, there was something pleasingly romantic about it. I smoothed down the skirt. It was amazing what Vera Wang internal corsetry could do—squashed internal organs or not, my waist had never looked so beautifully waspish. Mona gazed at me in silence. In fact, if I wasn't mistaken, she was slightly irked that I'd managed to look so damn good.

'Time's ticking! Are you ready for us?' Fran hollered through the door of another adjoining bedroom, where Mona had banished the crew while Beau was prepped for her 're-veal'.

'Yes, come capture our real bride with the fake one!' Mona shouted back, and the door opened to reveal Rob, dressed to kill in a sharp navy Tom Ford suit and skinny white tie borrowed from one of the ushers. He looked seriously hot—definite husband material.

'And here comes the groom!' Mona squealed, clapping her hands together. 'Alo-*ha*!'

As Rob and I looked at each other, my heart leapt with such vigour I let out a little involuntary gasp.

'You'll need this, though.' Mona thrust one of Trey's baseball caps into Rob's hand to make his disguise complete. Shaggy circled around us filming the decoy Beau and Trey, as we prepared to head off for the pretend wedding photo shoot on the beach.

'You look beautiful,' Rob said, his green eyes intent on mine.

'You scrub up pretty well yourself,' I replied, feeling my cheeks tingle. *Could today get any more surreal?* I took a deep breath and turned towards Mona. 'So, what happens now?'

'May I present Master Pinky, the ring bearer,' Mona called, arm outstretched towards the balcony, in full ham-it-up-for-the-cameras-mode. 'How does *he* look?'

Krystal appeared timidly, white Swarovski crystal–adorned lead in her hand, but no Pinky at the end of it.

'He, um, appears to have done a runner,' Krystal muttered, embarrassed, as both lenses zoomed in on her face. I felt for the poor girl.

'What do you mean, "done a runner"? How could that happen, have you seen the size of those trotters? He's hardly Usain Bolt. Plus—unless he's a trained high jumper as well—the balcony only has one exit, and that's through this door,' Mona ranted.

'I only left the balcony for a few seconds to check my phone,' Krystal stuttered.

'Pinky? Where are you, Pinky-pops?' Beau rushed through the balcony doors, narrowly missing falling flat on her face; the Dolce gown was so tight across her legs she could barely walk. 'Wow—don't *you* look hot!' Her gaze lingered for a second too long as she passed Rob, oozing sex appeal in his suit.

The doorbell to the suite chimed, startling us all, and Krystal scuttled over to answer it, keen to escape all the attention.

'Panic over!' she trilled, as the door was flung open. We all turned to witness Jason Slater carrying Beau's beloved pet into the living area, where he plonked him down, mini-tux in place, little silk purse bobbing as he trotted into the centre of the room. Jason covered his eyes, pretending not to have noticed Beau in her bridal gown, breasts undulating over the top of the tighter-than-tight corset. It couldn't have been a less virginal look—she was pure filthy sex.

'This little piggy cried, wee, wee, wee, wee, all the way home. Found him sniffing around the catering tent,' he joked, before snapping the lead back onto Pinky's collar and handing him to Beau. 'Don't let him out of your sight, angel.'

'I won't! Thanks, Jase,' Beau stammered, seemingly flustered by his arrival. Vicky seemed to have gone a bit misty-eyed, too. 'Don't worry, Krystal,' Beau said, 'I'll take care of Pinky now—the rings are in his pouch.'

Still mock-shielding his eyes, Jason backed out of the suite, the photographer clicking after him. 'Didn't see a thing, promise, ladies!'

'Beau, darling, you can't keep hold of that grubby little

thing whilst you've got a couture gown on. Give Pinky to
Amber, he's needed for the fake photo shoot, anyway,' Mona
instructed, prising the lead from Beau's fingers and thrusting it into mine. *I suppose it doesn't matter that I happen
to be wearing a priceless gown, too?* Vicky tapped me on
the back and surreptitiously handed me an open bottle of
champagne, presumably one that Mona had been quietly
working on all morning.

'Swig,' she ordered. Obediently, I took a large glug.

* * *

Outside the suite, against the clock now, as the real ceremony was due to start in less than thirty minutes, the female
section of the bridal party assembled to wave us off to one
end of the long beach on our mission. I'm sure it wasn't just
me who noticed a flicker of electricity as Rob offered me
his hand to step onto the golf buggy. Then I passed Pinky
to AJ, who clamped him under his arm and climbed onto a
second buggy behind us—he would be posing as the magazine photographer.

The resort was teeming with people. Florists carrying
boxes containing thousands of fragrant, fresh orchid petals crossed paths with caterers brandishing sealed metal
containers of food and burly men laden with lighting rigs
on their way to the marquee. With the wedding rapidly
approaching, a procession of golf buggies carried heavily
made-up guests to a pre-ceremony drinks reception deep
within the resort, away from any prying paparazzi lenses.
Rob and I giggled on the back of our cart as we weaved
through the maze of pathways in the opposite direction to
everyone else. Many guests did a double take at the bride
and groom whizzing past them, merrily shouting, 'Aloha!'
at all we passed. I allowed myself a dizzying moment to

imagine this was real—that I had the gorgeous Tiffany ring on my finger and was about to enjoy all the benefits of being Mrs Amber Walker, wife of Rob Walker; no more traffic light puns; the loveliest husband ever; mini-Walkers on the near horizon… Then Rob's phone rang.

He looked at it but seemed unwilling to answer. *It had to be her. Fantasy shattered.* He let it ring out and then turned towards me and shrugged. We both said nothing.

* * *

The carts finally crept to a standstill as we approached the main beach area, set up to resemble the scene of a celebrity photo shoot (complete with an oversized *Birth of Venus* shell that had been shipped in for the photos). After quietly disembarking, AJ ushered us in close. Rob and I listened intently.

'So, here's the plan,' he whispered. 'I had one of my guys put some piggy treats inside the shell, so we send Pinky out first, to attract the attention of the paps. I've got men positioned all the way down the beach to give us the nod, so when the paps take the bait and start creeping forwards, thinking the photos are about to happen, it'll be time for me to start snapping the two of you as you emerge from behind that group of palm trees.' He pointed at a cluster of rocks and trees a few metres away. 'Just come out onto the sand looking blissfully happy. You're going to need to really ham it up—hold hands, laugh, kiss, whisk her off her feet if you want to, Rob—whatever it takes to make it all seem real. Keep your veil pulled down over your face though, Amber, and Rob, wear the baseball cap the whole time, we don't want them to realise you're not the actual couple. And take your time, all this has to happen while the real ceremony is getting under way down the other end. They'll be snapping away, going crazy for you. Got it?'

We nodded sagely. Then the sound of a third buggy approaching made us all turn around, and Vicky jumped off the back.

'Mona's got it all under control with Beau. She won't let me within a mile radius of any of the bridal party—she clearly doesn't want me there—so I thought I'd come give you some moral support.' She giggled. 'I was thinking, I could pretend to be your stylist, if you like, Am—plump up your skirt for the photos and stuff?'

'Good thinking,' AJ agreed. 'The more authentic we can make it look, the better.'

Waiting for the nod, I peeked out from behind one of the beachside cabanas to survey the set. A sultry breeze blew in off the ocean and a canopy of hundreds of twinkling fairy lights shone above the giant conch. As the sun began its descent in the sky, we were ready to go.

'Three, two, one… Action!' whispered AJ, and Rob got ready to push Pinky out onto the beach, to snaffle the treats. Suddenly a wave of panic hit me—I darted forwards onto the sand and grabbed Rob's arm.

'Wait! Shit!' I held Pinky back by the collar, almost sending myself flying head over Wang. 'I've just remembered: Pinky's got the rings for the real wedding around his neck. We need to get them back!' I tugged firmly at his leash.

'Bloody hell—thank God you remembered,' Rob said, taking Pinky from me and holding him tightly as he tried to squirm free, his greedy little snout already picking up the scent of the treats.

'You'll have to take the rings back in the buggy,' AJ said, turning to Vicky. 'They won't be able to start the ceremony without them.'

As Rob restrained Pinky, I teased open the delicate silken

pouch. *That's odd.* It didn't seem to be holding anything of any weight. I felt around with my finger. There were certainly no rings inside, but there was a folded-up piece of paper.

'What is it?' Rob stared at me, Pinky clamped under his arm, a hand over the poor little mite's mouth to muffle his squeals of protest. I undid the paper. It had been folded at least six times, into a small tight triangle.

'It's a handwritten note.' A chill washed over me as I read it aloud, my voice trembling. I quickly realised it wasn't a love letter between Beau and Trey.

'"Angel, stay strong, remember the time and place—5:30, the ukulele bandstand. I'll be waiting with the car. Don't make a terrible mistake—not after last night, and all our amazing nights together. This is the first day of the rest of our lives. With all my heart, J."'

We all stood there for a minute, looking at each other: me, Rob, Vicky and AJ. Even Pinky had quietened down.

'J?' AJ finally said. 'Who the hell is J?'

'Who the hell do you think?' I stammered, my mind racing. 'It has to be Jason Slater.'

'Jason? You don't think he and Beau are planning to elope, do you?' For a security boss, AJ could be a little dim at times.

'No shit, Sherlock,' I replied, my mind racing.

'But how could she do this to Trey?' Vicky uttered.

Rob looked at his watch. 'I don't know. But it's 5:10 p.m., so we need to do something quickly.'

'But what?' I looked at him. My breath was quickening and I felt panicky—I desperately wanted to loosen this stupid corset. 'I *knew* there was something going on—I saw Jason put something into Pinky's pouch at brunch this morning—there was something dodgy about it then and it's dodgy as hell now.'

'We can't let her make a mug out of Trey,' Vicky announced. 'I've been cheated on before, and it bloody hurts. It'll hurt even more when he finds out his brand-new wife was cheating right up until five minutes before he married her. That is, *if* she goes through with it.'

'Trey's one of the good guys,' AJ said, shaking his head.

'We've got to tell him,' agreed Rob.

Everyone looked at me.

'Why are you all looking at me?' I protested. 'I can't tell him—he thinks I'm someone else, anyway.'

'Annie?' AJ asked. 'I did wonder, but I thought it was just something to do with you Brits and your weird way of speaking.'

'I can't do it.' I shook my head defiantly. 'No way. Rob?'

'Uh-uh.' He shook his head, too. 'A guy from a film crew, a guy he doesn't know from Adam, tells him he's not getting married to the woman he thought was the love of his life, on his wedding day? Are you joking?'

I turned to AJ. 'You know him better than all of us,' I said, feeling desperate; we were against the clock now.

'Trey's my boss. Would you tell your boss the best part of a million dollars he's just spent organising his dream wedding may as well have been pissed up the wall, because his fiancée is a cheat?' We all looked at the sand. 'Didn't think so.'

'There's only one person for it, then,' Vicky interjected, just as a blaze of flashbulbs erupted a few metres away from us on the beach. In all the kerfuffle, none of us had noticed Pinky freeing his lead from the rock Rob had wedged it under, and he was now sitting in the middle of the conch shell contentedly munching pig treats. At least half a dozen paps were swarming over the beach, all firing off shots of the happy ring bearer. 'We need to get hold of that pig.'

* * *

Having all piled into one golf buggy, AJ, Vicky, Rob, Pinky and I arrived at the entrance to the tiki torch-lit pathway at the other end of the beach. A hush had fallen over the congregation, seated on white chairs on the sand in a quiet, secluded bay. The whole area was bathed in a beautiful orangey glow, and a quartet of ukuleles were sounding the opening strains of Debussy's 'Clair de Lune'. Eight thousand pink orchid petals marked out the aisle. The female section of the bridal party hadn't yet made the short journey from the Presidential Villa to the scene of the ceremony. AJ had put his foot down, doing well over the 5 mph resort speed limit to get us to the ceremony ahead of time.

Taking a deep breath to steady my nerves, I stepped out of the buggy and slowly walked down the little path, Pinky strained on his lead ahead of me. Having loosened the top three clasps on the corset, I could at least breathe more easily, but I definitely wasn't calm. A few guests at the back turned and gasped at the woman, fully dressed as a bride, but clearly not Beau, walking towards the groom. When Trey looked up, aghast, I stopped.

'Amber—what the hell, babe?' Mona called out from her position, lying in readiness for Beau on one side of the seating arrangements. 'You're meant to be down the other—'

'Amber?' said Trey, stepping forwards. Confusion was etched across every part of his face.

I nodded. 'Afraid so.' At this precise moment Trey's discovering my real identity was going to be the least of his problems. There was a ripple of laughter from the unsuspecting guests as I let Pinky out of my grip and he gleefully ran down the aisle, straight across the petals towards Trey, his curly tail wagging excitedly. The pastor looked on, no doubt wondering whether this was all part of an elaborate, highly choreographed Hollywood performance to signal the entrance of the bride. *You never know what celebrities with more money than taste will do when there's a magazine deal on the table.* Fran, Shaggy and the magazine photographer were at the front, too, capturing it all.

I didn't take my eyes off Trey. 'Pinky's got something for you, in his pouch,' I said softly, as he crouched down to catch the pig at the other end of the aisle. 'I'm so sorry.' I turned and walked off slowly back towards the buggy, my stomach a knotted ball of nervous tension. A sad, sick feeling descended on me as I saw, with my mind's eye, a bemused Trey reach into Pinky's purse to pull out the note where his wedding bands should be.

'Amber!' I heard Mona call again, enraged that I'd had the cheek to ignore her in front of an audience. 'Come back here right now and tell me what the hell is going on!' But I kept walking.

When I reached the cart, AJ was in the driving seat, the engine running.

'Hurry, it's nearly twenty-five past!' He pointed at his watch, about to slam his foot down.

Quickly, I hitched up my ridiculously huge skirt and dived onto the back seat.

'Wait! Stop!' Trey came running up the pathway, Pinky under one arm, his face as white as the ascending full moon. We all turned to look at him as he stopped in front of the buggy, illuminated by the headlights. 'If what Pinky says is true, I need to get to the ukulele bandstand. Now.'

'Jump in,' AJ ordered. Trey squashed himself into the cart, next to Vicky and Rob, and we accelerated off. We made the two-minute journey in complete silence, none of us quite sure what to say, or what would await us at the other end. Though we knew it probably wouldn't be a bunch of ukulele players rehearsing in the moonlight.

* * *

As we neared the bandstand area, AJ stopped the buggy and turned out the headlights. As quietly as possible, we all scrambled out. I was glad I'd had the foresight to chuck my flip-flops in; the too-tight Cinderella shoes had done nothing for my bunions. Trey turned to Rob, settling Pinky into his arms, and then we all fell in line behind him as he silently marched towards the bandstand, which stood behind a gated wall covered in tropical flora. When he reached the entrance, he paused. AJ put out a hand to us:

'Leave him to do this alone,' he whispered.

Trey headed for the gate, only pausing once to look over his shoulder. His eyes fixed on me.

'You know, I never did believe you were Annie Liechtenstein,' he said. 'And you should know that Scorsese's next movie is shooting in New York, not Shepperton.'

'I'm sorry, Trey, I shouldn't have lied to you,' I whispered, a horrible burning sensation building up behind my eyes. 'It was wrong, and I hate myself for it. I'm so sorry.'

'Don't be,' he replied. 'If you hadn't been here today, who knows what might have happened? I could have ended up married to the lying bitch.'

Suddenly the sound of a car pulling up on the other side of the wall made us all stop. Trey breathed in deeply, slowly loosened his tie, undid his collar button, folded back his cuffs, and then purposefully opened the gate and disappeared from view.

* * *

The rest of us stood there, intrigued by how Beau might try and talk herself out of this one.

'Fancy using a poor, innocent pig like that,' Vicky muttered, stroking Pinky's soft belly.

'I'm getting quite attached to the little fella.' Rob tickled him under the chin. 'Wouldn't like to be Jason right now.'

The car engine was turned off. We heard a man's startled voice—it had to be Jason. There were a couple of exchanges, voices low and muffled; we couldn't clearly make out what they were saying. Then came a loud smack, the sound of a good, meaty punch, and a thud as a body fell to the ground, followed by a shrill shriek from Beau.

'Oh my God! Jason!'

We all looked at AJ.

'I think you'd better have a look,' I said, and he dashed past us and in through the gate.

From the other direction, a figure holding heels in one hand, a bottle of champagne in the other and walking with a pained expression, as if over broken glass, was approaching rapidly, her hair a giant ball of frizz in desperate need of some serum.

'Great—the last person we need,' I mumbled.

'Would you, Amber, like to tell me what the fucking hell is going on here, please?' Mona yelled, her voice slurred. 'We've currently got eighty of LA's biggest movers and shakers sitting around on the beach wondering when the hell this wedding is going to start, a bride who's gone AWOL, a groom on the run and ten bridesmaids wandering around aimlessly with less than half a brain cell between them.' *Huh—she's a fine one to talk!* 'And you're just standing here, flirting with Rob, thinking it's all a huge laugh?' She looked at Rob and Pinky and grunted with disdain.

I felt anger rise inside me in an unstoppable tidal wave. If anyone else needed knocking out this evening it was Mona, and it surely wouldn't take much—she was already half-cut. *Whose stupid idea had it been to put me into this dress in the first place?* Vicky placed a restraining hand on my arm.

'The wedding's off.' I scowled. 'You can ask Beau about it yourself, if you like. She's just through there, Trey is, too, and I believe Jason Slater is as well—if he's still alive.' I signalled towards the gate. Mona promptly dropped her shoes and the bottle by the side of the path and barged past us.

'Right, that's it—I need to see this,' Vicky announced, grabbing me by the hand.

'I'm coming, too, then.' Rob followed, his arms still full of pig.

As we turned the corner, the scene on the oriental-style ukulele bandstand looked like something from a horror movie. Still in her wedding gown, Beau was kneeling over Jason, who was lying on the ground, wincing as she wiped blood from his nose and lips with the back of her hand. There were mascara stains all the way down Beau's cheeks—her veil was off, her updo half down, her feet bare.

'Beau—for God's sake!' Mona shrieked, making a beeline for her. 'The dress! Whatever you do, don't get blood on the dress, it will never— Oh Christ, too late.'

'Oh, just fuck off, will you?' Beau spat at her in response. Sobbing, she put a hand under Jason's head and cupped the back of his neck.

'Ouch, not there! Just leave it, angel.' He grimaced, blood dripping onto his Hawaiian shirt as well as her wedding gown.

'But what about the magazine deal? The editor will go spare!' Mona screeched.

'Oh, I think that's well and truly off,' snarled Trey. 'Don't you, baby Belle?'

Beau let out a loud wailing noise and buried her head in Jason's chest.

We crept forwards to join AJ, who was standing, motionless, to the side of the bandstand. Rob set Pinky down, but instead of trotting over to comfort his rightful owner, Pinky remained rooted to his side.

* * *

Trey walked behind the bandstand to the waiting car and had a word with the bemused driver. He then coolly opened one of the passenger doors and called out:

'Beau, darling, the driver is ready to take you and Jason to the hospital now. Might I suggest you go with them, Mona? Oh, and don't bother coming back—any of you.'

'Wh-wh-what do we do?' Beau muttered to Jason.

'We go to the damn hospital. I think my nose is broken,' Jason replied, clearly in pain as he dragged himself into a standing position. Beau clung to his side, looking like the Bride of Chucky.

'Beau, I'm coming with you! You can count on me!' Mona slurred, desperate not to lose the only client she had left. 'Here, let me get your things.' She began scurrying around collecting up Beau's discarded Louboutins, veil and the two Louis Vuitton cases she had packed ready to elope. 'What about—er—Pinky?' she asked, pausing to look at the pig currently licking Rob's shoes.

'I don't want to see that traitor ever again.' Beau scowled. 'We're through.'

She and Jason hobbled over to the car and ungracefully got in, Mona taking the front seat after she'd stashed their belongings in the boot. Trey waved them off with a flourish.

'And I hope you'll be *really* happy together!' he called as the car slowly backed out of the resort, leaving us all reeling in its wake.

Chapter Twenty-Seven

The wedding guests were already inside the glittering reception marquee, where four hundred candles lit up the initials 'B' and 'T' at the entrance. Sumptuous serving stations with platters of fresh island catch and exotic salads were positioned along one side, and the mermaid theme continued with watery projections and more giant shells. The guests stood around, talking awkwardly as news of the cancelled wedding spread. When Trey appeared at the entrance, flanked by AJ, Vicky, Rob, Pinky and me, there was a blanket hush. Instinctively, Vicky and I held hands tightly. Though if I wasn't mistaken, she was also lightly touching Trey's fingers on her other side.

'Looks like a bloody Disney theme park,' Trey remarked, whipping a glass of champagne from a waiter's tray and necking it in one and reaching for another. 'What the fuck was I thinking?'

We all followed his lead in downing a glass—the entire tent had turned to stare at us. Trey made his way to the front of the marquee and stopped on the chequered dance floor, where he should have enjoyed his first dance as a married man. He unclipped the microphone from its stand.

'As you might have guessed, there's been a change of plan today,' he announced, his voice perfectly level.

Vicky squeezed my hand. 'He's so *cool.*'

'There will be no wedding,' Trey continued, 'because I have discovered that my fiancée has been having an affair with Jason Slater.' A gasp swept around the tent. 'Yes, the rumours are true. Biggest cliché in the book, huh! But, do you know what? It's okay,' he went on. 'They're welcome to each other, when Jason eventually gets out of hospital.' Gasps from the gathered guests. 'Oh, don't worry, Beau's okay,' he assured them. 'She's being looked after by her mad stylist, Mona Armstrong, the one who recently got caught shoplifting. They'll be fine together.' A titter went up from one section of the crowd. I looked over and saw Fran in the centre of it, next to Shaggy, who was still filming. 'But I do have one special thank-you to make this evening.' He beckoned over Rob, who walked forwards, pulling Pinky by his lead. Trey stooped down to pick up the pig. 'And that is to Pinky, without whom I would have made the biggest mistake of my life today. Thank you, mate.' He patted the bemused little creature on his head. 'Well, don't all just stand there gawping. This marquee is currently housing two hundred bottles of the finest Dom Pérignon, not to mention a bar stocked with every spirit under the sun, and I'll be damned if any of it goes to waste. Don't know about you, but I'm going to get rat-arsed!'

I spontaneously raised my glass into the air and cheered. As I did, glasses across the marquee were raised high, until we all found ourselves making a thunderous noise in support of Trey, Pinky and lucky escapes.

'Music, please!' Trey shouted above the racket, and the assembled band behind us struck up a perfectly apt Hawaiian version of 'Better the Devil You Know'.

* * *

Some hours later—I'd long lost count of the number of bottles of champagne and Mai Tais that had been consumed—the scene at the top table had become emotional. Vicky was locked in deep conversation with Trey, sitting in a compromising semi-straddle across his lap; Rob was playing 'who can slam the most tequila' with AJ; and there I was, squashed in the middle of both couples, a tuxedo-less Pinky asleep on my knees, bow tie loose around his neck like a partied-out playboy. I was perfectly fine with this set-up until I noticed a foul smell and a warmth in my lap. Pinky had done a widdle on the Vera Wang without my noticing. I shooed him off and went to tell Vicky, but realised that she and Trey were now full-on, tongues and all, snogging. I looked to my right and saw Rob slowly sliding lower in his chair. *Since when is a man mountain like AJ a good bet to take on in a drinking competition?* Maybe Rob wasn't as smart as I'd thought.

Wobbly on my feet, I quietly shuffled my chair backwards and weaved my way through the guests, who were mostly pulling expansive shapes on the dance floor, or draped over each other in various states of drunkenness. In one corner an inebriated Fran was directing a Jack Rabbit Slims Twist Contest between Shaggy—now wearing a grass skirt and little else—and the three hefty bridesmaids, all with their lipstick smudged. And, if I wasn't mistaken, that was Beau's mother up on stage, singing '9 to 5' karaoke-style with the Hawaiian band.

* * *

My memory from then on is patchy. I remember it feeling good to get some air—the night-time breeze was much cooler now, sobering. I ambled down a pathway towards the beach, with a few more 'Alohas' to Four Seasons staff en route, who looked bemused as they took in my outfit. *I'd almost forgotten I was wearing a wedding dress.* More than anything I wanted Rob to be here with me. *My fake hubbie!* My hand hovered on my phone, but I stopped myself; he would be too wasted to pick up, anyway. Instead, a few hundred yards from the back of the reception, I was distracted by a grunting noise near the catering tent. I struggled to see in the darkness. The grunting turned into a rampant snorting as I approached the side of the open tent and pulled back the canvas.

'Pinky!'

Beau and Trey's once-stunning five-tiered artisan chocolate-truffle wedding cake had been left on a table just inside a corner of the tent. Well, until Pinky had toppled it over and sat in the middle of the demolished dark chocolate sponge, happily munching away, his pink skin now a delicious shade of cocoa. I looked down at my pee-stained gown and laughed. Sitting down beside him, I scooped up a handful of the gooey mix from the untouched top tier, and started stuffing it into my mouth. *Man, I'm hungry.*

'Looks like it's just you and me now, my little friend,' I said aloud. 'What a day.'

Grinning, I thought of the hundreds of photos of Pinky in a giant shell, but no celebrity bride or groom, that would be landing on the servers of newspapers and magazines around the globe this evening. There'd be a lot of confused picture editors before the real story was eventually pieced together by a hack with a contact on the inside.

'What a drama you've caused, little piggy,' I teased. Pinky snorted in response. 'Tell you what, I'll adopt you if you like. It wasn't very nice of that evil owner of yours to just abandon you like that, was it? And I don't think you'd want to live with Mona—she wasn't really a pig person, was she?' I stroked his soft, warm body, not caring that I was coating myself—and the Wang—in chocolate, too. 'I think you'd like England—it's much colder than LA and Hawaii, but we've got lots of mud there and acorns, and I'll treat you to some truffles if you like. Maybe chocolate ones, rather than the posh ones though—you seem to like those best.' Pinky had an incredible appetite for an animal so small. 'I could make you a little pen in my bedroom and Vicky and I could take you to the pub with us—it'd be fun!' I chuckled as I used Beau's favourite catchphrase. Then I thought of my flat back home, the piles of junk mail in the hallway, eating hummus in front of the telly, going to The Chamberlayne with Vicky, my old clothes, my job at Smith's, getting the tube to work, even enduring one of Nora's recitals. I craved it all so badly.

I looked up, suddenly sensing I was being watched. There was Rob, walking towards us, slightly unsteady on his feet. I gazed blearily at him. When he reached our chocolatey corner, he stopped and lowered himself to the floor, sitting straight on top of a mountain of melted icing and ruining the Tom Ford suit.

'You know, I might have to fight you for adoption rights,' he joked, prodding Pinky, who looked kind of dazed, drunk on chocolate.

'See you in court, then.' I smiled.

'How's the cake?'

'Delicious.' I offered him a handful and he took a mouthful straight from my palm.

'Have you heard anything from Mona?' he asked between bites.

'Nothing. And I don't expect to, after all this. Besides, she's not my boss any more.'

'Probably for the best. Look at us.' He sniggered, gesturing to the chocolate around us and all over our clothes. 'What a mess. In every sense.' He tenderly brushed my jawline with his thumb, then he turned my face towards his bloodshot eyes. He had tequila breath and there was chocolate cake stuck to his lip.

'Do you remember that time, just before the BAFTAs when you were snogging the face off that American in Starbucks? You know, Poldark on steroids.'

I squirmed, chocolate squelched underneath me.

'Don't remind me. Worst kiss I've ever had.'

'Worst kiss I ever had to watch,' he remarked.

I turned to look at him, unsure what he meant. 'Did it look that bad from the outside, too?'

'I just hated seeing you with someone else.'

My heart leapt.

He pulled me a little bit closer, his green eyes now fixed on mine. *He's trying to kiss me. Oh my God, he really is.* A searing sobriety cut through the haze.

'Not like this,' I said, gently pushing his hand away, though I felt like my heart was shattering into little pieces.

He recoiled. 'I'm sorry.' We sat together as an awkward silence descended. My mind spun as the full impact hit me. *Rob just tried to kiss me. My Rob. And I said no.*

For Christ's sake, Amber. Oblivious to it all, Pinky finally stopped munching and snuggled sleepily between us, burying himself in my ginormous chocolate and wee-stained skirt. Seconds later Rob's head drooped and rested on my shoulder. I sniffed the top of his head; his brown hair still smelled clean despite the hours of tequila drinking. Half of me wanted to wake him up and turn back the clock. But I knew it wasn't right. *Besides, he might not even remember when he wakes up.* Before long, I had drifted off, too.

Epilogue

London, five months later

The windows were hot this afternoon. I knew I should have got in earlier to finish tweaking, before the sun peaked over the top of the buildings opposite and shone down, bouncing off metal and glass to heat up the window space like a greenhouse. We were enjoying a boiling-hot early July. I peeled off my cardigan. *At least dummies can't sweat.* I smiled, as I remembered how celebrities and their ratty publicists complained constantly about conditions—the rain, the cold, the temperature of their water.

The looks were coming together well; I was pleased. As I stood back to admire my handiwork, I thought how lucky I was to have scooped a job I loved so much: Selfridges Window Designer. *It's been three months and I'm still not tired of the sound of it. Finally, a job without the word 'assistant' in the title, a job to make my mum proud.* I was now in the fortuitous position of being able to pay not only half of the

rent for the flat I once shared with Vicky, but for a cleaner,
too. Since she moved out two months ago, Trey Jones had
continued paying her half of the rent, so they had a London
'bolt hole' and I had continued living there alone, though
I was still entertaining the idea of getting a kitten. *God, I
miss Vicky.* Nostalgia hit me for a moment as I remembered
the crazy times we had shared together as flatmates. Since
she moved to LA to make a go of it with Trey, our weekly
Skype chats weren't quite the same. I greatly admired her
spontaneity, though. She was always one to follow her heart.

I surveyed the mannequins again. My job situation could
have been so much worse. Imagine if I'd stuck with Mona?
I'd probably be in a rehab centre somewhere near Phoenix
right about now, having treatment for my nervous breakdown. I laughed to myself—then I thought of her for a few
moments. *I hope she's okay. I hope she's happy.* It's amazing what some distance can do. The last I'd seen of Mona
was just last week, in the pages of a glossy magazine, appearing in a world exclusive photo album of Beau Belle and
Jason Slater's wedding, bride and groom deliriously happy,
their newborn daughter Rainbeau Slater cradled in Beau's
arms on the cover. I had pored over the glossy thirty-page
feature and spotted Mona standing on her tiptoes in ankle-
breakers, her head arched to catch the camera, desperate to
be seen, towards the back of a number of stellar line-ups,
and later hitting the dance floor with a man half her age.
It meant that Beau had been over four months pregnant at
the time she was supposed to be marrying Trey in Hawaii.
What a mess.

A knock at the window made me turn around. It happens
sometimes; kids think it's funny to knock on the window
and run off. Sometimes Japanese tourists or fashion students

do it and snap my photo, before sending it into cyber space. Everyone loves the Selfridges windows—they're a destination in their own right. But this time, when I turned around, there was nobody there. I continued pinning an exquisite embroidered Prada dress to one of the dummies. I'd been working on the 'La Dolce Vita' creative for weeks: full-on fantastical Italian glamour set amongst the attractions of Rome, with models licking polystyrene ice-cream, reclining decadently against the Spanish Steps, power-dressed in Moschino, Armani and Versace, and wearing huge Prada sunglasses. In the next window, the Trevi Fountain flowed with a cascade of jewels from Gucci and Cavalli, while dummies dressed to kill in Fendi and Dolce & Gabbana trailed their fingers in the gold. It was all in celebration of Milan Fashion Week, of course. You can't be outrageous enough—the windows have to grab attention, even at a glance from the number 10 bus. It was such a buzz seeing it all come together—the creative director was going to be pleased.

The noise came again, this time lower on the glass. I spun back round, faster, and caught a glimpse of—*no, it can't be. Maybe I drank more white plonk than I thought last night?* A bad date and a bottle of appalling wine to get through it. But then it appeared again: a little pink pig trotted over and came to a halt in front of the window. It was wearing a smart brown leather harness, not a silly leather biker jacket like the miniature ones Beau Belle used to dress poor Pinky up in. I looked closer—that wet nose, tiny curly tail, brown patches around one eye and in the middle of his back. *It can't be, surely?* The pig made a grunting noise—whoever was holding the end of its lead was out of sight, beyond my line of vision. I watched it trot away from the window once more. Perhaps the Dolce & Gabbana I'd been pinning ear-

lier today had put Beau into my mind—the label still reminded me of her. *Perhaps she's in town?* I knuckled my
eyes. *I'm losing the plot, my imagination's running away
with me.* But within seconds, there it was again. I crouched
down. *It is, it's Pinky!*

I dropped to my knees and touched the window. The pig's
snout brushed it on the other side, leaving a wet mark on the
freshly cleaned glass. *Pinky!* I touched the window again
and the little pig nuzzled it, against my hand. My heart sped
up as I tried to fathom what this meant. Beau hadn't been
photographed with her once-beloved pet at all in the past
six months, and now Vicky was all loved-up with Trey, I
knew he didn't have the micro-pig, so who did that leave?
Not Mona, she hated the creature—unless she'd had a personality transplant? *How bizarre—I was only just thinking
of her.* A familiar panicky sensation began to wash over
me, starting in my stomach and slowly spreading upwards.
*Mona's come back to haunt me; she's prepping for London
Fashion Week and she's coming to get me!* I was tempted
to hide out the back until nightfall. Mona meant drama—
no question.

Then Pinky's lead began to shorten and a shadow fell
on the pavement—suddenly the person holding the lead
was there, right in front of the window, smiling at me. He
waved. My stomach lurched. *Oh my God. Rob.* Three pins
fell from my fingers, and I heard them land.

'Hi,' he mouthed. 'Surprise!' He bent down and scooped
up Pinky into his arms, holding his right trotter and making it wave. *The only thing cuter than a man holding a baby
or a puppy is a man holding a miniature pig, believe me.* I
couldn't help but beam.

I stood there for a few seconds, feeling paralysed. He

looked just as I remembered him: floppy hair, open face, green eyes, gorgeous, warm smile. I suddenly felt as conspicuous as the half-naked mannequin standing next to me. My breath felt short. My cheeks reddened. I hadn't dared to imagine it might be Rob out there. *Damn him for still having this effect on me.*

Rob wasn't moving, he mouthed: 'Pinky wants to see you!'

I froze. *What do I do with my limbs?*

He beckoned to me, and mouthed again: 'Come on!'

I couldn't believe it was Rob. It'd been months since I last saw him, at Kona Airport, following the disastrous wedding where he'd tried to kiss me in a pile of chocolate cake. At least I think that's what happened. I'd played that day over so many times in my mind, it had all got a bit hazy. I cringed. He must have known I fancied him. What a car crash I'd been, chasing a taken man. He's probably married now, with a baby.

Maybe I shouldn't go. I'm busy. Anyway, it's not fair of him to put me on the spot like this. I feared his rejection all over again, before it even happened, trying to pull me back and suck me under. I didn't want to go through that again. I'd done a really good job of getting him out of my system these past six months, dating lots, although I was still hunting for the One. I momentarily considered borrowing a ring from the window display and pretending I was engaged. *It would be so much easier if I had a fiancé to rave about.* But here I was—the same, single, Amber Green.

I looked back out of the window. By now, a few people had gathered around to admire the pig—Pinky always was an attention-stealer. Rob bent down so a little girl could pat the pig's soft pink belly.

How did Pinky end up with Rob? I was only joking when I'd mentioned adopting him. Has Rob actually gone through with it?

I pulled myself together. I had questions that needed answering; he owed me that, at least. *Think of him like an old work colleague, Amber—that's all he ever really was.* I put my cardie back on and ducked out of the window, grabbing my bag and coat from the cupboard next door. When I emerged through the shop doors, Jas from Smith's was standing on the pavement, too, and so was Big Al. Even Kiki was out there, along with a small crowd of shoppers, rubbernecking, wondering what all the fuss was about. After Kiki had recovered from the Miss P debacle and I'd told her the full story about what a nightmare boss Mona turned out to be over a lot of wine one evening, we'd wound up as friends again. She had even tried to set me up on a date with a mate of her current boyfriend. I eyed them all suspiciously. *Why is everyone staring at me?*

'What are you all doing here?' I asked Big Al.

'We just fancied a bit of air,' he teased, nudging Jas.

'A certain pig popped into Smith's earlier, looking for you,' Jas explained, indicating Rob and Pinky.

'You'd better go and see what he wants,' added Kiki, wearing a leopard faux-fur gilet, despite the temperature. 'We've only put up the "Back in Five Minutes" sign and I'm starving.' *Well, that was a first.*

For a couple of seconds Rob and I stood opposite each other in the street, just looking, before he pulled me close into a big bear hug, Pinky's warm body squashed between us. That smell: clean washing powder, aftershave with notes of cedar—plus a light whiff of pig. It all came flooding back. Rob was looking me straight in the eye, I mean *really* looking, like he had never seen anything so intriguing before. And then we both smiled at the same time, a big, proper, cheesy grin like a focused ray of light. *Aargh, so corny!* But neither of us could help it.

Then it was as if the world and all the people around us suddenly stopped what they were doing and were quiet and calm.

'You're very beautiful, you know, Amber Green.' He used his free hand to move a strand of hair from my eyes and tucked it behind my ear. I looked away, suddenly embarrassed. *Stop looking, people! Carry on shopping!*

'Don't be embarrassed—it's true.' When I peeked back to check, he was still doing the looking thing.

There were a trillion things I wanted to say. I had a sick-making flashback to the beautiful, glimmering diamond ring he had shown me just around the corner from here. It hurt then, and it still hurt now.

'I took the ring back,' he said, reading my mind. 'It wasn't the right fit.'

I looked perplexed. 'Oh, I don't mean size,' he qualified. 'I mean the person.'

I swallowed hard. 'So you're not married?'

'No, and I'm not a dad, either. Turned out to be a false alarm, thank goodness.' He glanced down at the little face between us, and Pinky's small, dark eyes looked back, innocently. 'I became a miniature pig's dad, instead.'

'You seriously adopted Pinky?'

'It takes forever to bring a pig from America, believe me.' He smiled, stooping momentarily to place Pinky on the ground, his lead wound tightly around one hand.

'Well, you always had a good rapport with him,' I teased. 'But why are you here, Rob?'

'I had to get some things straight. And then it wasn't hard to find you,' he replied, looking over to Jas and the Smith's crew. 'I had some help. And I've never wanted to kiss anyone more than I want to kiss you right now.'

Everything went into a sort of candyfloss mist as his free hand gently held my face and we smiled into each other's lips, melting into one another, right there, in the middle of Oxford Street. A delicious calm washed straight through me, from the back of my eyelids to the tips of my toes, as we shared the best kiss I had ever known; it was the most natural thing in the world.

A cheer went up from the assembled onlookers and when we came up for air we were still beaming. If I wasn't mistaken, Big Al wiped a tear from his eye. Even Kiki was smiling broadly. A bigger crowd had gathered by now, but all I cared about was him.

'You're not a bad kisser, Mr Walker,' I said.

'Not bad? I'll have to improve on that.' He tenderly brushed my cheek with his thumb—then his hand dropped and instinctively found mine, our fingers lacing together tightly. As Pinky lay down at our feet for an impromptu snooze, my heart swelled with happiness.

* * * * *

Acknowledgements

I must thank a few people without whom Amber Green and Mona Armstrong would almost certainly not have been brought to life.

My brilliant sister in law and agent, Jenny Savill, thank you for your ideas, encouragement and guidance, your faith in me made it possible and I admire you in so many indescribable ways; to Jill/Ruby Dawson for sharing your expertise – it was fate that we met in Marrakech, you are a true inspiration.

Thunderous applause to the team at Mira, especially Anna Baggaley for believing in *The Stylist* from the beginning and Alison Lindsay and Sophie Ransom for your enthusiasm and marketing and PR wizardry. You have all been a dream to work with and I am so grateful.

To my amazing husband Callum for not complaining when I spent hours at my screen during any free time and for appearing interested in red carpet fashion; to my incredible mum, for your endless support and holding the baby – literally – so I could get this book finished; to my wonderful friends for all the adventures we have shared which have without doubt inspired some of the situations in this novel. Especially to Chrissie, Mel and Michael, without whom I would have no understanding of what it is like to be monstrously hungover the day after The Oscars. And finally to my beautiful son, Heath, for arriving two weeks late so I could finish writing *The Stylist* and for being such a good boy as I tweaked it during your first year. There was nothing like the deadline of your arrival to get things done.

Loved this book?
Let us know!

Find us on **Twitter @Mira_BooksUK**
where you can share your thoughts, stay up
to date on all the news about our upcoming
releases and even be in with the chance of
winning copies of our wonderful books!

Bringing you the best voices in fiction

TWITTER